THE WAY YOU LIE

TWO WOMEN. ONE SHARED PAST.

KENNEDY BAKER

Cover Illustration by Alyce Dulaney and Book Cover Design by Alina Almeida.

Edited by Jessica L. Ross, Editor and Suzy Pope, LKW Editing.

Proofread by Samantha Jayne Proofreading.

ISBN: 979-8-218-87256-4 (paperback)

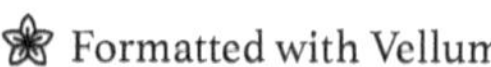 Formatted with Vellum

TRIGGER WARNING

THE WAY YOU LIE is a women's fiction novel with heavy themes of **physical, emotional and psychological abuse.** This novel is based on a true story, and portraying the accuracy of abusive partners and abusive situations is very important to us. However, your safety and well-being are equally important, and should ALWAYS come first. If you or a loved one is struggling with any form of abuse, please know that you are not alone and there is help.

The National DV Hotline: 800-799-7233

To Alyce,
for healing parts of me I didn't know were broken.

THE WAY YOU LIE

TWO WOMEN. ONE SHARED PAST.

KATE

I love being single. Aside from the occasional hookup, I told myself that I was going to live my twenties the way they were meant to be lived: unburdened. Dating apps are just a game, a distraction. Swipe left, swipe right. Read a cheesy bio, send a flirty message, maybe go on a date or two if the vibe is decent. My friends tease me about it, how I can find a date faster than they can find their car keys.

Ryan's profile on Plenty of Fish isn't remarkable. The first picture is a blurry photo of him standing in a garage, leaning over the hood of a car pretending to fix something, his biceps on display for the whole world to see. The second snapshot is a car engine, nothing more—just an engine. In the third picture, he's holding a beer while standing in the bleachers, and smiling at a NASCAR race or some sort of racetrack. *So he's into cars, then.*

Shifting on the couch, I adjust my sweatpants under the blanket. It's cold tonight, the winter air is chilling me to the bone. Winters in Michigan are unforgiving. I pick up my Budweiser from the coffee table only to find that it's empty. His bio is short: "Mechanic. Likes tacos, fast cars, and good conversation. Looking for something real."

It's so cheesy, I could throw up. I hesitate, almost swiping left, but I stop.

I've always loved the fixer-uppers. The kind of men who don't have it all together. A project, something to fix, and there's something about Ryan. He looks a little rough around the edges, a little bit dangerous. Like he would bring me back two hours after curfew, if I were a teenager living at home, smelling like cigarettes and bad decisions, and not give it a second thought.

But I'm not a teenager anymore. I'm a grown woman who likes to push myself to the brink of bad decisions just to feel something. Maybe it's because I grew up in a strict household, with a box strapped to the TV that bleeped out curse words when they were spoken. Maybe growing up on such a tight leash is what did me in.

"Let me guess, you're gonna tell me you can fix anything." It's the only clever thing I can think of. I regret it almost immediately.

He replies three minutes later. "Only the broken things that are worth fixing."

I shake my head, blushing. What a ridiculous response.

"How long have you been a mechanic?"

"As long as I can remember." His reply comes faster this time. "My family was unstable growing up, and cars were the only thing I could rely on. Something about having the ability to fix what's broken, being able to put it back together. Healed me in a way."

I stare at his message. It's deeper than I expected, especially to a complete stranger. "That makes sense, and I'm sorry to hear about your family. That must have been hard." Online dating is so awkward. I'm picking at my chipped red nail polish trying to think of something else to say, but he doesn't give me time to overthink my next response. My phone vibrates as another message comes through.

"I would love to get to know you more. Maybe talk about our past in person. Are you free next Monday? I can pick you up at seven." I can almost feel him smiling through the phone. "I hope you like Mexican food."

Very confident, and maybe a little cocky. Definitely my type. As I reread his message, I think back to my last *boyfriend*, Charlie. He was confident too, but it was so misplaced. He was not successful; he could barely keep a job, actually. But he was hot. That's all he had going for him.

My boyfriend before that was a DJ. Wild, unfiltered, and equally covered in tattoos. And my boyfriend before that was a drug dealer.

Yeah, I guess you could say I have a type.

I set my phone down, pretending to deliberate his invitation. I already know I'm going to go, but I want to send a response as charming as his. And I don't want to seem too eager.

I was born and raised here, but moved away when I was in high school, following my parents across the country. My dad was a pastor, but retired to take a job in technology. So, we moved to California for a fresh start. Then life happened.

I graduated high school and met the love of my life. I thought we were going to attend college together and be one of those gross couples who bragged at every college mixer about how we were so lucky to find our soulmate so young. But I was wrong.

I thought Danny was the one; I was sure of it. My parents were sure of it. He came from a good family, had a good head on his shoulders, and had big dreams involving a few kids and a golden retriever. But life had other plans. *He* had other plans. Those plans included breaking my heart and leaving me drifting through life lost and in desperate need of someone, or something, to anchor me. I never saw it coming, either.

That relationship broke me.

A few "situationships" later, *insert Charlie*, and I moved back to Michigan. Hoping to reset, to remember where I came from, to reconnect with my roots. *To grow up.*

I'm twenty-one now, and not in a hurry to settle down. Life is too unpredictable, and I like that. I like my freedom. I like drinking too much with my friends on a Wednesday and sleeping in late on Saturdays. I want to travel, I want to see the world. I want to get a few more spontaneous tattoos. I want to *live*.

One failed relationship after another has me thinking that maybe it's me. Maybe I am the reason none of my relationships work out.

Which is another reason I need to be single for a while... *I don't know who I am anymore.*

I am currently living with my high school friend, Steve, trying to embrace the change of scenery. When I moved back to Michigan, I wasn't sure what I wanted to do with my life, so I didn't want to rush into anything. *Not a huge fan of commitment, in case you haven't noticed.* Plus, his apartment isn't too far from the local mall, perfect for a temporary job. Crashing on his couch was only supposed to be temporary, but five months have passed and Steve seems to like the company.

"What do you think of this guy?" I lean over and ask, showing him Ryan's dating profile. "He's cute... but he doesn't have friends in any of his pictures. Is that weird?"

"Nah, I don't think so." He glances over at the photo and shrugs. "His friends are probably just better looking and he didn't want to be an eyesore."

"Gee, thanks!" I say, punching his arm lightly. "I guess I'll find out, I think we're going out next week."

Steve stands up to grab us two more beers from the fridge. He's only half listening. Leaning over the counter with a fresh one extended, he rolls his eyes. "You know I don't care about your love life, right? You have girlfriends for that."

"Listen—" I start as I swipe the beer from his hand, "the sooner I meet the love of my life, the sooner I'm off your couch." I shake my head jokingly.

Looking down, I wink at Bandit, the current love of my life—my three-year-old Pomeranian. "Don't worry," I whisper in his direction, "you're the only man for me."

Bandit cocks his head and smiles wide, panting aggressively in my direction. He licks the outside of my beer bottle, hoping to get a taste. "Yeah, yeah, don't get ahead of yourself, Kate," Steve says, bringing me back to our conversation. "You can stay as long as you want." He slams the last of his beer then wanders off to bed.

Alone with my thoughts, I turn back to my phone. *What is it about this guy?* He's not even really *that* cute, but something about him is edgy. I can't explain it, but I have to know more. Plus, who doesn't love a free meal?

"I love Mexican food. Can't wait." I take a deep breath as I watch my text bubble become a permanent fixture. Three little dots quickly appear in the chat.

I smile as I read his response. "It's a date."

KATE

The car is red. Not the cherry red of a convertible or the soft rust color of a used sedan—this is firetruck red, with a matte finish and an engine that growls like it has something to prove. When Ryan pulls up in front of Steve's apartment complex, the entire block seems to turn and look. I fold into myself, embarrassed. I hate attention.

I'm wearing my favorite vintage tee and a pair of red converse, complimenting my shoulder-length black hair. Although I'm a natural blonde, black hair is an ode to my wild side. Not to mention, it makes my blue eyes pop.

My style has an edge to it, bold and effortlessly designed to show off my ink. I covered my arms in tattoos when I turned eighteen, and didn't look back. *Sorry, Mom.* I'm tall, really tall actually, for a girl. Which makes dating hard. I have standards, like everyone else I suppose, but I refuse to date someone shorter than me. I tried it once before, and I just can't get into it. All it took was one date with a shorter guy, one hug where he came face to face with my boobs—I was all done.

He's so hot, it's captivating. And he is *definitely* better looking in person. He leans over, pushing the door open, and says, "Get in, Kate.

You're gonna love this place." As I step in, I notice, the passenger seat is low to the ground, the smell of oil and something I can't identify fill the cabin. The stereo is off, and he doesn't make small talk. Looking over at him, I survey how comfortable he looks. It's like he belongs here, with his left arm resting casually on the open window. His ripped jeans have a grease stain, and he's wearing a Carhartt hoodie, with his hat flipped backward. His hair is a shade lighter than mine—which is not my usual type. Charlie had blond hair and fair skin, but Ryan is the definition of undone, and I can't look away. The silence hangs heavy between us as the car rumbles down the road, and I'm not sure if I should break it or sit in it.

"So... how long have you had this car?" I finally ask.

"Built it myself," he says, eyes fixed on the road. "Took two years."

"Oh wow. That's... cool."

Other than a single nod, he doesn't respond. Then he revs the engine at a stoplight, loudly. "You like that?" he asks with a crooked smile.

I blink. "It's... loud."

He laughs like that's the correct answer. "That's the point."

Cocky. I feel my cheeks turning red. Instead of responding, I look out the window, watching the cars pass, one by one. *Why am I so nervous?* Men typically don't make me nervous. I can't remember the last time a man has made me feel anything other than annoyed. It's this car, I know it is. And his demeanor. And everything about him, really.

The restaurant is tucked into a little strip mall, unassuming from the outside, but it comes alive as you step inside. There are only a few tables with mismatched chairs and string lights overhead. It's warmer than I expected—cozy, almost. The kind of place that's probably been passed down from generation to generation.

We're greeted by an older gentleman who looks like he's in his mid-fifties, with the name *Christian* embroidered across his front right shirt pocket. His smile is warm and inviting as he leads us to a quiet table in the back. As we approach the table, he pulls out a chair for me.

"For the lady," he says, gesturing with his hand for me to sit down. I make my way to that side, sitting gently, returning his warm smile.

He sets down two menus before saying, "Your server will be over shortly."

When the server arrives, I'm convinced I've found the best items on the menu to try, when Ryan suddenly orders for me. Carnitas tacos, salsa verde, and two glass-bottled Cokes. When the server leaves, I half-smile and try not to be annoyed. "Do you do that a lot?"

"What?"

"Order for people."

"I just know what's good," he says. "Trust me."

I don't, not really. I don't know anything about him. But I smile anyway.

"Should we order a drink? Margaritas are my favorite."

He looks at me and a flash of something judgmental makes me pause. "I don't drink." My cheeks heat and I immediately regret asking. Okay then... I guess I won't have a drink either.

"Tell me more about your family," I say, desperate to change the subject. "Did you grow up around here?"

"There isn't much to tell. I grew up in a small town outside of Detroit. We lived in a trailer for a while. Me, my mom, and whoever her boyfriend was at the time. Most of them were assholes. She... wasn't well."

He doesn't say it like it's a secret. His voice is flat, like he's told this story a hundred times and stopped expecting anyone to ask follow-ups. I do, though. I always have questions.

"What do you mean?"

He sighs. "She was a schizophrenic. Diagnosed when I was a kid. She'd go off her meds and disappear for long periods of time. Then she'd come back thinking the government had bugged the TV. I didn't really know what was real or not for a long time."

"Jesus," I whisper.

"Yeah. I didn't know my dad. He left when I was two. I ended up living with my grandparents when I was twelve."

"Were they... better?"

He shrugs. "They were stable, at least. My grandma made sure I ate. My grandpa didn't talk much unless the game was on. Better than the trailer, I guess."

I look down, nervously fumbling with my hands in my lap. This is such a heavy conversation for a first date. I'm really, *really* wishing I had that margarita right about now.

I don't want to sound insensitive, but my childhood was so different. My dad was a pastor for most of my life, sixteen years of it to be exact, and it was... different. It was exhausting always being the dutiful daughter, having all eyes on you at all times. My parents might have been strict, but they were always present, always supportive. They loved me so much. I truly couldn't fathom anything else. It breaks my heart to know he grew up without feeling loved. Without feeling wanted.

Minutes turn into hours. I keep waiting for him to ask me anything, anything at all about myself. But the questions never come. He talks about the next car he plans to build, about racing on backroads late at night, about run-ins with the cops and how he could take apart an engine blindfolded.

"You'll have to come visit me at my shop sometime; it's not far from your place," he says, lifting a scoop of ice cream to his mouth. He took it upon himself to order dessert for us, too. I don't mind, though; I have a crazy sweet tooth.

Ryan's not shy, not really, but being with him is heavy. Like he's haunted. When he speaks, it's like trying to solve a puzzle. He's all locked doors and coded messages, and part of me—maybe the part that has always tried too hard in every relationship—is desperate to figure him out. He talks a lot, but with everything he says, there are even more unanswered questions filling the silence. It's... intriguing.

When we get back to Steve's apartment, he climbs out of the car, opening my door for me. *This, I could get used to.* Walking me to the door, he leans in to kiss me.

"I had a great time. I would like to see you again."

His words make me feel something, though I'm not sure why—he didn't learn a single thing about me. There goes his cocky confidence again. Assuming that I had a great time, assuming that I would want to go out for another date.

"Okay," I say, surprising myself. When I return the kiss, the butterflies in my stomach start doing backflips. He can probably hear my heart thrashing about in my chest. "I'll call you tomorrow."

Bandit whines behind the door, paw wedged beneath the welcome mat, begging for freedom. I turn to let him out before he manages to tear the door clean off its hinges. The second I throw it open, he bolts into the hallway running circles around Ryan.

"Well, hey there," he chuckles, bending down to give Bandit some ear scratches. "Who is this?" Looking at his wrist, I notice a thin, navy bracelet poke out from beneath the cuff of his shirt. *Bracelet* is a generous word—it's more like a piece of string held together by a few flimsy knots. It looks old, very old, like it fades more with each passing year. Something about it looks sentimental. I make a mental note to ask him about that later.

"This is Bandit," I say, admiring the view. "The current love of my life."

Ryan looks up and meets my gaze, eyes darkening as a smile spreads slowly across his lips. He stands up, pulling me in for another kiss. This time it was deeper and lasted a little bit longer.

"Call you tomorrow," he says again. The words linger on my lips as he turns and walks back to his car.

I usher Bandit inside and shut the door. Kicking off my shoes, I plop onto the couch with a sigh. The way he kissed me after one date, with such a bold declaration—it left my heart racing. He's possessive, but it's kind of sexy. Like he knows what he wants and he has to have it. Like he will settle for nothing less.

I go to bed that night not feeling excited, exactly. Not swept away. But I can't stop thinking about him either, and that feels like something.

KATE

"I've never had a serious relationship before," he says casually, leaning over me on the couch, reaching his hand into my bag of chips. We've been inseparable since our first date. I wasn't sure at first, but his energy is intoxicating. And his persistence is… adorable. He invites himself over to Steve's place almost every day.

Steve isn't thrilled, but he doesn't outwardly object either.

"Really?" That surprises me. "Not even a fleeting first love?" I bat my eyelashes at him teasingly. He's twenty-four, and that is definitely old enough to have a self-deprecating first love.

"Nope. After I graduated, I joined the Army. Only did four years, but that kept me busy. No time to date." *The Army?* Every time he opens his mouth, I learn something new.

It makes sense now. He's kind of reserved, and a little bit shy. Like he's seen things, more things than most. He wears his past like a shield. He's guarded like a wall I am determined to tear down, brick by brick.

"Wow, the Army? That's really cool. Why did you get out?"

Instead of answering, he turns, his hand gently guiding my face to look at him. He kisses me hard and fast. "I love your lips," he breathes. "I just can't get enough of them."

I forget what we are talking about as I let the taste of him consume me.

"Gross, dude," Steve says interrupting, walking out of his bedroom. "Get a room. Oh wait you can't—because this is my apartment."

I turn to him, glaring. Ryan laughs as he moves away from me slowly. The absence of his warmth sends a shiver up my spine. I've been doing everything within my power to keep this relationship casual. You can see someone every day and still remain casual, right? One time I told him I was busy, but he still showed up at my apartment an hour later. I didn't object because it felt nice to be missed. It feels nice to have someone want to be around you every waking moment. And it feels nice to be that person for somebody else. I haven't been that person in a long time.

Steve grabs two beers from the fridge before joining us next to the couch. He is in love with his worn-in armchair from college. I've only been allowed to sit in it twice.

With an outstretched hand, he offers me a beer. I look at him quickly, shaking my head ever so slightly. I don't mind that Ryan doesn't drink, at least that's what I assume, but it's definitely challenging. He makes me so freaking nervous that I would give anything to have a little bit of liquid courage. But things are still so new, I will not make a fool of myself this early.

"Okay then," Steve says, rolling his eyes. "More for me." He sets both beers down and kicks his feet up on the coffee table. "What are we watching?"

Sensing the distance growing between us, Ryan scoots closer and drapes his arm around my shoulder. I love that he always wants to be near me, touching me.

I toss the remote over to Steve. "We were just about to put a movie on. You can pick." I am grateful for Steve. Truly, I am. For letting me crash here until I get myself back on my feet. For letting me figure out what it is that I want to do with my life now. I'm grateful for the company, too. It's been nice to have someone to talk to since I left California.

But I wish he could be anywhere else right now.

He picks up the remote and turns on Netflix, not at all getting the hint. Horror films are our thing, so he puts on *Final Destination* without giving Ryan a say.

Not ten minutes later, Steve is out cold. Beer still in his hand, legs up on the coffee table with his head leaning back on the chair. I laugh as I pull up the camera on my phone and snap a pic so I can blackmail him with it later.

I cuddle up closer to Ryan. We are a mess of limbs tangled together trying to fit comfortably on this makeshift sofa bed. This couch is not at all big enough for the two of us, but I don't mind. He stays the night here and there, making himself right at home. I've never been to his place. I don't even know where he lives. I asked once if I could see his apartment, but he shrugged it off, saying that it wasn't very nice, that my place is better.

Steve's place is better.

He rubs my nose with his, our faces touching in the dark room. The glow of the TV shines in the background. I sit up for a moment, pulling my hair loose from the bun it was in.

"You are more than I could have ever dreamed of." He wraps his arm tighter around me as I lie back down. Pulling me closer into him, if that's even possible. "I could spend every night like this."

"I like the sound of that." I laugh quietly. Long after he falls asleep, I'm still absentmindedly drawing circles on his chest, listening to the steady sound of his breathing, his arm wrapped loosely around my waist.

I've gotten used to our one-sided conversations. Maybe he doesn't need to know about my past. Maybe he doesn't need to know about my ex, or my friends from high school. Maybe it's not that he doesn't care, it's that he likes me for who I am now. Maybe it's a simple kind of love, unburdened by details—or maybe this isn't love at all. I'm not really sure what I'm feeling, but I do know that it's too late to walk away now.

I am so in over my head.

The sound of his phone vibrating on the coffee table grabs my attention. For a minute, I think about seeing who it's from. But I stop myself because that's crazy, and I don't want to be *that* girl. I will be the first to admit that I have trust issues. Charlie cheated on me, multiple times, and I never really healed from the betrayal.

But it's okay to be a little secretive. It's okay to not want everyone to know every single thing about you. Boundaries are healthy, right? It doesn't necessarily mean he's got anything to hide. *Right?*

He's just guarded. I can live with that.

I close my eyes, letting the rise and fall of his chest lull me to sleep.

I have a feeling he is about to be my favorite mistake.

KATE

After a few weeks, I decide to visit Ryan at work. He always asks me to stop by, and I've got the day off of work, so I cave. Steve works from home and I try to stay out of his way when I can.

As I pull up, I watch him from the garage, the kind of place that looks half-abandoned but has a five-star Yelp rating because the regulars know better. His hands are covered in grease, his knuckles nicked and bruised from working. His baseball cap is turned backward and his white tee shirt is showing off a faded black star on his tricep. The kind of tattoo you'd get the second you turn eighteen, when you're young and desperate to mark your body with something permanent. My cheeks heat the longer I watch him.

He's so damn attractive, in the most laid-back, low-effort kind of way. Cool, without trying too hard. Confident in himself. I shake my head, trying to chase off the thoughts that have started to drift somewhere they shouldn't.

I open my car door, and Ryan looks toward the sound. Spotting me, he smiles. I climb out of my little Honda Civic and slam the door. Not the best car, but not the worst either. Reliable. Gets me from point A to point B, all I really need.

He starts across the parking lot, wiping his hands on a rag. I can feel my heart beating inside my chest. *What is it about this man?* I find myself wishing he would pick me up, carry me into the back room and have his way with me.

"Hey, Baby," he says casually, sweeping me into his arms—gently, trying to not get grease on my jean jacket. He tucks the rag into his back pocket as he looks at me with intensity. Like I'm the only person in the world who matters.

"Hey yourself." I give him a quick peck on the lips. Out of the corner of my eye, I see his coworkers staring at me. I stiffen.

"Ignore them," he says, sensing the change in my body language. "They're just jealous." He kisses me once more before heading back to the garage.

I'm turning red, I can feel it. I follow behind him, rushing to catch up. By the time I reach the garage, the wrench is back in his hand and his attention is on a beautiful '97 Chevy Impala. Leaning over the hood of the car, he says, "Kate, meet Joe and Garrett. Guys, this is my girlfriend."

I raise an eyebrow, eyes darting in his direction. *Girlfriend?* He's never called me that before. Girlfriend implies seriousness, girlfriend implies commitment. *Girlfriend...* means the opposite of casual dating. I lift my hand in a wave. "Hi, nice to meet you all." I wish they would stop staring at me. If they don't look away soon, I'm going to pass out.

"How long have you guys been working here?" Anything to change the subject.

Garrett speaks up first, clearing his throat as he says, "Uhh, about four years now. Going on five. Not a bad place to work... it pays the bills." He must be in his late forties. With sandy brown hair and bright green eyes, he looks like the kind of man who probably turned heads back in his day.

"I've been around since Bush beat Gore by a whisker," Joe cuts in, taking a drag of his cigarette, "and the courts made it official." I pause for a minute. I have no idea what he means by that. He coughs, a lifetime of cigarette odor clinging to him. His gut sags over his jeans like a deflated tire and he looks tired, really tired. Like he has dedicated every ounce of energy to this job… and to cigarettes over the past decade.

I'm about to respond when I notice Ryan digging his buzzing phone out of his pocket. He doesn't even bother to see who the call is from when he flips it open.

"Hello?" he says as he walks away, taking the call from the parking lot. I stand there watching him. The way he's smiling tells me he is talking to someone he really likes. *Who is it?* I wonder.

He just called me his girlfriend, so doesn't that make *me* the most important person in his life? I guess it could be his mom. But they aren't close, I already know that. And no one smiles like *that* on the phone with their mom. That's the way he smiles at me. I'm instantly spiraling and fuming with jealousy. *Why am I like this?* I need to get a grip.

I wish we weren't at the garage. I need to ask questions, or at least try and approach the question. Not knowing who is on the other end of the phone might eat me alive. *My perpetual distrust is telling me he's talking to another girl.*

Moments later he walks back to the garage. "Sorry, babe. That was my sister."

"Sister?" *Well this day is just full of surprises, isn't it?* I'm trying really hard to hide the shock from reaching my face.

Ryan has a sister?

We've talked about family multiple times over the past few weeks, sharing intimate details from our past, *at least one of us did*, and never once has he mentioned having a sister.

I would love to meet his sister. I'm a girl's girl, through and through. We could meet for coffee and bop around the mall together, talking about her silly brother who managed to convince such a babe to be his girlfriend.

"Yeah," he says, interrupting my daydream and turning his attention back to the Impala. "I told her I would call her later."

Nothing feels right. I shift on my feet. I can tell this conversation is over, and he doesn't seem inclined to offer any more details.

I turn back to Joe and Garrett, who seem to have forgotten we were talking. They are tinkering around in the garage, cleaning through piles of tools.

After standing in silence for a few minutes, I can't take it anymore. "Well I've gotta get home and let Bandit out," I lied. I took Bandit for a long walk right before I came to meet him. "I'll see you later, okay?"

He looks at me sideways, cocking his head. "Leaving already?" he says, curiously. "See you later."

He gives me a hug before getting back to work.

I smile nonchalantly and hurry back to my car. I can't get out of here quick enough. My body is shaking, and I'm fighting a sense of betrayal. If he has a sister, why didn't he tell me? All he does is talk about himself, and we have been dating—*apparently*—for over a month now.

I would know if he has a sister, wouldn't I?

I'll just ask him about it later. Like any normal *girlfriend* would do... which is another thing I need to address. Driving home, my thoughts consume me. I need to get my shit together. I need to stop this downward spiral before even talking to him first.

Love, or... whatever this is, isn't supposed to be this complicated. Is it?

KATE

"Can I ask you a question?"

He perks up and faces me, pulling his attention from the stir fry that I managed to cook, by the grace of God. "Sure, Babe. Anything."

"Why didn't you tell me that you have a sister?" I immediately regret that I decided to say anything. Why can't I leave well enough alone? *Charlie really did a number on me.*

Pausing, fork mid-air, he sets it back down slowly. "I'm sure that I did, you just forgot," he says without making eye contact.

"No," I say, cautiously. "I would have remembered…"

He looks at me like he is trying to decide if he should fight it more or admit he messed up. I'm holding my breath, waiting for his reaction. Without speaking, he stands up and walks around the table. Moving around Bandit, who follows his every move, he takes my fork and sets it down on the table. Grabbing my other hand, he pulls me up until my arms are wrapped around his neck. His face is inches from mine. I suck in a breath.

"Kate," his eyes are moving up and down my face, searching for something. "I love you. I'm sorry if I forgot to tell you. She and I don't talk very often. We aren't very close, so it must have slipped my mind."

He places his hands on either side of my face, forcing me to meet his gaze. His hair falls lightly in front of his eyes, and I have a strong urge to run my fingers through it.

"Ryan," I whisper. *He loves me? It hasn't been that long, has it? How can he love me already?* There are so many things I want to say, but nothing comes out. I should have known it was nothing, just my past trying to haunt me.

His gaze pierces straight through me. "Kate," he says again, softer this time.

I'm quiet for a moment. I am a walking contradiction. I just went from being convinced that he's cheating on me to professing my love. *What is wrong with me?* I didn't want this, this is the *opposite* of what I wanted, actually. I just wanted to have a fun, noncommittal relationship. But now that we're here, I realize that I'm happy. He makes me feel seen. He makes me feel *wanted*, something Charlie never did. He might have loved me, but he cared more about how our relationship looked on paper.

Maybe it wasn't another relationship I was afraid of, but rather losing another piece of myself, of my self-worth. Ryan makes me feel... loved. *Is that what this is? Love?*

When I find the words, I try to sound confident. "I love you, too." A grin spreads across his face. He rarely smiles. I hesitate, remembering how he smiled when he talked to his sister on the phone. *It's the exact same smile.* The smile he reserves only for me. When I look up, my eyes meet his again. They light up like nothing I've ever seen.

Seconds later, I smell something funny. *What is that smell?* Then it dawns on me. "Shit!" I gasp, racing over to the oven. When I open the door, the smell gets worse, and smoke fills the air. I completely forgot that I was baking a cake.

Ryan puts his hand over his mouth and laughs. "It's okay, Babe. Let me take you out for dessert."

I close the oven with a soft slam. "Yeah, I guess. I just really wanted tonight to be special." I shake my head, accepting defeat.

Walking over to the kitchen, he passes Bandit who is sitting by the oven, begging and blissfully unaware that I just ruined what he's waiting for. Taking the oven mitts off my hands, one after the other, he sets them on the counter. He spins me slowly around to face him.

"Baby."

Every time he says that, my breath catches in my throat. He has my full attention. "It *is* special, you made me dinner. Now let me take you out for dessert. I want to. Please?"

"Okay." *He wins*. I kiss him back, unable to stop smiling. "Let me just change out of these clothes."

He lets go of me slowly as I turn toward the dresser Steve is letting me borrow. It's smack in the middle of the living room, completely out of place, and not big enough. And it only holds a third of my belongings... maybe. My phone is resting on the dresser. I tap the screen to quickly check my notifications. One missed call from my mom... *I'll call her back later*.

I need more space. I need my own place. I really need to move out.

The absence of his hands on my face in just those few moments has me feeling empty—how does he do this to me? It's his quiet, delicate possessiveness that I like more than I would like to admit. I can feel his eyes watching me as I move through the dresser, pulling open a drawer, then closing it again. He takes a seat on the couch, waiting patiently.

I've never needed someone's attention as much as I need his.

I crave his calloused hands on my face, tucking a loose strand of hair behind my ear.

I crave his strong arms, wrapped tightly around my waist, pulling me into him.

I crave his voice calling me baby.

I'm definitely going to need my own place.

KATE

"It's not that bad, Babe," Ryan says sarcastically, peeling a piece of drywall with his finger. "We've got each other. That's all that matters, right?"

I smile at him half-heartedly. I got sick of sharing space with Steve, so I moved in with Ryan, who finally agreed after weeks of badgering. He lives in a small one-bedroom apartment on the outskirts of town, with peeling linoleum floors, a perpetually dripping faucet, and a weird smell I can't seem to locate. I see now why he always wanted to stay at Steve's apartment.

The off-white walls are dingy, and the cabinets are old and worn. The stove has a few permanent burns and one of the knobs is missing, but I guess it's fine because I don't know how to cook anyway. I have never lived somewhere like this before. It's not a dream home. Not even close... I always thought "scraping by" was a temporary phase people grew out of. But Ryan doesn't seem to care. He doesn't see the problem.

I tried everything possible to make it feel like home. I bought candles, cleaned night and day, taped up Polaroids on the fridge. Even Bandit is struggling to settle in, pacing restlessly, whining at shadows. I find myself avoiding video calls unless I can position the camera just right, to block out the stained walls. I told people I was just "settling in," but there was no settling happening—just sinking.

Things are different now, too. Ryan is always on his phone. Always. When we watch TV, when we eat dinner, even in the middle of conversations. But the screen is always tilted slightly away, the messages just out of sight.

But I notice. How he turns the screen off the second I lean into him on the couch. How he never leaves it unattended, it's always in his hand or in his pocket. How his face goes hard and unreadable when I ask questions.

It's been a long week, and I am desperately trying to hold onto the way he made me feel a few weeks ago. Before this apartment. Before we lived together. *I won't admit to myself that this might be a mistake. We love each other, right?*

I am trying. Trying really, *really* hard to be the perfect girlfriend. But tonight I can't help myself, I need to know. "Who are you texting?"

He looks over at me, pulling his attention away from his stupid phone. A cold expression hardens his face. "Why do you always need to know what I'm doing?" he snaps. "I don't ask you who you're talking to."

I pause. "But that's because I'd tell you." The second the words leave my mouth, I regret them. I've always been a little bit mouthy, always saying what's on my mind, consequences be damned, but I've never been good at reading the room.

"Yeah, well... maybe I don't need to explain myself every five minutes."

After that, the air between us turned cold. He got up, went to the fridge, grabbed a soda and walked out onto the balcony, shutting the door loudly behind him. I sigh, sinking further down into the couch. I shouldn't have asked.

Suddenly, my phone vibrates. It's Steve. Perfect timing, because I was about to go out there and apologize. *Again.*

"How's the new crib?!" he asks when I answer the phone. I swallow, pretty sure that he would be able to see right through me if I lied.

"It's alright... kind of a fixer-upper, but I'm working on it."

"Nice! Can I swing by tomorrow? You left a few things here."

"Sure!" I say. My excitement to see him is stronger than the embarrassment I feel about my new living quarters. "I'll text you in the morning and we'll figure out a time."

"Sounds good, catch you later," Steve says as he hangs up, not waiting for my reply. I glance across the room at Ryan outside on the patio. Bandit is curled up on his lap as Ryan takes a drink of his soda, his damn phone in the other hand. I think about heading out there to sit with him, but he looks content. Preoccupied with something, or someone, on his phone. *He looks like dynamite.* I can't explain it, but I feel sad. Deciding against it, I go to bed.

THE BIRDS WAKE me up early the next morning. I roll over, reaching for Ryan, but as I open my eyes, I realize I'm alone. Masking my disappointment, I get up to let Bandit out. *Where did he go?* I follow Bandit out the front door toward the parking lot. Our unit is in the very back of the building, far from absolutely everything. Not convenient for grocery trips, not convenient for much really.

Standing on the grass, I look around and realize that his car is gone, too. There's a hollowness in my chest, confusion laced with disappointment. *I hate this feeling.* He didn't lean over with a kiss goodbye or wake me to tell me where he was going.

I walk back inside with Bandit trailing behind me, wondering why it feels like he's already pulling away. But that can't be right. We just moved in together. We are in the newlywed phase, the "first apartment together" bliss.

Plopping my keys in a bowl, I hang the leash up and decide to make a coffee. I can't afford to spiral right now because I've got a shift later today.

I'm assistant manager of a store in the nearest mall, about forty minutes away. Some cute little boutique with the newest fashion. If I'm being honest, the job is pointless. I never save any money. I pour everything back into the store because I love fashion. Clothes, particularly. But it gets me out of the apartment and gives me something to do. Before Ryan, I was thinking about applying to cosmetology school. Now, I feel like it would be pointless.

I've missed the last two calls from my mom. I wasn't trying to avoid her calls, not really, but every time she called I was either with Ryan or on my way to see Ryan, and I didn't have the time to explain. They don't know that I'm seeing someone, let alone that I moved in with someone. They would die inside if they knew I lived with a man, *romantically*, outside of wedlock. They still think I live with Steve. Which was only acceptable because they know him, we've been friends for so long.

I look over at the clock. "Shit!" Slamming my coffee cup down on the dresser, I run to the bathroom. I'm going to be late for work.

It's a beautiful day in June, the sun is out, and there's a slight breeze. It's not too hot, not too humid. When I drove here from California, I only took what I could fit in my Honda. If it didn't fit in my car, I left it behind. Like my ex, like my friends. *I miss my friends.* My gaze landed on my favorite oversized jean jacket and a black dress. This will have to do.

Slipping on the black body-con dress, I shimmy around until I get it just right. I don't have much to work with. Because I'm tall, I barely have curves. I plug in my curling iron as I realize the state of my hair. There isn't much I can do at this point, but I'll try. After curling a few pieces I sigh, leaning in to put mascara on. I've never liked wearing makeup. I'm not really sure why, but I hate the feeling of anything on my face.

Admittedly, I'm very low maintenance. I mean, I love fashion, but most days, I fall somewhere between converse and floral prints, with only enough mascara to make my blue eyes pop.

My eyes land on my phone. I *really* need to leave.

Taking one last look in the mirror, I stare at my reflection. The woman looking back at me doesn't have any big plans or grand ambitions. Not anymore. She gave up her life and moved across the country for a fresh start, hoping to rediscover herself. Hoping to escape the memories of her ex lurking around every corner. She left her parents and her friends behind.

Now I find myself making decisions just to feel something, anything. I turn off the bathroom light and walk out to the living room. Slipping on my white vans, I lean down to give Bandit a few kisses.

I turn around, disappointedly surveying our apartment one last time and the life I chose. As I step out and lock the door I wonder if I will be happy with my new reality.

I wonder if it's too late. *What am I doing here?*

KATE

The longer we are together, the more it becomes clear: Ryan doesn't have anyone. No old high school buddies. No coworkers he hangs out with after hours. No "bros" he races with on the weekends, even though street racing is his entire personality. It's always just *him*. Alone in that big red car. *Alone, even when he's with me.*

It's Friday night, and I'm itching to go out and have some fun. Friday night should be the perfect opportunity to meet up with his friends. At least one of them. But instead, we're sprawled on the couch, watching TV, when I look over and ask.

"Should we go out tonight? We could go out with your friends, I'd love to meet them."

He looks up from his phone with a frown like I just asked something offensive. "I don't have time for fake people."

"What?" *What is he even talking about.* "What do you mean?"

He keeps going. "My *friends* all bailed when things got hard. Everyone says they're loyal until life gets inconvenient. I am the only one I can count on. I learned that the hard way." *There he goes again, talking but creating more questions than he answers.*

I press my lips together. I've always been a believer in second chances. I don't know if it's the way I was raised, but I've always allowed people to make mistakes. Possibly more than the average person. But something about the way he said it—it wasn't sad. It was *proud*. Like cutting people out made him stronger somehow.

"So... you don't have anyone that you hang out with? No high school friends or anything?" I should have assumed as much by now because it's been months and I haven't met a single person.

He eyes me with an intensity that gives me chills. "Why? Does it bother you?" he asks acidly.

I shift in my seat, debating whether I should be honest or if I should let it go. Maybe he's just hurt. Maybe no one has ever shown up for him the way they were supposed to. I think of my best friends, of the relationships I value so deeply. I have girlfriends from elementary school, girlfriends from high school. All so different, and all of them contribute to my life in their own way. I can't imagine life without any of them.

What happened to his high school friends? He is only a few years older than me. He grew up just a few hours away from our apartment.

Is there more that he isn't telling me? I shake off the thought before it takes hold.

I realize then that he is still staring at me. Looking away, I try to escape the heat in his gaze. This conversation took a turn and I'm not sure why that happened. "No," I say quietly, "of course not. I was just thinking that I would love to meet the people who know you best, the people you grew up with."

"Why can't you just let it go?" He stands up and starts to pace. I see it in him then, how quickly the switch can flip. He hates being questioned, in any capacity, and he managed to find the one girl who loves to have the last word.

"I was just wondering, Ryan..." I say passively.

I stand, thinking that maybe my touch will stop this situation from spiraling. As I walk over to him, I reach out and try to wrap my arms around his waist, desperate to take this conversation back in time just a few moments. He spins out of my grasp so quickly that I lose my balance and crash into the wall. My shoulder slams into the drywall with blunt force. He moved away from me like I was poison. Like my touch would infect him.

He's never done that before.

I stare at him, my eyes wide, with one hand pressed to my shoulder, as if putting pressure on it would stop the bruise from forming. Pieces of drywall form a circle around me like confetti, but no one is celebrating.

"I need to be alone," he mutters, heading for the front door. "I'll be back later. Don't wait up."

My voice comes out small. "I just thought…"

"God, leave it alone, Kate!" he shouts at me.

And just like that, he storms out, slamming the front door behind him. The picture frame hanging on the wall tilts to the side, knocked off-kilter from the slam of my shoulder. My keys, left behind in the bowl passed down from my grandmother, shudder. The whole apartment seems to vibrate with confusion. I'm still next to the wall, afraid to move. Gripping my shoulder, I slide to the floor. I cradle my head in my knees, letting tears roll down my face.

What just happened?

Through my tears, I see Bandit trembling in the corner, sandwiched between the TV stand and a plant that I let die. I try to force a smile. "Come here, boy. It's okay." My voice is quivering.

Slowly, he tiptoes over to me with his head down. He licks the tears from my knees and wags his tail, uncertain.

I'm not sure how much time passes as I sit in silence. The weight of what just happened is suffocating me. Ryan pushed me. *I can't believe he pushed me.*

And why? For asking if he has any friends? I feel the walls starting to crumble. For so long I let myself be swept away by it, by him. Brick by brick, I built the walls so high. Every little thing he did, every piercing gaze followed by my name on his lips, pulled me deeper into his castle where I felt safe, protected. *Loved.*

But now. *Now?* Every excuse, every half-truth, has me questioning everything.

Slowly, I get up off the floor and walk over to the couch. Sitting down, I let my body sink into the cushions. Bandit hops up next to me, resting his face on my knees. Staring at me. Waiting for me to do something, anything.

I pick up my phone, my body telling me that I should call somebody. *But who? And what do I say?* I open the lock screen and start scrolling my contacts list. Tears still falling, my shoulder still throbbing. The person I really want to talk to, I can never call.

I can never stand to hear the strain in my mother's voice, asking me what happened. She'll instantly pick up on the sadness through the silence. Wondering what happened to me, wondering how I let myself get into a situation like this, wondering how I let myself fall so far. And I could never lie to her.

I can never go home, either.

This might be my current reality, but it's still better than a life without constant judgment. Isn't it? Going home means facing the consequences of the choices I made that forced me to leave in the first place, and I'm not strong enough for that. Not yet.

I set my phone back on the coffee table, picking up the remote instead. As I turn on Netflix, I hope that a movie will distract me long enough so I can stop crying.

Barely ten minutes into the movie, my phone rings. I see *Babe* flash across the screen, and my stomach drops. After the fourth ring, I decide to answer it.

"Hello?" I say uncertainly.

"I'm so sorry, Babe. I never meant to hurt you. It's just… it was a long day at work and I wanted to relax and you know I hate when you ask me so many questions." *So this is my fault.*

I hesitate. His words sound almost like an apology. *But it's not.* I resign myself to just make peace… again. "It's okay. I'm sorry, too. I didn't mean—I was just curious." I don't know what else to say.

A sigh comes from the other end of the phone. I thought I heard a girl's voice, a faint laugh and the crash of balls rolling around on a pool table. It sounds like he's sitting in a bar. Did I push him to want a drink? Maybe this *is* my fault.

"How about I bring home some ice cream?" he says finally, breaking the silence. He knows there is nothing dessert can't fix.

"Sure. Cake batter with sprinkles for me, please," I request, trying to hide the sound of my sniffles.

"You got it, Babe. See you in a bit." He hangs up.

No need for anything further to be said. He apologized, sort of, and I need to move on. I need to stop being so difficult. Maybe I did push him too far? I can't find the fault line anymore, now I just feel confused.

It was an *accident*.

KATE

I t took a few days.
A few days for him to forgive me. A few days for him to look at me again like I'm the center of his universe. A few days of me apologizing for asking the wrong questions.

I stand on the edge of a makeshift racetrack, arms folded across my chest, trying to look interested. The smell of gasoline and burning rubber fills the air. I can see Ryan is in his element here. The rough, noisy crowd cheers as he adjusts the hood of his beat-up red car. It's his pride and joy—the only thing he truly cares about, aside from me, or so he claims. He's always so intense in these moments, eyes glued to the line, fingers lightly brushing the steering wheel as though the car itself is an extension of him. He's a different person at the race-track. Relaxed, not on edge. Content.

He never seems content with me.

One by one, cars line up beside ours. These evenings always start with a race and end with drinks in the parking lot. I watch as men climb out and position themselves in front of their vehicles.

Tommy walks by and slaps Ryan on the shoulder. "What's up, man? Hey, Kate!"

Tommy is a forty-year-old bachelor with a permanent five o'clock shadow and a receding hairline. He lives alone with his three dogs on an acre of land, spending his evenings drinking himself to sleep on the worn-out rocking chair on his front porch. The kind of guy who grew up in a small town and never intended to leave it. He never aspired to be anything or anyone.

I smile and shake my head. There are familiar faces everywhere. I try to remember all of their names, since we see them every weekend. Yes, *every weekend*. We have become a regular at this particular show, although "show" might be a gracious word for it. Men line their cars up to be gawked at as they sit around shooting the shit with a six pack of beer.

There isn't much else to it.

I watch Ryan, my heart in my throat. I don't care about the races. I don't care about cars. The smell of engine oil and the loud rev of the engines makes me dizzy. I only come because *he* loves it.

The first time I went with him, I felt so uncomfortable, so out of place. The atmosphere still makes me nervous. But Ryan was so happy. He smiled that rare smile—the one he reserves for me. The one that makes me feel like I'm part of his world.

I'm leaning against his car, his beautiful red Camaro, trying to immerse myself in the excitement. Slowly sipping on a cold beer, I'm pretending to care about the adrenaline, trying to fit in.

It only took me a few months before I felt comfortable enough to drink around him. I'll never forget the day that I came home with a bottle of wine after a rough day at work. He looked at me like I had just broken his most sacred rule, like I had somehow offended him. But drinking is the only thing that enables me to tolerate wasting my weekends at these shows.

Ryan is sitting in the driver's seat, watching the action from the shade. Reaching up, he grabs my waist and pulls me onto his lap, careful not to spill my beer. I wrap my left arm around his neck as his hands grip me steadily.

"You are so beautiful," he whispers onto my lips. As he leans in, he tucks my hair behind my right ear. When he kisses me, it's deep and passionate. Like I'm the only girl in his world.

I look at him, really look at him. At his thick, chocolate-brown hair and strong jawline. At his broad shoulders and muscled arms, flexing beneath his cotton tee shirt. At his olive skin and light brown eyes that sometimes looked hazel in the sunlight. At his hands covered in callouses, that are holding me as if I might disappear at any moment.

When he does this, it's hard for me to remember. The secrets, the stonewalling. It's like time stops. Nothing else matters but us and this moment. It feels right, letting those brown eyes ruin my whole life. *This is love.*

I faintly hear the whistle of men as they walk by. We are giving everyone a show, and I couldn't care less. I haven't felt this wrapped up in him in a long time. Ever since we moved in together, life with him has felt like a battle. I always feel like I'm walking on eggshells. It's almost as if he regrets the decision to move in together, even though it was his idea. But that can't be true. I refuse to accept that. I love him and he loves me. *I'm just being crazy.*

I pull away, but only long enough to tuck in my leg and swing around so that I'm straddling him. Lifting up his baseball cap with my finger, I spin it around backward. I flick his nose lightly.

"You are all that I want," I say softly, wondering when that became true. Wondering *if* that's true.

Outside, there's a flicker of sunlight left on the horizon. The sky is fading from orange to black. We've been tangled up in the front seat of his car, unaware of anything else, anyone else. I could kiss him forever. His lips are my favorite thing in this lifetime, and possibly in the next.

"Just you and me, Baby," he says, pulling back to catch his breath. He gives me a crooked smile, reaching behind me to start the car.

"Let's go home," he says, his eyes darkening. *Home.*

I give him another deep kiss before climbing off of his lap. Walking around the back of the car, I pass Tommy. "See you next week." I wave, the wind blowing my hair over my shoulder.

Tommy smiles at me, flashing me a toothless grin. "Later, Doll."

Most of the car community is older men, or rednecks. Let's be honest... they're old rednecks. I laugh to myself, wondering when I decided to spend my Saturday nights with middle-aged men.

As we drive home, I let that word dance around in my mind. *Home.* That is what we built. That's what he is, he is home. And I am in love.

~

THE AIR between us is still thick with desire when we arrive back at the apartment. I love when he is in one of these moods. It's like he has an appetite for me and only me. Like he worships me. Like everything is going to be okay. *Maybe it'll last this time.*

Ryan unlocks the door and holds it open for me. "After you," he says, voice low and warm.

I step inside, the familiar scent of home washing over me—the soft lavender scent of my favorite candle mixed with the lingering hint of motor oil. It's our home. Our shared life. And yet tonight, everything feels different. I feel loved.

He lets the door shut behind me with a gentle click, but the intensity between us doesn't ease. If anything, it thickens. I drop my purse onto the console table and turn. He's still watching me.

There's no teasing in his eyes, no smirk. Just the look he gives me when he doesn't have the words for what he feels. The look that makes my stomach flip and my chest ache all at once.

Without speaking, he crosses the space between us and cups my face, his touch tender, like he isn't sure if I'll let him kiss me. But I lean into it. Because he is my home, and I am tired of pretending that means anything less than everything.

I've been trying to say it all night." His thumb brushes my cheek. "I'm in love with you, Kate. So in love with you."

My breath hitches as I hold onto his every word. I don't need to say it back. He can already see it in my eyes. But I do anyway, because he deserves to hear it.

"I'm in love with you, too," I whisper.

He kisses me then—slow and deliberate, with the weight of every argument, every reconciliation, every night spent sharing this space and somehow still holding back. It isn't rushed. It isn't easy. It's real. A fierce kind of passion.

Our foreheads press together, lingering for a minute. When we finally pull apart, I wander into the bedroom to change out of my clothes and into something more comfortable. I walk back into the living room wearing one of his old tee shirts.

"I love you in my clothes," he says. Both of his arms are draped over the back of our couch. His body language is telling me everything I need to know.

I walk over to the couch, climbing on top of him, my legs straddling his waist.

"I'm not going anywhere," I say.

"I know," he whispers.

KATE

I haven't been avoiding my friends. Not really. Time just passes quickly when you're falling in love. Emma and Jade are my very best friends since elementary school. They stayed in our hometown, never left. The last time we saw each other, they came out to visit me in California after Danny broke my heart.

Finally, we're having a girls' night out. They are excited to learn about the small town I moved to, even though they don't understand why I moved here in the first place. It's not where I grew up. And they expected me to start over somewhere different once I was done crashing on Steve's couch. They didn't expect me to start dating. They didn't expect me to stay here. No one did, really. Not even me.

I pick up my phone when I see their names flash across the screen.

Jade texts first. "We're here! Can't wait to see you!"

Emma follows up with, "Where should we meet you?!"

I reply quickly. "Go ahead and park, I'll meet you there in ten!"

I smile, feeling giddy with excitement. These are my girls—the friends who knew me before I moved to California. The friends who partied with me in high school and who helped me through my first breakup. The friends who still remember me as the carefree, spontaneous Kate.

Jade, Emma and I spent our childhood summers up north at my family's cabin, swimming in the lake, eating endless amounts of Superman ice cream, and talking about boys. Happiness felt effortless. Life was easy and uncomplicated back then.

Ryan isn't home. He left earlier, and I don't know where he went. I didn't ask because it doesn't matter. The apartment feels empty without him, though.

I grab my purse and rush downstairs, eager to meet my friends. The movie theater is just a few blocks from our apartment, and as I sit with Emma and Jade in the dark, the familiar sounds of laughter and the smell of popcorn bring me to life. We talk through the previews reminiscing over stories from middle school and early high school. I haven't felt this carefree in months.

My dad pulled me out of school and moved us to California when I was fifteen, a few weeks before my sixteenth birthday. So while I grew up with these girls, I had to make new friends as a sixteen-year-old. It was hard, and I hated it. I didn't get to graduate with my best friends. I didn't get to go to prom. I missed out on so many things that feel like a rite of passage, especially for a teenage girl. So instead, I lived vicariously through Emma and Jade.

About thirty minutes into *Magic Mike*, my phone vibrates. It's Ryan.

"Where are you?" his text reads, just one question.

I frown, then quickly type back, "At the movies with Emma and Jade. I'll be home soon." Trying to shield the light on my phone from the rest of the moviegoers.

Before I can even set the phone down, another text comes through, this one more urgent. "I told you not to leave."

My stomach tightens. I don't want to deal with this, especially not now, but I respond anyway, trying to keep the peace.

"I'm just out with the girls. I'll be back in a few hours. Is everything okay?"

I watch the three little dots on the screen blink, then stop. It's like he's waiting for me to beg or apologize. I glance back up at the movie. Channing Tatum just made his debut and the whole theater erupts in cheers, but my mind is distracted.

My phone buzzes again. Another text comes in and my heart is racing as I slide my lock screen open. "If you don't leave and come home right now, I won't be here when you get back. I'll leave, and you'll never hear from me again."

My heart drops. *What?* I stare at the text, not sure if I'm reading it correctly. His words feel like a slap in the face. I can feel the blood rushing into my cheeks. My body is starting to sweat. My friends notice immediately.

"Everything okay?" Jade asks, looking at my phone in my lap.

"I—I have to go," I say quietly. "Ryan... he's acting weird."

Emma frowns. "What do you mean?"

"I'm not sure. He just—he wants me to come home."

They exchange concerned glances, but neither one pushes me to stay. Reluctantly, I grab my purse, apologizing for cutting the night short.

"Hey, we can hang out another time," Emma says, trying to lighten the mood. "It's okay. It's just one movie."

"I'm sorry," I apologize again as I stand up. "Thank you so much for driving out here. I'll call you guys tomorrow, okay?" I try to crouch over, so I don't block the view for everyone behind me. *I'm so embarrassed.*

It's only a few blocks, but the walk back to our apartment feels like the longest walk of my life. Every step feels like an anchor pulling me down deeper. I try to push away the nagging feeling that maybe Ryan is overreacting, but I've been here before—I know how this story goes.

When I reach the door to our apartment, I swing it open slowly. Ryan is in the living room, pacing. His eyes narrow when he sees me.

"Took you long enough," he mutters.

I open my mouth, but he cuts me off.

You disrespected me. You think you can just leave me here and go have fun like I'm nothing? I told you not to go. And you didn't listen. Now you expect me to be here when you get back?"

I blink slowly, as the conversation we are having takes a minute to register. "I told you I was just going to the movies. And you weren't even home," I say as my voice rises.

"You don't get it, do you?" he snaps, his voice low and dangerous. "You think you can just walk away from me like I'm some fucking afterthought? Like I don't matter? No, I'm *done*."

I glare at him, frustrated and confused and angry. "Ryan, why are you doing this? Why do you always have to make me feel like I'm doing something wrong when I just went to the *movies* with my *friends*? I didn't *do* anything."

He steps closer to me. His body is rigid, as though my words had physically hurt him. "Because I'm your life now, Kate. You should have remembered that before you decided to go out with *them*."

"I didn't know I wasn't allowed to hang out with my friends." Tears sting the back of my throat. "I didn't know that's what this was."

"You're mine," he says coldly. "And I'm telling you this because I'm the only one who loves you. They don't, *not really*. You'll see that when it's too late."

My heart shatters into a million pieces. I feel like I'm suffocating, like the walls are closing in around me. *I can't believe this is happening. I can feel the tears pooling in my eyes, but I refuse to let them fall. I am not going to let him do this to me.* I have to force the words out.

"You don't own me, Ryan. You can't tell me where I can go or who I can see."

He laughs, but I wasn't joking.

You'll get it sooner or later, Kate. You'll see. When I'm the only one left, you'll see." With a final, furious glance, he storms out, slamming the door behind him with a bang.

I stand in the middle of our apartment, heart pounding in my chest. *How did this go so wrong, so fast?*

I give him everything. I spend all of my time with him. I moved in with him. He calls me and I answer. Every. Single. Time. *Why am I not enough?*

I can't shake the feeling that somehow, this is all my fault.

KATE

Ever since I was a little girl I've loved surprises and presents. So when I receive a text from Ryan saying, "I've got a surprise for you, be home at 8:00 tonight," I can hardly wait. It's been weird since my movie date with Jade and Emma. He left me home alone, dwelling on our fight, ignoring all of my phone calls. When he came home the next morning, he ignored all of my questions and tried to pretend it didn't happen. I'm used to the whiplash, but God he makes me feel crazy sometimes.

I quit my job at the boutique last month because Ryan insisted on taking care of me. He said he wants to support me and provide for me. My manager didn't ask too many questions. I told her I had some personal things come up and needed to be home for a while. She didn't press it, which I am grateful for.

Glancing over at the microwave, the clock reads 3:47 p.m. What am I supposed to do for the next four hours? I pace around the apartment, put away some laundry, wash a few dishes, and take Bandit for a long walk. When I walk back into the kitchen to hang up the leash, I steal another glance at the clock: 5:13 p.m.

Time is dragging and I'm bored.

I miss everyone. *I feel so alone.*

I'm lost in the memories of my friends and the past, so I don't hear the door when it opens. Ryan peers around the corner.

"Hey," he says with a grin. "Are you ready?"

"Yes!" I force my legs to move, racing to meet him at the door. Ryan pushes it the rest of the way open to reveal a tiny Weiner dog curled up in his left hand. I look at the dog, then up at Ryan. By this time, Bandit has figured out that something is up and cocks his head, jumping off the sofa and joining us at the door.

Ryan sets the little hotdog down and steps back. She waddles over to Bandit and licks his face with one big motion.

"Oh my God, she's so cute. What's her name?" I bend down to scoop up the newest addition to our family.

"She doesn't have one. I thought you would like to name her," Ryan says, wrapping an arm around my waist and pulling me close.

He kisses my neck and watches me interact with the little brown puppy.

"What about Penelope? Penny." I smile down at the pup. "She looks like a Penny."

"Penny it is." He pulls me in closer, *as if I'm able to get any closer*. I set Penny, who is wiggling in my arms trying to break free, down.

Then Ryan kisses me hard and fast. His hands are on me, like he's trying to save my life. With my arms around his neck, I hop up in his arms, wrapping my legs tightly around his waist. He walks us over to the sofa and lays me down. His gaze pins me to the sofa. *I would let him have me right here, if he wanted.*

He pulls away for a second. There's a hunger in his eyes—like I am the only thing in the world that makes sense. Like I am the very air that he needs to breathe.

I pull him closer, already knowing how the night will end and not wanting it any other way.

THE NEXT MORNING, I look over my balcony and see a familiar blue Ford. A slow smile creeps across my face. *Steve.* My coffee cup is full to the brim and destined to be spilled all over the patio loveseat. I'm wearing one of Ryan's shirts and hot pink slippers—a sight to be seen. I'm not at all dressed for company, but I'm ecstatic someone came to see me.

It's been too long since I've seen a friend. I can't remember how long it's been since I've seen anybody, for that matter, aside from Ryan.

Steve hops out of the driver's seat. "What are you doing here!" I call down. Not waiting for his reply, I slide the patio door open, making my way inside and to the front door.

Peeking around the corner and into the hallway, I wait dramatically with my arms on my hips and my head tilted to the side. Somewhere on the second flight of stairs, I hear a "damn." I laugh to myself. He must really be out of shape. As soon as he rounds the corner on the third floor landing, I throw my arms around his neck.

"Hey!" He laughs. "I've missed you, too."

"Come in!" I say, stepping out of the way and dodging the two small dogs at my feet. Bandit is so excited to see his friend Steve. And Penny is happy because Bandit is happy. I'm smiling at the scene before remembering the state of the apartment. Looking around, I really wish I would have known he was coming so I could have cleaned up. The living room is a mess... clothes are strewn about, there's dog toys all over the floor, and a half-empty glass of wine is sitting on the coffee table—evidence from the night before.

"Uh... Love what you've done with the place..." he says with a side glance.

I smile, trying to kick the clothes out of the way. "Thanks," I say, laughing quietly. "It's a work in progress." I hope he can't see the sadness in my eyes. I still hate this apartment.

"Do you want a coffee?" I turn, preparing to head into the kitchen. Neither Ryan nor I cook, so our kitchen only ever has the essentials: coffee and condiments. And sometimes alcohol.

"No. I'm okay. Thanks, though." He sits down on the couch and waits. The look he's giving me makes me uneasy.

I grab my coffee and join him on the couch. "What is it? You're making me nervous."

Steve is silent for a minute. "Are you happy?"

I stare at him. Instinct makes me turn around to make sure someone isn't standing behind me. *I'm not sure why I did that.*

I swallow. "I'm... adjusting. We're figuring each other out. We are learning how to live together. I am happy... it's just been a lot of work."

He nods and looks down. "Look, Kate. I want to tell you something. I should have said something sooner but you weren't home, and then I could never find the right time to call."

I stop breathing.

"Do you remember when I came over a month or two ago to drop off some of your stuff? You were on your way to work, but you told me to leave it on the porch?"

"Yes." I force a nod.

"Well, when I pulled up to your apartment, I saw Ryan outside standing next to his car and talking to a girl. She had red hair, and I don't know... she was a few feet shorter than you, I think. I don't remember much of what she looked like other than her red hair. They were standing so close together. Their conversation almost looked intimate. I lingered in my car watching for a few moments. Nothing happened, but a few minutes later, she followed him up to your apartment. I didn't confront him, because I wasn't sure who she was. And the longer I sat on it, the more it bothered me. So I thought you should know."

I sit staring at my small, dimly-lit apartment. My eyes are imagining everywhere the other woman may have touched. The hope I was holding onto wavers, the love, the promises. *I'm not enough.*

I finally turn my head to look back at Steve, tears welling up and stinging my eyes. "Are you sure?"

He sighs. "Yeah, Kate, I'm sure. Like I said, I don't know who she was or what it meant, but the more time passed, I started to question what I saw, and I wanted you to know."

I'm not sure what I should say or do. My body goes numb and I can't feel my hands. I don't doubt what he saw. Steve would never lie to me, but there is absolutely no way *that* happened. Ryan would never do that to me. *Would he?*

I think about telling Steve to get out, but I can't. Besides, I don't want that. I know he's telling the truth. I just don't know what it means. And the sad thing is, I already know I will never find out.

"Let me go grab your things from my truck," Steve says gently.

I watch him from the window in my living room, the leaves on the trees blowing in the wind. The neighbor's dog is chasing a squirrel up a tree. The mailman is throwing newspapers up on each porch, his aim is worse with each throw. A woman is jogging and pushing a stroller along in front of her. *Life is passing by, and I'm stuck in this crummy apartment.*

Steve reappears shortly with a small box in his hands. He sets it by the couch and sits down. "Do you want me to stay for a while?"

I shake my head, turn from the window, and the motion brings me back to reality. My reality.

"No, it's okay. But thank you for bringing me my stuff, and thank you for telling me." When I finally look at him, his face says he's torn between staying put and bolting. Against his better judgment, he leans down to give me a hug. "I'll call you soon." He gives Bandit a gentle pat on the head before walking out the door.

Minutes after he leaves, I'm still not sure what to do. What I need is to hear his voice. That's the only thing that can calm the storm. I pick up my phone to give Ryan a call.

He answers on the first ring. "Yeah?"

"Oh, hey. Hi. I was just calling to say hi, and that I love you."

"I'm busy, I'll call you later." He hangs up without saying bye. He just hung up without saying the three little words that I need to hear—the three little words that would have fixed everything.

I stare down at my phone. I've never felt so alone. *Why am I not enough?*

KATE

THREE MONTHS LATER

I never asked Ryan about the redhead. Instead, he came home and said he got a job offer in Denver, Colorado. So, guess what? We moved to Denver. And ever since that night, everything has been harder. It's like we took a wrong turn somewhere a mile back but it took me weeks, no *months*, to notice.

Our condo in Denver is a step up, at least. We have a hundred or so more square feet. You can't tell, but it has to count for something, right? It's an older condominium community just on the outskirts of town. The building isn't old in the way that it should be condemned, *like our last place*, but it's full of character—charming, but dated. The floorboards creak, the trim is chunky, and the ceilings are tall. There's a winding, dramatic staircase that leads to the tiny bedroom on the second floor. Nothing in here matches perfectly, but that's part of its charm.

After weeks of careful negotiation, I convince Ryan to let me go back to work. I framed it as something temporary, so he reluctantly agreed. I don't know how we were able to afford our condo; I don't know how we're able to afford anything, actually. The eyeglass factory doesn't pay much, and it definitely isn't glamorous, but it pays enough to contribute, and it keeps me busy during the day.

My job is at the kind of place where time seems to stretch and fold in on itself, and I needed zero experience to land the position. I just had to bat my eyes at the right person... in this case, a middle-aged guy who's likely been married forever, has kids in college, and drives a sensible sedan back and forth from his home in the suburbs. I was hired the same day I walked in for the interview. Simple as that.

I work on an assembly line, packing up the eyeglasses once they come through on the conveyor belt. I am the entirety of the "packing and shipping" department. Well, not just me—there's also Jessica.

Jessica is a whirlwind. She's loud and brassy, with chipped nail polish and a flask always hidden somewhere in her oversized purse. She swears like a sailor, too. I liked her immediately. After months of feeling alone, Jessica's presence is a breath of fresh air. We eat lunch together and sneak out behind the building to smoke even though I don't. It's just good to talk to someone again—anyone. Jessica's boyfriend, Chris, is a character, too. He's also loud and swears a ton... landing somewhere between a redneck and a military brat.

There's a bar about four blocks down from the factory. It's the perfect spot for an after work nightcap. Jessica always asks me to stop by for a drink after work, but usually I'm in a hurry to get home to Ryan. One day, though, I finally said yes. Which led to Ryan inviting himself, and therefore Chris received an invitation, too. To my surprise, they really hit it off bonding over their mutual love of cars and engines. They don't really need to like each other; I'm not even sure if they do. They just need something to tinker with on Saturday afternoons.

Evenings with Jessica always end in the same way—with her slurring her words, me helping her inside, and Ryan rolling his eyes. But she is the closest thing I have to a friend right now, which is something I will not take for granted.

RYAN and I spend all day at Chris and Jessica's house. The guys are working on Ryan's car—something about a misfire, something about the timing belt—who knows? I stopped trying to understand the technical terms a long, long time ago. I lean against the porch railing, eyes heavy from the sun and the wine. Bandit and Penny are romping around the yard, making themselves right at home.

After three long hours of greasy work and passing stuff back and forth over toolboxes, Ryan waves me over.

"Hey, Babe," he calls. "Can you hop in and try to start it?"

I hesitate, looking around. Chris seems to have stepped away. "But I don't know how to drive stick…"

"It's just starting the engine," he says, annoyed. "Put your foot on the clutch and turn the key. That's it."

The pressure in his voice makes me nervous. I don't want to look stupid in front of our friends, and I don't want to disappoint Ryan, again, so I make my way off the porch and over to the driveway.

I slide into the driver's seat and do exactly what he says: foot on the clutch, hand on the key. But when I turned the ignition, the car jolts forward with a lurch and slams into the back of Chris's truck.

My stomach drops.

There's a sharp crunch of metal on metal, followed by a beat of absolute silence.

No one says anything.

Ryan doesn't yell. He clenches his jaw, his eyes flashing dark. But he doesn't yell; he doesn't even raise his voice. He walks over to the car at a slow, deliberate pace, checking the damage. I glance at Chris, who just returned from grabbing another beer. He rubs the back of his neck slowly.

"Chris, I am so sorry. I didn't mean to—I don't know how to drive stick."

He looks at me gently. "It's okay, Kate. Don't worry about it."

I feel myself starting to shake. Ryan is still glaring at me with an intensity that I'm afraid of. *I don't want to go home with him.*

An outsider would never know, but I know what that look means. I know that he's holding back because he will *never* yell at me in front of others. He waits until we're alone.

And just like that, it's time to go. Chris and Jessica both try to convince us to stay, but I don't dare suggest it to Ryan.

The silence on the way home is suffocating. Jessica and Chris only live ten minutes away, but the drive feels like an eternity. I keep sneaking glances at him from the passenger seat, trying to read his face, but he won't look at me. His hands are gripping the wheel so tightly his knuckles are white. I swallow and close my eyes, leaning back on the headrest, trying to breathe in and out. *In and out.*

We finally reach the condo. I climb out of the car, following him up to the door. Slowly taking each step, I make sure to keep my distance. He is unpredictable when he gets upset, that much I know. And I don't want to provoke him more than I already have.

We walk inside and he marches toward the stairs without stopping. For a split second, I think about sleeping on the couch, but quickly change my mind. That will only piss him off more. Kicking off my sneakers in the entryway, I quietly tiptoe behind him. I barely reach the second floor when he grabs my arm, hard. "Do you even listen when I talk? I asked one thing from you, and you fucked it up. It's like you don't even care." I can almost see the steam coming from his ears. It's amazing, actually, how he can go from calm to seeing red in the blink of an eye.

I try to pull away, confused, panic rising in my chest. "Ryan, I'm sorry. I didn't mean—"

It happens so fast. His hand comes down on my shoulder with force and he shoves me back—hard enough that I lose my footing. The breath rushes out of my lungs as my back hits the handrail. A sharp pain shoots up my spine, and I begin to tumble. Everything is spinning, until the room goes dark.

When I open my eyes, I have an excruciating pain in my right leg, my back feels bruised, and my head is throbbing. I blink a few times, trying to remember what happened and where I am. I squint and peer across the room and through the sliding glass door; it's getting dark outside. The sun was setting just a moment ago. *How much time has passed?*

My arm is bleeding and my right leg really fucking hurts. I try to pull myself up, at least to a sitting position, but the pain in my arm is too much. My head is killing me.

I look to my left and see Ryan crouched beside me. *Why are we on the ground?*

"What happened?"

"You're going to be okay, Babe. You fell, but it's okay." He searches my face, concerned. I close my eyes, furrowing my brows. This headache is quickly becoming a migraine. *Everything hurts.*

He cradles my head, moving to try and scoop me up. With one arm around my waist, he leads me slowly toward the stairs again. I hiss with pain, giving in to the limp. We climb the stairs, one-by-one. By the time we reach the top, I am out of breath and faint from the pain shooting up my leg.

Ryan slowly pushes our bedroom door open, and carries me gently toward the bed. Bandit and Penny are hovering in the doorway, confused. They aren't sure what happened, but they can sense the tension, and they know I'm hurt.

Once I'm seated on the edge of the bed, the dogs jump up beside me, one on each side. They're protecting me. They don't know why, but they just know they need to stay close. As I sit there, staring at the floor, tears prick at the corners of my eyes. *What happened?* My head feels foggy. I'm trying to remember anything, but it feels like a picture that's too far away, too out of focus to make out clearly.

Ryan doesn't say anything as he wanders into the bathroom. I can hear him rummaging around in the cabinets, opening and closing drawers. He's clearly searching for something. A few minutes later, he emerges with bandages and what looks like the makings of a sling. I refuse to let him see me cry, so I blink away the stinging tears and look away. He gently lifts my injured arm and begins to clean the blood. I hope I don't need stitches.

"You need to be more careful, Kate. I was so scared," he says quietly. "You had too much to drink."

Did I? His eyes are sad, like he feels genuine concern. I'm trying to hide the confusion on my face. "Yeah, I don't know what happened."

I know I didn't have too much, though. I only had one glass of wine with Jessica before he asked for my help with the car. One minute, I was at the top of the stairs, apologizing to Ryan for a *mistake*, and the next I'm crumpled up on the ground floor, face-to-face with the carpet.

A few bloody rags later, Ryan bandages my arm and wraps it in a sling. He takes part of the sling and wraps it around my shoulder. I wince from the pain. After that, he moves slower. The calluses on his hands contrast with how gently he is nursing my arm. I take a deep breath, trying to force myself to relax. My mind is spinning. I feel so confused, both afraid and relieved at the same time. He cleans up the bloody mess in front of me and then disappears downstairs. I hear a noise coming from the kitchen that sounds like the ice machine.

Did I fall? I wish I wasn't so confused.

I remember him being so angry. Flashes of his face in a twisted expression come into focus in my mind. *Why was he so mad over a mistake?* He has to know I would never wreck someone's car on purpose. How can he think I don't *care*?

But then Ryan comes back in from the kitchen, holding a bag full of ice, sidelining any of my doubts. "Come on, Babe. Let's get you to bed. You'll feel better in the morning."

He helps me up slowly with one hand on my waist and the other holding the bag of ice. I hiss in pain as I lower under the covers, contorting my body, trying to get comfortable. But everything hurts. He moves the pillow from his side of the bed and props it under my leg. Setting the ice down on top, he backs away. His voice is barely above a whisper.

"Sleep good, Kate."

He turns and walks out the door before I can reply. I close my eyes as the pain finally registers, and I let myself begin to cry when I hear the faint click of the door closing and the soft turn of the lock.

I sit up, as quickly as my body will allow, and stare at the door.

He locked me in.

ARIA

Ballet class ran a little long on this particular Tuesday. I recently graduated with a degree in fine arts and dance— ballet to be exact. I love the way ballet makes me feel. It's about the storytelling and the precision. When I was a little girl, I always wanted to be a ballerina, so I dedicated my life to being the best.

My days are consumed with working at a prestigious art gallery downtown, a job I was lucky enough to get because I was in the right place at the right time—something I will never take for granted. My evenings are spent at the ballet studio, studying rigorously for my application to the Paris Opera Ballet school. I've wanted to study ballet in Paris for as long as I can remember, and I am so close.

Wake up, rinse, repeat.

When class ends, I rush to grab my things. I slip on my sneakers and pull my peacoat over my lucky leotard, checking my phone for any messages. The first one is from my sister, Bryce. I'm meeting Bryce after ballet for dinner at a new little Italian place down the road from the studio, and I'm starved.

"Hi Aria, I'm here! Got us a table, but no rush. See you in a bit!"

I shove my phone deep into my tote, ignoring the rest of my

messages, and wrap my peacoat snug around my waist. May weather is always so unpredictable. It could be sixty and pleasant, or it could be thirty and snowing. You never really know—so you learn to prepare for the worst and live in layers.

Carmine's on Penn is only a six-minute walk from the studio, which is only a thirteen-minute walk from my apartment. Living downtown has its perks—everything is very conveniently located. It keeps me in shape, too.

Not that I really need it. I'm tall and lean—exactly what you picture when you think of a ballerina. I eat, a lot actually, but you'd never know it.

When I arrive, I look inside and spot Bryce seated at a booth in the back, swirling her glass of red wine, studying the backside of the menu. Bryce is three years older than me, named after Bryce Canyon National Park, where our parents were when they found out they were pregnant with her. I'm fortunate to have a sister who I am close to, despite our differences. Where I am quiet and refined, she is loud and colorful.

Pulling out my chair, I plop into the seat. I'm starving. Class kicked my butt this evening. "So," Bryce says playfully. "Are you ready to get back out there? I think it's time."

I roll my eyes. Not even a *hi Aria, how are you* first.

It's been eight months since my last relationship ended. It's not that long if you ask me, but no one did. Apparently, it's been long enough for everyone to think I should move on already.

"I don't know... I'm just so busy right now." I reach for my water, taking a few long sips. "I'm working so hard at the studio. I only have a few more private lessons before I apply to the Paris Ballet, and I won't let anything derail that. Especially not a man," I say leaning back in the chair and rolling my eyes.

I hate being badgered like this. If it's not coming from Bryce, it's coming from my mom. If it's not my mom, it's my roommate. Everyone thinks I'm so unhappy, so lonely... and I mean sure, maybe I am a *little* lonely, but I also have goals, and I'm focused.

I'm not unhappy. I'm just dedicated.

"Yeah, I know. But what's the harm in going out to dinner? You don't have to marry the guy. Just get out there. Let him buy you dinner." Bryce turns her head to the side, waiting for me to dig deep for another excuse. "Talk to someone other than Daisy for a change." Daisy is my four-year-old shepherd mix.

Fine," I say, inhaling deeply. It would be nice to go out to dinner every once in a while, and share some intentional conversation with someone other than my dog. Nothing more, though. Ballet comes first.

Reaching down into my tote, I fish out my phone. "Just dinner." I open up Tinder, which my roommate Marissa made me download last week by threatening to throw away my Chinese takeout that was wasting space in the fridge. After a few swipes, a mechanic comes across my screen. Ryan is his name. His profile isn't particularly flashy—just a few pictures of him in a backward baseball cap, standing next to a car, smiling with a crooked grin. His one-liner reads, "Looking for something real. Faith, family, fast cars."

I laugh to myself. He is *definitely* not my type.

I am drawn to men who are accomplished and a little too focused on their career, like me. My last boyfriend was a doctor, if that tells you anything. It was steady, and we were happy, but there was no future for us. He didn't want a family, and I thought I could be happy with him and only him, but I want more out of life. I want children. We were together for years, long enough that most people would start anticipating a ring, but that just wasn't us. We never lived together, because we both wanted our own space to focus on the most important thing—our careers. Instead, we shuffled back and forth between each unit, clearing out nothing more than a drawer for each other. I never saw a problem with it, even though Bryce liked to tell me otherwise. It just wasn't that kind of relationship. I didn't have time for *that* kind of relationship.

"What do you think of this guy?" I pass my phone to Bryce who eagerly snatches it out of my hand.

"Now we're talking," she says quietly. She scrolls across his profile for a moment, reading his cheesy one-liner and swiping through photos of vintage cars.

Our waiter approaches the table, interrupting silently. "Hi there. Can I get you anything to drink? Perhaps wine as well?"

"No, water is just fine for me, thanks." I smile, trying to remember the last time I had a glass of wine, or any alcohol for that matter. Just another thing that I won't let derail my training. The waiter nods, slipping away to make his rounds.

"I mean, he's cute," Bryce says finally, looking up. "But he's not really your type."

"Maybe that's the point..." I hesitate before adding, "If I'm ever going to settle down, I need someone not so focused on their career. Someone who sees a future with me. Someone who wants a family like I do. I want kids one day, after I'm done being a ballerina." I let myself think about my future for a minute.

I'm in my prime, the proper age to be accepted into prestigious programs. Even then, only ten to fifteen percent of applicants are accepted. But I've dedicated my life to this. I don't go out, I don't even really have fun. I can't remember the last time I had good, old-fashioned, reckless, twenty-one-year-old fun.

Ballet is my entire life. But when I can no longer dance, I want to be a mom. That's it, just those two things. That's all I want out of life. Is that too much to ask for?

"Then I say go for it," Bryce quips, swiping right on Ryan's profile. As she passes me my phone back, she smiles. "I did it for you so you wouldn't change your mind."

A wave of panic rushes over me. "You are so annoying," I whisper.

"I know," she counters. "But you'll thank me later."

Our conversation turns from my love life—or lack thereof—to Bryce's job. She is a special education teacher at one of the most sought-after private schools in the district. It's a difficult job, and the pay is terrible, but she loves it. We talk about Mom's birthday coming up and the new coffee shop opening up in my neighborhood.

When the waiter returns, I order chicken fettuccine alfredo, and Bryce orders chicken parmesan and a second glass of wine. Once a month, we try a new Italian place in Denver. It's one of our sister traditions, and something I really look forward to.

I've never had many friends. I have one or two friends still from high school, and my roommate, Marissa, whom I met in college. Aside from them, my sister is all I've got. I've always kept my circle small and put my goals first. Besides, having more friends would mean less time for ballet.

Yawning, I steal a glance at my phone. It's been three hours and I have work early in the morning. Bryce could talk for hours, so I'm going to have to find a way to cut this short. I have an early morning at the art gallery, which isn't a lie—but it's not a good enough reason for Bryce. The waiter brought our check over an hour ago.

He must have seen me yawn, because a moment later he swings back by our table. "My shift is done in a few minutes, and we're closing up shortly after. Can I get you one last glass of water?"

Thankfully, Bryce takes the hint. "Oh no, we're just leaving. Thank you!"

On my walk home, I hear a faint ding coming from my pocket. Reaching into my peacoat, I see a message from Ryan flash across the screen. My stomach drops.

I stop dead in the middle of the sidewalk, earning me a few cuss words from someone who nearly crashes into me from behind as I read the message.

"Hey. Want to catch a movie on Friday night?"

A movie? A movie feels more intimate than dinner. No stimulating conversation, no talking at all actually. Just awkward side glances and uncomfortably sharing a bucket of popcorn. He didn't even introduce himself first.

I stand still, considering his question for a minute. People are moving around me to the right and left, grunting in annoyance as I block the path.

My emotions are playing tug-of-war. I don't really want to go, but... I have no plans on Friday night. Friday is my night off from ballet.

What can it hurt?

KATE

I open my eyes. I haven't slept well since that night. I wait until Ryan falls asleep, then move downstairs to the couch. Then I set an alarm so I can crawl back into bed before he wakes up and pretend to be asleep as he kisses my cheek and leaves for work.

I'm adapting, though. I measure my tone more carefully, and I don't ask questions. I feel stupid for still holding on to him. I don't know why I'm even doing it. *Why haven't I left?* I run through reasons in my mind, each one feeling more like an excuse and not a valid reason. I should run as far away as I can. *But I don't.* I don't want to be like everyone else who's let him down. Everyone else has given up on him, left when things got too hard, and I won't do that.

I chose him, so I need to unlearn what I'm used to. I can fix this. I can fix *us*.

He starts work so early, getting to the garage hours before I even wake up. I've been holding on to the little moments I get each morning before work. I revel in drinking my coffee in peace, curled up on the couch with the pups. Centering myself before I go about my day. I had to take a few days off of work after the *incident*, which I downplayed as a four-wheeling mishap. My manager didn't ask questions, and I didn't offer anything more.

Leaning over, I throw the comforter back and reach for my phone. I rub my eyes, confused by a bright orange sticky note on top of the screen. I pick it up and hold the phone above my face, praying I don't drop it. I would be lying if I said that the little scar below my lower lip didn't come from this very thing. I lost my grip on the phone and *bam!* My phone smashed right into my face.

"Let's start here. I've got a surprise for you. Go check the fridge—where the cold drinks live."

That's odd.

I slowly peel myself out of bed, giving in to the limp that's still there. It's been a few weeks and my right leg is mostly healed, but every morning it's stiff and sore from sleeping. *Or lack thereof.* My ego is really the only thing that's still bruised.

Shuffling into the kitchen, I open the fridge, spotting the second note.

"Cool, right? Now go to the bathroom and look in the mirror. You're gonna want to see that cute face of yours."

I look around the apartment, confused. Ryan isn't home, and I'm not sure what these sticky notes will lead to. He is never playful like this anymore, so something is definitely up. Standing by the coffee machine, I lean against the counter waiting for my coffee to finish brewing and pondering all possible scenarios.

Taking my coffee, I head *back* upstairs to the bathroom. Right above my toothbrush holder is the third sticky note.

"Looking good, Baby. Now go find the place with your candles, books, and all your random stuff (yeah, even the bobby pins)."

I think for a moment, setting my coffee on the counter. That can only be one of two places. After deciding that it must be my bookshelf, I make my way back into the bedroom and start rummaging around. I am rearranging everything, trying to find the hidden message, when I finally spot the note tucked behind the cover of my favorite book.

"Almost there. Check where the laundry hangs out. You know, the basket you pretend doesn't exist."

I roll my eyes. Typical. Of course Ryan throws in a slight dig wherever possible… even when he's trying to be nice. Bending down, I lift the heavy laundry basket off the floor and onto our bed. Moving through the clothes, I fish around for a small orange square.

"You're so close. Go to where our fur children beg—look under their bowl for the real surprise."

I'm starting to get annoyed of walking up and down the stairs. It's early, and I haven't had multiple cups of coffee yet. I don't mind the playfulness, and I love surprises, but not first thing in the morning. I need a minute, or rather an hour, before I am awake and happy and ready to start my day.

I see Bandit and Penny waiting patiently for their breakfast. Slowly I lift their bowls, my heart threatening to burst out of my chest. I lift it to see a small velvet box with an embossed design decorating the top. Flipping it open, I gasp.

The ring is *huge*. Princess cut, solitaire on a white gold band. My whole body goes still. I realize I've been staring at it for too long when I hear whimpering coming from my left. "Oh, sorry guys." Snapping out of it, I set it down and give them breakfast.

I pick up the small box again. *How did he afford this? And when did he have time to do this?* It's been less than a year. Picking up the phone, I dial Ryan's number. *He wants to* marry *me?!*

"How…?" I start without saying hi.

Ryan cuts me off with a chuckle. "Don't worry about it, Babe."

He mumbles something vague about "savings" and "working extra shifts." I don't press him further. I know better than to ask too many questions. "Is that a yes?"

My "yes" comes automatically before my heart or my head have a chance to weigh in. It feels like the only *correct* answer. To say no would have cracked open the very fragile peace we've built. To say no would mean that everything was for nothing, and I've never been one to give up or quit.

I can practically feel him smiling through the phone.

"I love you. I'll see you after work."

Once he hangs up, I sit at the kitchen island, looking down at the ring on my finger. It sparkles like something out of a magazine. I want to love it—I want to be the kind of girl who jumps with glee, who calls all of her friends to scream the news, who takes selfies and posts captions like *"I said yes!"*

But my phone sits untouched. There are no calls to make. I've drifted so far from everyone I used to know. *Am I allowed to cry?*

RYAN COMES home from work early. The door swings open as he steps inside with a bouquet of flowers bigger than anything I've ever seen. I glide out of the kitchen to greet him, setting my glass of wine down. His face lights up when he sees me.

Picking me up with one arm, he swings me around in a circle.

"I love you," he whispers before giving me a kiss.

"I love you, too," I say, kissing him back. "And the flowers are beautiful."

He smiles and walks into the kitchen, looking for a vase, when he notices my glass of wine on the counter. "I see you didn't wait for me to start celebrating."

I freeze. My body tenses with familiarity, remembering the last time he used that tone. I move around him in the kitchen, running my arm along his shoulders and softly ignoring his comment. "I'll pour you a glass." I don't know why I bother. I'm going to end up drinking his glass, too. I've still got a little limp, so I move slowly, putting as much weight as possible on my left side.

He catches a glimpse of my ring as it glistens in the kitchen light. Reaching for me, he takes the bottle out of my hand, setting it down. He's careful not to use too much pressure on my arm where the wound is barely being held together by the stitches I needed after *falling* down the stairs.

He brings my hand up to his lips. "Mine," he whispers, kissing me softly.

I smile. Trading him a glass of wine for the flowers, I look down at the bouquet. Roses. *My least favorite flower.* For a brief moment, I wonder what it would be like to receive a bouquet of my favorite flowers. *I wonder if he even knows what my favorite flower is.*

Setting the flowers on the kitchen table, I grab my wine glass and we go sit together on the couch. He hangs his arm around my shoulder, pulling me in close.

"So I was thinking," I clear my throat softly. "What if I went back to school? We're starting over in a new place. What better time than now to make a career change... or pursue a dream?" I'm trying not to ramble, something I've never been good at. "I've been thinking about cosmetology school."

He looks at me grimly. "Why would you want to do that?" His arm tightens around my shoulder ever so slightly. "Aren't you happy?"

I swallow. "Of course I am," I say, quickly wishing I could take my question back.

"Let's pick a movie. Your choice," he suggests. *So, we're changing the subject. Got it.*

What a wonderful idea... anything to not be alone with my thoughts right now. I pick a horror movie, hoping it will drown them out. But even the blood and screams can't hold my attention. His either, apparently. I catch him stealing a few glances at his phone. Like he is waiting for a text or checking the time.

My gaze keeps wandering to my ring. It's not the ring I can't stomach—it's what the ring represents. It's the idea of forever with a man who doesn't even know my favorite flower. Forever with a man who can push me down the stairs and then say it's my fault.

This proposal isn't about love. It's about control. I twirl the ring around my finger, spinning it around and around in circles, hoping he doesn't see.

Later that night, I place the ring carefully on the bedside table, like it might burn me in my sleep.

ARIA

He's late.

Not that I mind, because I'm still putting the finishing touches on my makeup. Over the past few days, our conversation has moved from casual messages on Tinder to more consistent texts throughout the day.

It's been nice, I'll admit, having someone check on me throughout the day.

I just sat on the couch to slip on my shoes and wait when I feel my phone vibrate on the cushion next to me. "Downstairs. You can't miss me," his text reads.

I smile. *He's kind of charming.* I bend down to give Daisy a scratch behind her ear as I grab my purse, closing the door behind me. Down my apartment stairs and out the main door, the crisp night air rushes to greet me. Summer evenings in Colorado are absolutely perfect. And he's right. I can't miss him.

In front of me, idling in a handicapped parking spot, is a bright red Camaro. He climbs out of the driver's side and walks around the front of the car. And *wow*. He's even better-looking in person.

He's dressed casually, wearing faded jeans and sneakers with a sweatshirt that looks like it was made for him. He's tall, with dark hair and a red baseball cap on that complements his olive skin. Once I'm able to peel my eyes off of him, I quickly glance down at my own outfit, immediately wishing I wore something casual, too. Instead, I landed on fitted jeans that complement my figure, my favorite black sweater, and leopard print flats.

I look good, don't get me wrong, but he looks downright *sinful*.

Reaching down, he opens the passenger door for me like it's second nature. The gesture startles me. I can't remember the last time a guy opened my door for me.

"You look beautiful," he says as I brush past him and into the passenger's seat.

He slams the door before I can respond, walking around the front of the car to the driver's side. "Thank you." I look over at him and smile.

His smile is gentle.

"So..." I clear my throat. "What movie are we seeing?"

"It's a surprise," he says. His crooked smile is bigger this time.

I hate surprises.

"Tell me about yourself." His eyes never leave the road.

I hesitate for a minute. "Well... I love ballet. I've been training my whole life to apply to ballet school in Paris. Other than that, I don't know..." Looking down, I twirl one of my rings around my finger. I hate talking about myself.

"I spend time with my roommate and my dog, Daisy. I'm kind of a homebody."

"So am I." Then he adds without hesitating, "And I would love to come watch you dance sometime."

The declaration warms my heart. My ex never came to watch me dance. Never, not once. He was always too busy, or had some other excuse. "I would love that."

Before I know it, we reach the theater. It's across town, nestled into a worn-down plaza in between a hole-in-the-wall taco joint and a Hobby Lobby. He pulls the car into park.

"I know, I know," he says, watching my expression as I take in the exterior. "But they have the best popcorn in town. Trust me."

I don't trust him. I mean, I just met him, but I want to. I nod slowly, reaching for the door handle that's slightly worn from too much use. Briefly, I think about the other girls he's had in this car, in this seat. *How many of them has he taken on this very same date?*

And why are first dates so awkward? I forgot about this part. Walking side by side, with your arms brushing but not holding hands, because it's too soon for that. That's a step, a declaration, and we've only just met. So instead we walk awkwardly, elbows bumping every few steps, each pretending we don't feel anything.

He pulls out his phone so the attendant can scan our tickets. We are seeing *Mission Impossible*. Which one? I couldn't tell you. There's too many to keep track of, and I think I've only seen half of them—even that might be generous. Action flicks are not my typical movie choice, but I don't say anything because it doesn't really matter.

"Do you want popcorn?" he says, breaking the silence.

"Yes, absolutely."

Stepping into the line, he grabs a pack of Red Vines off the shelf, too. "Great, I'll get a large one we can share."

Our seats are good—not too close, but not in the very back either. My chest tightens, appreciating his good choice in seats. It's a small thing, but it doesn't go unnoticed. If you're a frequent moviegoer like me, you appreciate things like this.

The previews start, one after another, when he leans over and whispers into my ear, "Can I hold your hand?"

My heart is in my throat.

First, I can't believe he asked. It's so polite—too polite. *Who does that?* Second, because I haven't held someone's hand in a really, really long time, and I want to hold his hand, too.

I'm so thankful the dim theater lighting is hiding my blushing cheeks.

He's been holding my hand for thirty-six minutes now, *not that anyone's counting*, drawing circles on the top of my hand with his thumb. His calloused hands are sending shivers through me with every slow pass. I'm finding it hard to focus on the movie, so instead I watch his hand as it moves slowly over mine. After a few minutes, I notice a fragile piece of navy string, frayed at the edges. It looks personal, like it holds sentiment or memories. It's at odds with every other piece of his carefully constructed appearance.

When the movie finally ends, I'm trying not to feel relieved.

He lets go of my hand as he moves to gather up the trash, and I frown. He turns to me, his face so close to mine that I suck in a breath. "Want to go get milkshakes?"

It's nice that he doesn't want this date to end, either.

"Yes, please."

Making our way back out to his attention-seeking vehicle, he tells me about a little diner down the road. He says they're known for the best milkshakes.

And he asks me to trust him, *again.*

If I'm being honest, I didn't taste anything special or out of the ordinary about that popcorn, but the fact that he thinks it's the best is adorable.

OH WOW, this really is the best milkshake I've ever had.

This diner is like a scene from a movie. The walls are adorned with vintage red booths, and a retro jukebox stands comfortably in the corner. Sitting on the counter barstool, I spin left and right, sipping on my strawberry milkshake, appreciating my surroundings. I'm imagining a world where I'm Audrey Hepburn and he's James Dean, and I'm in awe of him.

How could he possibly know the best place for everything? First popcorn, now milkshakes. What's next? *Does he spend his free time trying every movie theater and diner in town?* I immediately regret my train of thought, as my mind wanders, again, to him on this exact same date with someone else.

"So, tell me about yourself," I say before I hurt my own feelings.

He spins his stool to the right until he meets my eyes, resting his chin on his palm. "I'm not sure what there is to tell. I don't really have a family, it was always just me and my sister. My mom was unstable when we were kids so we learned to take care of ourselves. Eventually we ended up with my grandparents, but it wasn't much better." He pauses for a second to take a sip of his melting shake. "Then I joined the Army."

He continues. "That's why I fell in love with cars, I think. They became something I could rely on. And if they broke, you could fix them, and they would be good as new. Better, even."

The words pour out of him like a dam, and as soon as they come out, he can't stop them. He takes another sip of his milkshake as he squares his shoulders. "It kept my hands busy, and my mind from troubled memories. I became so involved with my project that I didn't worry about where my next meal would come from."

I picture him as a child, sitting on the couch, starving, alone for days. I can feel my heart cracking open. No child should ever have to experience that. I reach out and grab his hand. "I'm so sorry."

He gives me a soft smile before slurping up the rest of his milkshake. Standing abruptly, he walks across the diner to the jukebox, flipping through pages of music. I can tell by his body language that he's uncomfortable with the emotional tone of our conversation.

As I watch him at the jukebox, I really look at him. I can already see the way the world has hurt him. I can see the weight he carries in his shoulders. The sadness and the pain are etched into him like scars. And I find myself wanting to be the one who brings light into his darkness.

KATE

Date nights have a different ring to them now. Literally.

It's Wednesday night. Ryan came home early with big plans, which he *never* does. "Let's go get Mexican food for dinner. What do you think?" he says, looking at me apprehensively. "It's been months since we had Mexican on our first date, and now look at us. Engaged." A mischievous grin spreads across his face. "Then maybe tattoos?"

I notice his eyes quickly dart to my right foot, to the tattoo on the right side, before coming back to my face. Following his line of sight, I see *Daniel James*. I stupidly tattooed his name on my foot one drunken night years ago. It doesn't bother me anymore, but I wish I could say the same for Ryan.

I don't really have regrets, though. It's one of the few things I've been able to learn and hold on to in my life. Life only gives you what you can handle. And look at me, *handling*.

Looking up at him tentatively, I smile. "Sounds like the perfect evening to me."

I stand in front of the closet with my hands on my hips, staring at my drawer of vintage tees. Spotting the one on top, I pull it out. *I have an idea.* Fifteen minutes later, I wander out to the living room. Ryan looks up from his phone. His gaze sweeps over me slowly.

"You wore that on our first date," he says quietly.

Blushing, I do a slow spin. "You remembered." *How does he still make my heart feel like it's going to explode inside my chest?*

He stands up and steps slowly over to me. "I could never forget. I wanted you so damn bad... I knew right then that I needed to have you."

He kisses me, rushed and intense. All the excitement has Bandit and Penny playing tag around our legs. Laughing, I reach for my purse. "Be back soon guys."

A little Mexican restaurant comes into view. The paint needs a refresh, and there are a few plants out front that could use a drink, otherwise it looks like any other hole-in-the-wall taco joint.

He reaches over and holds my hand, lacing his fingers with mine. No one would ever guess the dreams that had taken root, *and the ones that had withered away,* over a side of guacamole.

Ryan parks right out front. It's pretty dead for a Wednesday, especially for the Wednesday before Labor Day. There's a banner outside blowing lazily in the wind—four-dollar margaritas and two-dollar tacos. It doesn't get much better than that.

We climb out of the car and head straight for the patio. It's a beautiful evening. Not too hot, perfect patio weather.

I immediately spot the hostess straightening up a stack of menus behind the stand.

"Table for two," Ryan quips, holding two fingers up. She smiles at me, then at Ryan, holding his gaze longer than normal, before leading us through the patio doors to the farthest table in the corner. Ryan is walking in front of me, his hands in his pockets. Stopping abruptly, he leans down to pull out my chair. I raise my eyebrows. He never does that. He hasn't done that since we first started dating.

When she passes me a menu, I laugh to myself. I haven't ordered for myself in so long, I don't even remember what I like anymore. Ryan will order for me like he always does. I take it from her anyway, appreciating the gesture, but when she meets my eyes, I'm caught off guard. The warm, inviting smile and the welcoming gesture are gone. Now her eyes look almost... sad. When she looks at me, it's like she sees something that I don't. Like she knows something that I don't.

She is gone as quickly as she appeared. *What was that about?* I think to myself as I set the menu down.

Moments later, our server appears. Before he can get a word out, Ryan cuts in. "Hey, we'll get four carnitas tacos, salsa verde, and two glass-bottled Cokes please."

He looks at me quickly, silently asking if I need anything. I shake my head, hoping he doesn't press it further and that Ryan doesn't notice. Thankfully, he jots our order down quickly and turns back toward the kitchen.

"So, where are we going for tattoos?" Ryan may not know my favorite flower, but Ryan does know that tattoos are my love language.

He laughs. "I heard about a little shop about twenty minutes from here. Someone came into the garage last week and told me about it. I checked it out online and their work isn't bad." He takes a sip of the Coke that was just delivered.

"Sounds perfect." I reach across the table and grab his hand. If I'm not holding him, he might slip through my fingers. At least, that's how it feels. I'm constantly checking to make sure this isn't a dream. Because they say you aren't supposed to feel pain when you're dreaming.

He smiles that crooked smile he reserves only for me.

Slowly tucking a strand of hair behind my ear, I smile back.

The server brings our food and we eat in silence. It's a familiar silence... the kind of silence I've gotten used to. It's not uncomfortable anymore, just expected. Ryan has always been a man of few words, and it took a while, but I learned how to match his energy. Sometimes, there isn't anything that needs to be said. *Sometimes, it's safer to stay quiet.*

"You ready?" He nods at my half-empty plate, growing impatient. It hasn't been that long, but I am a slow eater. I've been that way since I was a little girl. I'm always in a hurry—in the car, when I'm walking, basically in every other instance aside from when I'm eating.

I decide to leave behind what's left of my tacos. Otherwise, Ryan will just stare at me, tapping his hand on the table until I'm finished. "Yeah, let's go."

We pay our tab and walk out to the parking lot as Ryan's red car comes into view, standing out among the other cars like it has something to prove. He takes off in a little jog, opening the passenger side door with the sweep of his arm. "After you, Baby."

I skip the final few steps, closing the distance between us.

"Woooooow," I say sarcastically. "What's gotten into you tonight?"

He laughs, even though I wasn't really joking. He grabs my butt playfully in a silent answer. "I'm crazy about you," he says, more seriously this time, as his eyes melt into me. "I'm the luckiest man in the world."

I stand up on my tiptoes to kiss him, even though Ryan is only an inch taller than me. A little unnecessary, but I like the drama of it.

He laughs again. I haven't heard him laugh this much in a long time. *He's in a good mood tonight.* I wonder why. *Why can't it always be like this?*

Climbing into the car, I blow him a kiss. He pretends to catch it, quickly shoving it in his pocket before he closes my door. I shake my head and laugh; he can be so charming when he wants to be.

The tattoo shop is small. A neon sign flickers out front, buzzing with anticipation. It's cozy and a little worn-in. It's the kind of place where artists come and never leave, finding home inside these four walls. As we walk in, I immediately notice trophies lining the wall to my left. The steady buzz of a tattoo gun is music to my ears. I feel at home here, like Ryan does on the racetrack.

"Hey, folks." The voice comes from an older gentleman with *Rhett* displayed across his chest, embroidered into the worn-out fabric of his shirt. He looks up from the middle-aged man he's tattooing. "How can I help you?"

Ryan waves. "Hey, man. Do you have time for two tattoos this evening?"

"Sure thing, I'm almost done here. How big are you thinking?"

He looks at me and shrugs. "Not too big." Lifting his hands, he motions a size with his left hand. Roughly outlining something bigger than a quarter but smaller than a baseball.

Rhett nods, returning his focus to the man in front of him. "Give me about thirty minutes and we can get started."

I walk over to the wall, my eyes scanning high and low. There are sample drawings covering every inch of this shop.

"What should we get?" I whisper in Ryan's direction.

"I have an idea." He smirks, bumping me with his hips. I look at him curiously, but he doesn't offer anything more.

When it's our turn, Ryan goes first. He's talking to Rhett so quietly that I can't hear what he's saying. *So, it'll be a surprise then.*

After twenty minutes, a shape starts to appear. I stare at the piece of art forming on his bicep. It's an infinity symbol with an anchor closing the loop on one side.

"Because you are my anchor," Ryan says as he looks up, his eyes meeting mine. "I was drowning before, and you saved me."

I look at him. He doesn't smile. He doesn't say anything else. He just looks at me with his big, beautiful brown eyes. That look tugs on my heartstrings.

I'm at a loss for words, and that doesn't happen to me very often.

I stare back at him. "It's perfect," I say, suddenly remembering how to speak. I've spent my whole life waiting for a love that consumes me.

When it's my turn, I get the exact same thing. I'm such a fool for him.

What's one more tattoo I'm going to eventually regret?

If this was a test, I think I aced it.

ARIA

Wednesday usually consists of our regulars eager to see the new pieces on display, but not today. We've only had two visitors all day. As I sit here, my chin resting on my hand, lost in thought and bored to pieces, my phone lights up. A text from Ryan appears on the screen.

"Got plans Saturday? Wanna see something cool?"

I smile, thankful my boss isn't around. Ryan's been on my mind a lot since last weekend, since our first date. It was nothing special or out of the ordinary because he is ordinary—Levis and a ball cap kind of ordinary—but something about that feels safe. My ex only cared about himself and his career. We both knew it. But Ryan is different. I'm drawn to him in a way that I can't explain.

Picking up the phone, I type my response and send it more quickly than I mean to. "Yes, absolutely."

His response comes instantly. "Dress casually. We might get a little dirty."

My cheeks heat up. *Why am I blushing? Because he used the word dirty? Jesus, Aria, get a grip.* Before I have time to overanalyze what he possibly means, I get another text. This time it's from Bryce.

"Are you alive? I haven't received an update on your date with Ryan."

I roll my eyes. Her timing has always been impeccable. "It was good... really good actually. We're going out again on Saturday." A smile creeps across my face as I feel my cheeks blush again.

IT TAKES us about forty minutes to reach our destination, driving into the dusty outskirts of Denver. The racetrack appears like a mirage—bleachers are filled with people holding beer cans, engines are screaming in the distance, the scent of burning rubber fills the air. I glance down at my outfit, thankful that I wore an old pair of vans and worn-in jeans. A little dirt won't hurt me. Ryan's wearing a black tee shirt today, cuffed at the sleeves, showing off two black ink tattoos. One is a faded star that looks really, really old, and the other is an infinity symbol with an anchor inside that looks brand new. The ink is bright and it's peeling a little bit. *I should ask him what it means.* I don't have any tattoos... just one more thing we don't have in common.

I've never been anywhere like this before. I'm used to classical music and ballet studios, not grease stains and bleacher seating. I feel like a kid experiencing Disney World for the first time.

I find myself sinking lower into the passenger's seat, wishing I had more experience in social settings. I wish I actually knew how to have fun, instead of feeling uncomfortable in my own skin.

Ryan climbs out of the car, walking around to open my door. From his relaxed stride, I can tell he is in his element. He looks much more relaxed than he did on our first date. After helping me out, he takes my hand and leads me effortlessly past a row of cars, nodding at people who seem to know him. I love the way he lights up when he talks. There's something boyish about him here, something genuine. Like this is the one place in the world he feels at peace. Like he's known these people his whole life. Like they're family.

We quickly stop at the snack shack positioned at the front gate next to the parking lot. With fries in one hand and a Coors in the other, I follow him up the bleachers. He stops near the sixth row, close to the action, but far enough away to talk without having to shout.

He leans back, draping one arm around my shoulders. "You ever think about having kids?" he asks suddenly. I blink, unable to mask the surprise on my face.

He glances at me and laughs. "What?"

Clearing my throat, I shift in my seat. "Um, yeah—I mean, yes. I would love a family one day. I have career goals I would like to check off first. But the short answer is yes." *Stop rambling, Aria.*

He smiles slowly, his eyes on the track. "Me too. More than anything, actually." Pausing, he rubs the back of his neck. "But I can't. There were... complications after an accident back when I was in the Army." His voice drops a decimal, letting the words sink in.

I see the vulnerability written all over his face. The declaration makes me feel trusted, like he's chosen me to hold this sacred truth. It doesn't seem like something he'd share openly, and I find myself wondering if he's ever told anyone before. My heart aches for him, but also for the small minuscule part of me that was entertaining the idea of a family with him. How selfish of me. And ridiculous. *I just met this man.*

"I'm sorry," I say gently, reaching for his hand, hoping my voice doesn't carry any pity in the words. "Everything happens for a reason. And hey, if you really want a family, there are other ways."

My words must have caught him off guard—not in a bad way, though. I watch as that deep permeating sadness fades away just a little bit. He shrugs and sits up a little taller. "You're right. Doesn't matter how it happens—adoption, fostering... whatever. I just know I'm meant to be a dad." He smirks, lacing his fingers with mine as he takes a swig of his beer.

From our seats, I look around the racetrack. There aren't too many people here even though it's the weekend. Most seem to be regulars. Normally, I would be lying on the couch reading a book or doing my second load of laundry for the day. It feels nice to be out of the house doing something different.

"Would you like another beer?" Ryan asks, bringing my thoughts back to the present.

"No, I'm okay. Thanks, though," I say, smiling up at him as he scoots past me to get a refill. I never drink. And when I say never, I mean literally never. Because I never go out and have fun. I caved when I agreed to the one, and this one is already making me feel a little tipsy. I refuse to embarrass myself in front of him on our second date.

As I watch him walk away, he turns back and winks at me. "I don't usually drink much, but 'when in Rome,' right?" He smiles. *Don't be a snob, Aria... it's just a couple beers at the racetrack. Lighten up.*

He reaches the beer stand in no time, and I can't take my eyes off him. His hands are in his front pockets, and he stands with confidence, but it's a shy kind of confidence. And wow, *his butt in those jeans.* He turns around to head back to the bleachers, and I realize I'm staring. Our eyes meet for one second before I look away.

Okay, I could not have made that more obvious.

My cheeks are probably bright red. Turning toward the racetrack, I pretend to be invested in what's happening when Ryan scoots past me and back to his seat.

He hands me water, and as I reach for it I realize that he's moved so close to me that our knees are practically touching. At that moment, I imagine what it would be like to raise kids with someone who wants it so badly. Someone who tells bedtime stories and teaches lessons from the garage. Someone who buys me a bouquet of sunflowers every Sunday and makes me coffee each morning.

I shake the thought away quickly. I'm getting ahead of myself. For one, this is only our second date. I need to relax. Two, I am going to Paris. I won't even be here for a year or so.

"Tell me something about you," Ryan says to me. I didn't realize how long we were sitting in silence. He might have asked me other questions while I was lost in thought about my future with him. *A complete stranger.*

I swallow, unsure of what else to say. I told him about ballet on our first date, and that's really the only interesting thing about me.

"Hmmmm. Well, I love to bake. It's just a hobby, but I love being in the kitchen."

He grins. "I bet you're very good."

I blush again as I look down. "Thank you, yeah, well... no one's been poisoned yet."

He laughs, tipping his head back. Then, his attention snaps back to the race. Something big happened, but we missed it. I look around confused, hoping to get a grasp of what's happening, but I don't see anything.

On the drive home, the car is quiet. He doesn't turn the radio on and he doesn't talk, either. His hand is resting on my leg, his thumb running small circles across my knee.

When we pull up in front of my apartment, I keep waiting for the kiss goodnight, or maybe an invitation back to his place, but neither come.

"I'd invite you over," Ryan says, hesitating. "But my cousin's asleep. She's got early shifts and I don't want to wake her."

Something in me deflates. Trying not to show my disappointment, I nod. He's trying to be respectful, and it's nice. His thoughtfulness is one of my favorite things about him.

Sitting in his car for a while longer, we talk about nothing and everything. Movies we love, places we want to visit. The past, present, and future. A natural quiet sweeps over the car when he finally leans in to kiss me. It catches me off guard, but I let myself sink into it. His lips are so soft, and he's looking at me like my kiss could save him. I don't remember climbing out of the car. I don't remember walking up the steps to my unit. I don't remember changing into my silk pajamas.

I don't remember anything but the lingering taste of his kiss on my lips.

KATE

Ryan emailed my dad.

He didn't call. He sent a cold, impersonal email asking for permission to marry me. Like it was just a formality to check off the list. A little too late, I might add.

My dad responded with a firm, unapologetic, "No."

I'm not surprised. My parents have never actually met Ryan. Their life is still in California, and mine is now in Colorado. They don't even really know what my life has become—not the town I live in, not the tiny condo.

Early on, I shared a few photos with my mom and told them about the mechanic I'm seeing, but as things shifted, I started sharing less. I didn't want the judgment, the questions. I didn't want to hear the worry in my mother's voice, so I painted a version of my life that was easier to digest. Easier to defend. But even from a distance, my dad must have sensed something. So he said no. Zero hesitation, just no.

Ryan didn't mention the rejection directly, but I could tell that it upset him. He became more withdrawn afterward, more clipped in his comments. The man of few words became a man of even fewer. I tried to bring up the idea of waiting to get married—maybe giving my parents time to come around—but he shut me down immediately.

"We don't need their blessing," he argued. "We've got each other. That's all that matters." And that was that.

That next morning, we stand in the cold courthouse, waiting our turn like we're at the DMV. My dress is simple, something I found on clearance at the mall. It's not really my style, and definitely not what I envisioned for the day I get married. But Ryan came home last week wanting to just go to the courthouse and skip a wedding entirely, so I didn't have much time to find something better.

There are no flowers. No music. My parents aren't here. They don't even know I decided to go through with it. My friends didn't call. I invited Emma and Jade, a casual text out of the blue, telling them that Ryan and I decided to get married. I hoped they cared enough about me to make the trip. But they didn't. They didn't even reply.

It's like the world collectively agreed to pretend this isn't happening.

Jessica and Chris are the only ones who show up—Jessica in jeans and a tee shirt, Chris in a camouflage sweatshirt. Ryan's sister didn't show up, or his mom... Come to think of it, I wonder if he even told them he was getting married.

The courthouse is slow on this particular Friday. There's one person in front of us, determined to get out of a parking ticket that *wasn't her fault*.

Moments later, I hear our number called. It's our turn.

As we walk up to the front, fingers entwined, Ryan squeezes my hand. My mind is darting back and forth between bliss and confusion. I feel happy, and then I'm back to *how did I get here anyway?*

The civil worker mumbles something about *happily ever after* and *finding your soulmate*. But I'm not listening. My thoughts have drifted to Danny.

I know, *not the time or place*, but as I listen to the faint sound of my freedom slipping away word by word, I imagine what he would say if he could see me now. We talked about marriage, before everything came crashing down. I wonder if he would try to be happy for me, or if he would laugh. At Ryan, at Charlie, and at the endless string of bad choices that came after him. He wouldn't be the only one.

After a few short minutes, I hear, "You may now kiss the bride." Ryan's movement draws me from my daydream. He moves quickly, cupping the back of my neck with both hands.

It happens in an instant.

I close my eyes, and Ryan holding me upright is the only reason I am standing right now.

Ryan.

The man I just vowed to spend the rest of my life with. He pulls back finally, smiling like he just won the jackpot. Smiling like he knows something I don't.

What have I done?

I've never felt more alone in my life than I do right now, with my husband.

"Congrats, man!" Chris claps Ryan on the back as Jessica rushes over, handing me a beer. "Newlyweds!" she says as she gives me a hug.

I take the beer out of her hands and crack it open. I toss it back, finishing the whole thing in one sip. Ryan looks at me like he wants to say something but hesitates. He shakes his head, declining the beer Chris is offering.

There's something about toasting with beer—the absence of champagne is everywhere. The absence of elegance.

I'm not sure what a wedding is supposed to feel like, but I'm sure this isn't it.

We stand outside the courthouse celebrating for a bit—an hour, maybe two. I don't remember any of it.

I black out as the minutes pass, lost in the fantasy of a version of myself that is so deeply and madly in love with the man of her dreams. But that guy isn't him and that girl isn't me.

The ride home is quiet. The courthouse is about an hour from our condo. Ryan seems content, driving with one hand on the wheel and the other resting lazily on my knee. I reach into my purse and dig out my phone. Opening my photo album, I scroll through the photos Jessica took on my phone. Staring at the photos, I look at my face—really look—and I don't recognize the girl looking back at me. My smile is empty. I look like I'm drowning in a room with no water.

Selecting the best one, I open up Instagram. I guess it's time to share the news. I look at my feed. I haven't posted anything in months. Four, maybe five. I disappeared, like a ghost.

After typing up the caption, "K+R 🖤 ," I hit post, closing my phone quickly. I turn my phone face down on my lap. I don't want to see the reactions, the questions, the comments. Everyone will be so shocked. *And why wouldn't they be?*

I keep my life so private. I don't talk to anyone anymore.

I look out the window, feeling sick from drinking the cheap beer on an empty stomach. Minutes later, my phone begins buzzing in my lap. I hesitate as I flip it over, nervous to see who it's from.

I'm in a group chat with Emma and Jade. Our thread has been around since middle school. The first text is from Jade. "I know we haven't really talked in a while, but we are still happy for you."

Seconds later, from Emma, "We miss you." Tears well up in my eyes. I click my phone closed and look back out the window.

I feel my heart break as rows of trees pass by me in a blur.

What have I done? What can I tell them after so much time?

How can I tell them that it wasn't my choice to let our friendship fade? It wasn't my choice to stop calling or to stop making plans. And then we moved across the country. They will never understand, and I can never explain, not really. I don't even understand.

Ryan squeezes my leg as he turns to face me, taking his eyes off the road for a brief second. "We should order pizza for dinner, *wife*." His hand is tracing lazy circles on my knee. I can tell that he loves the sound of that word on his tongue.

I force a smile. "Sure." *Pizza, at home, after our cheap courthouse wedding.* I will not fall apart right now.

"I love you," he says before turning his attention back to the road. Even his best intentions are still so deceptive.

We're about twenty minutes from home, so I flip my phone back over to call Dominos. I notice more messages on my phone screen, making me pause.

"Dude, you got married?? WTF?" from Steve.

"Girl! I saw your news! We need to catch up, I hella miss you," from Janelle.

I close my eyes and take a deep breath. The car is starting to spin. Or maybe it's me. I don't know how to pretend this is okay when it's not.

I take another deep breath, forcing myself to pull my shit together. At least until I get home and can lock myself in the bathroom. I dial Dominos and order a large pepperoni pizza. Our usual.

Ryan pulls into our parking spot, number 32, and as he parks, I can't help but feel cheated. I was cheated out of what a wedding should be. I was cheated out of what a marriage should be. There is no wedding night magic. It's just the same silence, the same worn-out couch, and the same cramped condo in an unfamiliar town.

I follow Ryan through the front door feeling utterly defeated. Our pizza arrives shortly after, thanks to my impeccable timing. We eat in more silence. He doesn't ask about my hopes and dreams. We don't talk about the future we are going to build together. Instead, we share our attention with Ryan's phone.

KATE

R yan's been arrested, just thought you should know."

That's all I hear before the call ends. I look at the phone in my hand, thinking maybe my ears are playing tricks on me. *Arrested? What?*

The voice sounded tight, nearly breathless. When I hang up, I see that I have a dozen missed calls, all from unknown numbers. *What in the world?*

I'm at work, spending my morning cleaning the eyeglasses that come through on the conveyer belt one by one and lost in thought about my conversation with Ryan last night. I mentioned maybe wanting to go back to school, and Ryan changed the subject without answering me. Jessica is out sick today, so it's just me holding down the fort.

Slowly, I pack up my things, and I tell my boss I don't feel well so I can leave my shift early. My mind is spinning. There is no way I heard that correctly. *Arrested?* My how the mighty have fallen. *Wedding yesterday, arrested today.*

By the time I reach our condo, something feels off. I skip across the parking lot, as if shaving off seven seconds will change anything. I walk inside and everything is different. Things are not in their proper place. The couch is moved ever so slightly, DVDs are tossed on the floor, and the lamp next to the sofa is knocked off the side table. *What happened here?*

Bandit is pacing by the front door, and Penny is cowering in the corner. Making my way over to the couch, I sit. I begin calling every number I can think of—so basically I call Jessica, and she doesn't answer.

Huffing, I grab my laptop from our bedroom. I flip it open and pause. I don't know where to start. I've never been in this situation before. Finally, I track Ryan down through the county courthouse's online records. *Burglary. Pending trial. No bail.*

What the fuck. *Burglary?*

That doesn't sound like Ryan. Sure, sometimes he does questionable things… but burglary? No bail? The court document I managed to find online mentions stolen tools and car parts from a private residence in town from an address I don't recognize. I sit back on the couch as I reread the accusations one by one, picking them apart in my mind and trying to piece the story together. *How did I not know any of this was happening?*

Ryan has been working later nights than usual at the garage, yes, but I thought it was just to avoid being home with me. We usually come home just in time to have dinner together. Then we go to bed. Things aren't exactly blissful, but there's no chaos, either. And the absence of chaos is almost enough to trick me into thinking this is happiness.

Our things are thrown all over the place. I'm so confused. *Why would he need to steal tools?* He has plenty. And he works in a garage. There are plenty of things he can borrow there, too. It makes no sense.

Scooping up Penny with Bandit close on my heels, I walk across the hall to our neighbor's door. After pleading and dodging a few questions about why the police ransacked our place earlier, he agrees to watch the pups for a while.

Ryan is being held at a jail twenty minutes away. I feel so anxious, I might be sick. Outside, the sign reads, "Denver County Jail." I sit in my car for a few minutes, trying to steady my breathing, but it's no use.

Walking up to the door, I swallow and give it a hard push. I've never been inside of a jail before. The fluorescent lighting is bright and sterile. The phones are ringing off the hook. It's so loud. Women are crying and men are yelling. It's chaotic everywhere. I look around slowly, standing frozen like a deer in the headlights.

As if sensing my fear, a woman walks up to me and puts her hand gently on my shoulder. "Can I help you, honey? Who are you here to see?"

I swallow. "Ryan. Ryan Langford. I think he's here…" My voice trails off as I look around again.

"Oh, yes. Ryan." She clicks her mouth. "We brought him in a few hours ago." She almost looks disappointed. "Head down the hall and wait in the first room to the right. He'll be in shortly."

Eyes look up at me from every desk and from every direction. Eyes with silent questions. I do not belong here, and everybody knows it. Even I know it.

After walking for what feels like a mile, I finally reach the room the officer directed me to. Inside there is a cold, metal table with one chair on either side. The walls are brick painted a miserable gray color. One side of the wall is a large two-way mirror. I've seen this room before, in every true crime show that's ever existed. I gulp, pulling out the chair closest to me. This chair is so cold, I can feel the chill through my leggings, making its way up my body.

I thought the officer said shortly? It feels like an hour has passed, maybe two.

Finally the door swings open, and Ryan walks in, handcuffs on his wrists and ankles. The voice behind him says, "You've got ten minutes, make it count," before slamming the door shut.

The silence is delicate, like glass on the verge of breaking.

I expected Ryan to explain, to apologize or even make an excuse, anything. But he just looks down at the table, at his wrists chaffing within the too-tight handcuffs.

"Ryan, what is going on? What happened?" I try to whisper, but it comes out louder than I intend. "Talk to me."

"I didn't do anything," he says, looking up. "I didn't do what they accused me of. Chris set me up."

I freeze. "Chris? What do you mean?"

"He told me that house belonged to a friend of his. He asked me to pick up some tools for him." He sighs. His voice is strained, barely above a whisper. "I'm going to kill that asshole."

I pause. None of this makes any sense. Why would Chris do that? Does Jessica know? They are our best friends, our *only* friends. Jessica didn't answer when I tried to call earlier... but that doesn't mean anything. She could have been busy.

They came to our wedding. This has to be some kind of misunderstanding.

I look back at Ryan, trying to make eye contact. I need to feel a connection—anything to ground me, because I feel the rug being pulled out from beneath me. But he won't look at me. And I have the sinking feeling that I am going down with the ship.

Clearing my throat, I say, "So what happens now? When can you come home?"

My voice breaks when I say *home*. Something about that word and saying it out loud makes me think back to our wedding day—about the vows we spoke and the promises we made. *Was it all a lie?* It feels like Ryan took a hammer to everything. And I'm tired of feeling this way.

Ryan looks at me then, his eyes clouded with sadness. "I have to stay here, Babe. At least until the sentencing."

I lean back into my chair. The truth hits me at that moment, staring ahead at nothing, at everything. *Why doesn't he get bail?*

I want to believe him, I really do. But there is a nagging feeling inside of me saying there is more to this story. And that part of me is *mad*. Mad that he didn't put me first. Mad that he didn't think before acting.

Play stupid games, win stupid prizes.

Shifting in my seat, I manage to get out, "Do I need to call a lawyer?"

"No, I've got that handled."

"What does that mean?" I say, confused. "Are you sure? Let me help you."

"Drop it, Kate. I said it's handled," he says tersely.

There's a weight in my chest from everything he's downplaying. I want to lash out at him. I want to make him feel how he makes me feel, if only for a second. But I say nothing. *I do nothing.*

It's a waste of breath to try and console him. I should know that by now.

A knock on the door makes me jump, and the officer enters the room. He reminds me that our ten minutes are up. I stand up slowly, every bone in my body telling me to bolt.

Turning, I take one last look at Ryan. My eyes burn like the room is on fire with invisible smoke.

ARIA

I'm losing my mind.

It's been four days since I've heard from him. Four days since he dropped me off from the racetrack. Four days since *that kiss*. Four days since our amazing date.

At least, I thought it was amazing.

Rolling over, I see Daisy patiently waiting by the door. I should get up.

I slide my feet into my sunflower slippers as I crawl out of bed, tossing a sweatshirt on. Daisy runs into the kitchen, straight to her leash. She brings it to me, just in case I think about making myself a coffee before taking her outside.

Marissa is rummaging around the kitchen, doing dishes it sounds like. I wander through the room, lifting my hand slowly to wave. She smiles, knowing better than to try and talk to me this early without coffee.

Our apartment is on the second floor, something I fought tooth and nail for. I didn't want to be on the first floor, because it's unsafe for two females living alone, and not higher than the second floor because of Daisy. She spots a squirrel the second we step through the door and takes off running, leash whipping behind her down the stairs.

"Daisy!" I'm yelling as loudly as I'm capable this early without any caffeine coursing through my veins yet. "Get back here!" I chase her down the stairs to the big oak tree in front of the complex. When I catch up to her, she's waiting patiently, eyes glued to the branches.

"Jesus, Daisy," I whisper, out of breath. "It's too early for this."

I look down at the phone in my left hand. I have the volume on and vibration turned off for the first time in four years. *Why doesn't he call?*

Dragging myself up the steps, I follow Daisy as she leads the way to our unit. Swinging the door open, Marissa eyes me up and down as she leans against the counter. "You okay?" she asks, lifting her own coffee to her lips.

"Yes." I force the words out, gritting my teeth. "Is there more coffee?"

She nods her head to the left where the freshly brewed pot is sitting on the counter.

I whisper thank you as I trudge toward the coffee maker when I see that she's set out a coffee cup for me already. Our coffee cup collection is full of funky patterns and sassy quotes, picked up from miscellaneous farmer's markets and Hobby Lobby's all over town. Today's choice reads: *Don't talk to me until I've had my coffee.*

Cute, I think, giving her a glance.

Following her out onto the patio, we sit down on the loveseat overlooking the city. Marissa and I don't have much in common other than our love for dance and our apartment balcony. It's the best view in the city. She loves the outdoors, hiking, and drinking on patios, and I love baking, quiet nights on the couch with a good book, and Daisy.

We bonded over dance in college, and the rest was history.

"So what's on the agenda for today?" she says through sips of coffee. "Are you planning to stay home and brood some more?"

I glare at her. "I'm not brooding," I say, deflecting. But that would be a lie. My phone never leaves my side. I keep telling myself not to overthink it. Maybe he's busy. Maybe he's the kind of guy who doesn't believe in constant contact. Maybe he just doesn't like texting. It's only been two dates after all. And I don't want anything serious, *so why does it matter?* But still… something about the way he looked at me on the bleachers, the way his hand squeezed my thigh when he talked about family, it felt real.

It was real, wasn't it?

As if it hears me talking, my phone dings. Quickly lifting it to my face, I notice the text is from my mom. Groaning, I set it back on the cushion. I need some separation, because this is unhealthy.

"No, no brooding today," I repeat, trying to convince us both. "I need to go by the gallery for a few hours and help Leslie with something, then I've got ballet."

"You could take a break, you know," she says hesitantly. "From ballet. You do deserve a night off every once in a while."

I shift on the cushion, adjusting the throw blanket over my legs.

"I know, but I'm so close." I pause, taking a sip of my coffee. "Only a few more lessons until I'll feel ready to apply to Paris."

She smiles, knowing this conversation is pointless. Nothing is more important to me than ballet. Not even Ryan.

"What are you up to today?" I ask, coming back down to earth. I've always been an anxious over-thinker, and ballet has been the only thing that quiets the noise. Otherwise, silence fills in the blanks with fear.

"I need to get ready for work in a bit, then John and I are going to the movies tonight." John is her needy, slightly neurotic boyfriend. He's a little bit odd, but he loves her desperately. Because of that reason alone, it's hard to not like him. They've been dating since freshman year of college, so at this point they really just need to take the next step. But neither of them will say or do anything about it. *We're happy*, Marissa says, *why complicate it?*

I lean down and give Daisy some ear scratches. She fell back asleep after waking me up ridiculously early to go outside. *Must be nice.* Looking out over the city, I watch the cars lined up in traffic, the hustle and bustle of city life.

Denver is a busy city, busier than it gets credit for. Most people move here and live as close to the mountains as they can get, but I like the city. I like being able to walk to work and the ballet studio. I like to take Daisy for long walks around the town, stopping at a new coffee shop each time. I'm a city girl through and through.

Staring over the balcony, I make myself a promise. I promise I will put myself first and never let another man waste my time again.

KATE

I don't remember pulling into our parking spot, or changing into different clothes, or pouring myself a glass of wine. But when I come out of my daze, I find myself sitting on the floor in the living room, wearing Ryan's tee shirt. The dogs are curled at my feet, snuggled up in a blanket.

The version of Ryan I convinced myself to believe in is slipping through my fingers like sand, and there is nothing I can do to stop it. Reaching across the floor, I grab my phone. My heart feels heavy.

If Jessica did hear about Ryan's arrest, she didn't feel compelled to call me back, and that conversation is more than I have the energy for right now.

It's moments like this where the reality of my isolation consumes me. Moments where I want to call someone, anyone, to let them in, and I realize that I have no one to call. Not anymore.

As I sit in the dark, I feel myself starting to spiral. I'm sitting here alone, looking out the window at a world I don't recognize, talking to the walls that are closing in on me. It's pathetic.

I am nothing without him. He made sure of that, and I let it happen. *And we both know I will never leave.*

~

THE COURTHOUSE IS GRAY, square, and cold. Not just in the physical sense, but in the way it sits on the street like it doesn't want to be noticed. As if it absorbs every ounce of hope that passes through its doors and buries it in cement. The last time I stepped foot in this courthouse was on our wedding day. The irony is stifling.

I haven't seen Ryan in eleven days. It took eleven days to get a court date scheduled. Eleven days to decide his fate. I am here early, really early. As I round the corner, I spot his car in the parking lot. The red one, polished and shining, as if it were the one on trial and not the man who drives it. They left it here for me to deal with in case the trial goes sideways.

Inside, the courthouse is sterile and thick with tension. Beige walls and harsh fluorescent lighting. People are sitting in silence or whispering in corners. I stand in the security line feeling like a child in an adult world I don't understand. I clutch my small purse and shuffle forward, my eyes darting around, searching for something familiar. But it all feels so foreign.

I find an empty bench outside the courthouse and sit down, smoothing the wrinkles from my skirt. I dressed carefully this morning—neutral colors, light makeup, hair pulled back. Not my normal style, but I want to look respectable, presentable. Like someone who couldn't possibly be married to a man accused of these kinds of things. Someone who makes good choices, including the man she married.

Or, maybe they will take pity on me. Either one is fine.

Ryan comes through the side door a few minutes later, his expression unreadable. Still in handcuffs, still wearing a bright orange jumpsuit. He glances in my direction as he walks past me into the courtroom, escorted by two guards. Barely above a whisper, he says, "Don't worry, Kate. It'll be fine."

But I don't believe him. It won't be fine. *None of this is fine.*

When it's time, I walk through the doors and into the courtroom. I'm not sure where I should sit, so I pick the third row. Not close enough to be in the action, but not so far back that it seems like I don't care.

The judge is already seated. Ryan is sitting up front with his court-appointed lawyer, who looks like he just graduated from high school. My vision is foggy. People are moving like shadows, shuffling papers and adjusting microphones. It feels like a play I haven't rehearsed for. Everyone knows their roles, and I'm just sitting here, terrified, hands curled into fists in my lap.

I keep thinking, *six months. It'll be six months. We'll get through it. It'll be fine.* That's what the teenage lawyer had suggested. It's a first offense in a small town, the judge will go easy on him. He said those things like they were promises.

It's really hot in here. Lifting the base of my sweater slightly, I start fanning it up and down—anything to create a little airflow. I'm starting to sweat, and it's not a good look.

Ryan stands at the front, flanked by his public defender. He doesn't look back. Just stands there with his hands folded in front of him, the same dead calm he always wears when things get too real. I wish I could see his eyes. I wish I could feel a connection to him, even just for a second.

I hear the judge ask him if he has anything to say, and he shakes his head once.

Of course he has nothing to say. Silence is his chosen language.

The prosecutor lists the charges—burglary, breaking and entering, possession of stolen property. I can't understand half of what's being said, as if the charges are being read underwater. I try to understand, but I can't. My heart feels like it's trying to claw its way out. I stare down at my hands as I start to shake.

The judge begins speaking again. Something about the seriousness of the charges, about prior infractions that were never formally pursued, about the need for consequences. My vision goes blurry. I blink rapidly, trying to focus. *Prior charges?*

The judge looks directly at Ryan as he says, *"Six months to twenty-two years in state prison."*

KATE

Six to—wait. *What?* I heard the words, but they aren't registering.

I glance at Ryan, but he doesn't move. He doesn't flinch. He just nods, once, as if he was prepared. That's when it hits me—maybe he was. Maybe there's more to this than I was ever allowed to know.

He guards his secrets like a luxury. That isn't shock on his face; it's acceptance. Familiarity. The realization twists in my gut like a knife.

If he knew this could happen, *why didn't I? How could he do this to me? To us?*

The room suddenly feels miles away, like I'm looking at everything through a tunnel. *Six months to twenty-two years.* That's not "we'll get through it, Babe." That's... my entire twenties. That's maybe forever.

Is this what I have to look forward to?

What if I want kids?

What if I want more out of life than just someone waiting for the man she loves to come home from a prison sentence?

Memories flash before my eyes in a fury, one to the next. The months I sacrificed, the dreams I buried beneath the weight of him, all vanish in the span of a few seconds. It's not just about the next few years. It's the next decade—possibly two. It's the rest of my life, slipping away like sand through my fingers.

This must be my own personal hell.

Lost in my devastation, I didn't see the courtroom clearing out around me. I didn't see Ryan get hauled away. I didn't get to look at him one more time. Didn't get to see that crooked smile, or hear him tell me that everything will be alright. Because it won't.

I'm the last one here. Standing slowly, I walk out of the courtroom. The world has already forgotten about me, about Ryan. I'm lost in the shuffle as the next group files into the courtroom, ready for the next case. I can hear the echo of my flats against the tile, and notice the way my hands feel as I clutch the metal railing on the staircase, exiting the building. I feel so small.

I will not cry, not yet.

Outside, the sky is dull and gray. I sit down on the front steps of the courthouse for a while, staring at nothing, when I start to laugh. Nothing is funny, but I can't seem to stop laughing. Because it is funny, the whole thing. *Isn't it?*

My love life is like a horror movie and I'm just the first one to die.

Climbing in the front seat of my car, that's when it hits me. I can't hold it back anymore. I start to cry, shoulders shaking violently as I sob. Hyperventilating, I let it all out.

I never got the chance to say goodbye. They whisked him away, hauling him off to prison before I could catch my breath, before I could ask what comes next. By the time I realized what was happening, he was long gone. Just a figure swallowed whole by the system that claimed him.

And the worst part is, I have **no one.** I can't call my parents, or my friends. Ryan made sure he was all I have, that my entire world revolves around him. And then he left.

He *left* me.

I should hate him. I should, but I can't. I'm not strong enough. Not anymore.

I rest my forehead on the steering wheel, tears streaming down my face.

The words echo in my head like a bell tolling.

Six months to twenty-two years.

KATE

"Hello?" a voice comes through on the other side of the door.

"Hey," I say quietly. "I know we don't know each other well, but would you be able to watch my dogs for me? If you could feed them, and let them out a couple times a day, I would really appreciate it."

The door swings open to reveal my nosy neighbor who had a conniption when our condo was ransacked after Ryan's arrest. He looks at my door behind me and answers quickly. "Okay."

"Thank you. I'll be home in three days." He closes the door just before I start to cry. *All I do is cry.* After all this time, I should be a pretty crier.

Walking back across the hall, I plop down on our sofa with a big sigh. Bandit jumps up on my lap. I squeeze him tight. I'm cashing in all of my PTO, hoping the distance will help me escape, if only for a minute. The idea of being here alone and putting on a brave face at the factory is too much to bear. I rush to get things in order, quickly shoving my things into a suitcase. There is one flight today from Denver to California, and I am determined to be on it.

I am long overdue to visit my parents. They still live in Southern

California, about twenty minutes from the beach. And a hug from my mom is exactly what I need.

It's all my fault, I know that. I pulled away. They don't know what happened to my life. They don't know that I decided to get married. They don't know anything.

But this is one relationship I can fix.

I finish packing in record time, throwing every pair of shorts I own into a tiny carry-on. I really, *really* miss the beach, and long drives with the windows down, and feeling the salty air on my skin. As I take one last look around the condo, it feels hollow. The lack of Ryan is everywhere.

As the miles stretch between me and the town we used to call home, I feel no relief. I'm in a haze, moving through the motions without purpose.

My heart is broken, and the wound won't close.

Los Angeles is exactly how I remember it. Palm trees line the streets, swaying lazily in the ocean breeze. The city is alive—there's distant noise from a rooftop party, and the chatter of beautiful strangers walking the streets. LA feels like a movie set.

My parents live in a two-bedroom apartment, fifty minutes out of the city, closer to the beach. They prefer suburbia to the hustle and bustle of city life.

My dad works for a tech company, writing software programs, iPhone apps, things like that. My mom doesn't work, hasn't worked a day since I was born. I used to think that I wanted to be a stay-at-home mom, too, following in her footsteps. Now the thought threatens to bring me to my knees—the realization that I might never get to have a family.

She's standing outside waiting, unable to contain her excitement as my dad parks the car. She hardly waits until I climb out of the car before she says, "Are you eating? Why are you so thin? Come inside, let's get you some dinner."

I roll my eyes. "Yes, Mom, I'm eating." Following her inside, my dad trails behind us with my overweight suitcase.

The apartment is exactly the same—nothing has changed. The same dark green sofa. The same bird decorations on the mantle. The same picture frames filled with my senior pictures, covering every shelf in sight.

"Come and sit down! Dinner is just about ready." my mom says, wandering back into the kitchen. Pulling out a chair, my dad gestures for me to sit. The same seat I always used to sit in. The same spot at the same dining table. I smile. It's nice to know some things will never change.

"So how's life, Honey?" my dad says, scooping some potatoes out of a bowl. "How's the job?"

Nervously pulling at my sweater, I look at my empty plate. "Oh, it's good. Nothing too exciting, but it keeps me busy."

"That's good. How are things going with that guy?" He looks at me for a moment, silence filling the void with the words he doesn't need to say. *That guy.* The guy who has a name that no one bothered to learn. The guy who asked for my hand in marriage through email. A moment we all remember, but don't feel the need to revisit.

"It's complicated..." I say, reaching for some green beans, desperate to focus on anything that will keep me from spinning out. "I haven't seen him in a while."

Not a lie, not really.

"Good."

Reading the room, my mom changes the subject. "What do you want to do while you're here? You're here until Sunday, right?"

"Yeah." I force a smile. "Just a few days. And I'm not really sure, I haven't thought much about it. I might call Janelle, see if she wants to grab a coffee. Other than that, just hang out with you guys. We can go for a drive if you want."

My parents love being in the car. They love mini road trips, little drives to anywhere, nowhere.

"Sounds good, Honey. Let's go for a drive tomorrow. We found a new restaurant on the coast we would love to show you," he says, handing me a bowl of chicken pasta, followed by the bowl of potatoes.

They are really trying to fatten me up.

"That sounds good, Dad. I can't wait." I force a yawn. "I'm tired from the flight, so I'm gonna head to bed. I'll make sure to have an alarm set for the morning."

As I get up from the table, I turn around and look at my parents. They are still so in love, after twenty-something years of marriage. You can see it in everything they do. In the way they look at each other, in the way they hold hands. In the way they joke—their playful banter keeps the spark alive. If I'm honest with myself, I'm jealous.

Alone in my room, I pull out my phone. I push my suitcase off to the side as I scurry onto the bed. Crawling under the covers, I pull them over my head. What I really want at this moment is to hear his voice.

I dial his number, letting his voicemail message consume me, if only for three seconds. "Hey, this is Ryan, leave me a message." Beep.

I take a deep breath.

"Hey, it's me. It's been a few days since they took you away, almost a week I guess. And I miss you. I still don't understand what happened. I just miss you." My voice breaks. "This wasn't supposed to happen. We were supposed to have a future. You promised me you would never leave me. You *promised*. Just you and me, remember?" A tear rolls down my cheek.

"I'm trying, Babe, but I don't know what to do. I don't know how to do this without you. I can't do th—" I'm cut off as the voicemail ends, reaching capacity.

Setting my phone down, I put my hands over my face, crying quietly. I don't want my parents to hear. I don't want questions that I can't answer.

Tears soak my pillowcase. I roll over, letting the sadness sweep me into a deep sleep. I dream of a time before this, before I met Ryan. When life was simpler.

KATE

The weekend passes in a blur of fake smiles and empty thoughts.

I don't sleep much, and I eat even less. I stare at the walls in my parents' apartment, feeling disconnected, like someone whose identity has been completely erased.

It's a miracle that my parents can't see what's going on beneath the surface. I can't talk about it, not yet. Not because I don't want to, not because I wouldn't love advice or to be comforted, but because I'm too unstable. I can't think about Ryan without breaking down. I'm in hell every time I close my eyes.

I spent the weekend missing Bandit and Penny, and wondering if I should reach out to Janelle—her husband is Danny's best friend. Two years have gone by since the fallout, and I didn't expect anyone to pick sides. The whole thing became awkward after a while. If I want to see her, now is my chance. I can't put it off any longer.

I lay back in the bed, grabbing my cell phone, scrolling to the J's. Finding Janelle, I click on *Text Message* and start typing.

"Hey girl! It's been a while. I'm in town this weekend visiting my parents, and I want to see if you're free to grab a coffee. I need to head to the airport later this afternoon, but I'm free until about one o'clock."

I take a deep breath, setting my phone on the nightstand. Turning my attention back to the piles of clothes around the room, I feel annoyed. I severely overpacked for a weekend trip. Now I have to deal with cramming everything back into my way-too-small suitcase.

I really, really need a coffee before I tackle this mess. I hear my phone vibrate on the nightstand just before I climb out of the bed.

"Hey girl! Happy birthday! Ah, wish I could but I gotta head to work in a little bit. I miss you though, I'll try to fly out and visit you sometime soon!"

I stare at the message. *I forgot it's my birthday.*

My mind drifts to a conversation I had with Ryan weeks ago. I wanted to fly back to Michigan and spend the weekend in Traverse City. "Anything you want," he said. "Anything for my girl."

The memory is like a knife to my heart.

I didn't know that my world would come crashing down a week later. A soft tap on the door brings me back to the present. I look back at my phone, at the message. Oh well, it's probably for the better anyway.

My parents slowly open my door. "Happy birthday!" they say in unison, my dad holding out a coffee for me. "Twenty-two today. Do you feel any older?"

I do, actually. I feel battered and bruised, like this year has taken everything from me. Determined to not ruin this moment for them, I put on a fake smile, taking the coffee cup from my dad. I wrap my arms around both of them. "A little bit." I laugh. "Thank you for the coffee, and for letting me stay this weekend. It was exactly what I needed."

"Sure Honey, anytime," my mom says. She looks like she might cry. Why, I'm not sure—probably because her daughter is another year older. The kind of thing that gets you when you have children. *A feeling I will probably never know.*

The weekend went too fast. As I load my suitcase back into the car, I make myself a promise. I will come and visit more. I will fix the relationship with my parents. I will make more of an effort, and I will not push them away.

Then one day, I will tell them everything.

As soon as I swing the front door open, Bandit greets me, tail wagging. Penny is curled up on the couch, staring at me with wide eyes. I smile at the scene. At least I still have them. *I wonder if they miss Ryan, too.*

I drop my bags by the door. Moving takes more energy than I have. I am so tired. Forcing one foot in front of the other, I join Penny on the couch. My body aches are becoming familiar. I've started to look forward to them because they remind me that everything was real. As I look around the empty room, the realization hits me like a ton of bricks. *My husband is in prison. And I deserve this, don't I?*

I chose to marry Ryan. I said yes. No one held me at gunpoint.

I reach for the remote, turning on the TV, hoping the noise will drown out the thoughts violently rattling around in my head. I can't move forward, I don't know how. I feel untethered, drifting through my life, and the feeling is overwhelming. I've been consumed with Ryan, with our relationship, for so long—trying to fix him, trying to make it work—that I lost myself in the process.

And now with him gone, there is nothing left but pieces of a life I can't recognize anymore. Bandit looks over at me, as if he hears my heart breaking.

I am lost, and I don't know how to find my way back.

Maybe I've always been lost.

KATE

Ryan is finally allowed visitation.

The prison is hours away from our condo, tucked in a secluded part of Colorado, far away from the town where we once tried to build a life. Far away from civilization. The drive itself feels surreal, as though I'm traveling to a different world entirely.

I keep my eyes forward and my mind empty, not wanting to think about what is waiting for me at the end of the road.

And then there's the overwhelming number of rules. I have to check my emotions at the door and remember every detail: what I can wear, what I can't bring. Everything has to be approved. No jewelry, no tight clothing. Nothing that can be perceived as "distracting." I can't even bring my purse. Just a small clear Ziploc bag with a few essentials—keys, my ID, and a handful of quarters I'm allowed to bring for the vending machines. It feels like stepping into an alternate reality, and I barely recognize myself.

When I finally reach the prison, I'm stunned to see tall iron gates. I know what a prison looks like (I have seen *CSI*), but the building is much larger than I imagined. The slow crawl of the opening gate causes my heart to beat faster. I feel small and insignificant in the vast expanse of it all.

Pulling up to the window at the gate, the guard asks for my ID, so I reach over and pull it out of the Ziploc bag. I hand it to him, my hands shaking. His eyes are hard and cold, like he has to stay emotionless and distant to get through his days.

My car slows to a crawl, and I park directly in front of the prison. There are three cars to my left, and that's it. When I walk through the front door into the prison, that's when it hits me: the silence, the concrete walls, the heavy metal doors that clang shut behind me. The air smells like bleach and something stale, and the guards' eyes on me are almost more than I can bear. Like they are judging me. They don't make any effort to hide, either.

I check in at the front desk, adding my name to the list of visitors. Finally, I'm let to a visitation room after waiting thirty minutes past my appointment time. The room is sterile and cold, with a long table stretching down the middle.

Ryan is already seated, waiting for me. His eyes meet mine as soon as I step inside, and for the first time in weeks, I see something that resembles familiarity. But he's different now. The man sitting across from me isn't the same one I married.

The distance between us is palpable, like the last few weeks have hardened him. I want to touch him, but I've already been warned— no physical contact. The absence of his touch is all over me. An ache on my side where his hands should be, and down my cheek where his fingers used to graze.

He tries to smile, but it's strained, like a reflex more than a genuine expression. I miss his crooked grin. *I would give anything to know what he's thinking right now.*

"Hey, Babe." His voice is soft, but it sounds hollow. He reaches for me, for my hand across the table, but stops himself. Remembering. Disappointment flashes across his eyes as he pulls his hands back. "I miss you so much. I would give anything to touch you."

I match his disappointment. His eyes darken as he looks at me, watching. As if he's trying to remember, trying to remind me how we used to be.

"Me too." I look down, fidgeting with my hands. "I wish you could come home."

"How are you?" he asks. *Awful, thanks for asking.*

"I'm okay. I took some time off and went to visit my parents over my birthday weekend." I pause before adding, "Our neighbor says hi every now and then."

I look up and meet his gaze then, and I swear, just for a moment, a flicker of jealousy flashes. I try to be vague, not wanting to reveal how broken I am. I don't want to admit that I'm drowning. I've been waiting for him every day since he's been gone. I just want it back the way it was before.

"How are you?" I wince immediately. What a stupid question. "I mean—what do you do all day?" Our conversation doesn't flow the way that it used to. Our small talk is forced and uncomfortable. A faint echo of something that no longer exists. The small moments of connection are gone. There is nothing left to talk about. Without his touch, without his influence, we are nothing.

"Well." He laughs half-heartedly. "I got your name tattooed on my ass the other day."

I blink. "You what?"

"You heard me," he says, slightly annoyed that he has to repeat himself. "That's about it. We do chores, eat, and have a little bit of recreation time to work out, stuff like that."

I nod. I can't relate to his life anymore, even if I try. He interrupts my train of thought. "Will you come visit me again soon?"

I nod again.

My head and heart are at war, and I'm caught in the crossfire.

"I wish you would talk to me," he whispers. He is desperate, I can tell. I'm sure he feels me pulling away, a detachment that wasn't there before.

"I'm trying." My voice threatens to give out. "I don't know what to say."

I feel nothing but emptiness. Nothing I can say will change this.

This is our life now. A chill goes through my body. My instinct is to grab his hand, lace his fingers with my own. I think about it, *consequences be damned,* but the thought is fleeting.

The visit is short. Too short. The guards are already signaling that our time is running out, and I barely managed to find a connection in our conversation. As I stand up, about to leave, I feel the weight of the prison pushing me down. Ryan looks at me one last time, his face a mix of longing and frustration, but I can't bring myself to speak.

So I just walk away.

But as I get in my car, ready to drive back home—completely alone—I can't help but wonder. I wonder if I just dodged a bullet.

Because isn't this what my future will be if I stay?

A few hours here and there, fragments of a connection that will never be enough. We will never have children, never buy a big house, never settle down. Flashes of the past come back to me in a blur. The night I *fell* down the stairs, the dent my shoulder left in the drywall. The way he told me that I got it wrong, that it was all in my head. The way he made me feel small and insignificant. And I can't quiet the corner of my soul that feels... *relieved.*

KATE

The sunlight pouring through my window wakes me up early this morning.

Bandit and Penny have commandeered the space on the opposite side of the bed where Ryan used to sleep. We've gotten into a rhythm, the three of us. Mornings curled up on the porch, and long walks around the neighborhood. I couldn't go back to the factory. I couldn't face Jessica. Not after everything. She never bothered to check on me either, so I decided to leave it alone. If Chris did have something to do with Ryan's crimes, I'll never know and I'm sure I don't want to anyway.

I have a little bit of money saved. Not much, but enough to give myself a minute to figure out what it is that I want to do with my life. That, and I plan to sell my wedding ring. That should bring in a pretty penny. *Hopefully.*

I feel like I'm finally able to breathe now, like the fog has lifted. The silence doesn't feel quite as heavy now. I've taken our picture out of all the frames. I've packed up his clothes, his piles of tools—all remnants of him—and boxed them up, storing them in the closet. It hurts too much to see them day by day. They were preventing me from getting any closure.

Christmas is next week, and although I'm not excited, especially because I'll be celebrating alone, it's nice to have something to look forward to. I'm going to go buy a Christmas tree today. A little late, but better late than never I suppose.

Curled up on my sofa, I look at my phone discarded beside me. I want to reach out to Emma and Jade; I've wanted to for weeks. But I could never force myself to do it. It never felt like the right time, and I never knew what to say after all this time. Today, though, I'm feeling... giddy. *Like my old self.* Or like someone spiked my coffee this morning.

After staring at my phone for another minute, I pick it up, scrolling until I find our group chat. "Hi! I miss you guys. Are you free for a happy hour FaceTime later?" I hit send and immediately feel nauseous. *What if it's too late to fix things? Or what if they don't reply?* That would be so much worse than me not saying anything at all.

I groan, leaving my phone on the couch as I wander into the bathroom. I grab my toothbrush first, washing away the taste of coffee. I've moved onto my hair, trying to cram the flyaways into an extra-large hair clip, when I hear my phone ping from the other room. Penny barks, the noise scaring her out of her nap.

I skip over to my phone with my heart in my throat. It could be anybody, like my mom— it might not be from them. I swallow before bending down to pick it up. I see the text from Jade first. "I'd love that. I'm free around 4:00!" Then, the text from Emma. "Me too!"

"Sounds perfect. I'll call you both then!" I'm smiling. *I can't remember the last time I smiled.* I glance over at the pups lounging on the dog bed in the corner of the room. "Everything's going to be okay," I whisper.

I rush into the bedroom and weed through my closet, yanking shirt after shirt off the hanger looking for the perfect one, when I see it. The faded band tee, the one I wore when I made the biggest mistake of my life. *The one he loved.* Without hesitation, I rip it off the hanger, carry it all the way into the kitchen, and toss it straight into the trash can.

The afternoon came and went. I've spent the last hour putting up my skinny Christmas tree, adorned with a pack of bow ornaments from Target. I stopped through the liquor store on my way home for a fresh bottle of Chardonnay, because I can't get through this FaceTime without some liquid courage.

It's 3:58 p.m. I take a deep breath, and dial their numbers. My phone is propped against the candle on my coffee table and I'm curled up on the ground wedged between the couch and the table with my legs sprawled out in front of me.

Jade joins the call first. *She looks exactly the same.* Emma joins next, and I can't stop the tears as they start to fall. "I missed you guys so much," I choke out between sniffles.

"We missed you more," Emma says. We make eye contact and the look in their eyes tells me everything I need to know. *All is forgiven.* We don't need to apologize or explain. We can just pick up where we left off.

"Tell me everything I missed."

KATE

I want a divorce.

It's been fifty-seven days since I visited him in prison. Fifty-seven days filled with moments that were all mine. In hindsight, I can see Ryan and I were oil and vinegar, and we just didn't mix. After talking with Jade and Emma, it finally clicked. I talked and they listened. And now it's as if, without Ryan here to fill every corner of my life, I'm finally able to breathe. It took fifty-seven days, but I'm sure.

I didn't go back to the prison. I couldn't. The sight of him would shatter everything. He calls, but I don't answer. At least not the first few times.

In every voicemail, he begs me to hold on just a bit longer, insisting that once he gets out of prison, everything will be different. He promises he will change, that the man he was isn't the man he wants to be. The words are always the same—empty promises that carry no real weight, nothing to back them up but his unconvincing tone trying to pull me back into the world that I left behind. The world where he controlled everything. The world I escaped the moment he was dragged off to prison.

There were moments when I almost believed him, when the

desperation in his voice and his promises to change made me question everything. But as much as I wanted to believe him, deep down, I knew it wasn't the truth. I can't keep waiting for a version of him that doesn't exist.

And I think in some small, masochistic way... I actually enjoyed it. I enjoyed the thrill of not knowing which version of him I would get each day. The highs were high and the lows were low, but the rollercoaster was what kept me going. The adrenaline was intoxicating. It's so twisted, I know. I know that *now*, as least.

Tonight, as I watch my phone ring with a 1-800 number, the temptation to answer gets the better of me. "Hello?" My voice comes out quiet.

"Kate?" he says, as if he doesn't believe that it's really me, as if his voice is playing tricks on him. "I'm so glad you picked up. How are you?"

I'm praying that he can't hear my nervousness through the phone. "I'm fine, Ryan. Getting by." He doesn't deserve to know anything about my life now that he's no longer a part of it.

"Kate." This time, his voice comes out small, broken. "Don't do this. Don't throw us away. Just... take a little time to think. Think of the life we've built." He pauses. "We can make it work. I know we can."

He's pretending like somehow *I'm* the asshole in all of this for abandoning *him*. He doesn't say anything else as he waits for me to respond.

"That's not fair." My voice breaks. "I don't want this life, Ryan. I don't want to spend my days missing you, and my weekends visiting you in prison. I want more out of my life—you have to understand that." When I finish speaking, I'm shaking. I practiced those words in private, too many times to count. I never thought I would be brave enough to tell him, though.

"Please don't do this," he begs. *I'm not used to the sound of him begging.* "I need you. I *need* you to wait for me."

Something inside of me snaps. I realize that in this moment I am safe. Safe behind the walls of this condo. He can't reach me. He can't hurt me. He is miles away locked up in a cold prison cell. So I clear my throat and tell him everything I've always wanted to say, but was too afraid to utter.

"You *broke me*, Ryan. You took a girl full of life and light, and you broke her. You told me you loved me and then you hurt me. You physically hurt me." I pause, but only long enough to catch my breath. "You don't hurt someone you love. You made me cut off my friends and my parents. You spent months isolating me, making me think that no one would ever love me as much as you did. I gave you everything and you gave me *nothing*. Nothing but lies and infidelity."

I stand up now, starting to pace. I can't stop. It's like the dam has broken open. Everything I was holding in and everything I was holding back comes pouring out all at once.

"And the saddest part is that I believed you. For so long, I believed you. I wanted to be the center of your world so badly that I believed you. Worst of all, I defended you. And in the end it doesn't even matter. You didn't care about me, you didn't put me first, you didn't change. I will not wait around for you to break what little is left of my soul. I am done."

I hear a smash from the other end of the line. It's faint, but it's there. It sounds like he smashed his fist into a brick wall. I stop pacing when I hear the loud crack of knuckles shattering against the stone.

I can't believe I managed to get everything out without breaking down. I can't believe I managed to find my voice—the voice that he silenced. I don't know where the strength came from. Maybe it's been building up over the past year, or maybe I've finally just had enough.

I swallow again as I close my eyes. I take a deep breath and then exhale, willing myself to hold on to that sliver of truth. "I would wish you the best, but you and I both know you already had it."

For a minute I think he hung up, but then I hear a muffle from the other end. "You will regret this Kate. I will be waiting for you when you realize the mistake you just made."

I look down and notice that my fingernails are gripping the back of the kitchen barstool so hard, they punctured the fabric. Bandit and

Penny are curled up on the sofa, making themselves comfortable in Ryan's old spot, and snoozing quietly. If they missed him, they don't show it. The line remains silent for another minute.

His voice is hoarse, barely above a whisper. "For what it's worth, I do love you. I've always loved you. Bye, Kate." *Click.*

I can't believe it. It's over, it's really over.

I'm free.

ARIA

I nearly drop my phone when it buzzes.

The name on the screen makes my breath hitch. After seven months of silence, Ryan finally texts. After seven long and grueling months of driving Marissa insane, I woke up this morning fully prepared to let him go and move on.

I've spent the last seven months doing anything possible to keep my mind busy. I signed up for double the ballet classes, and I painted my room then repainted it again three months later. Anything to distract myself from a guy who ghosted me after two dates.

I'm going to Paris, and I *finally* feel ready.

"Hey Aria, sorry I've been MIA. I've been dealing with some family stuff, and I wanted to reach out... but the time... never felt right."

I stare at the message. I should be mad. I should definitely ignore it, at the very least. *Who ghosts someone for seven whole months?* "Family stuff..." What a horrible excuse. I thought he didn't *have* any family. "The time never felt right?" He could have easily texted me on a lunch break to let me know he was dealing with some sort of *emergency*.

He presses on. "You free this weekend?"

The nerve of this guy. I quickly start to overthink what this could mean in my head, before I land on curiosity. Maybe I should hear him out? Maybe he has a really valid reason, or *excuse*, for being quiet *for months*. Unlikely, but I need to know.

My fingers move faster than my thoughts. "I'm free tomorrow." *Come on Aria, why?*

He responds quickly. "Cool. Pool day at my place? It's supposed to be warm. I'll order food after."

Hesitating, I remember how he wouldn't let me in last time. Maybe I'll get to meet his cousin? I imagine a box of tools by the front door and vintage car posters in the living room. A few grease stains on the couch from nights stretched out in his dirty work clothes, devouring a pizza.

"Sounds good. Is your cousin still living with you?" Can't hurt to ask, right? Maybe his family emergency had something to do with her.

"No, Alicia's gone. It'll just be us," he responds, with a wink face emoji.

So, her name is Alicia, then.

SUNDAY ARRIVES, cloudless and hot. I pack my tote with sunscreen, snacks, and a towel, and drive across town to his condo complex. His pool is small and surrounded by cracked concrete, but it's quiet, tucked away behind the building, half-shaded by an old pine. It doesn't *technically* open for another week, but Ryan said they don't monitor it closely. The idea of breaking a rule makes my insides twist up into a bunch of knots, but I don't say anything. I won't be a buzzkill.

Ryan greets me shirtless and barefoot, a lazy grin spreading across his face like he didn't just go silent for seven months, causing me to question all of my life choices.

"It's about time we got some sun," he says, handing me a cold can of soda.

I reach out to take it, admiring the view. "I know, it's been raining so much lately." I laugh quietly, setting my things down on a lawn chair.

I wish I had some color right now, even just a little base tan. I'm about to blind him as soon as I take my shirt off. Being this pale is just embarrassing.

He takes a dive into the deep end, splashing me as his feet hit the water.

"Hey!" I say. "No splashing!"

A wide grin spreads across his face. "Why don't you make me, then?"

Oh, it's on now. There's no time to worry about being pale. Quickly, I rip off my shirt and shimmy out of my shorts. With a running leap, I bound into the deep end, so close that I nearly land on top of him. He throws his head back and laughs.

God, I forgot how beautiful he really is.

Everything feels so easy. We swim, we laugh. He makes fun of my dog paddling, so I dunk him under the water in retaliation. For a few hours, I forget about everything.

I let myself admire the sun glistening on his skin and his brown hair tousled from being dunked under the water. The sound of his Bluetooth speaker plays low in the background. I love how playful he is. I love the side of me he brings out.

Another hour or so passes, and my stomach growls. Somehow it's already dinner time, and I'm so hungry. Ryan laughs. "I heard that! Let's go inside and order pizza."

He swings the front door open, saying, "Leave your shoes anywhere, Babe. Make yourself at home."

Babe. I love the way that rolls off his tongue. His place is small and pretty plain, actually. It isn't at all what I envisioned. There's two stories, a bedroom and a bathroom upstairs, and then the living room and kitchen on the main level. No car posters on the wall, no decor of any kind.

I notice immediately a photo of him and another girl on the fridge. *That must be Alicia.* She is really pretty. I set my tote down and pull out one of the stools at the counter, taking a seat. I can't help but stare at the photo of them across from me. She has fair skin and jet black hair, with lips painted red. *They don't even look related.*

Ryan orders us a large pepperoni pizza and plops down on the couch, turning on *Criminal Minds.* He smiles and lifts his arm up, gesturing for me to come sit next to him.

"I've got a surprise for you," he says moments later. I turn and look at him, eyebrow raised in question. *Maybe now is a good time to tell him that I hate surprises.*

He moves his arm, pulling out the drawer in his end table. Sitting there is a jewelry box. It's long and rectangular, like it holds a necklace, or maybe a bracelet. *Or maybe another time.* I don't even realize that I'm holding my breath when he picks it up and hands it to me. "For you." His eyes darken.

Moving slowly, I open the lid—a necklace. It's beautiful. Simple, but beautiful. It's silver, with a chain link and a monogram "A" charm dangling in the front, accompanied by a turquoise bead.

Jewelry? After ghosting me for seven months? It's a nice gesture, but it's a little odd. There's no way he could have known I would text him back. Most people would cut their losses after seven months. Two dates isn't enough to hold out hope for over half of a calendar year. *Unless you're me.* I'm quiet as I contemplate what this means. Finally, I force the words out.

"Thank you, it's beautiful."

ARIA

I wake up to more texts than normal today, which is weird for me. I only ever hear from my mom, Bryce, or Marissa anyway, but it's never all three of them and never this early in the morning. Setting my phone down before I read the messages, I decide to go visit Ryan at work first. I'll respond to them later.

I spend extra time getting ready to go see Ryan—I want to look just right. I'm wearing jeans and my favorite zip-up crop sweatshirt from Lululemon. It's rare when I actually look at the weather ahead of time and dress accordingly.

By the time I pull into the lot, it's late afternoon. The sun is hiding behind the clouds, getting ready for afternoon showers. The auto shop is a low, flat building with faded red bricks and rows of cracked pavement leading up to the garage bays. The air smells like oil and rubber and heat. I'm halfway through parking when my phone buzzes in the cupholder.

"Actually, never mind—today's crazy. Come tomorrow instead?"

I frown. The message is abrupt and rushed. I stare at the screen, my engine still running. *But I'm already here.* I'm already dressed in the outfit I picked out for him to notice. I already made the drive.

Shutting off the car, I step outside with my phone still in my hand. Maybe I'll just say a quick hello.

The sound of voices and the metallic clank of tools carry across the lot. I walk toward the open garage when I see them.

Ryan is leaning against the workbench, jaw clenched at something a woman says. She's tall—taller than me, even—with shoulder-length black hair and black jeans cuffed at the ankle. Her arms are covered in tattoos. She is *gorgeous*.

As I watch them, I'm fighting the feeling of déjà vu. She looks familiar.

Wait... Is that Alicia?

There's a smudge of something on her arm—grease, maybe—but she doesn't seem to notice or care. *Like she's been here before.* Her posture is rigid, and her body looks tense. Ryan doesn't notice me. He's too busy trying to charm the other woman.

I freeze just outside the bay, half-shielded by the side of the building. My heart is beating hard in my chest. I don't know what I'm looking at.

Something about the scene grips me—the way Ryan's face softens when he looks at her. The way her body tenses when he flashes his most seductive smile. Even from here, I can tell they have history, or at least it seems that way. I can't explain it, but he seems so content around her. I hear the girl say something, but it's too quiet to make out the words. Whatever it is makes Ryan glance down and rub the back of his neck. Their body language isn't flirtation. It's something else. Something unfinished, maybe?

Honestly, it's confusing. I realize I've been staring, so I quickly turn around. I don't want to see any more. I don't text him back, because what do I even say? The walk back to my car feels like it will never end.

Climbing in, I shut the door softly behind me. I start to shake as my hands grip the steering wheel. Tipping my head back, I let myself stare at the roof of the car for a minute, still processing the scene.

I have no idea what I just saw, but I do know what it feels like.

What is it they say? *Always trust your gut?* My gut has never led me astray, not in my twenty-one years of life. *That's got to mean something, right?*

I'm going to throw up.

Finally I turn the car on, putting on music as I let it comfort me. On the drive home, I replay the scene in my mind on repeat: the way the girl leaned in to get his attention, the way Ryan smiled but not with his mouth—with his eyes. Like he was remembering something no one else in the room could see.

It's fine. I shouldn't be jealous. I am not his girlfriend, not officially.

I reach to my neck, picking up the necklace he gave me between my pointer and index finger, sliding the charm up and down the chain. There is something he isn't telling me. Maybe secrets that deep are reserved for a girlfriend. Maybe I don't deserve to know.

Maybe the girl with the black hair is part of the secret.

I spend my evening curled up on the couch with Daisy watching *Grey's Anatomy.* It's our favorite way to spend the evening. I never drink, but tonight I do. *Twice this month, actually.* Marissa has half a bottle of red blend sitting on the counter, so I pour myself a glass.

I'm only twenty minutes into the first episode when my phone buzzes. Ryan sent me a stupid photo of his dinner to break the ice. "I missed you today. Work was nuts. Are you free tomorrow?"

I don't bring up the girl at the shop. I know what it looked like, and I know what it *feels* like, but I don't want to know. After crying my eyes out on the drive home over a stupid man I barely know, I decided I don't want to know why Ryan looked too comfortable standing beside another woman. I don't like confrontation.

I'm having fun, I'm *living,* for the first time in a long time, so I'm going to let it go. I am going to focus on ballet and on my career. If he wants to date other girls, that's fine. I can date other people, too. I can be *unserious.*

"It's okay," I say, feeling a little disheartened. "I'm free after five o'clock."

"Perfect. Wear something comfy," he says. "You'll see."

So I say yes—because when you think too hard, eventually it starts to hurt.

ARIA

I told Ryan casually on our first date that I was obsessed with animals as a kid, and that proof still decorates my bedroom to this day. An array of stuffed turtles line my bookshelf, accompanied by delicate, small glass dolphins given to me by my grandmother on every birthday as a child. She would search far and wide for unique dolphin figurines, and we would go antiquing together on the weekends. It was our thing.

Ryan picks me up at five o'clock on the dot. We drive across town with the windows down, and the evening breeze flows through my hair. He doesn't tell me where we're going until we pull into the parking lot—The Downtown Aquarium in Denver.

Inside, everything changes. The building is cool and quiet. Blue light is reflecting off glass and water. The calming rhythm of swimming creatures, the slow drift of jellyfish, and the laughter of children create a feeling of deep serenity within me.

Ryan is leading me—walking beside me with his hand low on my back. We take our time as he points out his favorite displays, and he is just as excited as the children to pet the stingrays. The sight makes me laugh.

In this moment, he feels reachable, and I feel a happiness that reaches down to my core.

By the time we make it through the building for the second time, we take a detour at the gift shop. Striding through the room with intention, he heads straight to the back where adorable plush sea creatures of all kinds are lined up along shelves on the wall. Picking up a sea turtle, he carries it over to the cashier.

"For your collection," he says, pulling me in for a kiss. A grin slowly spreads across his face and he stands up a little bit straighter, like he's proud of himself for remembering.

My heart slowly melts. My ex didn't remember the little things. He didn't know my favorite flower, or my favorite animal, or my favorite color. I don't think he knew anything about me at all. But he knew the right things to say, and exactly when to say them. So I stayed. I stayed and wasted years of my life.

I will not make that mistake again.

"You remembered." I kiss him back, letting his arms wrap around my waist. "Thank you."

He pulls away from me after a minute, cold air filling the space where his body used to be. I follow him out the door, my hand linked in his, as he leads me down the sidewalk. For a minute, I let myself imagine that I'm enough and that I'm the only girl he needs. Because as much as I hate to admit it, I hate picturing him with anyone else.

I don't know how to be unserious.

We reach a little Mexican restaurant, just three blocks from the aquarium. According to Ryan, they have the best carnitas tacos, and those are his favorite.

He asks for a table for two, somewhere quiet in the back of the restaurant. He leads me again, and I let him. I like his desire to be in control. It's protective in a charming, chivalric way. It's like he needs the world to know that I am his. My ex didn't care enough about me or anything that I did to bother showing me off.

Pulling out my chair, he gestures for me to sit down. I smile, taking a seat. Turning, I hook my purse on the back of my chair.

When I face forward again, I notice he's staring at me. I see the look in his eyes, and I bite my tongue. Ouch.

I try not to wince as I feel my mouth filling up with blood. *I'm so clumsy.*

Thankfully, he doesn't notice. He reaches for my hands, moving the salt and pepper out of his way. "You are so beautiful," he says, staring at my lips.

I blush. *Always with the goddamn blushing.* I'm fair-skinned—there's no hiding the flames creeping into my cheeks.

The server approaches our table with two menus when Ryan cuts in.

"Hi—we'll have two orders of your carnitas tacos and two margaritas on the rocks." He orders for me, and I don't think he realizes how sexy it is.

I don't want a margarita, but I'm going to drink it anyway. I smile at the waiter, passing the menu back to him. I didn't even get a chance to open it, but I like it this way. I like being taken care of.

I feel Ryan hook his leg around my ankle. "So," he says, clearing his throat. He looks nervous. "There's something I want to ask you."

My heart is in my throat. I hate surprises. But he doesn't know that, because I still haven't told him. Because I always seem to be at a loss for words around him, and I never know how to speak up for myself.

"Will you move in with me?" He says it so matter-of-factly, like it's no big deal, but I hesitate. "I've been thinking about it, and it feels like the next step forward."

Already? He knows my ex let me down. He knows that as soon as it became time to take the next step, the stars suddenly unaligned and nothing made sense anymore. I look around the restaurant, anything to avoid eye contact. I can't imagine my things scattered throughout a new place. *What about Marissa?*

I've only just gotten used to the idea of Ryan again. The idea of cohabitating feels... like a leap. I think about him all the time, but the timing cannot be worse. I submitted my application to the Paris Ballet two days ago.

What will happen if I get accepted?

I've worked my entire life for this. *But what happens to us?* I swallow. *Us.*

This feels like a problem for another day. I've never had someone *want me* this way, and it's intoxicating. He's watching me with apprehension, as if he can see me weighing the options in my mind.

There is nothing going on. Not when he looks at me like this. Not when he buys me jewelry. This man is not capable of hurting me.

So I tell him yes and pack my bags.

ARIA

I peer around the curtain and spy Ryan sitting in the front row, holding a pamphlet. My studio puts on quarterly performances. It's just a simple recital for us to practice our skills—and show them off. Sometimes, scouts will make a special appearance, but not tonight.

Which is better, honestly, because I couldn't handle the pressure of a scout and Ryan here at the same time. I would probably pass out.

He's looking around the studio now, so clearly out of his element, when we make eye contact. He smiles at me with a crooked grin, a grin that makes me feel all the feels deep in the pit of my stomach.

He's so sexy.

Suddenly the lights dim. That's my cue. I give him a wink, then close the curtain, moving to take my place among my peers. Poised in first position, en bas, I close my eyes and inhale deeply. Ballet is the one thing in my life that I've done right. But I'm still wearing my lucky leotard, just in case.

When I open my eyes the crowd is cheering. People are standing and clapping—you know it's good when you get a standing ovation. I look around for a minute, smiling at the audience, when my eyes land on Ryan. He is beaming. He's shaking his head back and forth in disbelief.

I've never smiled so big in my life.

I exit the stage, moving through the room to gather my things, slipping into linen pants and a pulling sweater over my leotard.

Before I can grab my tote, I feel two arms wrap around my waist, pulling me in tight. *I would know those arms anywhere.*

I hold my breath for a minute before I hear Ryan whisper in my ear. "You were... incredible." He kisses my ear then my neck as he makes his way down. I rest my head on his shoulder, breathing deeply, letting myself feel him on every inch of my body.

Then he stops, pulling away to catch his breath. "Let me take you out to dinner?"

I twirl around until I'm facing him, feeling so small under the weight of his gaze. Feeling small in his arms. "I would love that."

He smiles again, kissing me on my nose as he turns to lead me out of the studio, hand linked with mine.

There's a little Indian restaurant tucked in the corner between the studio and an interior design firm. It looks quiet, almost uninviting from the outside, but the regulars know better. They have the best chicken tikka masala in the Denver area.

It's the one recommendation I was able to bring to this relationship and even Ryan agrees—it is the best. *Omg is that what this is? A relationship?*

We slide into a booth in the back. Out of the public eye, hidden from the commotion. The waitress brings us two menus, and before she can get a word out Ryan interrupts. "Can we see your wine list? We're celebrating." I look at him and smile.

He orders us a bottle of Pinot Grigio, a bottle local to the California Central Coast. The waitress pours us each a glass, then resumes her rounds. Lifting his glass up, he turns to look at me. His beautiful brown eyes are glistening, and I can see him scanning my face, searching for the words.

"Aria." He pauses. "I've been waiting for the right time to tell you this."

I think I forget how to breathe.

"I love you." He starts to shake ever so slightly. "I've known for a while now... I'm in love with you."

Tears pool up in my eyes. My hands are shaking and my heart is racing. He makes me so nervous.

He loves me? When did that happen? And why did I allow this to happen? My mind quickly flashes to the girl at the garage, but the thought is fleeting. He was supposed to be someone I only spent time with when I was bored or lonely. It was never supposed to go this far. *How will I leave for Paris now if I get accepted?* How am I supposed to follow my dreams if that means breaking the heart of the person I love? Because I do... love him. I fought it *hard*, God knows I did, but it was no use.

"I love you too, Ryan," I whisper, lifting my glass up to meet his. "To us."

He clinks his glass with mine. "To us."

ARIA

Loving Ryan is like drinking red wine on a white couch. It's exhausting and exhilarating, all at once.

I've been settling into the condo, *our condo*, learning the rhythm of Ryan's world. I used to see him two, maybe three times a week, but now I am fully immersed in his life and his schedule. I've grown used to the peace of his daily life, the way he spends his evenings tinkering with old tools or watching racing documentaries on TV.

For the most part, Ryan seems excited. He has no qualms about the transition. He's eager to cook dinner together, settle into a routine, and build something that feels like stability. He says he's excited to come home to me every night, me and Daisy, who feels right at home. But sometimes I can't shake the feeling that the shadows of the past are still clinging to the walls, even though the lingering smell of lavender in the living room is the only reminder that another girl used to live here.

The condo is... fine. I didn't pay too much attention to it the first time I was here. I was too busy panicking over receiving jewelry after seven months of radio silence. It's definitely not the kind of place you imagine when you're a little girl with big dreams for the first time you live with a boy, but it's fine. The floorboards are slightly uneven, and the doors are heavy, solid oak that get stuck when I try to open them. The narrow, Victorian staircase is the best part. *I miss Marissa, though.*

She's trying to be happy for me. "If it's what you want," she said when I told her. Deep down I think she's happy, though. This allows John to move in, forcing them to take the next step, since neither of them want to talk about the future.

It's a Friday afternoon, and Leslie let me leave early from the gallery today. She said something about holding a private showing. I don't know. I didn't ask too many questions, I'm just grateful for a few hours at home to get some cleaning done before Ryan gets off of work.

Carrying my overflowing laundry basket up the winding staircase into our bedroom, I set it down on the bed. I'm standing in front of our closet, about to put up a fight with the door, when I notice a tiny piece of paper shoved under a loose floorboard in the corner. *Huh.* It looks like it was hastily crammed in there. The edges of the paper are ripped and the ink is faded and sloppy, like it was written in a panic. I read it slowly.

If you're reading this, you're new.

He will tell you I was crazy, but I wasn't. You aren't crazy either.

He will make you feel like you are.

He will apologize. He will buy you gifts.

He will say you're different.

I was different too.

I flip the note over to reveal one last sentence.

Watch the doors. He locks them from the outside.

What... the actual fuck? A chill rattles up my spine. There's a faint smear on the page. It could be mascara but it looks more... crimson. *Omg. Is that blood?* No, *don't be crazy Aria*, it's probably just red nail polish or something. I flip it back to the front side and notice a date scribbled in the top corner, 5/2. As I stare at the message, my legs give out and I slump down onto the floor.

Ryan and I matched online four days later. My hands begin to tremble as I reread the message. *Is this some kind of joke?* This has to be a joke. I *just* moved in with him... There is no way. Absolutely no way he is *this* kind of person. It's not possible.

My thoughts are racing. I read the note again and again, hoping that the next time I read it, the words will change. But they don't. I think back to Ryan's words and how he's always kept his life so private. I remember the way he's always avoided introducing me to his so-called cousin. Every lie comes crashing down.

Alicia wasn't his cousin, *if Alicia is even her name.* They were dating. Dating... at the same time he was seeing me. This was *her* condo. *Their condo. What happened to her?* The words on the paper swirl around in my mind, and nothing makes sense. But I am looking at proof, cold hard proof, that things aren't what they seem. I always felt like he was hiding something, but I could never put my finger on it. My "A" charm necklace tightens around my neck, suffocating me. *Was it even for me? Or did he buy it for her and then decide to give it to me instead?* The overwhelming feeling of betrayal makes me feel sick.

I look down one last time at the ominously vague warning. Without thinking any further, I stand up and walk to the closet. Throwing my things into a bag—well, the important things, I don't care to organize anything. Clothes, shoes, makeup, toiletries, all go into my bag in a panic.

I need to leave. I need to get out of here right now.

It feels like the walls are closing in on me.

By the time I finish, I'm shaking. My sadness has turned into anger. This apartment isn't mine. Ryan isn't mine. It was all a lie.

Grabbing my bag and my car keys, with Daisy on my heels, I look around the condo one last time. Nothing looks the same now. I rip the photo of him and Alicia off the fridge and shove it in my bag, along with the note, and close the door behind me.

STANDING by my car outside of my parents' house, bag at my side, my phone buzzes again; this time it's a voicemail. That's the sixth voice-mail in thirty minutes.

I put it up to my ear, listening to Ryan's voice, frantic and pleading. He arrived home from work to discover me and my things long gone, and he's been spiraling ever since.

"Please, Aria. Please come back? I'm sorry, okay. But you've got it all wrong."

I can hear him stammering, his voice cracking with the weight of his words.

"Aria, please," he begs again. "From the moment I met you, I knew you were the one."

I grip the phone tightly. The pain that's been simmering in my chest, the betrayal that has been building like a storm, finally breaks through.

"It doesn't matter, Ryan," I finally text back, my fingers shaking. "You lied to me. You led me on, and now you want me to believe that it was an accident?"

His response comes instantly. "I love *you*, Aria. Not her. My ex was crazy."

The words from the note hit me like a gut punch. *She told me that you would say that.* I wonder if even he believes his own lies? But it doesn't matter, I've already made up my mind. "No, Ryan. I don't believe anything you say. I will never believe you again."

As I'm breathing heavily in the night air, I feel a strange sense of relief wash over me, even as the tears begin to blur my vision. This isn't the life I wanted, anyway.

I'm standing outside the house I grew up in for what feels like an eternity, trying to absorb the reality of this moment. Eventually, I take a deep breath. Wiping the tears from my eyes, I turn off my phone and toss it into the passenger's seat. I climb in, slam the door, and begin to drive.

Ryan's words are echoing in my mind. The realization cuts me like glass.

I may have been his, but he was never mine.

ARIA

Ryan doesn't stop.

Text after text. Call after call. Voicemails spill over into the next. His name becomes a constant on my lock screen. He is ruining my peace, distracting me from ballet practice. He is consuming my every moment, and it's always the same thing.

"Please, Aria."

"You mean everything to me."

"My ex was crazy."

"You're the one."

I haven't spoken to him in almost a week. Bryce told me to block him, and my gut is telling me to do the same. But my heart... my heart is still wounded. For every lie he told me, there's also a memory of his laugh, or a kiss, deep and all-consuming. As the week goes by, my anger lessens a little. Now I'm just confused, which isn't much better, honestly.

I don't know how to reconcile the two versions of Ryan in my head—the one who broke my heart, and the one who taught me how to have fun again, how to love again. It's giving me vertigo.

And why do I even care? I'm so annoyed with myself. Any normal person would see these red flags, take the warning for what it is, and run, but no... not me. And why? What *is it* about Ryan that has my judgment so clouded?

Sitting on the couch, I wrap my legs in a blanket. Marissa let me move back in with open arms and zero questions. I called out of work this week, telling Leslie I have bronchitis. I knew the lie would work; she would never allow me to get her sick. Honestly, even though it feels good to be back home with Marissa, I don't feel better... just numb.

I've been staring at the TV pretending to watch *Grey's Anatomy* for a few hours now. It's the episode where Izzy loses Denny, one of my favorite heart-wrenching episodes. I've restarted it three times because even though I'm staring at the TV, my mind is somewhere else entirely. I can't focus.

His next message, the third text in an hour, comes with an offer. "Let me cook you dinner. Just one dinner. If you still want to walk away after, I won't stop you."

I hesitate for a moment, considering. He's never cooked me dinner before. I didn't even know he knew how to cook. Part of me wants to see that in person because I don't believe it.

I can't seem to quiet the little voice in my head asking me if I got it all wrong. I don't even know Alicia. She could be lying to me. Maybe it's not what I think? Maybe there's more to the story? Maybe his quiet and mystery is really just passion and devotion.

Or maybe the bad ones are just my weakness.

Unable to control myself, I text back an hour later and tell him yes. I tell myself I can still walk away if I want to. I'm still in charge of my own life.

Peeling myself off the sofa, I walk into my old bedroom. As I look around the room, vacant aside from a few leftover boxes sitting in the corner, and a few of John's things that he has yet to unpack, I remember what my life used to be. John sure took no time turning my old room into his personal oasis. I haven't been gone that long, but it looks completely different in here. *I wonder if he'll pop the question to Marissa soon.*

I might not have been living before, not really, but I was happy. *Wasn't I?* Happy enough. I have a good job, and I am on my way to study ballet in Paris. Then I met one stupid boy, and he changed everything.

I haven't bothered to unpack the overflowing bag I left with last week because unpacking makes everything real. I haven't been to ballet in a few days, either. Taking a seat, I crisscross[SJ1] my legs in front of my bag and rummage around for anything semi-clean and decent to throw on. I will not dress up for Ryan. I refuse. He can have me as-is—hair up in a messy bun, with leggings and a tank top on. *He's lucky I even agreed to come over.*

Giving Daisy a kiss on the head, I grab my purse and head to my car. If I don't go today, *right now*, I never will. *I don't even know why I am going.*

Pulling up to the condo, I'm hit with a wave of nausea.

I should not have come.

Willing myself to climb out of the car, I force myself to put one foot in front of the other. I walk slowly up to the door, telling myself that I won't stay long. After one knock, it swings open. He doesn't say anything; he just looks at me with sadness and longing.

"Hey," I say, quietly.

I really shouldn't have come. But those arms, and that smile... Seeing him in person has me almost forgetting why I was upset in the first place—almost.

"Hey," he says back. Peering around him, I notice spaghetti on the kitchen counter. The garlic bread looks overcooked, and the side salad looks a bit wilted. But he tried. He's never tried before, and he tried. That counts for something.

We sit at the counter, eating in silence. I study his face as he eats. He looks tired.

"I didn't lie to hurt you," he says finally, voice low. "I just... I didn't know how to leave that part of my life behind. It was over with Alicia the moment I met you, I swear. You were different. You *are* different." He looks desperate.

Twirling the pasta on my fork, I think about his words. *Different.*

Then I think about the words scribbled on the note, the warning. I haven't taken a bite yet; my stomach's too tight. But Ryan's on his second helping already.

"Why didn't you just tell me?" I ask. "Why didn't you tell me you lived with your ex, if that's what she really was?" *Not your cousin.*

"I don't want to lose you," he whispers. "And I was scared that if you knew how messy I was, you'd run. I thought... I could just keep her a secret until she moved out. Because then it wouldn't matter. I was trying to figure out how to have a fresh start, with you."

I'm quiet for the rest of the meal. It kind of makes sense... kind of. There's a wildness in his eyes I've never seen before, like he is frantic to keep me tethered to him. He's not wrong, I don't have time for drama—my life has always been drama-free. I keep my circle small on purpose. I'm driven, focused on my goals. If I would have known the truth about Alicia, would I have stayed? I don't know anymore. Ryan has awoken so many emotions in me, emotions that I didn't even know I was capable of feeling.

My heart aches. I want to believe him so badly. I've always been forgiving, maybe too forgiving. A big part of me wants our story to end in redemption. I want to be the girl that he changes for. Love isn't perfect. And maybe this is what forgiveness looks like.

"Please come back home," he whispers again. "Things will be different, I promise. No more lies."

I swallow. Glancing up, I realize that he's been staring at me, waiting for my reply. Waiting for me to say anything at all. This would be a good time to ask him what happened to her, but I'm too scared.

"I don't know, Ryan." I force the words out.

"Please, Aria." His voice cracks. "I love you."

I MOVE BACK in the next day.

Everything looks the same, but it feels different. I keep telling myself it's a fresh start. That forgiveness, real forgiveness, means choosing to move forward.

Ryan sends me a text, mid-afternoon. "I've got a surprise. I'll be home at 8:00."

I sigh. *I still hate surprises.*

Walking into the kitchen, I decide to bake some cookies to pass the time. Baking is my favorite way to clear my head, and I'm actually really good. I used to help my mom bake desserts for every family holiday, and one of my favorite memories is the time I helped her make cookies for my elementary school bake sale.

Opening the fridge, I grab the ingredients I need—milk, eggs, and butter—and I set them on the counter next to a massive bag of flour. Walking into the pantry, I dig around for my cookbook, the one filled with my favorite desserts. A few minutes later I find it, crammed between two boxes of cereal.

There's nothing chocolate chip cookies can't fix, not even heartbreak.

I deliberate for a minute. Should I make one dozen or two? I don't really *need* to make two dozen cookies, but I could always give some to Bryce. I head into the living room to grab my phone off the couch, opening Spotify to put Kelly Clarkson on shuffle.

Letting myself be consumed by the flour and the mess, I don't even notice that four hours have gone by. The door flings open, and when he walks through our door, there's a little puppy tucked under his arm. A French bulldog—round-bellied, sleepy-eyed, black with a white splash down his nose.

I blink. "Who is that?" My arms are covered in flour.

He grins, full and wide like the man I remember falling for. "His name's Beau. He's ours. For our new beginning."

He sets the puppy down, and Beau stumbles forward with a little huff. Picking up a kitchen towel, I wipe my hands before kneeling down to pet him, caught somewhere between surprise and surrender. The puppy's soft fur warms my hands. His tiny body presses against my leg like he's always belonged here.

Daisy senses something awry and jumps down off the sofa. Crouching low, she's confused but also curious. She tiptoes slowly toward the tiny puppy. Beau barks, full of excitement, and runs up to Daisy then runs his sloppy tongue up the side of Daisy's face.

Ryan kneels beside me and kisses my forehead. "I want this to work, Aria. Us. I want to get it right this time."

I look at the dog, then at the man beside me, then back again.

Maybe this is what second chances look like.

ARIA

My day has been quiet.

"Daisy. Beau," I call over to where the dogs are snoozing. "Let's go for one last walk before Dad gets home." Daisy's head shoots up at the word "walk." Beau has no idea what's going on, but he follows Daisy wherever she goes.

With their leashes on, we walk out the door. Daisy is visibly frustrated at the pace we have to go for Beau and his little legs. What should be a ten-minute walk takes us thirty minutes.

On our way back, I swing by the mailbox. We never get anything good in the mail. Mostly bills and a few car magazines for Ryan. As I'm shuffling through the bills, I notice an ivory envelope with Aria Cassidy written in beautiful calligraphy. The top left corner is embossed with POB in big, bold letters.

"Oh my god," I say under my breath. "Oh my GOD!" Jumping up and down, I can hardly contain my excitement. I've been waiting to hear from the Paris Opera Ballet for weeks. I quickly fish my phone out of my jean shorts. Scrolling until I find Bryce in my text messages, I pull up our chat. "YOU ARE NEVER GOING TO GUESS WHAT I JUST GOT!"

Her response comes less than a second later. "Omg omg omg. OPEN IT. RIGHT NOW!"

I jump up and down on the sidewalk, squealing as my neighbors move around me to the other side of the street. The scene that I'm causing has Daisy and Beau in a tizzy.

Racing up the sidewalk, we reach our apartment and rush inside. Out of breath by the time we get inside, the pups collapse by the water bowl and I set the letter on the table. Staring at it, I don't move for a minute.

Everything I have been working for comes down to the response in this letter. My future is determined by this letter. It's surreal, really. With shaking hands, I tear the envelope open and unfold the letter.

Dear Aria Cassidy,

Thank you for your interest in the Paris Opera Ballet. We are pleased to inform you that you have been accepted into the 2015-2016 school year. Please respond immediately to acknowledge your acceptance, as spots are limited. Additional information to follow.

Tears start pouring down my face. I can't believe it. Through blurred vision, I reach for my phone and reply to Bryce.

"I got in. I can't believe it... I got in." All those evenings spent at the studio, staying late when class ended to study with my instructors. The summers I worked so hard in highly competitive programs when the rest of the girls my age were traveling or tanning by the pool. It all paid off.

I was accepted into the Paris Opera Ballet.

I scroll to find my mom's number next and send her a text. "Mom, I got in."

I can't wait to tell Ryan. Wait... *Ryan.*

What am I going to do? How am I going to leave for a year to study in Paris, or possibly longer?

Then the door to the apartment suddenly swings open so abruptly, it makes me jump. I've still got tears in my eyes, my hands are still shaky, and the letter is sitting open on the table.

Ryan steps inside with a leash in hand, and behind him pads along a dog I've never seen before. A small off-white Pomeranian with watchful eyes. Beau immediately perks up and lets out a bark. Daisy lifts her head in confusion.

I pull my attention from the letter in front of me to Ryan in the doorway, quietly tucking it in between a few magazines on the counter.

"Hi... who's this?"

He drops the leash without a word at first, crouching to scratch the dog behind the ears. "This is Bandit," he says casually, as if that explains anything.

"Okay..." I wait. "And Bandit is...?"

He gives me a short, nonchalant shrug. "My old dog. From a long time ago. Alicia made me get rid of him. It's a long story."

Alicia. I can't help but flinch at the name. That wound has never healed. Ryan stands, brushing off his jeans, grease stains covering the front of his left pant leg. "The people who have him now—old friends of mine—they let me see him sometimes. Just for a night or two. Thought I'd bring him over because it's been a while."

I furrow my brows, watching the way Bandit moves slowly through the apartment. "Wait," I say as the pieces start falling into place. "He's... staying here for a night or two?"

"Yes," Ryan says lightly, but there is an edge of irritation in his tone. "It's no big deal."

I want to ask more—*why now?* Why has Ryan never mentioned his old dog, if he's still somewhat in the picture? But I keep my mouth shut.

His clipped reply tells me the conversation is over, and I need to let it go.

Bandit curls up on our living room rug. His gaze lands on me like he can see something that I can't. Ryan looks at me, and I manage to peel my eyes from Bandit to meet his stare.

"Why are you asking so many questions?" he says, irritated. "Don't you trust me?"

"Of course," I stammer. "I'm just curious, that's all."

After taking his shoes off by the door, he walks to the kitchen for a beer. As I watch him moving effortlessly through our apartment, living peacefully behind his wall of secrets, I glance back down at the kitchen table where my acceptance letter sits.

The excitement I was feeling just a few moments ago has turned into dread. I consider for a moment about telling him, about letting him celebrate this moment with me. But then I decide against it. A few weeks ago when I told him that I sent in my application, he didn't react with anything more than a half-hearted, "That's great, Babe."

Deep down, I'm not sure he'll be happy for me. I'm not sure if he'll come with me, either. And suddenly I feel so tired. The adrenaline and joy I'd been feeling drained out of me.

Walking over to the letter, I fold it up, slide it back into the envelope and tuck it into my planner sitting on the counter. It'll have to wait.

ARIA

Lying in bed, I stare up at the ceiling. It's been two weeks since I was accepted into the ballet school of my dreams. And for two weeks, I've been keeping it a secret from Ryan.

I can't decide what to do or how to tell him. So I just haven't. It is not the right call, I know. But it just feels easier to keep it to myself.

I finally climb out of bed as Ryan's oversized tee shirt falls off my shoulder. As I walk to the bathroom, the nausea hits me harder. I reach the toilet just in time to spew the contents from last night's dinner everywhere.

"What the heck," I mumble to myself. *Why do I feel so terrible?*

Out of the corner of my eye, I notice a tampon sticking out of my toiletry drawer, tucked between a box of Q-tips and my curling iron. That's when it dawns on me.

When was the last time I had my period?

Another wave of nausea hits me as I crouch over the toilet. After gagging for a minute, I finally compose myself enough to sit up, pulling my body closer to the drawer. Moving things aside, I dig to the bottom and locate the box I'm looking for.

Every twenty-something-year-old girl keeps a pregnancy test

lying around, just in case. I bought it when I was with my ex, a scare that nearly caused us to break up.

I dump the box out and the contents fall to the floor beside me. Unwrapping the test, I peel my sweaty body off the floor and onto the toilet seat. My heart is pounding so loudly, it drowns out every other thought in my head. I set the test on the counter to the right of me face down, unable to get up.

Two minutes turn into five when I notice my phone light up. Ryan's name flashes quickly across the screen. "Good morning, Babe." He's usually gone by the time I wake up. The garage opens a few hours before the art gallery, so I spend my mornings alone, getting ready slowly, enjoying my coffee in peace.

My phone is taking up space on the counter next to the test I refuse to look at. Standing, I reach for my toothbrush, desperate to rinse the taste of vomit out of my mouth. Looking up at my reflection while I brush my teeth, I'm alarmed at how pale I look.

I rinse the toothpaste from my mouth as I lean forward on the counter. My arms are shaking as they struggle to hold me upright. I take a few deep breaths before I flip the test over.

Two pink lines.

Clear. Bold. Unmistakable.

Pregnant.

Gasping, I drop the stick like it might burn me. It clatters on the counter, bouncing for a minute but landing right side up.

My knees begin to buckle. *This cannot be happening.* I am about to go to Paris. I can't have a baby. I can't be a mom right now. I'm only twenty-one. I have no idea how to do this.

Snapping a picture of the test, my hands are still shaking as I text it to Ryan. The only thing I can think to do is send him a photo. Maybe his excitement will curb my shock. A few minutes later, my phone buzzes with his reply.

"Are you sure it's mine?" That's it. That's all it says.

His words are like a punch to the gut.

What? He's kidding, right? His dry sense of humor always comes out at inappropriate times, so why should this time be any different. Annoyed, I stare at the screen and wait.

But there is no further typing bubble.

As I sit on the edge of the bathtub, phone clenched in my fist, I stare down at his message. *Are you sure it's mine?*

Not *I'm so happy.*

Not *oh my god* or *I love you* or *I'm coming home so we can celebrate.*

Just doubt. Accusation. I sit with that for a minute, with the realization that he actually thinks I could cheat on him. *Why would I do that?* I left once before but I came back. I chose him. *And when would I even have the time?*

The sun is peeking through the blinds, casting long stripes of gold across the tile. There's a lingering smell of coffee coming from the kitchen. Walking out of the bathroom, I spot Daisy and Beau pacing by the front door. They don't understand what's happening, but how could they? I bend down to clip on their leashes and walk barefoot out the front door. Looking for my sandals is more energy than I have right now.

I WAIT for him to come home like someone waits for a storm they can already smell in the air. When the door finally opens, it's later than usual. He steps inside like he doesn't live here—he doesn't look at me. He doesn't say hello. He just drops his keys onto the table with a clatter and moves past me toward the fridge.

I'm watching him like he's a stranger. "Hey," I offer quietly. "Can we talk about this?" He pops open a beer, takes a drink, and doesn't answer. Swallowing, I try again. "I guess I just thought that you would be excited."

That's when he turns. Something in his eyes are different.

"Celebrate?" he spits. "Why the hell would I celebrate?"

I freeze. "You said you wanted a family."

"I said I wanted to *try* one day." His voice rises. "But I didn't think it would actually happen."

I step back a little, suddenly uncertain about everything. "I don't understand. You told me on our second date that you wanted kids more than anything."

"I say a lot of things," Ryan mutters, pacing now, jaw clenched tight. "I love you, Aria, but do you think I'm ready for a kid right now?"

"The timing is not ideal, I know..." My voice cracks. "But it's still the family that you—"

"I can't believe you did this," he cuts in.

"Did what? I didn't *do* anything."

He throws his beer bottle hard into the sink. The glass explodes into a thousand pieces as sound rips through the apartment. My heart is pounding now. "Ryan..." I flinch as he steps closer to me.

"You don't get to talk to me like that," he says, his voice a low growl.

"I—I'm pregnant," I stammer, silently pleading as I back into the kitchen cabinet.

"I KNOW," he barks. "And whose fault is *that*?"

Everything goes still.

I shake my head, feeling dizzy now. "I didn't do *anything*, Ryan!"

"You trapped me," he hisses. "You wanted a baby so bad, you'd do anything. I should've known."

My chest heaves. "You're not making any sense. You said—"

"I SAID I didn't think I could have kids!" He slams his hand on the counter, his voice shaking the room. "And now you're here pretending like this is some fucking miracle?"

"No," he continues. "You always do this. You twist everything. You make it about you." It happened so fast. He shoves my shoulder, and I stumble backward. My hip hits the kitchen island, and my wrist slams against the sharp corner of the granite. A sickening crack. The pain is white-hot, instant.

I cry and drop to my knees, clutching my arm.

"Ryan—"

That's when his face shifts. For a moment, he looks at me like he stepped outside of himself and woke up in the middle of the damage.

But he doesn't help me, either. He doesn't kneel, or apologize. He just stands there, staring. And then, cold as ever, he says, "You'll be fine."

I can't breathe.

I cradle my wrist, blinking through the blinding pain. Ryan walks away, up the stairs, disappearing into the bathroom. I hear the sink running and then silence.

Trying to get up, I fall without having both hands to support me. I look around the apartment, every instinct telling me to grab a weapon. Anything to protect myself. When my head turns toward the living room, I see Beau cowering beneath Daisy. Both of them are hiding behind the couch. The sight breaks my heart.

What am I supposed to do right now?

The pain in my wrist is worse now, the throbs matching my every heartbeat. Shifting one knee in front of the other, I scuffle over to the couch and manage to lift myself up. Daisy and Beau quickly jump up next to me, one on either side.

Pulling a blanket off the back of the couch with my one good hand, I drape it over the three of us and lay down. My tears silently soak my sweatshirt. I think back to Alicia's warning... "Be careful." *I wonder if she knew this side of him?*

Faintly, I hear the shuffle of footsteps, and the bedroom door clicks shut. I guess he's going to bed. *What more is there to say, anyway.*

I feel so alone.

ARIA

My wrist isn't getting better.

I try convincing myself that maybe it's just a bad sprain, that the swelling and purple bruising don't mean anything serious. But deep down, I know. When I finally get to urgent care, the x-ray confirms what I've been dreading: my wrist is broken.

Ryan broke my wrist.

The doctor looks at me with a tight-lipped expression, asking careful questions in that clinical, polite way. Lying through my teeth, I answered no when he asks if I might be pregnant so I could get the x-ray. When he asks how I broke my wrist, I murmur something about an accident at work. I can't bear to see pity in a stranger's eyes.

The doctor puts my wrist in a brace and sends me home with instructions to rest, use ice, and follow up with an orthopedic specialist. I can't think about any of that, though.

I can't think about anything other than the baby. *Our baby.*

Every conversation we have twists into something ugly, something I don't recognize. We fight more than we talk these days. We try, *if you want to call it that*, to discuss the pregnancy. What we would do if we kept it.

Ryan changes his mind by the hour. One moment he's affectionate, apologizing, telling me he can see us raising a family together. The next, he's cold, detached, talking about how "now isn't the right time" and how we are "too young to screw up our lives with a baby right now."

I'm so exhausted—physically, mentally, emotionally. Every time I think about the tiny, fragile life growing inside me, my chest tightens until I can't breathe.

A week later—a week of fights and conversations that went nowhere—I decide to call my mom. I haven't talked to her in a while. The phone rings, and I hear a quiet shuffle, then a voice comes through the line.

"Aria?" my mom says, confusion lacing her tone. "Is everything okay, honey?"

"Mom." My voice cracks. "Something happened." There's silence on the other end. I can hear her breathing patiently, waiting for me to go on.

"I'm pregnant. It was an accident... but now I don't know what to do."

"Oh, Aria," she says. I know her well enough to know that she is debating the best way to handle this. "First, you know that your father and I will support you no matter what." She hesitates. "But what about Paris?"

I close my eyes, tears pooling under my eyelids. *Paris.*

I completely forgot about Paris. I never even told Ryan.

So that's my choice then? A baby or Paris?

I nod even though she can't see me through the phone.

"Yeah," I sniff, forcing the words to come out. "You're right. I'm going to think about it more. I'll call you tomorrow, okay?"

I can sense my mom hesitating on the other end. Like if she lets me hang up, she doesn't know what will happen. What I will do. I don't know, either.

That night, Ryan finally says the words out loud. We're sitting on the couch, eating leftover pizza in silence. He isn't looking at me. He hasn't looked at me in over a week.

"I think you should get an abortion," he says flatly. "I'm not ready to be a dad."

I feel my stomach bottom out. My hand flies instinctively to my abdomen.

"Ryan... I—" My voice cracks. "I don't know if I can do that."

He finally turns to look at me, his face hard. "You want to ruin both our lives over something we aren't ready for?" *Ruin our lives.*

Every piece of me that was holding onto a future with him, every part of me that was imagining him pushing our kids on the swings or teaching them to ride a bike, comes crashing down at that moment. I want to argue. I search deep within me, searching for the words that would make him change his mind. But I already know those words don't exist. He won't change his mind.

So I say nothing.

That night, I lay awake in bed, staring at the ceiling. Ryan is curled up on his side—he falls asleep facing the wall. Both my wrist and my heart ache more than I thought possible. I have no idea what to do.

Can I raise a baby alone? Will my salary from the art gallery even support a child?

Will Paris let me push my acceptance by a year?

If I'm lucky and they agree, how will I support myself and my child? Will I stay here or go to Paris anyway?

How would I afford a nanny in Paris without a job?

The questions keep coming, and there are no answers in sight.

The fear is overwhelming. I cry myself to sleep, paralyzed by the choice I'm about to make.

ARIA

In the end, fear won.

The next morning, I sit alone in the waiting room feeling numb and terrified, praying that my boss doesn't fire me for calling out of work again. *If only she knew.*

The clinic smells like bleach and sadness. Ryan isn't with me. I sent him a text as soon as I woke up, letting him know that I made my decision. He didn't ask what time my appointment was. All he said was, "I knew you'd come around. You'll feel better when it's done."

I don't think I'll feel better ever again.

My hand cramps from filling out the paperwork, still stiff from the brace. Minutes later, they call my name. My legs feel like Jello.

But somehow, I move anyway. One foot in front of the other.

Walking into the room, I see a gown sitting on the table, accompanied by a scratchy, wool blanket that isn't big enough to cover anything at all.

"Get undressed, please," the nurse says, smiling at me sadly. "The doctor will be in to see you shortly."

I nod, unable to find the words. That's been happening to me a lot lately.

Twenty minutes feels like sixty as I lay there naked and cold under the too-small blanket. The feeling of being completely alone, of making such an important decision, is swallowing me whole. I reach across to the chair on my right, where I threw my purse and discarded clothes. Digging through my purse, I feel my phone and pull it out, hoping to see a text from Ryan.

My heart sinks when I click the home screen button and see nothing from Ryan, just a text from my ballet instructor. "Aria, how are you doing? We miss you around the studio. You should be hearing from Paris any day, shouldn't you? Hope to see you in class on Monday."

The walls are closing in around me. I can't breathe.

I set my phone in my purse and turn back to face the ceiling. She's right, at least I have Paris. I repeat the words like a prayer until the doctor comes in. *At least I have Paris.*

The procedure itself was a blur of bright lights, medical terms, and cold metal. If I'm being honest, I don't remember most of it. Surprising actually, how quickly you can take a life out of this world.

I feel like someone scooped out everything inside of me and left the shell behind. The doctor required me to stay in a recovery room for a few hours to make sure I was well enough to leave. The deep sadness I feel is an ache that I know will never fully heal.

Sharing a room with three other women, I stare at the cheap linoleum flooring, surrounded by the quiet sniffles of the other women around me. No one says anything; we just sit in our own silent grief, separated only by a plastic curtain.

How did I get here? At least I have Paris.

I close my eyes, listening to their tears fall. I can't cry, I'm too numb. Instead, I let the sadness lull me to sleep. A few hours later, I wake to a nurse gently tapping my shoulder. "You are free to go whenever you'd like. Take your time." I wish I could look away from the pity in her eyes. It was probably empathy, but I'm too broken to tell the difference.

It takes more strength than I have to peel the blanket back and crawl out of the bed. Bending down, I quietly gather my things and trudge out slowly, without looking back.

Ryan isn't waiting in the parking lot. Seven hours have gone by since I entered the clinic, and he hasn't texted. He hasn't called.

I get into my car by myself, my body aching, my heart bleeding out somewhere I can't reach. I pull the seatbelt across my lap with trembling hands and stare out the window, wincing from the pain caused by the pressure of the seatbelt, when it starts to rain.

For the first time today, I let myself cry.

Not silent tears—full-bodied, soul-wrenching sobs that shake me to my core.

I cry for the baby I let go.

I cry for the girl I used to be.

I cry for the love I thought I had.

When the tears finally run dry, I pick up my phone. Opening my email, I locate the follow-up message from the Paris Opera Ballet that I received weeks ago. I was too busy then to read it with everything going on. Without hesitation, I type "I accept" and hit send. Turning the key in the ignition, my car rumbles to life. Despite everything, I smile as I wipe the last tear off my cheek.

I'm going to Paris. I'm leaving this life behind, even if it takes everything I have left.

ARIA

I stare at my phone... the tiny fluorescent screen showing an email displaying the sentence that threatens to unravel the last piece of me that's being held together.

"I'm sorry, but the acceptance window has passed. Please try again next year."

I blink, absolutely sure that I am reading this incorrectly. I rub my eyes, just in case. I read it again.

Please try again next year.

Without a second thought, I jump off the bed and bolt through the condo, racing into the kitchen like my body is on fire, ignoring the parts of my body that are aching from the procedure yesterday.

Grabbing my planner, I flip it open and pull out the initial acceptance letter, looking for the date. Scanning the letter, I'm looking for something to stand out, anything.

Then I see it.

"Please reply within two weeks upon receipt to confirm your acceptance." I slide down the length of the cabinet, my butt hitting the floor. As I lie there, slumped against the island, I remember.

I forgot to accept when I got the letter. I *forgot.*

I was so excited, and then I found out I was pregnant. And then Ryan happened.

And I forgot. *I completely forgot. How could I just forget my entire life?*

And now it's too late.

This was my one chance, and it's gone. I will be too old next year. They would never be so crass, but I know. Acceptance is favored for students between the ages of seventeen and twenty-one. Everyone knows that. Next year, my spot will be offered to someone younger in pique physical condition who has been training their entire life to attend ballet school in Paris, *just like I did.*

Someone who will give up everything to be there.

I let out a blood-curdling scream. Standing up, I stomp over to my ballet bag, sitting on a bench by the front door. I force the zipper apart, locating my slippers. Without hesitation, I wrap my fists around them and chuck them across the room at full speed. They hit the wall with a thud before falling to the floor.

Daisy yelps, the sudden noise scaring her out of a peaceful nap. I'm panting, and as I look around the room, it clicks.

No Paris. No baby.

In the span of a week, I've lost *everything.*

I want to cry but instead rage bubbles up inside of me.

Storming up the stairs and into the bedroom, I reached for my duffel bag. I open my dresser drawers, yanking them out and flipping them upside down, dumping the contents into the bag one by one. *This feels familiar.*

Ryan is already at work. He's always at work; he's never home anymore.

He didn't take the day off to make sure I was feeling okay after the procedure yesterday. He didn't pile up a few books and snacks on the couch for me. He just went to work, business as usual.

I pause for a moment, imagining him coming home to an empty home. *Again.*

The moment is fleeting. I don't know what I need right now, but I know I can't be here.

So I don't leave a note, I just leave.
Following the dogs, I slam the door behind me.

ARIA

Ryan doesn't stop me this time.

He doesn't beg for me to come back. Instead he says, "If you need to clear your head, go ahead. I'll be here when you're ready to come home."

So that's what I did. I moved back into my old bedroom at my parents' house, even though the ballet posters on the walls and the yellow comforter feel like memories from someone else's childhood.

It's the one place where I can simply be. Where I can grieve, and mourn, and feel however I want to feel without flinching, without waiting for the constant backlash.

I attempt to clear my head, but it's not going well. I'm not sure how to function.

I can't eat. I don't sleep.

I stopped going to ballet. My instructors reached out for a while, but then they stopped. I'm sure they put the clues together that I've quit.

Instead, I come home every day directly from work. I'm lucky to still have a job after taking so many random days off with no explanation.

Sometimes I drive by Ryan's condo on my way home, just to make sure it's still standing. Just to see if he's moved on without me. Once, I thought I saw another car parked out front. But it doesn't really matter, does it? Nothing matters anymore.

Bryce comes over every Sunday for family dinner now. I haven't worn anything but sweatpants in weeks—she tried for a while to get me into real clothes, but her attempts failed. And after a while, she stopped asking. So she comes over to the house instead, trading in our Italian dinners for movies and family puzzles.

Slowly, time and Bryce's company are healing my broken heart. But a piece of me is gone. It's too broken, and I know I'll never be the same, not ever.

She and I are sitting on the couch snuggled up under a blanket. We're sharing a bowl of popcorn when my phone chimes. I reach down, seeing Ryan's name on my screen.

He didn't disappear, not even close. The morning after I left, I woke up to find a latte waiting on the porch. Then came the texts.

"Miss you, babe. Come home soon. How are the pups doing?"

Then the calls. His voicemails are full of longing, each one reminding me that he hasn't actually let me go. He's still waiting.

He showed up one afternoon with flowers tucked under his arm and that boyish grin I used to love so much. Sunflowers, my favorite. "No pressure," he said, holding them out. "Just wanted to see you."

I accepted them because it felt easier than refusing. As I placed them on my nightstand, I tried not to look at them as they wilted day by day.

Meanwhile, Ryan found a new roommate—some guy from the shop. *It's only temporary*, he said. Just someone to help cover the rent for a while. He mentioned it casually, like it was no big deal.

But all I heard was *you're replaceable*. Life goes on without you.

Pulling my thoughts back to my phone, I read his message. "It's been weeks, Aria. Will you please come home?"

As I scroll up through the long string of texts from him, I stop on another one.

"I woke up thinking about our baby. I had a dream about him. In my dream, it was a boy. And you were the most amazing mom. Just got me thinking about what could have been."

Pain sears through my heart at his words. Pain and fury. I don't understand how he does that. He's furious one moment and heartfelt the next. *Because ultimately it was his decision, wasn't it? He called the shots. He wanted me to get an abortion. So what choice did I have in the matter? What was the alternative—staying in a resentful relationship or trying to raise a baby on my own?*

And another one.

"I'm sorry you missed the opportunity to go to Paris. I am. But we have each other. That's all that matters, right?" He will never understand. How could he?

I sigh, closing my eyes, resting my head on the back of the couch. Bryce squeezes my hand without saying anything. A silent reminder that she is here and that I'm not alone.

Some of the messages are sweet. Some of them remind me of the man I fell in love with. Or the future I almost had. But mostly, they just make me feel lonely and heavy under the weight of my reality. The reality that he will never understand what it was like to walk into a clinic alone and say goodbye to our baby. He will never understand what it's like to train for something your whole life, only to have that dream slip through your fingers.

He's spent the past few weeks dangling pieces of our life in front of me—a memory, a joke, a promise—and no matter how hard I try, I find myself being reeled in. Almost stepping forward without thinking, like a dog trained too well to the sound of a whistle.

If I give up now, what do I have left?

My phone buzzes again. "I'm outside, I just needed to see you. Please come out."

Heading for the front door, I grab a sweatshirt off the armchair and pull it over my head. I catch my reflection in the mirror, and I pause. I don't recognize the girl looking back at me. My skin is so pale, paler than normal, reminding me that I haven't been outside in days, weeks maybe. My hair is a tangled mess, reminding me that I'm due for a shower, too. The bags under my eyes make me look like something that crawled out of *Night of the Living Dead*. *What happened to me?*

I straighten, adjusting my hair tie, trying to erase the image from my mind.

Ryan sits on the porch swing, swaying gently. I walk over, and as I sit beside him, he slows the swing to a stop. "How are you?" he says without looking at me. He's fumbling with his hands in his lap. I haven't seen him in so long, I almost forgot what he looks like. And it's kind of cute, how nervous he is right now.

Kind of.

"I don't know, Ryan. I feel empty, broken. Like I am drifting through life with no purpose now." I see him flinch under the weight of my words. "I'm sorry, I'm not trying to make you feel bad." Immediately, I try to take it back.

"I just feel numb. I don't even really know how to explain how I'm feeling."

He reaches over and grabs my hand. I shudder. His hands are so warm. I haven't felt his touch in so long. "Come home, and we can figure it out together." He's doing everything short of begging. "I don't know what's next; I just know that I love you. And I need you to come home. We will figure everything else out as it comes. Together."

I look at Ryan. My eyes are running up and down his face. He looks so desperate and sorry. Like he actually feels bad for me, for us —for the past few months and everything we lost.

I'm tired. I'm just so very tired.

So I let my hand close around his, lacing our fingers, and decide to stop fighting.

ARIA

.

Ryan's been hinting at it for weeks.

Little things dropped casually in conversation, like when we're watching TV and a commercial for Kay Jewelers comes on. He mentions that someday he wants to make it official, and that he can't wait until I'm his wife.

This week he's been acting quieter than usual. He's never particularly chatty, but this week he seems anxious, nervous almost.

I moved back in right before Ryan's birthday, just in time to help with his next project. He's building a drift car. Not fixing one, but building it from the ground up.

Ryan has a way with engines, with grease-stained hands. I learned by watching him at first, then by doing it myself. He taught me how to change spark plugs and rewire tail lights. He even showed me the delicate art of sanding down rust without stripping the metal. We spent weekends shoulder to shoulder in the garage, music low, tools scattered, the scent of oil clinging to the air.

The trips are my favorite part. We get in the car and just drive, visiting random towns I've never heard of, driving for hours to dig through junkyards and old barns for forgotten parts. He lets me pick the playlist, and he laughs with his whole chest when I sing off-key.

There is something sacred in those drives—like time doesn't exist out there, just the hum of tires on pavement and the feeling that maybe we're building more than just a car. Sometimes we don't even find what we were looking for. But it never really matters. It's about the hunt. It's about the shared glances and gas station coffees, about getting lost and not caring, because we are together.

I spend all of my paychecks, and my savings, on this project, on our drift car. I decide to believe that if I pour enough love into him, into us, that maybe I can glue the shattered pieces back together. I cling to it like a raft—desperate to shift our focus to something else, something lighter.

I've been floating all week, dreaming of the day I get married. Deep down, I think this is what was missing before. That maybe he will want a family, that he will want all of those things he told me about on our second date. Maybe the timing was wrong before; maybe he just wanted to be married first.

Or maybe he wanted to wait until I wasn't so focused on my career.

Yesterday, I went to the mall with Marissa with no agenda, just a casual girls' day, when I stumbled upon the most perfect top. It was black, with an open low-cut back and a white bow adorning the seam. It would go amazing with my favorite skinny jeans. So of course I bought it, just in case.

"What will you say?" she asked me between sips of her iced caramel latte. "If he proposes."

I stopped and turned to look at her. "I would say yes, of course." I raised my eyebrow at her, slightly annoyed at her question. And her tone.

She shrugged. "I mean, you two have been through a lot. I think it's normal if you hesitate, even for just a minute." Picking up a shirt from the rack, I turned it around, pretending to inspect the design as I let my thoughts ruminate.

She was right, more than she knew, actually. She knew about the baby and Paris, but I never told anyone about the night he broke my wrist. Not a single soul.

We've been better since I stopped living and breathing ballet. Without ballet, Ryan's been my main focus. I've poured everything into our life together. I've been baking more, too, and spending more time at home with him and the pups. It's been good, and I've been happy. I decided right then that I had no reason to say no.

"I'm happy if you're happy," she continued, filling the silence.

I look at her and smile. "I am happy."

"Okay then."

She dropped it as she turned to walk out of the store. That's one thing I've always appreciated about Marissa—she speaks her mind. She isn't afraid to ask questions, or give her two cents. *I wish I could be more like that.*

That night, Ryan came home, and he was more fidgety than normal. "Let's go out to dinner tomorrow," he said, spinning his beer bottle around in small circles on the countertop. "Let's go back to our little Indian place. The place where I first said I love you."

He watched me, eyes darkening with a longing I can't quite explain.

"I would love that."

Which brings us to today.

I barely slept. I wake up, have my morning coffee with the pups on the patio, then go straight to the nail salon.

I look down at my freshly manicured nails. I chose a soft pink, something light and delicate, just in case. I feel hopeful for the first time in a long time. And I don't know what to do with this feeling.

The last time I felt hopeful was the day I was accepted into the Paris Ballet. For a moment, sadness sweeps over me for the life I had before, and for the life I thought I wanted. But it wasn't meant to be.

This life is what is meant to be. Ryan.

I put on some music and decide to curl my hair. That should kill a little bit of time. After I finish my hair, I get dressed. I pull the top over my head, and I adjust the straps, maneuvering until it fits just right.

It's perfect, just like I knew it would be. This top with my favorite jeans and my most comfortable flats. This is the perfect outfit to get engaged in.

Then I hear the front door swing open. I swallow, taking one more look at myself in the mirror. The color has started to come back in my cheeks. Once I stopped fighting and started accepting, I became an entirely different person.

Turning off the light, I walk out in the living room to meet him when I hear a soft thud. Ryan dropped his keys. I look up and see him stopped dead, eyeing me up and down. "Wow." He pauses, at a loss for words. "Babe, you look... incredible."

I do a little spin for him.

He walks over to me and picks me up, kissing me so hard that my feet lift off the ground. I can feel his hands tremble ever so slightly as he grips my face. I kiss him back, again and again. We are wrapped up in each other and lost in this moment when I hear Beau sneeze. I pull away laughing, throwing a hand over my mouth.

Way to ruin the moment, buddy.

Ryan smiles at me and grabs my hand, leading me out the front door. I close the door softly behind me, taking one final glance at our home.

When we return, I will be engaged.

THE RESTAURANT LOOKS THE SAME.

It's busier here tonight. There's a large party in the front celebrating someone's birthday. A man and a woman are tucked off to the side, laptops out, deep in a work discussion. I follow behind Ryan as we're led to our same booth in the back of the restaurant.

After the waitress rambles through the list of wines, Ryan orders a bottle, quietly letting her know that we're celebrating.

My stomach is doing somersaults. The anticipation might kill me.

She returns shortly with a bottle of '82 Bordeaux, pouring us each a generous glass. Ryan takes a big sip, finishing half of the pour in one swallow, before standing up. He slowly smooths out the front of his pants, pausing for a second to take a deep breath. Then, he drops down on one knee.

Suddenly the whole room stills. Everyone is watching us. No one says anything, no one moves. I'm not sure that I'm breathing, either.

"Aria," he says, voice shaking. "I love you. Will you please, please marry me? You complete me. I've never loved anyone the way I love you." A tear slips out, falling down his cheek. "I need you."

He holds up a box. For a moment, I think to myself that it's smaller than I imagined it would be. Then he cracks the lid open. I stare at it, then at him, then back at the box, blinking through my tears. For a second I can't move, and I forget how to speak.

The ring is simple, silver with a round diamond that winks at me under the dim restaurant lighting.

"Yes," I say quietly. "Yes, I will marry you," I say again, a little bit louder this time.

A single tear falls down his cheek as he stands, pulling me deep into his arms. The whole restaurant starts clapping in unison, and I forget that we aren't alone.

This is it.

This is the moment every awful thing we have ever survived is finally worth it.

ARIA

TEN MONTHS LATER

I look down at my phone and see a text from Bryce. "I'm out front!"

She is picking me up for one last Italian night before I'm a married woman.

I can't help but smile when I read those words, *married woman.* We decided to get married in my parents' backyard. They have a huge garden shaded by beautiful oak trees. It's perfect for a candlelit dinner under the stars. The festivities will be intimate, laid back, and exactly what I want.

The reception tables will be covered in ivory linens and sunflowers. But deciding on the food was the hardest part. Mexican is his favorite and Italian is mine, so we compromised and settled on Mexican, tacos and a nacho bar.

We're expecting about thirty people to come. We only invited close family and friends. Well, my family and friends. Ryan doesn't have anyone. He invited one coworker, but that was it. His grandparents have passed, and I suggested that he invite his mom, but he shot that idea down as quickly as I brought it up. It's a little strange he doesn't have anyone to invite from his family or even a childhood friend, but I'm used to it. He's never had anyone.

Ryan and I are lost in conversation about the next step. I want a big house. We're getting married, so we should start looking. A bigger house is the next step, and I'm sick of this tiny condo. "Sure, Baby. Let's move. What if we moved out of state? What about Texas?" He lifts an eyebrow, as if trying to sell me something like a car salesman. "A fresh start for our new chapter. A new adventure." Despite the heat, we're sitting on the sofa together with our feet on the coffee table. He winks at me and reaches out to take my hand in his.

I hesitate. It's intriguing, but I've never lived anywhere else other than Colorado. This is home. The thought of starting over is scary. *But that's what you do when you get married, right?* You make big, life-changing decisions. Or at least, you become more open to them.

"Yeah, maybe... I just want us to have a real fresh start. I want out of this condo. I want more space and a yard for the dogs."

"I love it." He wraps his other arm around my shoulder. "Let's do it." He flashes me that grin, the one that promises he will take care of it.

I shake my head playfully, giving Ryan a kiss on the cheek. "See you later, Babe. Bryce is outside."

He turns to face me, giving me a real kiss, deep and slow. "Miss you already."

I feel my insides turning to mush.

Pulling away I whisper, "I love you."

"Took you long enough," Bryce says as I slide into the passenger's seat.

I roll my eyes. Reaching out, I playfully shove her shoulder.

She laughs as she puts the car in drive. We decide to go back to Carmine's on Penn, the place where she first told me I should reach out to Ryan. Where she said I should "just get out there and enjoy a date night... I don't have to marry the guy." I can appreciate the irony.

The hostess sits us at a table in the back. It's quiet, and we're tucked between a wine cellar and the open floor. I'm pleasantly surprised to see the same waiter we had last time.

He strides professionally over to our table. "Hi ladies. Nice to see you again!" He remembers. I smile. It's nice to be remembered.

"What are we having this evening? Are we celebrating anything?"

"We are, in fact," Bryce cuts in, nodding in my direction. "She's getting married next week! So we'll take a glass of your best champagne, please."

I shrink into my seat as my cheeks heat.

"Congratulations! I'll be right back with two glasses of our best, on the house." He leaves before Bryce can order an appetizer to go along with it.

She looks at me as I fidget with my necklace. I always do that when I'm nervous. I fuss with my hands or my jewelry. Ever since Ryan gave me this necklace, it's been my favorite piece to fidget with.

"Are you okay?" she says quietly.

"Yes." I clear my throat. "Yeah, I just hate attention. You know that."

She nods slowly, not believing that for a second. "Most people are overjoyed to be engaged, you know—to be getting married."

I stare at her. She's always been bold, but I can sense there's more to that statement. "I am happy, *overjoyed* even," I say, mocking her.

She raises her hands in playful defeat. *Why do people keep suggesting that I'm not happy?* First it was Marissa, right before I got engaged, now Bryce. I am happy.

The waiter returns quickly with two overflowing glasses of champagne. I take mine and throw it back, drinking the whole thing in one large gulp.

Bryce stares at me, smiling hesitantly at the waiter.

I am happy.

ARIA

top.

I hear the word, but as I look around, I'm not sure where it came from.

I look back at Ryan and he's staring at me, concern lacing his face.

As I turn to look at the crowd again, sitting quietly in wooden chairs watching the ceremony under the shade of a big oak tree, I notice they are all staring at me, as if they heard it too. But it's silent, aside from the officiant and the sound of my heart beating through my chest. No one said anything. The voice came from inside my head.

This morning I cried for no reason. The makeup artist had just finished my makeup and the dam broke loose. I was unable to control it. She gave me a reassuring smile, like it wasn't the first time she'd seen a bride cry on her wedding day.

Yesterday I was fine. I went to bed feeling happy. *Overjoyed*, just like I told Bryce at the restaurant last week. Ryan and I sat on the patio loveseat, curled up in each other, watching the sunset, talking about the future.

But today I feel anxious, confused, and out of touch with my feelings.

Ryan grips my hand tighter, as if he's afraid that I will slip through his fingers. Or run.

As I look at the faces in the crowd, I notice my mom. She looks sad and almost defeated. Like this is the last possible thing that she wanted for me. Like she woke up praying I would get cold feet. She wanted me to study ballet in Paris, I know that. She wanted a different life for me. I look at my sister next, and her face mirrors my mom's. Their expressions make my already racing heart jump.

Why are they looking at me like that?

I am a pathological people-pleaser. I know that, too. I put everyone before myself. I put Ryan's needs before my own. *Is that what people see when they look at me? Someone who can't stand up for herself?*

I catch a glimpse of my reflection in my dad's sunglasses. My dress is form-fitting with an A-line bust and pearl beads trailing down the back. It's beautiful and makes me think of being a ballerina. The kind of dress that was made for someone else... not me. My hair is half up and half down, with loose waves flowing down my back. My makeup is simple and just the way I like it. Bryce got me a pair of turquoise earrings to match the necklace Ryan gave me—my something blue. She knew I would be wearing the necklace today like I do every day.

Looking away from my family, I turn back to Ryan. He's watching me curiously. Like he has questions, or things that he would love to say but he won't, not in front of everyone. I just want to scream, but that would be dramatic of me. I wouldn't dare cause such a scene. I wouldn't dare embarrass Ryan. Instead, I sway on my feet, side to side like I'm standing on quicksand.

My head starts to spin, and I feel like I might faint. It's hot today, and despite the incessant heat we've had, we hit a record high today. The four glasses of champagne I downed this morning aren't helping, either.

It's then that I hear the officiant's voice, far away as if it's coming from inside a tunnel. "Do you take this man..." His words trail off, but I know what happens next. I've seen this movie a million times.

He finishes reading and looks up. I feel every single eye on me, and everyone in the yard is waiting. I swallow, and in a barely audible whisper, I say "I do." The words feel like they got caught in my throat.

Ryan smiles at me like he knows something I don't. *Because he's always three steps ahead of me, isn't he?* But the officiant seems satisfied. He looks down and begins to read again, and this time the vows are directed at Ryan.

Ryan's eyes are on the officiant, like he's hanging on his every word.

I look back at the crowd, at my friends and family. My eyes move from one person to the next, scanning every seat, every row of chairs. Every single guest is wearing black. *Is this a wedding or a funeral?*

Suddenly Ryan grabs my face, pulling it toward his, forcing my attention back to what is unraveling in front of me. He gives me a big kiss, wet and sloppy. He opens his mouth, slipping his tongue inside. It's passionate, and dominating. Like he's letting the world know that I'm his. *That he won.*

I feel like I'm going to be sick.

When he pulls away, I see a gleam in his eye. He smiles that crooked grin I used to love so much, and locks our hands. Leading me forward, he drags me down the aisle. I keep waiting for people to clap or cheer, but the lawn is quiet. People are smiling, but no one cheers. The joy doesn't reach their eyes. It feels like acceptance instead of happiness, but Ryan doesn't seem to notice.

The rest of the night goes by in a blur. I'm here, but my mind is somewhere else. He cuts the cake and it cuts me like a knife. We share our first dance, but my head won't stop spinning. I can't quiet the part of my heart that feels like I just lost the last piece of myself. I've been losing parts of myself, little by little, over the past year and a half, but my independence was all I had left. My freedom. *What happened to me?*

I grab another glass of champagne and walk around to the front of my parents' house. Their porch swing is always where I come to think and to quiet my thoughts. This porch has watched me grow up. I've fallen in love and had my heart broken on this porch. I'm convinced that world hunger could be solved on this porch. There's nothing this porch hasn't seen or heard.

Taking a seat, I hear the sound of my wedding dress crunch beneath me. This dress is beautiful, but man is it uncomfortable. I lean my head back and close my eyes, using my legs to move the swing forward and back just a little bit.

I feel sweat drip from my neck down the front of my dress. The heat is merciless. The breeze from the swaying porch swing is cooling me down, but only slightly.

I'm not sure how much time has gone by. Ten minutes, maybe twenty, when I open my eyes to see Marissa tiptoeing around the side of the house.

She spots me and smiles slowly.

"Hey," she says gently. "I was looking for you."

I try to force a smile but when I do, my lips wobble. My eyes pool with tears. I close my eyes, trying to blink them away, but it's no use. They start trailing down my cheeks. Marissa sits down next to me, looping her arm through mine. "Oh, Aria." I lay my head on her shoulder, letting my tears fall as I look down, spinning my wedding band around and around.

What have I done?

ARIA

I didn't plan to stop by the garage.

But it's Tuesday, and Tuesdays are usually slow. I thought maybe Ryan and I could go grab lunch together. You know, something that married couples do.

It's been a few weeks since our wedding day and we have been settling into our "newlywed bliss." It's been a few weeks since I lost the last piece of myself, handing him what's left of my life.

When I pull into the parking lot, I notice the flashing red and blue lights. A few cop cars are parked at odd angles outside the shop, and uniformed officers mill around talking to the mechanics. For a split second, I think maybe there has been a break-in or an accident and my stomach flip-flops.

But then I spot Ryan standing stiffly near the service bay, his arms crossed and his jaw tight. An officer is speaking directly to him, his voice low but firm.

I stay in my car, hands frozen on the steering wheel, watching. My stomach is in my throat. Finally, I make myself get out. The air feels thick, heavy with the weight of something I don't understand.

Ryan sees me approaching and his eyes widen, not in relief, but in panic. I slow my steps, confusion coursing through my veins. "What's going on?" I ask as soon as I get close enough. He cuts me a sharp look, barely shaking his head. Not here. Not now.

The shop owner, Barry, stands nearby, his arms folded across his chest. He isn't yelling. He looks... disappointed. Angry. Eventually, the cops pull away, leaving a tense silence in their place. Ryan mutters something to Barry, and Barry just nods grimly. *What is going on here?*

Ryan drags me to the back office and behind closed doors, he finally tells me. Not willingly, of course—no. He doesn't volunteer any information. I have to drag it out of him.

Ryan has been taking the tires off the books, selling them to people for cash, and pocketing the money. It wasn't a few bucks here and there, either. He's stolen fifteen thousand dollars' worth of inventory.

My mouth goes dry. *Fifteen thousand dollars?*

I can't even comprehend a number that big, not when we barely have enough to cover rent some months. We live comfortably enough, sure, but we aren't loaded.

Where the hell did that money go?

Out of the corner of my eye, I catch my engagement ring sparkle in the light. I shudder. *Did he use that money to buy my ring?* Ryan is looking at me like he expects sympathy, like he deserves it even. But I can barely meet his eyes. "What were you thinking?" I whisper loudly, horrified.

Barry gave him an ultimatum: pay it back in full or go to prison. It's as simple as that. He shrugs defensively. "It's not like he needs the money. Barry's loaded."

"That's not the point, Ryan!" I cry, my voice breaking.

"We will talk about this more at home," he says, his voice low, threatening me with his tone. I look back at him, stunned. Words escape me. *Who is this man in front of me? Am I married to a thief?*

Without saying anything else, I storm out of the office. I'm unable to hide my frustration. It's always something with him. *Why am I not enough?* Why can't he just settle down and live a peaceful, married life with me? He has everything. A loving wife, a good job, adorable pups.

Correction... he *had* a good job.

I drive home in silence. The windows are down, and there's no music playing. The fresh air is keeping me grounded. The drift car is the answer. It's the car we built together, side by side—the project that's taken months, countless late nights, and all of my savings. Piece by piece, I bought every part. The turbo kit. The new racing seats. Every upgrade. Every shiny bolt. And now we have to sell it, because of him, because of a choice he made without me and a choice that put everything we built in jeopardy.

Not the Camaro, no. Not his baby. Selling that car is out of the question. So, we list the drift car online the next day, and within forty-eight hours, a buyer comes with fifteen thousand dollars in hand. I watch in silence as the man loads my car onto a trailer. A piece of my heart goes with it.

Ryan doesn't seem to care. If anything, he acts like it's just another transaction, another inconvenience to move past. We hand Barry the money a few days later. It's a clean slate, Ryan says. No record. No jail.

But I feel filthy and complicit somehow. It's like I am tethered to a sinking ship I didn't even realize was going down. It makes sense now, why Ryan suggested moving to Texas. He's not looking for a fresh start and he doesn't want an adventure. He's running. And somehow, without even knowing it, I am running with him.

"THEY WANT ME BAD," Ryan says, his chest puffed up with pride. "If it goes well, they'll probably make an offer on the spot." I stare at the empty suitcases on our bed, heart pounding as Ryan packs up a bundle of clothes. It happened too fast—a call, an interview scheduled, a plane ticket booked for Texas.

I force a smile. "That's amazing," I say, because that's what I'm supposed to say, right? Because that's what a supportive wife would say. It doesn't matter that I don't have a say in anything. It doesn't matter that I don't want to move away from my home. I was entertaining the idea, but things feel different now. I don't know who I am anymore and living in Colorado is the only piece of my identity that remains. I find myself wanting to hold onto it with a white-knuckled grip.

Thanksgiving is just days away. Families are baking pies, buying turkeys, stringing lights along their rooftops. And here I am, standing alone in our condo, wondering if I am being left behind.

When Ryan boards the plane this afternoon, he barely looks back. No kiss goodbye, no last hug. Just a quick, distracted wave as he disappears into the crowd.

The silence is deafening. I spend the evening curled up on the sofa, half-watching reruns of *Criminal Minds*, waiting for my phone to light up. Waiting for an *I landed safely* or *I love you* text. They never come, though.

The next afternoon, I finally receive a text. "Got the job, Babe! I gotta stay, I start in two days. Start packing." That's it. No *I miss you*, no *can't wait for you to get here*, just an order.

As I stand in the middle of our living room, looking around at everything we've collected together—the photos, the vintage record player, the furniture we slowly replaced piece by piece—I feel like I'm drowning. Ryan isn't coming back to help. He isn't flying home to move with me. It's all on me. *How am I supposed to move an entire condo by myself with no help and no money to hire movers?*

Feeling defeated, I head to Home Depot. I buy a stack of cardboard moving boxes and three rolls of tape, hoping it's enough to put a dent in things.

At first, I pack methodically: kitchen stuff in one box, living room items in another. But by the second day, my body aches too badly to think straight.

Ryan has barely texted me since he left. When he does send a message, he asks how much I've gotten done. There is no love or emotion, just business. *When did that happen?*

Is this what love is? It's nothing like in the movies... the girl doesn't get the white picket fence, and she doesn't live happily ever after.

Why am I the only one working at this relationship?

My mind conjures images I don't want: Ryan at some Texas bar, laughing too hard at some stranger's joke, brushing a hand against another girl's hip, bringing her back to the house... the house he got for us. *Our house.* It makes me physically sick.

I am constantly fighting the urge to check his social media every hour. I'm constantly fighting the temptation to call and catch him off guard.

But I know better by now. If he wanted to tell me, he would. I can't make him talk. And if I show too much insecurity, or if I push him too hard, it will just be more ammunition for him to use against me later. So I keep my mouth shut, pack, and wait for him to reach out first.

By the fifth day, exhaustion fills my every bone and muscle. There is a hollow ache in my chest every time I box up another memory. My hands are raw from carrying boxes, and I haven't slept in days. My arms are bruised from hauling boxes by myself.

No one offered to help. *I also didn't tell anyone I needed it.*

A week later, I rent a U-Haul and load it myself, item by item, trip by trip from the condo to the truck, my muscles screaming in protest. Anything I couldn't lift myself, like the couch, and the bed, I leave behind. After hours of watching YouTube videos on "How To Tow A Car: For Dummies," I had to beg an unsuspecting bystander to help me secure my car to the back of the U-Haul, just one more thing I shouldn't have to deal with. Ryan told me not to worry about his precious Camaro, something about a coworker handling it for him. I didn't ask questions even though I would have loved to know why the same person couldn't bother to help me move. But it doesn't matter, because he wouldn't have given me a straight answer anyway.

The sky is dark by the time I finish. The street lamps buzz overhead as I wipe sweat from my forehead with a trembling hand. Before I lock the door for the last time, I turn to take one final look at our home. It's stripped bare now, just blank walls and scuffed floors staring back at me, no sign of the dreams I clung to. *I wanted to get out of this condo, but not like this.*

I drive away that night from Colorado, heading for Texas and whatever version of my life is waiting for me on the other side. I brush away the tears that blur my vision, push on the gas pedal, and turn up the radio. My heart aches with every mile I put between myself and the life I once had.

ARIA

The Texas sun is different—sharper somehow, hotter even in the fall.

When I pull into the driveway of the house Ryan rented, I'm bone-tired from driving through the night but filled with a fragile and reluctant kind of hope. I reach our house just before noon, and I notice the Camaro already in the driveway. That's interesting... *how did it beat me here?*

The house is small but cute, tucked into a quiet neighborhood with tidy sidewalks and streets lined with similar houses. It's got a fresh coat of white paint, a little porch with room for two chairs, and a sturdy oak tree shading the front yard. The mailbox is worn and the driveway is short, but it's quaint.

It's not much, but it is a new beginning.

As I climb out of the U-Haul, my body is aching from the long drive and my legs are stiff and sore. I stand for a minute, letting the cement ground me. I desperately need coffee. Daisy and Beau file out after me, sniffing around and already marking their territory. The air smells different here—warmer, like open fields and wildflowers and possibility.

I step up onto the porch, looking around, taking in all of the possibilities, when Ryan flings the door open. He picks me up and twirls me around, giving me a big kiss.

Thank God. I feel relieved. Everything happened so quickly, and now we're here. The interview, the move. Ryan and I haven't truly connected in over two weeks, and I need him. I need to feel the tether, otherwise I spiral, second-guessing everything.

"I can't wait to show you around," he says with excitement in his eyes, finally setting me down. Lacing his fingers with my own, he leads me through the living room. I get a tour of the master bedroom, the guest room, the full bath, the half bath attached to the living room, the kitchen, even the garage he wants to turn into his own personal workshop. He's thorough, very thorough. I'm slowly taking it all in... the blank walls, the empty rooms, the wide-open spaces that haven't been filled with memories yet, good or bad.

This could be it. This could be where we start over.

I let myself think back to a few months ago to the paint colors I researched and the Pinterest designs I saved as inspiration. From the new kitchen mixer I want to buy, to the garden I want to plant, and the dog house I want to build for Daisy and Beau. I'm still daydreaming when I notice Ryan through the living room window. He took the keys to the U-Haul and has the back opened up, maneuvering through boxes, sorting through things and figuring out the best way to unpack.

Daisy and Beau are racing circles around him, playing hide and seek between the boxes, and he's smiling, chasing them around. The sight makes me smile and the weight of the last week begins to lift. My phone rings. The sound is coming from the pocket in my hooded sweatshirt. It's Bryce. "Hello?" I answer.

"Hey! Did you make it?"

I smile. "I did, about an hour ago. It's nice here... really nice."

She hesitates on the other end of the phone. "Good," she says quietly. "I hope you get the fresh start you are looking for."

"Me too," I whisper. "I love you. I'll call you tomorrow."

"Love you," she echoes.

I slide my phone back into my pocket and head outside to help

Ryan with the boxes. I haven't felt this light in a long time. Not since the early days.

Here it's just us.

Aria and Ryan.

Ryan and Aria.

There's no ugly history bleeding through the walls, and no ghosts lurking in the corners.

The first box I carry in has my art supplies. I pick a sunny corner in the guest bedroom and plop the box down gently, dragging out my sketchbooks and canvases that have been packed away for far too long. I can't remember the last time I had the urge to draw something.

For the first time in over a year, I can almost imagine a new life. A life where I spend my days baking while our three-month-old naps, a baby we both want and love deeply. Sketching on the porch, watching the sunset, while Ryan tinkers with our car in the driveway. I will build a garden while he ties up a tire swing for our toddler.

It's peaceful. A slow, simple life. The life I dreamt I would always have after ballet. I am going to take pictures and hang those pictures on the walls.

Texas isn't home yet, but I am determined to make it so. There is something intoxicating about the anonymity of it all. Here, no one knows what happened between us. No one knows about the cracks that spiderweb just beneath the surface.

We can be whoever we want here. We can be happy.

As I walk back into the living room carrying the empty box in both hands, I see Ryan sitting on the porch, watching the leaves blowing in the trees, lost in thought.

This is it, I tell myself.

This is the clean slate I prayed for.

I just have to believe in it hard enough.

ARIA

"What do you think about a honkytonk?"

Ryan peeks around the corner and into the guest room, into my little art studio. The corner of the room is piled high with paints and canvases, sketchbooks and pens. "What?" Confused, I lift my head, pulling my attention from the sketchbook in my lap.

"Let's go out tonight," he says. "We're in a new place. Let's go out and check out the town." I look at him for a minute, considering.

We've been here for a few weeks and I finally feel somewhat settled. The U-Haul was returned and the boxes are broken down. We've painted a few rooms, hung a few pictures. Ryan's been settling into the new job, and I've been applying to art galleries around the area. We do deserve a night out.

I can't remember the last time we went out for a fun date night.

"Okay, let's do it." I grin, standing from my ivory armchair.

"I'm gonna run to the store real quick. We'll leave when I get back." Slowly, he shuts the door behind him.

Setting my sketchbook down on the ottoman, I look at the image on the paper. It's a beautiful cake, a wedding cake crafted for a special occasion. It's got three tiers, and it's adorned with hot pink flowers and textured frosting.

Sometimes I let myself dream about opening a bakery.

It will probably never happen because I wouldn't even know where to begin. *Where would I even bake, for that matter? Out of the kitchen in our rental home?* Ryan would hate that.

Putting my dreams on pause, I dig my phone out the pocket of my sweatpants. It's 6:15 p.m., and I have precisely one hour until he gets back, taking into account that it's Ryan and he gets distracted doing absolutely anything at all. He could run to the store for one thing and take an hour and a half, browsing every aisle. With him, there's always zero sense of urgency.

Daisy and Beau are whimpering in the other room. Opening the door, I walk into the kitchen to give them a treat. Daisy sits patiently, waiting. She's learned by now. Beau looks from me to Daisy and back to me. I laugh, digging two doggy biscuits out of the jar on the kitchen counter.

"Sit," I say gently. Daisy is still as a statue and doesn't move an inch. Beau tries and gives a valiant effort, but he can't help but wiggle in anticipation of a treat. I laugh, setting both treats down on the ground in front of them.

I walk away, wandering into our bedroom, listening to the sound of chewing coming from the kitchen. *What does one wear to a honkytonk?*

My style is clean and classic, black and neutral, casual but a little bit more formal. Though I haven't danced in months, it's typical fashion a ballerina would wear. Immediately, the thought wounds me.

I don't think of ballet much anymore. I didn't even bring my leotards or slippers with me in the move—they got left behind with my mom. *Why take up space in the U-Haul?* I miss it, I do. But I can't go back. It's been too long. My feet aren't calloused anymore, and my legs are out of shape. If I went back now I would have to start over completely.

Looking at my closet, I try to find something that's not formal, something with maybe a little color, but I find nothing. No color, no patterns.

Sighing, I settle on a white tank top and jean shorts. I have one pair of cowboy boots left over from a themed dance senior year of high school. They're red with white stitching up the sides.

Slipping them on, I stand in front of the floor-length mirror in our bedroom. Turning my head to the side, I examine the girl looking back at me. The light is starting to come back in my eyes. I almost look like myself again. I almost look... happy.

I'm curling my hair in the bathroom when I hear the front door open. Ryan opens the bathroom door a minute later with flowers in his hands. His eyes light up when he sees me.

"Wow. You look..." He pauses, searching for the right word. "Sexy."

I laugh. "Yeah, right."

"You do." His voice gets low. "Texas looks good on you."

He hands me a bouquet of flowers. Sunflowers, blooming on full display.

My favorite. "Are you almost ready?" he says, still watching me as I smell the flowers.

"Just let me put these in water, then we can go." Taking one last look at myself in the mirror, I flip off the light.

Following him out of the bathroom, I open every cabinet in the kitchen looking for a vase. I can't remember where I stashed them. I did bring one with me, didn't I?

I'm walking around in circles, reopening the same cabinets, slowly getting frustrated, when Ryan opens the small cabinet atop the fridge. Reaching inside, he pulls out an opaque, pastel yellow vase.

"Here, Babe." He hands it to me slowly, smirking. I sigh, taking the colorful vase from his hands.

"There," I say, setting the vase down gently on the ledge, separating the kitchen from the living room. "It's perfect."

I grab my purse from the ledge, and link my arm through Ryan's. I'm ready for a night on the town.

Nothing could have prepared me for a honkytonk.

I didn't know what to expect, I'll admit, but even my imagination steered me wrong. A neon sign illuminating the large words "Billy Bob's Texas" decorates the front of the building. The parking lot is loaded with lifted 4x4s, and our little sports car feels wildly out of place.

Inside there are lights coming from every direction and more cowboy hats that I can count. So many cowboy hats. Hundreds of cowboy boots shuffle along the wood plank floor, which is littered in sawdust and peanut shells. The air inside is hazy, beer glasses are clinking at the bar, and a Luke Bryan song blares from the speakers mounted in the corners of the ceiling. We are so out of place, but without hesitation, Ryan grabs my hand and spins me out onto the dance floor. He's spinning me around and around. We don't know the moves but I don't care.

I toss my head back and laugh.

I love this little life.

ARIA

Three months. That's how long it took. Three months.

Three months in Texas. Three months at his new job. Three months in our new home. Three months into our new beginning. Three months before the job that brought us here disappeared like smoke. Three months until the life I loved was gone.

Ryan comes home early, slamming the door behind him so hard that a newly hung picture falls off the wall in the living room. I look up from my laptop at the kitchen table as a pit forms in my stomach. A kitchen table that cost a pretty penny, I might add.

"Fucking idiots," he spits, tossing his keys onto the counter. "They don't know a good mechanic when they see one."

"What happened?" I ask cautiously.

"One of our regulars came back with an issue after I fixed his headlight. The boss blamed it on me, but really it was a defect with the manufacturer." He grunts, like that explains anything at all. "I tried to explain, but he called me a liability."

I want to believe him. *God, I want to believe him.*

But I can't help feeling like he isn't telling me the full story. Too many pieces of the puzzle don't fit. *He was fired after one mistake?*

That's a little dramatic. He always paints himself as a victim, betrayed and misunderstood. Everyone is always out to get him.

I swallow. "What are we going to do?"

His fist slams down on the table, hard. "Why would you ask me that right now?" he yells. "Give me a Goddamn minute to think." He storms off into the garage, where a beer and his car await.

I release the breath I didn't realize I was holding in. The question is still lingering in the air. What are we going to do for money?

How are we going to pay rent or afford groceries? For a second, I feel like I might throw up.

The feeling is fleeting, though. As quickly as it leaves, I stand up, going to retrieve my phone. If we don't have money, then we need to get money, and fast.

I start taking pictures of everything. The vintage record player we bought the night after we got engaged. The couch that my mom gave us one weekend after deciding to upgrade the couch from my childhood to a newer one. The ceramic dinnerware given to me by my grandmother before she passed. Everything in this house holds a memory and a story. I feel my eyes welling up with tears as I take picture after picture, unable to imagine parting with these things.

But what choice do we have?

Ryan isn't going to take this seriously. It's going to fall on my shoulders like everything does. Just like the abortion did, just like the move did.

I've had no luck hearing back from any of the art galleries in town, even though I have just over of three years of experience. Leslie wrote me a letter of recommendation, praising me for my time spent with her. I'm thankful for that, and I'm really hoping that letter earns me a call back soon. But that doesn't help me right now.

Ryan walks back into the living room then, the garage door slamming into the wall with force. He watches me, positioning items just right, taking photos of our personal things. "What are you doing?" His voice is cold.

I pause, turning to face him. "I don't know what other choice we have, Ryan."

He starts to pace like a caged animal. "You could at least feel bad for me, you know. Before you make it all about you." He stares at me with a twisted look in his eyes. "I'm the one who just lost my job."

I stop, not sure that I heard him correctly. *Make it all about me?*

That night I lie awake, staring at the ceiling fan spinning overhead, wondering how the dream rotted so quickly. Wondering how I had convinced myself, even for a second, as if a fresh coat of paint and a new zip code could fix anything.

ARIA

I should have left hours ago.

Ryan has been tense since losing his job. He's angry and cold. He goes out every day to drive around town and look for work. He's been applying in person and doing who knows what else to fill his days, typically coming home just before dinner.

It's been nine days since Ryan lost his job. I managed to sell a few things on Facebook Marketplace to pay for gas this week and groceries. But it's just a temporary solution. He knows it and I know it.

A fight has been brewing since this morning, simmering under every word. The final thread is threatening to snap. *What's it going to be this time?*

It's always something, and it's always "my fault." It's always things I say, the things I don't say, the things I do, or the things I don't do. Tonight, it's the way I asked him to turn down the TV a little bit so that I could sit on the couch next to him and read. That's it, nothing more.

He turned down the volume, but he didn't say a word. I watch as his arms move stiffly, lifting the remote slowly and setting it back down afterward.

I look over at him and try to give him a reassuring smile that says thank you, but he won't look at me. His eyes are glued to the TV, pretending to watch the shapes dance across the screen.

As I climb off the couch, I set the throw blanket down, tossing my book on top of it. I walk down the hall, heading for our master bathroom, when I hear a shuffle come from the living room. Ryan stands up to follow me, and I hear his voice sharp, coming from a few feet behind me.

"What makes you think you can talk to me like that?" His words slash, and I can already feel his anger rising with every step he takes toward me.

I look behind me toward him. Ryan is quickly gaining speed with every angry step. I try to shut the bedroom door behind me, thinking maybe I can lock it in time, but he's faster. *Shit.* All I did was make him more furious with me.

He shoves the entirety of his weight through the doorframe, and suddenly the room feels small. My back hits the wall as I stumble backward. I can't stop the fear that grips me. Here we are again. *I know what comes next. Don't I?*

He stands close, too close. His breath is sour and his eyes are empty. He's only a shell of the man I love.

He reaches out, not to touch me, but to lift me in a chokehold. His hand wraps tightly around my throat as my feet leave the floor.

"Ryan," I try to force out as I gasp for air.

I can't scream. I can't breathe. I can't... *breathe.*

The ceiling swims above me as he lifts me higher and higher[SJ1] . I can't make a sound. I can't call for help... not that anyone would hear me. *How did I get here?* The closer I get to the spinning ceiling fan, the more I accept what is happening and I succumb to the numbness.

For a split second, I start to pray. I pray that he makes it quick.

I've stopped fighting. I don't know when it happened, the subtle shift to acceptance. My vision starts to darken when I hear the faint whimpering of Daisy and Beau coming from the doorway. *Did I ask for this? Is this somehow my fault?*

Maybe this is my penance for what I did to our baby. My baby.

Maybe I deserve this. *I wish he would just do it already.*

The last thing I feel is the impact of my body hitting the hardwood with a force that snaps through me. I hear the sound and feel the crack of my ribs before it all goes dark.

WHEN I COME TO, everything is quiet, save for the ceiling fan, still spinning on a loop. The room is dim, and the air is cold. I'm in our bed, my head is pounding, and my mouth is dry. Ryan is beside me leaning against the headboard with a damp cloth pressed gently to the back of my head. He's whispering something I can't make out and lightly stroking my hair, another useless apology.

Everything hurts. I don't know what to do. My instinct is to readjust and release pressure where it hurts, but I can't locate the source. It's like my entire body is pulsing. I try to sit up, but he's holding me firmly where I'm lying.

"No, Babe," he says like it never happened. Like he's the one who found me broken instead of the one who broke me. "Don't try and move. Just rest."

"I need to go to the bathroom," I whisper. My voice doesn't even sound like my own. He accepts that, like that's a good enough reason for him, so he moves to help me. Sitting up slowly, he tucks one arm around my waist as I try to stand. Sliding each leg off the bed, one after another, I pull the full weight of my body with me as I stand.

When I'm upright, he lets go. I tiptoe, slowly shuffling my legs as I make my way to the bathroom, like I'm walking across broken glass. I feel him watching me from behind. His eyes are burning into the back of my head.

It takes me an eternity but finally I reach the door, closing it quietly behind me, locking it quickly. I wait until the door is closed before I flip the light on.

When the light illuminates the room, I gasp. There's an outline of a handprint on the front of my neck. It reaches the whole distance, covering every inch of my skin. Bruises form quickly when you're fair-skinned. I stare back at my reflection, at the broken girl in the mirror, and I see the truth.

It's a miracle I'm still alive.

I turn the sink on, letting the running water drown out my sobs as they slip through. I don't know how much time has passed as I tremble, watching the girl across from me. He could have told me to jump off a bridge, and I would have done it. I would have done anything for him, anything he wanted. That's the person he made me.

And I let him.

That's the worst part. *I let him.*

I wipe my eyes before opening the door. Ryan is sitting on the bed in the same spot, scrolling through his phone. He looks up when he hears the door open.

"I think I'm going to try and get some sleep," I say quietly.

He smiles at me. "I think that's a good idea." He stands slowly, pulling the covers back as I make my way over. I crawl into the bed as quickly as my body will let me. Daisy jumps up beside me followed by Beau. They curl up into a ball at my feet, protecting me.

I close my eyes, listening to the ceiling fan spin around and around, when I hear him slip out of the room. The door clicks gently behind him. It hurts to breathe.

When he's gone, I open my eyes and turn onto my side. I wince from the pain, when I notice my phone discarded on the floor in the corner of the room, the scene of the crime. Without thinking, I throw the blanket back, forcing my body out of the bed for a second time. I drop down to my knees, the weight of my body slamming my knees into the ground harder than I intend.

I pick it up, quickly scrolling to the text thread with my mom. I don't hesitate as I type out "Mom, I need you," and press send. My hands are shaking so hard I can't control it.

I shift my weight from my knees and onto my butt, sliding my back against the wall. As I pull my knees up to my chest, I cry out in pain. My ribs are definitely broken.

But I let myself feel the pain. Because if I don't feel the pain, if I don't feel the gravity of this moment, I might pretend it never happened. I might make an excuse, I might justify his actions. *Because that's what I always do, isn't it?* He promised me the last time would be the last time. And it's always my fault. It's always my tone. It's always *me*.

But not this time.

My phone lights up. It's late, and I don't know why my mom is still awake, but I'm glad. "I'll be there tomorrow," is all the message says. I close my eyes, hot tears streaming down my face.

Somewhere in the back of my mind, I picture a different version of us. Somewhere in a parallel universe I'm so madly in love with the father of my child, who picks me fresh flowers every Sunday and pushes our son on the tire swing. But this isn't love. If it ever was, it isn't now. It's a cage, and I'm not safe inside it.

I let my shoulders sag, keeping my body curled up tight as my shoulder meets the floor. And I fall asleep, curled up in a ball on the floor.

I know what I need to do.

ARIA

Everything hurts. My neck, my ribs. *My pride.*

Ryan is gone before I wake up. When I open my eyes, I notice a sticky note on a cup of coffee that says, "I love you." But the coffee has gone cold, just like our love. Looking down, I see Daisy and Beau curled up at my feet. They look as uncomfortable as I feel. I don't know what I would do without them.

I feel my phone jabbing into my side. Sliding my hands underneath my back, I pull out my phone. The battery has only five percent left as I open the text from my mom. "My flight lands at 9:30 a.m. I'll see you at the airport."

I glance up at the time stamp in the corner of the screen. It's 8:15 a.m. Peeling my broken body off the ground, I shuffle my feet in the direction of the shower. I let the hot water burn my body as I think about my mom, about the conversation I'm about to have. *What am I going to say to her?*

A war is raging inside my head. All the voices who told me a variation of *I told you so* over the past two years. But I've lived in chaos for so long, I don't know what peace looks like anymore.

Twenty minutes pass as I stand there. The water comes close to melting the skin off my body. Slowly, I turn the water off. I need to leave soon if I'm going to get to the airport in time.

I drive in silence. My thoughts are spinning. I feel like I could be sick again. The fear has me in a chokehold. The feeling is as real as it was last night when Ryan attacked me.

Am I really doing this?

Sitting in my car, I wait. The Austin airport is busy today, but I find a spot in the back. I'm waiting and looking for my mom as I slide the bead on my necklace up and down the chain.

Then I spot her. She has a backpack on and a small tote bag. She packed light, because she knew she wouldn't be here long.

I can't stop myself. I throw the car door open and begin to run, my feet pounding through the pain. My mom meets me halfway, throwing her arms around my body. My knees buckle, threatening to give way until I'm a heap of bones and broken dreams on the curb of the airport terminal.

WE DON'T TALK, because she already knows. I think she always knew. And if she didn't know before, there's a handprint across my throat that's giving it away now. Pulling into the house, we walk inside and go right for the closet. We each grab a suitcase, throwing in as much as possible. I grab my clothes and my toiletries, dumping out each dresser drawer into the open bag. *I'm getting good at this.*

My mom grabs my light yellow mixer, my art supplies, and a few vintage pieces of dinnerware given to me by my grandmother. She moves through the house, quietly and with purpose, grabbing the things that she knows I just can't leave behind.

On the way out to my car, I grab a few of Daisy's favorite toys and Beau's favorite pillow, throwing them in the trunk with the rest of my stuff crammed into a too-small suitcase. Walking back into the house, I head straight for the garage. I can't help myself.

I open the door, walk inside, and let out a scream, a gut-wrenching scream, as I pick up a hammer and start swinging with what little strength I have left.

By the time I'm done, I'm out of breath and my stomach is in knots.

I step back, examining my masterpiece. As I look around the room, my eyes bouncing between objects, I realize I don't know what any of this stuff is. Sports trophies from when he was a kid, but I couldn't tell you what sport he played. A stack of records, but I couldn't tell you his favorite artist. Boxes of papers that I've shredded and torn to pieces. For being his *wife*, I don't know a single thing about him.

Quietly, I hear my mom shuffle in the doorway. I turn and look at her as a tear slides down my cheek. A single tear, because that's all that he deserves. She looks at me and her mouth quivers. The suitcase she packed is sitting behind her on the floor. I take one last look around the garage, at the broken pieces of his life, of everything he loves that I shattered.

I pull my phone out of my pants pocket and set it on the counter. If I am going to do this, and really do this, I have to accept what that means. If I'm going to run, that also means I'm going to hide. I will need a new number, and a new car. If I want to be free, I need to leave every single piece of *this* life behind. My life.

I glance at my phone covered in a sunflower case, a case that's chipping at the corners, and I walk away. With Daisy and Beau close behind, I walk away from this house. From this life. From this marriage. From Ryan.

I don't cry as the car pulls away with my mom behind the wheel. I don't smile, either. I gave up everything for this. My hopes, my dreams. I fought for this until I bent further than I could go, and I eventually broke.

My thoughts grow louder. I don't know what I did to deserve any of this. Even on my worst day, all the hell that he put me through: the mistrust, the gaslighting, the abuse. I did everything for him. I gave him everything. My heart, my soul, my body. I was so Goddamn faithful.

Sitting in the passenger's seat, I turn around looking at Daisy who is curled up into Beau, comforting him, and whisper, "Life is about to get so much better, just you wait."

PRESENT DAY

KATE

What time is it? The sun is streaming in through the window, making a bright yellow square on the carpet next to the bed.

I close my eyes and rub them hard, trying to massage away the deep ache in my skull and give my eyeballs a thorough massage. I throw my legs over the edge of the bed, stand up slowly, and wander to the bathroom for a new pair of contacts. I trip over a pair of sneakers on my way there, discarded in the middle of the hallway after the bar last night. Bandit hops gingerly over the pile, following on my heels as I reach the vanity drawers and rummage around for my contact solution. Being blind is annoying—really annoying.

Popping the contacts in, one eye after the other, I sigh as the state of the bathroom comes to focus in front of me. It's a disaster in here. There's a half-empty coffee mug on the counter from yesterday morning and a pile of dirty clothes in a heap on the floor... evidence of my ADHD is everywhere.

This is my fourth apartment in five years. Every year, I move apartments when my lease is up because consistency makes me uncomfortable. Every time I think I should maybe buy a new rug or a shoe rack so I stop kicking my shoes off just anywhere, I know it's time. I need to know that if anything is going to change, it's because I allow it to. I need to know that I'm in control, so I never let myself get too comfortable or complacent. I've been in this particular apartment for six months and four days, and it's already starting to feel like I've been here for too long. Not that I'm counting.

The last guy who stumbled out of here said my life was chaotic, but I prefer the term *highly energetic.*

Suddenly, I hear my phone faintly buzzing, and the sound snaps me back to the present. *Where is it?*

I circle slowly around the living room, trying to remember the last time I saw it. I got back from the club late last night, *later than I wanted*, but one drink led to five, and here we are. Picking up my purse, I dump it upside down and spill the contents all over the coffee table. Not here.

I lift one couch cushion, then the next. Not there either. Walking back to the bathroom, I lift my skinny jeans up off the floor, and I hear a loud *thud* as it drops out of the back pocket and onto the linoleum. "Jesus," I whisper to myself. *My head hurts.*

Opening my lock screen, I look at my texts. I have a few missed messages from my friend, Kayla. I met her at a concert eight months ago, and we've been inseparable ever since. Are we best friends? No, I don't think so. She's not the first person I would call in an emergency, but she is my favorite person to let loose and have a good time with. I don't know what it's like to be a real friend anymore though, not really. I spend most of my time alone, with Bandit, or with my clients. I have one friend, maybe two, who made it through everything this decade threw my way, but that's it.

"Did you make it home okay?" That text was from *nine* hours ago. Whoops.

"Call me as soon as you wake up. Let's go out to breakfast and debrief on last night." I glance at the time stamp and see that she sent this text just thirty minutes ago.

I respond, "I'm up! I'll meet you at Snooze in an hour," and hit send. *Breakfast... and coffee.* What a great idea. I don't think I ate dinner last night. That must be why I got so drunk so fast.

Back to my dirty apartment. Walking over to the contents from my purse, which are still strewn across the coffee table, I pick up my AirPods and pop one in my right ear. Opening Spotify, I search for Gracie Abrams and put it on shuffle. I grab my discarded items one by one and toss them back in my purse—my wallet, my favorite Burt's Bees lip gloss, my keys, and a pack of gum all file back in, immediately followed by my AirPods case.

After I wash off last night's mascara, I apply a new coat, swiping on the absolute bare minimum. I throw my hair up in a messy bun, save for a few pieces framing my face. Sometimes I miss my black hair. Sometimes I look in the mirror and feel like I'm looking at a blonde stranger.

I look down, deciding that the leggings I slept in are good enough for this outing. Removing my oversized tee shirt, I throw on a workout tank and my favorite quarter-zip from Lululemon. Taking one last look in the mirror, I shrug. This will have to do.

My feet slide into my discarded sneakers before I bend down to give Bandit a few kisses. I pick up my purse on my way out the door, slinging the strap over my shoulder, locking the door behind me. I nearly bump into Mrs. Carter, who is carrying a large brown paper bag stuffed with groceries.

Mrs. Carter lives alone with her overweight tabby cat, Ziggy, and her collection of fiddle-leaf figs. She moved into her apartment after her husband passed a few months ago, hoping for a change of scenery and a quieter life. Aside from her nuisance of a next-door neighbor, who stumbles home at three a.m. more often than not, she seems happy.

She shakes her head at me as she comments, "You know, you would have heard me coming without those *things* in your ears." Her gaze lands on the tattoos creeping up my left arm, and she pauses to stare pointedly at the "Eat Me" cookie in my Alice in Wonderland sleeve.

I laugh and force a polite smile. "So sorry, Mrs. Carter. I've got to run, though. I'm meeting a friend for breakfast." I give her a small wave as I move around her and out to the parking lot.

I always have music playing. *Always.* I can't handle silence. Because if it's too quiet, I can hear my thoughts playing on a torturously unending loop. If it's too quiet, my anxiety bubbles up violently into my chest, reminding me how many years of therapy I've avoided. If it's too quiet, I start to feel trapped.

I *need* the noise.

The AirPods were the first thing I bought for myself after *him*. It was a gift for myself—no, a necessity. The AirPods helped me embrace my fresh start, and I've used them every day since.

SNOOZE IS BUSY TODAY. Denver has way too many people as it is, and there are only so many brunch spots, but it feels extra packed on this particular Saturday. It takes me much longer than I want to find a parking spot. I spot Kayla immediately at a booth in the back. She's waving her right hand at me furiously. I wave back as I maneuver through the bodies and the tables.

"It's good to see you're alive," she says by way of greeting.

I chuckle. "Yes, I'm alive. But not fully, I need coffee."

When I sit down, I notice an overflowing iced caramel latte waiting for me on the table. I pick it up, taking a huge sip. *An absolute angel.* "I don't deserve you," I whisper, letting the caffeine course through my veins as my eyes roll back into my head. *This is exactly what I needed.*

"So, tell me about the guy," she says without hesitation. "I've been waiting all morning for the details. Spill."

I scoot back, letting my back rest against the booth as I inhale deeply. "I don't really know what there is to tell... We danced, we flirted. He bought me a few drinks and followed me around for a while."

"Yeah, I noticed," she cuts in.

I give her a look saying *stop interrupting me if you want to hear the story,* and she raises her hands in defeat, so I continue. "He bit me."

She coughs, choking on her coffee. It takes her a moment to regain her composure before she says, "He did what?!"

I laugh as I watch her eyes bulge out of her head. "Not like that. He was just flirting. I think? He pulled me in to whisper something into my ear and bit my neck. It was playful." I shrug. "And kind of hot."

"Wow. How do I get a guy to bite my neck?"

I laugh again, this time feeling it deep in my core. "Well, he did say he'll be back next weekend... maybe he'll bring his best neck-biting friends with him."

"A girl can dream."

The waitress marches over to take our order, and our conversation turns from my flavor of the week to her job, which is *draining every ounce of joy from her body* according to her. I'm only half-listening as I think about the guy from last night, and I realize that I'm looking forward to seeing him again. I haven't had this much fun in a while. If he wants to flirt, I can flirt right back. I majored in non-commitment.

Let the games begin.

ARIA

Sitting on my parents' porch with a fresh cup of coffee in my hand, I sway back and forth slowly on the swing, looking out into the mountains.

I made the biggest mistake of my life on this very porch swing.

No one really talks about the aftermath or about how hard it is to start over from ground zero. I changed my number and bought a new car. I avoided coming to my parents' house for the first nine months of being back in Colorado just in case he came looking for me. I did everything I could think of. I did everything to make sure he wouldn't *find* me if he did come looking. Every time I heard the rev of an engine or saw a bright red car out of the corner of my eye, my heart would stop beating for a few seconds.

I still remember the day I got a restraining order, just in case.

I've spent so long being scared and wishing I was invisible. It's difficult to put a finger on this feeling—wanting to die while also wanting to make it to another day.

Wretched is about as close as I can get.

I don't sleep through the night anymore. I'm too scared to close my eyes because I see his face every time I do. So instead I lie awake, reliving all my bad decisions and turning over every single choice that I made, overthinking all the things I never said to him but should have. It's like a nightmare that won't stop replaying in my head, except it really happened and it led me to where I am right now... which is nowhere. Doing nothing. My therapist calls it *cognitive hypervigilance,* which basically means I'm in a constant state of fight or flight.

I bring my cup up to my lips, letting the coffee burn my tongue. I've grown to like pain, look forward to it even. The pain reminds me that it was all real. Glancing down, I notice the scar on my wrist, remembering how *real* it actually was. Remembering the moment the dream splintered into the nightmare that won't let go.

I hardly recognize myself anymore, but I guess that's the point.

I sigh, kicking my leg out to stop the swing from moving. Every Friday on my way to therapy, I stop by to have coffee with my mom. We both look forward to it, and I couldn't stop now even if I wanted to. Sometimes we chat about life and if Bryce will ever settle down and start a family. Other times, we sit in silence, letting the gravity of the past keep us grounded, each reflecting in our own way.

My stomach grumbles, reminding me that I skipped dinner last night. I wasn't hungry after I watched a movie with Kate Winslet that turned out to be more of a drama than a light-hearted rom-com, leaving me emotionally devastated.

My therapist is on the same block as my favorite breakfast place, so I think I'll swing by for a breakfast burrito to go. Trauma is much easier to discuss on a full stomach.

It takes me ten minutes to find a parking spot.

By the time I walk inside, my food is waiting for me on the counter, probably at room temperature by now. I'm not used to it being this busy here, especially on a Friday. Denver has way too many people. *When did that happen?* It changed so much in the two years I was gone. Now it's bumper-to-bumper traffic and lines out the door.

As I turn to leave—takeout in one hand, to-go chai latte in the other—I hear the most infectious laughter from across the restaurant. I look back and notice two women sitting at a booth, deep in conversation. They look like they are debriefing after a girls' night out, the bags under their eyes giving away their lack of sleep.

Then I hear the laugh again. One of the women throws her hand over her mouth, trying to muffle the sound coming from deep within her core. Her laugh is so magnetic. It's the kind of laugh you would gravitate to if joy itself had a sound. The kind of joy that makes your face hurt from smiling. She looks vaguely familiar, but I can't place it.

I smile, remembering when things used to bring me joy, and when I was capable of feeling unbridled happiness.

Then I remember why I no longer smile, and turn on my heels, letting the door close loudly on my way out.

My therapist is waiting for me when I arrive.

"So, how are you? Tell me about your week."

I shift in my seat. Therapy doesn't make me nervous, at least not anymore, but it's the lack of bringing anything to the conversation that always makes me uncomfortable. My days don't change. There's never anything new or exciting. Last week a bird almost pooped on my shoulder, but missed me by three inches, and that was by far the most interesting thing to happen to me in weeks.

I've created a careful routine for my life, which results in a controlled sense of freedom and reliable consistency. So there's never anything new to report. I go to the same grocery store where I know every exit and every aisle like the back of my hand. I visit the same coffee shop where they know me and my order. My therapist says my need for order comes from a place of fear. He's probably right. "It's been good. A normal week, I think. Nothing special happened."

He nods, writing something down on his notepad. I know he has to take notes, but I hate when he does that. It makes me feel like I answered incorrectly to a test question.

"How often do you still feel the need to look over your shoulder?"

His question makes me pause. It's stupid because we're in a tiny office with no windows, but as soon as he asks, I resist the urge to turn around. It's a reflex at this point. "What do you mean?"

He lets out a small sigh as he crosses one leg over the other. "I just wonder if you are waiting for something, Aria. A sign maybe? I think your waiting might be preventing the wound from fully healing."

I sit with this for a minute, letting silence hang heavy in the air. *Is he right? Am I waiting for something?* Sure, I would love to see an engagement announcement, confirmation that he's moved on. Even an obituary would be fine. It's not knowing where he is or what he's doing that still scares me.

"I don't know that I'm waiting," I finally respond. "I'm just sad. I still don't sleep through the night. I still have a mild panic attack every time I see a red car." Taking a deep breath, I continue. "How am I supposed to know when I'm ready? To move on, I mean."

He tilts his head, considering the question.

"Moving on isn't linear, Aria. It doesn't mean that you need to date again, at least not right away. It won't erase your past, and it won't erase all the work you've done. No one gets to make choices about your life again. No one but you. But allowing yourself the option... it means that you are opening yourself up to the possibility of enjoying life again."

He pauses briefly. "I just want you to think about it. You are twenty-six, you have your whole life ahead of you. You're too young and too talented to live in this state of purgatory for the rest of your life."

Sometimes I wonder if sadness is contagious. I wonder if people cross to the other side of the street when they see me coming, just so they don't catch it. I didn't used to be sad. I used to be bubbly and full of life. My mother used to call me a blonde Mary Poppins. *But now?*

He made me hate Indian food. He made me hate the color red. *He made me hate myself.* I ignored every red flag because of my own insecurity and now I'm on the run, living in fear, hiding from the monster I let into my own life. But I don't say any of that. Instead I nod, promising him that I will try.

KATE

I t's Thursday.

Thursday means no cover and free drinks at my favorite club, Rain. Thursdays at the club also means fewer crowds and stronger pours. And hot guys who bite your neck.

We hardly said anything to each other that first night. We only flirted and danced, but as I stumbled toward the exit to head home, I heard him yell, "Same time next week?" And I vaguely remember giving him a thumbs up, high above the crowd.

Standing in front of the mirror, I study the girl in front of me. My hair is getting long and for the first time in a long time, the ends sit below my collarbones. I throw some waves in it, leaning into my *effortlessly put together* look. I'm wearing my favorite black dress, the one that's short enough to show off my long legs but long enough to leave something to the imagination. Opening my mascara tube, I apply one more coat to each eye. I take one last look in the mirror. My ride should be here any minute.

As soon as I climb into the Uber, I see a text from Kayla. "Ugh can't make it tonight. My boss has me working late on some stupid project that's not even due tomorrow. Say hi to the neck-biter for me." Her comment makes me laugh when I realize what that means. I wasn't prepared to not have backup tonight. Not that she would even really help me with anything, but just knowing that she's there would make me significantly less nervous.

I wonder if I should clue him in to his new nickname.

THE UBER DROPS me off down the block. When I reach the front, I wave at the bouncers. They all know me here, something I like more than I should probably admit. They wink at me as I bypass the line, skirting by the girls showing too much skin.

I see him then, standing near the bar with his back against the wall. There's *something* about him in his dark jeans and his Adidas sneakers that has my heart beating out of my chest. I take him in this time, memorizing his features before the alcohol starts flowing. He's taller than any man I've ever seen, with light brown hair that curls at the ends and dark brown eyes. He's lean, with a body like a runner. There's an intimidating stillness in his posture that's alluring, drawing me to him for a reason I can't explain.

I've always been drawn to the tall ones, but I've never seen a man this tall out in the wild before. He has to be six-eight or six-nine. I'm tall, and he still towers over me. He spots me immediately and uses his leg to kick off the wall, drifting over to where I'm waiting in line for my dirty martini.

"You again."

"Me again." I smile as I let my eyes trail up and down his body. *He's so hot it physically hurts.* "I never got your name."

He looks at me for a minute as he debates on whether to keep the illusion or tell me a sliver of truth. "It's Benson." His lips curl into a smile as he takes a drink of his craft IPA—*typical Coloradan.* "My friends call me Ben. And you are?"

Before I can answer, it's my turn at the bar. My favorite bartender, Scottie, is working tonight, and I'm thrilled. "Hi Kate!" He's always just as excited to see me as I am to see him. We bonded one night because we were both born in Michigan, and the rest is history. "The usual?"

He doesn't break eye contact or wait for my answer as he starts moving swiftly behind the bar, reaching for the green olives. "You're the best, Scottie. Make it a double." I wink at him as Ben's eyes dart back and forth, watching this encounter unfold. I can't tell if he's jealous or just curious.

Scottie hands me my extra dirty martini as Ben chimes in, "Hey, man. Put it on my tab."

He shakes his head, laughing as he begins typing behind the bar. "Have fun, Kate, and be safe." His look traps Ben in place before coming back to meet mine. "See you later."

"So it's Kate, then." Ben answers his own question as we move from our place in line closer to the corner of the room. "Are you from Denver?" He leans in, really invested in my answer.

"No." I smile back, my favorite seductive smile. "I'm from Michigan. I don't like it here much, if I'm being honest."

No. Colorado was never part of my plan. There's too many people here. Everyone smells like weed... like rotten plants and zero ambition. But no one knows me, no one knows what I've been through or what I've endured, and I like it that way. *So I stayed.* I shouldn't have, but I stayed.

I glance away for a minute, but when I turn back to face him, he's giving me a look. "I bet I can change your mind."

Well that's presumptuous of him. Little does he know that I see this going nowhere. I'm looking for a one-night stand, and nothing more.

I will never let anyone all the way in again. That is how I stay in control, by being one step ahead and in full and total control of my heart and my emotions. I let my guard down once, and it cost me everything. No, I've already made up my mind. I'm better off being alone.

"Oh yeah?" I grin a little bit wider. "I guess we'll see."

"I guess we will." His gaze travels up my legs, pinning me in place on the dance floor. His eyes go from my sneakers to my dress, lingering on my chest before meeting mine. "You are beautiful," he says. Heat pools in my stomach. This particular dress looks best in a heap on someone else's floor.

I'm used to attention, but I crave it now. I've learned what to wear and what to say to get what I want, always remaining in control. But something about Ben makes me feel out of control. His eyes look like they're casting flames, and it's intoxicating. My hands start to shake, which is not a feeling I'm used to. I'm not used to holding back.

I'm not sure who moves first, but before I know it I'm caught up in the moment as we begin making out on the dance floor. My arms are wrapped around his neck, with one hand trying to keep my drink steady so I don't spill vodka down his back. We're both breathing quickly, too quickly. He has one arm wrapped around my waist, pulling me in close and the other gripping the back of my neck, his hand tangled up in my hair.

All eyes are on us. At least it feels like it.

And, I have to pee. *God, the timing could not be worse.*

Still breathless, I pull back and manage to say, "Don't. Move."

I slip away quickly without looking back, leaving him panting in the middle of the dance floor. There's only two girls in front of me, so the line moves quickly. I touch my lips and laugh, moving forward a few steps. *What the hell was that?*

Before I know it, it's my turn. My chin rests on my hand inside the bathroom stall as I think about Ben. There are only two ways this can go. One, I bring him home with me and never hear from him again. Two, I invite him home and he says no. *Unlikely.*

Standing, I shimmy my dress back into place and yell, "Should I invite him over?!" I listen as girls from every stall chime in with some variation of, "Hell yeah, girl!"

It's settled, then.

Scottie is making the drinks strong tonight. I know I asked for a double, but this feels like a triple. I exit the bathroom door, stumbling a bit when I spot Ben in the middle of the dance floor, standing exactly where I left him. Couples are grinding around him but he's standing still, waiting for me.

From across the room, I watch as a girl intentionally bumps into him and then blushes as she apologizes for spilling beer down his leg, clearly looking for attention. He gives her a curt smile, acknowledging her apology, and looks back toward the bathroom. His eyes light up when he sees me.

When I reach him, I pull him back in for one more kiss, short and gentle this time. "Will you come home with me?" I breathe onto his lips.

He studies me again like he can't help himself. "Yes." His voice is deep, full of desire. He leads me out of the club, his fingers linked with mine. I feel sixteen again, drunk on his touch. As we approach the curb, I lean against a light post, letting the cold metal steady me as we wait for our Uber. Five minutes turn into ten as we watch cars come and go. I feel useless, not knowing what type of car we are supposed to be looking for.

Without warning a red sports car pulls up, and my body tenses. I feel the alcohol churning in my stomach as I fight to keep it down. I'm standing still, painfully aware of every part of my body and ready to bolt if I need to. I'm not sure how far I would make it because I'm pretty intoxicated, but I'm sure I could at least get a head start.

Ben notices the change in my body language. "Hey, are you okay?"

I didn't realize I was holding my breath until the driver climbed out of the car. *It's not him.* No, it's just a blond-haired frat boy wearing a purple polo with a little alligator embroidered on the chest pocket. I exhale, closing my eyes in relief.

"Yes. Yeah, I'm fine," I say when I open them again, giving Ben the most reassuring smile I can muster. I will my legs to move as he opens the back seat door for me, gesturing for me to climb in first. He climbs in after me, draping his arm across my shoulder and pulling me in close.

He took *everything* from me. And I'll be damned if I let him steal one more moment of my peace.

So I lean into Ben, draping my legs across his lap, letting myself feel excited for the first time in a long time.

ARIA

The birds are chatty this morning, and the air outside is warm.

I roll over and see Daisy and Beau at the bottom of the windowsill, sitting still as rocks, watching the bird dance outside on the tree branches. My house is in a quiet neighborhood on the outskirts of Denver. I chose the house with the biggest shed in the biggest yard. The pointed posts on the picket fence are as sharp as thorns. They guard my sanctuary—*my fortress, really*—from the outside world. I have neighbors, but they are quiet and non-intrusive. Just the way I like it.

Climbing out of bed, I turn and fix the floral comforter, pulling it up over my pillow and smoothing it down with my hands. My pink nail polish is chipped, only a few tiny spots of color remaining. I am long overdue for some self-care.

The beep from my coffee maker makes me turn and go back into the kitchen. I open my cupboard, quickly scanning my coffee mugs. I had to leave all my old ones behind. The mugs with fun, quirky sayings and mismatched patterns was the collection I grew with Marissa. They didn't make the cut that day when I had to flee for my life. So, my collection was replaced by a ceramic, hand-painted set of six from my mother. I look from the blue one to the pink one before I land on the green one with little vines and leaves wrapping around the base. Filling the cup to the rim, I carry it over to the couch, flipping on *The Kelly Clarkson Show*.

Before I sit down, my eyes float across the living room to a cardboard box buried in the closet, half open and covered in dust. Inside the box are my old ballet slippers and leotards, my acceptance letter to the Paris Opera Ballet, a sonogram, and a dainty silver necklace. The box holds all the things that remind me of the life I once had, the life that I lost, the life I was forced to run from. I haven't opened it in over a year, but I often find myself sitting on my couch with nothing but that old box in my line of sight.

The lingering grief haunts me every day. *I miss who I used to be.*

My mornings always start this way—zoned out to some mindless daytime television show, sipping my morning coffee alone, with nothing but the sound of Kelly Clarkson and the birds chirping outside the window. But then I crave the silence. The quiet peacefulness allows me to reconnect with myself after being drowned out by someone else's voice for so long.

The recluse spider only comes together with another recluse to mate. The arachnid avoids contact with humans and even with other spiders. They spin messy webs to retreat to instead of using them to hunt and trap food as other spiders do. Their endurance is remarkable, and they survive for months without food or water. A recluse prefers to stay hidden, blending into its environment, present but unseen. It moves through life silently, surviving on nothing but resilience. I think that is fascinating.

My mom let me isolate for a few months before she sat me down one day and told me my behavior wasn't healthy. She told me I was allowed to heal, but I needed to move forward at the same time, even just a little bit. So she pulled me off the couch and forced me to bake with her. We would bake cookies for the neighbors and pies for the local nursing homes. We baked to keep our hands and our minds busy.

One day our neighbor, Denise, stopped by. She had an old overgrown oak tree with branches that hung over our fence that always shed leaves into our yard. Denise told us that her daughter, Marie, was getting married. She asked if we would bake a two-tiered cake for the wedding with simple white frosting for the design. Nothing too intricate, but simple and elegant. I agreed to bake the cake because I had nothing else to do. Denise and Marie loved the cake so much that Denise recommended me to a few of her friends whose children were also getting married.

Somewhere along the line, people started calling me and asking me to bake their wedding treats. A year later, I had enough saved to move out on my own. The first thing I did was buy a house. I chose this house because of its detached studio. It was originally intended to hold a lawn mower and other appliances, but I turned it into my own special bakery, Aria's Cakes. The second thing I did was replace my mom's sofa with a new one—something without the shape of my body permanently imprinted into it.

Mixing the ingredients together—flour, butter, sugar, eggs, vanilla —I can lose myself for hours at a time creating edible masterpieces. I can spend an entire day crafting delicate and colorful macarons, swoon-worthy cheesecakes, and towering layer cakes. Kneading fondant or swirling buttercream frosting across a fresh cake feels cathartic while I focus on smoothing the cake's sides and edges to perfection. My favorite part is creating whimsical sugary shapes to top a tiered cake. Nothing is too imaginative—dainty butterflies, silky ribbons, ivory pearls, and exotic flowers make each confection a unique expression of myself.

Breaking from my reverie of baking and setting my coffee cup down, I walk to the bathroom. I take a deep breath in the mirror. It's easier to bake with my hair thrown up in a ponytail out of my face, and I've got three cakes I need to bake today.

I'm perfectly fine, safe in my carefully constructed routine. But my routine is starting to feel like a cage despite my love of baking, and this is just a house. It's not a home because I have no one to share it with. I sigh—a long, drawn out breath that stretches through my chest.

I've worked so hard for the freedom I have now. And I hate to admit it, but I'm lonely.

EVERY WEDNESDAY NIGHT, Bryce and I host an art class at the local foster home. It's something we started doing shortly after I returned to Colorado to give back and do what I love without allowing myself to be too vulnerable. The innocence of the children at the foster home helped me heal.

The way those kids trust so openly, the way that believe every brushstroke matters—it healed me. Being around them reminds me that love can be simple and safe instead of dangerous and threatening. They allow me to show my affection freely, just by wiping paint from small cheeks and little fingers. There is no risk of being taken advantage of because they ask for nothing in return. The children remind me of myself as a child, before I grew up and life taught me some hard lessons.

Wednesday nights with these kids are the best thing I've ever done for myself, and I love that I can do something for them.

As I slip my apron over my head, I look out into the room at all the shining, innocent eyes looking back at me. Bryce and I pushed plastic folding tables together and draped tablecloths across the length of them, with brushes fanning out in every direction next to large mason jars filled with water and pallets holding every paint color you could imagine.

The project today is simple: paint the sky. We tell the kids to paint a rainbow, the moon and the stars, a sun and some clouds, anything their heart desires. Anything that makes them feel alive.

Bryce moves from table to table, opening paint tubes and refilling water cups. She doesn't have an artistic bone in her body, but she comes anyway. She shows up every week. She loves to be here, even though she throws her canvas in the trash the second we lock up for the night.

I'm so grateful my art supplies were one of the things my mom packed for me that day. She knew I couldn't be without them. I had already given up ballet, and I think she knew that giving up art, too, would be something I couldn't come back from.

Looking across the room, I watch as Jamie dips her brush in the pink paint, then red, then yellow as she smears a huge glob of this glorious orange color across her canvas with the biggest grin across her face. Then I look at Nicky, with his glasses two inches from his canvas, outlining a bright yellow sun with intense precision.

I make myself a promise as I watch these children create their masterpieces, so pure and uncomplicated.

I'm going to start living again.

KATE

When I was a little girl, I created a rigid schedule for every family vacation. I planned surprise birthday parties for my friends. I lived for Friday nights and color-coding my monthly planner. It's the one thing I've always been good at.

So when I was forced to grow up and really look at my future after *him*, it was a no-brainer. I wanted to be a wedding planner— Jennifer Lopez sold me the dream.

I studied late every weekend, took online courses, and every time someone I knew got engaged, I would ask them if I could help plan their wedding, just to dip my toes into the water. Before I knew it, I had six weddings under my belt, and my business was taking off.

There's a catharsis in watching couples start a new chapter and something healing in the way a bride glows or a groom weeps when he sees her walking down the aisle in her wedding dress. It's fulfilling to give these couples the wedding I never got to have.

But I don't believe in happily ever after. Not anymore. It took long enough for me to stop crying at weddings. Now I approach them tactically, as a job I need to get done. I'm in full control of my emotions in a way I never was before.

Standing in the back of the room, I watch as the wedding party pairs up, one by one, and walks toward the altar, following my direction. Tucking my clipboard under my arm, I lift my iced coffee to my lips. A few minutes later, it's the bride's turn. She loops her arm under her dad's, lips quivering with the realization of what she's about to do.

The bride's mom approaches from the side, carrying a bouquet of bright red roses, and hands them to the bride, using the tissue in her other hand to wipe her eyes. The roses complement her bright red lipstick.

I hate the color red.

She takes the roses and holds them directly in front of her belly button, tilted outward. *Just like I showed her.* I smile as I watch her put one foot in front of the other, walking toward her future.

I like wedding rehearsals. They give me a chance to get to know the family and the wedding party on a deeper level, positioning myself as someone they can trust.

I'll never forget the second wedding I ever planned. The father of the bride could not take his eyes off of me. I'm not sure if it was my age, or the fact that I was covered in tattoos, but he wasn't sure about me from the start. After three drinks though, and a few compliments on his custom tux, I finally won him over.

I watch as the bride and groom stand at the front of the room, holding hands as they face each other. The officiant is carrying on about the proper timing to be handed the rings, and the wedding party is trying their best to not to look bored.

I wish that I hadn't stayed out as late as I did last night because my head hurts. But it's not my fault. I have no control when it comes to Rain on Thursday nights. After I make my rounds, saying goodbye to the parents and reminding the wedding party to not get too drunk tonight or they will absolutely regret it, I make my exit.

I climb into my car, taking one last look as I drive away. I love this venue. It's tucked in the foothills of the mountains about thirty minutes from my downtown apartment. The exterior is white and pristine with large white pillars framing the front door. It's timeless—the kind of place Elizabeth Taylor would get married.

Bandit greets me excitedly when I open my front door, jumping as high as his little body can manage. I scoop him up with one arm, tossing my purse onto the coffee table and kicking my shoes off in the hallway as I carry him into the bedroom. I set him on the bed, watching him make himself comfortable as I pull out every single drawer in my dresser, searching for my favorite hoodie.

"What should we do tonight, hmm?" I ask, still digging. Bandit cocks his head to the side, probably wondering why I still carry on conversations with him after all these years, as if he's ever once been able to respond.

Finally, in the very last drawer, I locate the ratty oversized hoodie I've had since high school. It's not even really mine. It belonged to Steve, and it has the number four ironed onto the back in a large block number, his old varsity number. I stole it one day and never gave it back, and it's one more wash away from unraveling completely.

Now that I'm comfortable, I pick Bandit up, carrying him back out to the living room as we both plop down on the couch. I pick up the remote, turn on the TV and flip through the channels looking for a horror movie, when I hear my phone buzz. It's a text from Ben. "Chinese takeout and a movie marathon? I'll buy the food; you provide the couch."

I smile as I read the message. He's charming. In a different kind of way. He makes me laugh, and *he's safe*. We've been talking for a few weeks, moving on from Thursday nights on the dance floor to Friday night takeout. It'll be Saturday morning breakfast soon if I'm not careful. *What am I doing?*

I smile as I type my response. "See you soon."

I've been researching bakeries for weeks. My bride, Laura, wants a stunning four-tier cake with ivory fondant and hand-drawn designs, and she insists on having the best. She must have the best planner, the best cake, the best everything. After narrowing it down, I'm confident I've found just that.

Not to mention, cake tasting is my favorite way to spend a Sunday afternoon.

Walking up the path, we arrive in front of a house with a sign that says "Aria's Cakes" out front, with an arrow pointing to the left. Following the sidewalk around the corner of the house is the cutest detached studio I've ever seen. The exterior is painted buttercream yellow with market lights hanging in front of the door. The sign on the front door is detailed with the most intricate designs and colored with beautiful pastels.

"I'm so excited," Laura whispers under her breath.

"Me too. I skipped lunch for this," I reply, tapping lightly on the door. Laura smiles at me, laughing. If only she knew how important dessert is to me. "Cake for breakfast" is my mantra.

Seconds later, the door swings open and an adorable blonde sashays into the room. She's wearing a yellow sunflower apron stained with flour and chocolate, and her long blonde hair is tied up in a bun on top of her head. Her glasses are a light brown tortoise shell pattern, and she has the most welcoming smile I've ever seen. She looks... familiar to me. But I can't place it.

"Hi, Kate and Laura! You're right on time. Please come in! I'm Aria." She steps to the side and motions beside her to reveal a charming tasting room.

She has shelves upon shelves of vintage tasting plates, glassware and flatware. There's a large refrigerator over in the corner and a countertop in the middle of the room. *That must be where the magic happens.*

Off to the right, there's a seating area and a mini wine fridge, bursting at the seams with bottles of Sauvignon Blanc, Chardonnay, and Riesling. The whole room is brought to life with flowers blooming and plants in every corner as the scent of buttercream frosting fills the air.

It's not very big, but it's so warm and inviting. Her bakery feels like I've walked into a familiar place to catch up with an old friend.

Laura is the first to show her excitement. "Thank you! We are *so* excited."

I lead the way to the wooden counter-height pub table with two stools standing on each side. In the middle of the table are six pieces of cake, all Aria's signature flavors, with a stack of forks nearby. The table is adorned with a vase of sunflowers and a bottle of Chardonnay; the complementing wine glasses are etched with little sunflowers and swirls throughout the glass. Leaning down to pull out a stool, I take the first seat. Laura slides in next to me as Aria walks around to the other side.

"We are so excited to meet you, Aria! We've been looking forward to this tasting all week," I say as I set my tote down next to my feet. "I've been researching bakers for weeks, and I was overjoyed when I found you. You come highly recommended."

Aria smiles, blushing a bit. She's soft-spoken—quieter than I expected. "Oh, thank you. You are too kind." She picks up the first piece of cake and sets it right in front of Laura. "We will start with 'White Wedding' and work our way through the rest! 'White Wedding' is a lemon lavender cake, layered with a zingy fresh lemon curd and iced in a lavender vanilla bean buttercream." Handing Laura a fork, Aria says, "Let's get you some wine to go with that."

Laura does not hesitate. She quickly scoops a piece onto her fork and I can practically taste the flavor of the cake through her facial expression. "OMG," she says with her mouth full. "This is the best thing I've ever had."

Aria giggles, pushing an overflowing glass of wine in her direction.

"Kate, you have to try this," Laura mumbles as she shoves another piece in her mouth.

I pick up a fork and push a healthy piece onto it and then into my mouth. *Holy shit.* This is the best slice of cake I've ever had. The frosting is not *too* sweet, the lemon curd has me drooling, and the cake is perfectly moist. "Aria, this is insane. I've never had anything so good."

Aria is beaming. "I'm so glad you like it!" After pouring herself a glass of wine, she joins us at the table. "Now talk to me about the design. What are we thinking?"

Leaning down, I reach into my tote and pull out the magazine I stashed there. "Okay. Yes, we have *so* many ideas. We would love to know what you think. Give us your professional opinion." Flipping through the magazine, I land on the page I'm looking for and hand it to Aria. "We absolutely love the intricate piping details on this one."

"That one is my favorite," Laura says through her mouthful of cake. "Please tell me you can do that."

SIX PIECES of cake and two glasses of wine later, I glance down at my phone. Two hours have passed as we girls bonded over life, love, and desserts.

"Laura, how are you ever going to choose?" I ask her.

Laura moans as she throws a hand over her stomach. "I have absolutely no idea because I want them all. And I am so full I could burst!" she laughs. "Aria, may I use your powder room?"

"Definitely!" Aria turns around to point across the room. "It's in the back off to the left. You can't miss it." Laura smiles as she peels herself off the bar stool, moaning as she slowly waddles to the back of the studio. I laugh under my breath.

"How long have you been a baker?" I ask Aria as she cleans up the fourth plate of cake, sweetly named "Happily Ever After."

Aria smiles, setting down her wine glass after she neatly tosses back what was left of the pour. Her eyes look apprehensive and almost sad. "Professionally? A little over a year." She pauses for a moment before continuing. "I used to be married." She shakes her head as soon as she says the word *married*, like she's trying to get the bad taste of something sour out of her mouth.

"Long story short, I survived. Afterward, I spent some time trying to put my life back together. Baking has always been my favorite hobby, so it just fell into place. The rest is history."

I smile sadly back at her. "I have a similar story. I married an asshole, too. Healing definitely takes time. I'm sorry that happened to you... but look at you now."

Aria glances around the room, taking in her quaint little studio and the life before her, the light not quite reaching her eyes though she is smiling. "Yeah, I guess you're right."

We hear the faint sound of a door close as Laura wanders back to the tasting table. "Oooh, all that sugar and wine... I'm a little bit tipsy." She giggles as she stumbles slightly, pulling out the bar stool with more force than she intends. I shoot a glance at Aria and she stifles a laugh. "But I had some time to think about the flavors while I was peeing. Let's do the bottom tier 'White Wedding' and the top tier 'Chocolate Veil.' I think Jeremy will really like that one."

"You got it!" Aria says as she slides a glass of water in Laura's direction. "I will email you a proposal this week."

"That sounds great! Kate, I need to run. I've got work in the morning and I guess I should figure out dinner." She takes a sip of water, then leans in to give me a hug. "Drive safely!" I tell her.

"Thank you so much, Aria. This was wonderful, and I can't wait to have you be a part of our wedding." A smile and a wave, and Laura's out the door.

"Would you like to stay for one more glass?" Aria asks me, reaching for the near empty bottle of wine.

"Oh, absolutely." I smile as I lift my glass in her direction. The room is glowing from the sunset shining through the windows. It makes the already warm space that much more inviting. There's no way I can say no.

Aria pours what's left of the bottle into our glasses and raises her arm in a toast. "To Laura and Jeremy."

"To Laura and Jeremy!" I say in return, taking a small sip. With her arm extended, I can see a horizontal scar on her wrist. It's faint, but it's large enough to be a constant reminder that time can mend some things but not erase them completely.

Before I can say anything more, Aria fills the void. "I'm so happy to finally meet you. I've been in the industry for a little while now, but it's been hard to make friends."

I feel the exact same way. The wedding industry is so large and oversaturated, especially in Colorado, but there's a lot of competition. It should be easy to make friends, but it's really not. I know exactly what she means without her needing to say any more.

"I completely agree. I have a love-hate relationship with this career. I love being a wedding planner, but I hate the drama that comes with it."

Aria nods and looks down at her wine glass. "When I was with my ex, I lost all my friends. I had some of those friendships for my entire life," she says quietly, her voice fading. "He took everything from me."

I nod, letting her words sink in. She has no idea how much I understand.

For a moment, I think about changing the subject before this conversation turns too heavy. But then I realize that I haven't talked about that time of life to anyone in a very long time.

In fact, I can't remember the last time I had an intentional conversation with anyone about anything other than music and the weather. I am the queen of small talk, always keeping people at an arm's length and never fully letting them in. For years, it was just a way to protect myself from things I couldn't face, but now I think it's become second nature.

There are some things that I never breathed a word of, not to anyone. I buried them down so deep and convinced myself that if I drank enough liquor and never uttered the words out loud, the trauma would just disappear. But that's not how it works, *unfortunately*.

Aria is opening up to me. For some reason she trusts me, or maybe she just has a few things she needs to get off her chest and no one else to talk to. Either way, she is sharing her truth with me, and I feel like I owe her the same.

"The same thing happened to me. My ex was so controlling. I used to think that being needed meant being loved. I used to really believe that no one would love me the way he did. But I think deep down I knew that I was playing a part, and that I was pretending."

I hesitate, wondering if I should pump the brakes, using this opportunity to take a sip of my wine. I don't know Aria, and I don't want to scare her away by oversharing. But the moment of hesitation is fleeting, because as soon as I start talking, I can't stop.

"I'd just gotten so good at it, I wasn't sure who I really was anymore. He erased my identity completely before I knew what was happening." I don't know why, but I just *know* that Aria will understand. She's been divorced, like me. She doesn't have many friends, like me. I can't seem to quiet the little voice inside that's telling me to open up and to let someone in who might understand, so I don't have to carry the weight of the past all alone anymore.

My mouth feels dry, but I continue. "After Ryan, I had to completely start over. I was so young, too, so I had absolutely zero idea what I wanted. I was floating through life with no purpose. It was really, really hard. Some days, it still is." Saying his name feels like lighting a match. Just uttering the syllables out loud makes me want to throw up.

Aria's face drains of color.

"Did you just say Ryan?"

ARIA

Is this a joke?

I fight the urge to look around, expecting someone to jump out from behind the curtains and yell *gotcha!* There is no way we are talking about the same Ryan. It's not possible. But I can't ignore the nagging pit in my stomach. I have to ask her.

Kate laughs—sort of—but something in her voice cracks. "Ryan Langford."

I sink into my seat feeling suddenly lightheaded. I've had a little too much wine, and realizing that we are speaking about the same man hits me like a freight train. "Oh my God."

"There is no way," Kate keeps going. Her voice softens, and she speaks cautiously now. "Mechanic? Quiet, but like too quiet? Born in Michigan? Raised by his grandparents?"

I'm staring across the table at Kate, stunned and unable to move. I'm unable to speak. It's been years since I've heard that name. My heart is racing, and I can't seem to stop the sudden trembling in my jaw. I manage to nod slightly.

Kate is so different than I am. She has a voice I can never seem to find in myself. She has an energy that draws others to her. Her personality is so magnetic. She's strong and confident and so sure of what she wants. *How were we married to the same man?*

"No fucking way," Kate says finally.

We sit in silence for a minute. The room feels like it's losing oxygen as neither of us moves. *What are the impossible odds* that I would meet someone who was married to the same garbage heap of a human that I was?

It's almost laughable. *Almost.* Our conversation unfolds like a confession.

Kate speaks first. "I married him in 2011. We divorced when he went to prison."

I blink, fast. "Prison? He was in prison?" I gasp.

Kate nods slowly. "Six months to twenty-two years. Burglary. I... didn't even know he was capable of it. Well, I guess maybe I did. I just didn't want to believe it."

I reach for my wine glass like it's a lifeline. *Of course.* The seven months of silence, the "family emergency," the lies—it all makes sense now.

We stare at each other like survivors finding each other in the wreckage. The red flags are too similar to ignore. The control. The silence. The isolation. The feeling of being owned instead of loved.

"When did you get divorced?" Kate asks finally, her voice still rough with shock.

"A few years ago," I say, clearing my throat. "We were together for almost three years. I always wondered what he was like before me... If he was paranoid and angry, or if it was just me who brought it out of him." Shifting in my seat, I'm suddenly very uncomfortable.

"It wasn't just you," Kate says again, her voice stronger now. "He was always like that. Secretive. Controlling. He made me feel like I was crazy half the time, and I'm sure he didn't get any better after going to prison."

The silence settles between us again, the weight of it anchoring us like a boat being tossed by the waves. I nod slowly. "Me too. He would punish me with silence. Or he would just vanish for a night and never explain where he'd been. But then he'd come back and act like I was being dramatic for caring." My voice sounds faraway.

Kate exhales. "God, the gaslighting."

We talk for over an hour, trading stories like war veterans. We compare timelines, habits, phrases he used, the subtle tactics he repeated. He told us both we were the only ones who understood him. That we were dramatic. That we *made* him behave the way he did.

I discover matching bruises in our memories, and it takes everything in me to not crumble to pieces.

"Didn't you just hate how he would always say things like 'he just *had* to have you'?" Kate asks at one point, swirling the wine around in her glass, disgust written on her face. "At first, I loved it. I thought it was sexy and possessive."

My breath catches as I cringe. "So did I, but I realized very quickly that he wasn't trying to be a protector. He was a dictator."

By the time the sky outside fades to navy, we've forgotten about Laura's wedding and about everything except each other and this shocking revelation.

"I don't know how to describe it," I say, wrapping my arms around myself. "But it's like... no one ever understood what it was like. Until now."

I look over at Kate, still unable to believe that fate brought us together. I knew from the moment Kate walked through the door that something about her felt... familiar. Not her face or her laugh, exactly. It was something deeper.

"I know," Kate says. Her voice cracks. "I know exactly what you mean."

It wasn't *just* that we both survived Ryan. It was that we survived being completely and utterly *alone*. Each of us walked through hell thinking we were the only ones. Now, sitting across from each other in the glow from the candle I lit in the center of the table, we aren't alone anymore.

I glance down at my phone. *How is it 9 p.m. already?* I have a full day of tastings tomorrow, so I really need to find some food and clean up this mess.

"I've got a long day of baking ahead of me tomorrow, but can we get coffee sometime?"

Kate smiles at me. "I would LOVE that. Text me anytime." She excuses herself to the bathroom, then grabs her tote. As she heads for the door, she turns to look at me one last time.

When our eyes meet, it's like looking at a reflection. For the first time in a long time, I feel seen—not as a victim, not as a mistake, but as a woman who had made it out. A survivor.

KATE

I look across my kitchen table at my mom, who is rummaging through my living room, tidying up my mess and organizing my piles of clutter. She just can't help herself. Every once in a blue moon she invites herself over, just so that she can find something to meddle in. She usually comes over on days when my dad wakes up early to go fishing. He leaves her home alone, and she can't stand to be at home by herself for more than a few hours.

Once she finds the general vicinity of the couch acceptably tidy, she takes a seat, pulling out the book she always keeps neatly tucked into her purse.

Mom and Dad learned that I married Ryan by accident. Without thinking, I listed their address when I was filling out a piece of paperwork to change my last name. I didn't even realize I'd done it until they called me one day out of the blue. Sprawled out across my Colorado apartment floor, painting my nails, I answered the phone and received an earful. I can only imagine what they thought, and how hurt they must have been to be treated that way by their only daughter. But I was ashamed, and still am. They moved out to Colorado shortly after. They never told me why, or at least not the real reason—*Dad got a new job*, and *we felt called to be near the moun-*

tains. But with them living close by, our relationship slowly began to mend.

"So," my mom says, pretending to be invested in the words on her page. "Are you ever going to get back out there? It's been years Kate." She clears her throat, lubricating her pipes so that she can drive her point home. *I still haven't told her the truth. I wonder how differently this conversation would go if she knew.*

"I'm not getting any younger you know, and I would like grand-kids one day."

Oh, here we go. "Mom," I say, giving her a look.

"What? I'm just saying Kate, you're not getting any younger."

"Mom, I'm only twenty-nine."

"I realize that honey, but don't you want to at least get out there? Meet a nice man? You will be thirty this year."

"Don't remind me," I whisper under my breath. "Actually..." I start again, and the words come out before I can stop them. "I did meet someone a few weeks ago."

Her eyes go wide as she waits for me to continue. *What am I doing? Stop talking, Kate.*

"His name is Ben, uh... Benson." I stand then, opening the fridge to get a snack even though I'm not hungry. "I met him at a bar, and he's great... really great." As soon as I say the word bar, I cringe. I'm sure my mother, the wife of a retired pastor, is dying inside to know that her daughter met a man at a bar. Peeling back a string cheese wrapper that I am not intending to eat, I add quickly, "I don't know where it's going yet. But I like him, I think. If it turns into anything, you will be the first to know."

She forces a smile, turning her attention back to her book, a look of satisfaction written all over her face. I find myself still standing in the kitchen, leaning against the island, fidgeting with my string cheese wrapper.

Sometimes I let myself wonder what would happen if I let my guard down. What would happen if I let myself fall for someone again? What would happen if I gave Ben a *real* chance and he didn't hurt me. He's already so different than Ryan. He's easygoing and uncomplicated. I like that. Not to mention our chemistry, which is undeniable.

My mom turns the page of her book, the sound of the paper folding beneath her fingers. I watch her for a minute, trying to imagine what kind of man she hopes I end up with. *Smart? Successful? A banker? Someone in tech like my dad? Someone my age? Someone older?*

I think my mom would really like Ben.

The thoughts swirl around in my head as I watch her making herself at home on my sofa. She's so lucky to be she married to my dad, to her soulmate. Never questioning their happily ever after. It's such a foreign concept to me to not have to second guess everything.

I CAN'T STOP THINKING about Aria.

I've been distracted ever since we met at the cake tasting. She texted me yesterday and asked if I want to grab a coffee today, and I said yes. *Of course I said yes.*

I need to know more about her. I barely slept last night antici-pating our get-together. There are so many unanswered questions and so many things I want to know—no, that I *need* to know. Espe-cially now that I know there is someone else out there in the world who knows exactly what I went through. Also, *is she okay? Like genuinely okay?*

The sun is still out when I finish up at a micro-wedding, spilling through the wide windows of the event venue, casting golden lines across the whitewashed floorboards. The last vendor has packed up, and only a few scattered remnants of the day's wedding—floral petals, ribbon scraps, and a single silver heel someone will surely come back for—remain behind.

Aria is meeting me at the coffee shop, and then we're going to walk a trail behind the venue. I arrive early, trading in my black dress for my favorite Lululemon leggings, something a little bit more comfortable for our walk.

We get our drinks to go—an iced caramel latte for me and a chai tea latte for Aria—and head down the narrow dirt path through the pine trees. The sky slowly melts into sherbet streaks as our shoes crunch softly over the gravel. The silence isn't awkward, though. It's breathable.

I'm quiet for a while, not really sure where to begin. I want to know everything there is to know about Aria. Not only is she one of the nicest people I've ever met, but we share something no one else will ever understand.

"I have so many questions; I'm not really sure where to begin," I say after a few minutes, laughing half-heartedly.

Aria laughs in return, huffing in a breath. "I know. I feel the same way." She pauses for a minute, catching her breath. "Tell me everything. Start from the beginning." Then she adds quickly, "But only if you're comfortable."

I nod, sipping slowly on my latte. "Okay, right... the beginning. Let's see. We met on a dating app. Honestly, I didn't think he was really anything special. He looked so ordinary, but there was a mysterious allure to him, you know? Something quiet and complicated, and I've always loved a fixer-upper."

I hesitate for a moment before I continue. "We weren't together that long, though, not really. Just long enough for him to ruin my life, but he went to prison less than a year into our relationship. That was my out." The last sentence makes me choke on my coffee as I'm reminded of that phone call.

"I still can't believe he went to prison," she whispers, dragging her feet. We walk a while longer in silence. The trees close in around us, draping the trail in curious shadows. "Did you ever think it was your fault?" she says, turning to look at me.

"Of course. I always thought it was my fault." My jaw tenses. "That's how he kept us. He didn't have to chain us up if he could convince us we deserved the cage." My throat goes tight. "I haven't said this out loud to anyone, but... when he was sentenced, part of me still felt like I had betrayed him. I think deep down, I knew that I didn't, but I couldn't stop those intrusive thoughts. He really did a number on me."

I stop walking, taking a moment to catch my breath. I turn slightly toward Aria. "Can I ask you something? You don't have to answer."

Aria stops beside me. She doesn't speak; she just gives me a small nod.

"What was your moment? The one when you knew it was over. The moment you knew you couldn't keep going."

The trail stretches quietly before us. The sound of birds comes from somewhere overhead, and I hear traffic humming in the distance.

Aria takes a long breath. "I don't talk about it. Like... ever. Not even in therapy. But... there was a moment."

I wait, gently, silently.

"We were fighting," Aria says, her voice just above a whisper. "One of those nights where nothing I said was right. I had just found out I was pregnant." She pauses. "I was terrified. But there was a part of me that was... hopeful."

I feel my stomach drop.

"He grabbed me," Aria continues. "It wasn't new, it was never new. But he shoved me so hard that I flew back and hit the kitchen counter. He broke my wrist. And I knew—right then—I knew what my future held." Her voice cracks.

"Shortly after, I went into the clinic, alone. He insisted, and I refused to bring a baby into that. I wasn't even sure what was happening."

I look down and notice my hands are trembling. Even though I know Ryan is capable of terrible things, I can't believe he did that to *her*. The rage bubbling up inside me threatens to make me sick. My eyesight goes blurry for a moment. When Aria finally comes back into focus, I see she is crying. I see the quiet sobs and all the weight she is carrying in her shoulders.

I reach out and wrap my arms around her. "I'm so sorry. You are worth so much more. Don't ever forget that."

Aria blinks fast, forcing back the tears. We stand still for a long time, watching the leaves sway on the trees. The forest is still apart from the slight breeze, and there's not another soul out here. Nothing but our memories are here with us.

"I think that's when I knew," Aria finishes slowly. "That if I stayed, there'd be nothing left of me. I had already started vanishing, and that was the nail in the coffin. Even though it took me a long time to gain the courage to leave."

My own memories swell inside me. The night I "fell" down the stairs. The way I cried in our bed with Bandit curled at my feet, listening to the sound of the door lock with me trapped inside. How I had convinced myself it was an accident because that was easier than admitting the truth to myself. I pull away from Aria and wipe away my own tears.

Briefly, I remember the guilt I felt and the days I spent thinking it was just me. That maybe I was just not good for him, that maybe he would be better for someone else. Those thoughts almost made me stay.

"They always say it's an accident," I mumble, finding my voice. "They chip away at you, smiling as they do it. And the scariest part is... the world doesn't always see it. It's not always a bruise you can point to. It's the way your voice goes quieter. The way you stop laughing. The way you flinch when someone raises their voice, even if they're not yelling at you."

Aria agrees, shivering as if she feels it in her bones. "You are so right."

We resume walking. No destination, just forward. Up ahead, we spot a bench.

"I still have dreams about him," I admit, wishing I had something of weight to offer after her admission. "Not nightmares, really. Just... dreams where I'm still with him. And I wake up in cold sweats and panic. I feel sick to my stomach. I get the same panicky feeling when I see a red car, or anything red for that matter."

"I used to dream I never left," Aria says. "And those nightmares scared me more than anything."

When we reach the bench at the end of the trail, we sit down facing the sunset. Neither of us speaks for a long time. Finally, Aria looks at me and says, "Thank you. For listening."

I smile, tears pricking my eyes again. "Thank *you*. For surviving and for sharing it with me." I loop my arm through Aria's as she rests her head on my shoulder. I barely know her, but I feel like I've known her my whole life. "You are the strongest person I've ever met. I don't know if anyone has ever told you that, but it takes an unbelievable amount of courage to walk away from someone like him. To choose yourself."

I don't know what else to say. I don't think there is anything else I could say that would help, anyway.

We sit like this, side by side, watching the sun set. There is an unparalleled understanding between Aria and me. Someone who now sees all the things that were once invisible. But it's more than that. It's a promise.

We are no longer each other's past. We are each other's future.

ARIA

Daisy and Beau trip over each other as they scramble out of the driver's side door, nearly leaving a dent in the car beside me. They know where we are the second we arrive. They take off, racing through the gates to the dog park as I grab my water bottle and lock up the car.

I set my stuff down on the nearest bench, claiming it for the next hour or so. Kate is meeting me here with her dog, Bandit. I pull my legs up onto the bench and cross them underneath me. It's a warm eighty-two degrees today. The sun in Colorado is so strong, within five minutes I can feel the sweat dripping down my neck.

Daisy is running circles around a black lab, threatening to steal its tennis ball. Beau is already across the park, stalking a poodle from a safe distance. They love it here.

Looking to my left, I see Kate climb out of her car with a small, wiggling poof in her arm. She holds him close until she crosses the threshold. As soon as his paws hit the dirt, he takes off lightning-fast across the grass.

Waving my hand over my head, I signal to her from my spot on the bench. She smiles, walking in my direction. "Hi!" she says when she gets close enough.

"Hey!" I return the smile.

Our last conversation was heavy. We had too many questions about each other, about Ryan, and about everything in between. There were so many things we each wanted to know. So many things that needed to be said, things we never told anyone. Now, I really just want to get to know her. I don't know anything about her, *yet*, but I think we could be great friends. I hope so, anyway. We already have so much in common.

"Do you have any weddings on the books this weekend?" Kate pulls her knees up to her chest, turning slightly to face me.

"Only two, thankfully." I laugh. "I'm really bad at overbooking myself, and even worse at setting boundaries."

"I know, same. I'm always caught between needing the money and wanting a weekend off to relax. It's impossible to navigate."

Boy, do I know. "It's so hard to work for yourself."

I take a sip from my butter yellow Stanley, the water already luke-warm from the summer heat. "What do you do?" I look over at her curiously. "I mean, when you aren't working."

Kate takes a minute to respond, tilting her head as she really ponders her answer. "Honestly? Nothing. Well, I am seeing someone. I think? I don't really know what I'm doing…"

"Oh?" I peer over at her. "Tell me all about him."

She sighs deeply, almost annoyed. Not at me, but at the situation. "I met Ben at the bar a few months ago. I didn't really expect it to go anywhere, I didn't want that. It was just harmless flirting." She laughs. "But I haven't been able to shake him. He's nice, and caring, and funny. So funny." Her eyes light up when she talks about him.

I elbow her playfully. "So then what's the problem?"

"I don't know." Kate sighs as she tucks her knees closer to her chest. "Do I really want to be with someone again? That's the big question. I gave up on the idea of marriage and children. I told myself I would never settle down again, not after Ryan. I was sure of it. But then I met Ben, and he is so different—in the best way. It's easy, like too easy." She sighs. "Sometimes I wake up with the urge to call it off, and end whatever *this* is, but then he does something sweet and I allow it. His charm has completely clouded my judgment."

I purse my lips. "I totally get it. I haven't dated since Ryan. Not one date. I haven't gone out, or even put myself in a situation that could lead to harmless flirting, so I get it. I really do. But maybe you should just let yourself see where it goes?" I rest my head in my hand, facing her. "What is it they say? *Give the advice you wish to receive?* Healing and working through the trauma is important, but it's equally as important to live your life… to not throw in the towel over one experience. All men aren't the same, according to my therapist."

"Okay, but what if they are?" Kate says sarcastically, forcing out a laugh. "I'm really proud of you though, for going to therapy. I never did. I've still never gone, not after all these years. I couldn't talk about it and I didn't want to until I met you." She puts her legs back on the ground, stretching them out in front of her. "Maybe I should see a therapist, though. Yours sounds like a genius."

"He is," I say teasingly. "And I'm proud of you for even entertaining the idea of being with someone else."

"Thank you, thank you." She waves her arm in a small curtsy. Groaning loudly, she adds, "All right, fine. Just for you, I'll see where this goes." I laugh again.

"What do you do when you aren't baking?" Kate asks.

I hate this question, for no other reason than it takes me back to ballet. Back to a time when I used to do what I loved. I do love baking, but it's not the same. And it's not something I can easily explain.

"Baking is my life. Baking *and* these mutts over here." I nod to Daisy and Beau panting heavily as they lay in a heap in the shady grass. "I used to practice ballet. I was really good. I was training to go to ballet school in Paris, actually." Her eyes light up slightly. "Until, you know, Ryan happened."

Kate shakes her head. "What a dipshit. I'm so sorry."

"It's okay. It's been years now. I miss it, but I've mostly put it past me now."

Leaning my head back and lifting my eyes upward, I rest my neck on the edge of the bench. The wind has kicked up, blowing my blonde hair around in circles. We sit in silence for a minute, listening to the sound of the dogs panting, paws digging in the dirt, and barks of excitement.

Kate breaks the silence. "I used to have black hair."

"What?" I turn my head, looking at her. She looks... amused. I study her, trying to imagine what she looked like with black hair.

"YUP. I was *edgy*. Black hair and red lipstick was my signature look. At least my twenty-one-year-old self thought so." She laughs. "It was a phase. And now, I fucking hate the color red." She laughs again. This time the sound vibrates from deep within her core. My eyes widen as a montage of memories crash over me. I've heard that sound before—months ago, picking up a breakfast order. The girl with a laugh that stopped me in my tracks. The girl with black hair at the auto body shop, all those years ago. The girl in the picture on the fridge, *Alicia*. They are one in the same. *It was Kate.*

I decide to keep this little kernel of information to myself. The corners of my mouth curl upward as I realize fate was pushing us together this entire time.

KATE

Ben looks at me across the kitchen table, watching as I sip my morning coffee.

Saturday morning breakfast. I sigh. We got here a lot faster than I intended.

"I have an idea," he says, lifting his own coffee to his lips. I set mine down, my curiosity getting the better of me. "What if," he says and then pauses, leaning into the dramatic emphasis. "What if, you moved in with me?"

I can only imagine the look on my face because he immediately follows it up with, "Don't freak out." I think of Aria and hear her voice in my head telling me to *give him a chance*. I fight the urge to roll my eyes and chuckle because now would not be an appropriate time to laugh.

Instead, I look around the room, trying to lock eyes on something, anything to ground me. I come up short, my gaze returning to Ben. The look on his face, the way he's looking at me, I can see how important this is to him. Like this is the first time he's ever wanted to take this step with someone. I can tell that he's serious. I can tell that he's been thinking about this proposition for a while too, probably feeling too scared to ask.

"I think…" I pause, trying to find the right words. *What are the right words?* Living with Ben would not be the absolute worst thing in the world. He makes me happy, and we have a lot of fun together. I could get used to fresh coffee every morning waiting for me on my nightstand. And I would love to share rent with somebody. But it's so soon. It's only been four months—or is it six months? I don't really know how long it's been but it doesn't feel long enough to take a step like this.

I'm brought back to the last conversation I had with my mom—the one where she grilled me about finding a man so that I can think about giving her grandkids in her lifetime. *What if Ben is the one? What if he's not? But what if he is… and how will I know unless I give him a chance? Give us a chance?*

I dredge up the courage from somewhere deep within me. "I think," I say again. "That I would really enjoy waking up to you every day." I cross one leg over the other and plaster a grin on my face. "But there needs to be some ground rules."

The *look* on his face… He is beaming. His beautiful brown eyes light up brighter than anything. "Anything," he says without hesitation. "Anything you want."

"I will move in with you…" I say slowly. "My lease is up soon, so it's perfect timing." He rolls his eyes, forcing a laugh. "But I need us to move slowly. I can't commit to anything more than that. Not right now." I swallow, trying to find the proper words to get my point across. "I am excited to see where this goes, but we just need to move slowly. Okay? Also I want fresh coffee every single morning. If you miss a single morning, even just one, I'm moving out." I smile at him coyly as I speak the last few words. Ben shakes his head, laughing this time as he leans across the table, pulling my face in for a kiss.

"You got it," he breathes onto my lips.

When he sits back down, I look at the plate of pancakes in front of me, and I feel a sudden roiling in my stomach. I set my fork down and lean back in my chair. *Am I going to be sick?* I wait uncomfortably to see if I am in fact going to throw up all over this table. That's when it dawns on me.

I'm *excited*. This nervous, uncomfortable feeling in my abdomen —it's *hope.*

Ben lit a spark inside of me I thought was long gone. Somewhere along the line, he reminded me of a part of myself I thought I'd lost forever.

"And," I add, looking across the table into his deep brown eyes, "you have to help me pack up this apartment. It's a disaster in here."

"You got it, Babe," he repeats, laughing this time. "It wouldn't kill you to be a little bit neater..."

I stand up, punching his shoulder lightly as I walk to the Keurig. "Keep it up and I'll stay here, living in my filth, and you will no longer be allowed to come over."

He raises his hands up in playful defeat. "Okay, okay. My lips are sealed."

He stands up, joining me at the counter. He pulls me in tight, wrapping his arms around my body. His broad shoulders tower over me, keeping me pinned comfortably in place. I rest my head on his chest, letting myself relax. *Am I really doing this?*

I HOLD up two nail polish swatches—one is hot pink and one is black.

"Okay, little miss emotionally unavailable," Aria says, rolling her eyes. "It's summer. Let's save the black for when our seasonal depression kicks in."

I roll my eyes at her, although she's right. "Hot pink it is." I hand the swatch to the nail tech. I love our girl dates. I'm drawn to Aria like a magnet, like fate had this grand plan for us all along and now the pieces are snapping into place.

"So," I slip my feet into the burning hot water, "I told Ben about Ryan last night."

"What!" She practically screeches, startling the woman next to us trying to enjoy her pedicure.

"Okay. Relax. I didn't *tell him,* tell him. Not all the gory details. I wouldn't even know where to begin, but I did tell him I was married once before." I swallow. "We were watching a movie and it weirdly kind of just felt like the right time."

She's staring at me, waiting for me to continue.

"He was... strangely okay with it." I lift one foot up and rest it on the pedestal. "Because he proceeded to ask me to move in with him. This morning actually, over breakfast."

Her eyes bulge further out of her head. She looks like a character from one of those Saturday morning cartoons I used to watch as a kid, sitting on the sofa with a bowl of Fruity Pebbles in my lap.

"I kept waiting for some sort of jealous reaction, or twenty questions, but neither came. He just said, 'I can't be upset because otherwise we never would have met' or something like that."

"He's so cheesy," she says, rolling her eyes. "Okay, and then..."

"Then I told him that you and I were both married to the same man."

She's still staring at me. I don't think she's blinked in over five minutes. I can't tell if she's upset that I shared something personal about her, something that wasn't my information to share, or if she's just in shock.

Finally she says, "You did not."

"I did, but don't be mad," I say quickly, lowering my foot back into the water. "You are going to meet Ben eventually, and it felt like something he should maybe know. He would have asked how you and I met, and sure I could have just said *through weddings*, which would have been true, but it felt weird to omit a huge part of our friendship. Yes, we work together in a general sense, but it's so much deeper than that—"

"I'm not mad." She cuts me off from my rambling. "Not at all. I understand why you did it. I'm just surprised, that's all. You chose of your own free will to open up to a man..."

She's right. A year ago I never would have let someone in like I have with Ben. He has become woven into every fiber of my being. He's immersed himself so deeply into my heart and my mind, that I don't even think twice anymore before letting him in. *When did that happen?* "You're right," I whisper quietly, lifting my other foot up out of the water.

She turns her head, giving me a look. "It's not a bad thing you know."

Aria is the real reason. I knew it from the moment I met her. Once I realized who she was, I knew that she would change me. Aria makes me want to be a better person. She's so kind and so thoughtful. She makes me want to be the kind of person who hosts an art class for underprivileged kids in my free time. She is genuine in everything that she does. Anyone who meets her feels it and knows it instantly.

I stopped letting people in a long, long time ago. I built myself a cage of sarcasm and bad decisions, and I became comfortable there. But Aria makes me want to be different, better. I smile over at her, "I know it's not."

Aria picked a light blue color for her toes. She loves yellow and blue, any pastel color really, and I love pinks and purples, anything bright and colorful. *Aside from red.*

"What do you think *he's* doing, right now?" I change the subject abruptly. Normally I don't have anyone to share my innermost thoughts with, so I take advantage of my time with her.

"He's probably ruining someone else's life," she says without hesitation.

I laugh even though she's probably right.

ARIA

Chinese food on Mondays has become our routine.

Wine is poured without asking, and shoes are kicked off at the door. Kate's apartment is my second home. Or should I say, Ben's apartment?

Ben is funny and charming—a real homebody with a love for Italian food, video games, and Kate. Where she is loud and colorful, he is quiet and calculated. He complements her—I love watching their relationship. Their playful banter is so effortless. He lights up the spark inside of her, and to witness it makes my cheeks hurt from smiling.

It's a typical Monday, and I'm sitting on the floor of Kate's living room, with *The Vampire Diaries* blaring on TV and Chinese food in takeout boxes between us on the carpet, when Ben pops into the kitchen. He grabs his teriyaki chicken and gives Kate a quick kiss on the cheek. "Hi Aria," he says with a brief smile as he turns on his heels and heads for the stairs, video games waiting.

"Hi!" I try to wave in return, but he's taking the stairs two at a time and is long gone before I can reply.

Kate plops down on the sofa, wine glass in hand. "When did you and Ryan meet?"

I blink, walking around the corner of the sofa to join her. We've been getting together once a week, at least, for the past few weeks, but it feels like no matter how much time we spend together, we are always uncovering new facts. New lies buried in the truth we thought we knew.

"We went on a few dates, and then he ghosted me for seven months." I still remember receiving that text out of the blue with a vague, non-explanation of his absence.

Kate's mouth parts slightly. Her hand freezes, wine glass hovering midair. "Wow. That must have been because he was in prison." She throws her head back, sighing loudly, eyes scanning the ceiling for something only she can see. "We were definitely dating when you two met."

I look at her and force a smile, turning my head to the side. "It's not your fault." I pause for just a beat. "It's not mine, either." Suddenly, I have an idea and reach quickly for a notepad. I pull one from my bag, sticky with frosting, and draw a line across it. I write *Kate* at one end and *Aria* at the other.

"Let's see what overlaps," I say calmly. Because I already know. *Don't I?*

We begin piecing it together. Month by month. Year by year. Each date drops like a stone in a still lake—the ripples just keep going. Every memory brings echoes.

She twirls a piece of teriyaki chicken at the end of her fork. Bandit is hovering three inches away, eyes wide and waiting for that piece of chicken to fall.

"Can I ask you something?"

She looks at me curiously. "Of course, anything."

I don't even know how to form the question out of the words that are swirling around in my mind. There is probably a more delicate way to phrase this, but I need to just get it out before I regret it. "I visited him at work one day, at the beginning of our relationship. Our relationship *after prison*, I guess. And you were there. I didn't know it was you at the time, but I saw you two. Talking."

Her eyes widen as she looks at me. She remembers that day well, clearly.

"I only watched for a minute, before I became overcome with jealousy and had to leave." I manage a weak laugh. "Why were you there?"

She sets her fork down dramatically before lifting her wine glass to her lips and finishing the whole thing in one gulp. "I was there trying to get him to sign divorce papers."

"I stayed in his condo for a while after he went to prison, because he paid the rent in full for the year, and I thought he owed me that much. It's the least he could do after everything. I didn't know why he did that at the time, but in hindsight I bet he knew he would likely be going away and wanted his place ready and waiting for him when he got out." She huffs, shaking her head.

"At first, I didn't care about a divorce. He was in prison and I was free. But once I got wind that he was released early, I started thinking about it more. About my freedom, on paper. I woke up one day, took a Xanax, and decided that cornering him in public was my best chance."

I open my mouth but it comes out strained. "I'm so proud of you." We sit in silence for a minute, watching Caroline pretend that she isn't in love with Klaus. Looking at Bandit, begging three inches from Kate's face, I laugh. "You know..." I pause, scooping some rice onto my fork. "I met Bandit once."

She looks perplexed. I can tell she has no idea what I'm talking about. My words come out dry. "I didn't know he was your dog, though. Ryan didn't tell me anything."

Her hand is still wrapped around the empty wine glass when her knuckles turn white. The glass looks like it could shatter at any second. Something clicked just now, and her expression changes from confused to full-on livid.

"Bandit went missing years ago, just for one night. I was at my parents' for the afternoon, for a BBQ. I brought Bandit with me and he snuck out of the fence somehow. I almost lost my mind. I drove around the neighborhood fourteen times, until well past midnight. I couldn't find him anywhere and I was devastated." She looks somber as she remembers.

"The next morning I was shattered and completely alone in my apartment when the doorbell rang. I opened the door and there was Bandit. Smiling and wagging his tail. No note. No nothing. He just… *appeared*."

She continues. "I had another dog… a puppy that Ryan gave me right after he proposed, after a long fight. He gave me that puppy with the promise that things would change," she whispers quietly. "Her name was Penelope. She got hit by a car and died five days before Bandit went missing. That was the worst week of my life. I was swallowed by grief, and I blamed myself that I allowed Bandit to get out of the fence." She looks defeated.

"Oh, Kate…" My heart hurts for her. I picture Beau lounging on my couch at home, likely annoying Daisy to death. I can't even imagine. Those two are my entire world and the only thing that got me through the years.

A tear slips from her eye, but she wipes it away quickly. "I can't believe he took Bandit." Her face turns serious as she connects the dots. "Because I showed up, asking for a divorce. He wanted to show me that he still had the power."

"Omg," I whisper. *Did he have something to do with Penny?* My mind conjures unwanted images of Ryan doing the unthinkable. "It wasn't your fault, Kate." I don't know if she believes that, but she hears the words all the same. I move into the kitchen quickly and snatch the bottle of wine.

We keep going. We map the chaos, and every detail confirms what we already know in our bones. We aren't crazy. He really did live two lives, maybe more. Everything Kate went through, I went through too in a similar version, like a pattern. And it makes me sick knowing there is likely another girl out there, falling victim to the same pattern.

He was different with me," I say after too long. "I don't know what he faced in his life that turned him into a monster. At the end of the day, I just assumed it was my fault."

"It was NOT your fault," Kate says through bites of food. "I always knew Ryan wouldn't stay frozen in time while I moved on. I knew prison would change him and harden him in ways that would make the next girl's life feel like a battle they didn't enlist in. But now that I know that girl, now that I know *you*..." She pauses, hand tightening around her wine glass. "The thought of him hurting you makes me want to smash my fist through a wall."

Kate got the cold manipulation, the calculated gaslighting—but I got something else. Something raw. Ryan's unfiltered rage. And it wasn't her fault, of course it wasn't. And it wasn't mine either. Deep down, I know that. It's just the hand I was dealt. It's what prison did to him. But I hadn't known, and it almost killed me. *Literally*.

"I was twenty-one when we met. I was a child. I like to think that I did the best I could with what I knew at the time—it helps me sleep at night." She sighs drastically.

"I was twenty-one, too. Do you ever wonder how many there are? How many more girls just like us?" I ask as I stand, moving into the kitchen.

Kate doesn't have to think. "Every day. He gets older, but I bet the girls stay the same age." She winces. "I wish we could help them."

"Me, too." I nod, slow and sure. "And you know what?" I grin as I pull a hot pink Tupperware tray out of my bag, turning to face the couch. "I brought your favorite dessert."

"WHAT!" Kate squeals, eyeing the goodies in my hands. "You didn't."

I bounce back into the living room with the tray of salted chocolate chip cookie dough sandwiches. The cookies are one of my signature treats and Kate's personal favorite.

She reaches for one and takes a huge bite. "Mmmmm," she says as crumbs fall out of her mouth and onto the sofa. "You are a baking wizard."

Bandit is instantly up on the sofa a second later, shoving his nose between the couch cushions in search of crumbs, desperate for a taste of the treat.

I lift a cookie in a playful cheers, causing more crumbs to fall as the cookies clash.

"To being the other woman," I say.

"To being the other woman," Kate echoes, fighting back a laugh.

Suddenly we hear Ben's voice coming from the loft upstairs. "Hey! Save some of those cookies for me!" I'm still laughing as the room grows still. We stay like this for a long time. Two women and a past filled with ghosts. Without warning, Kate picks up the notebook, rips the pages out, crumples them into a ball and tosses them across the room, straight into the trash can. She looks over at me and smirks.

Pulling a blanket over my lap, I reach for another cookie. Kate cranks up the volume, and we let the Stefan, Damon, and Elena love triangle consume us for the rest of the night.

KATE

My parents are so persistent.

As soon as I told them I was moving in with Ben, they insisted on meeting him. Actually, they demanded it, which brings us to today. Ben and I are sitting around my parents' dinner table, subjecting ourselves to twenty questions. I've got to admit, he is handling it like a pro.

"So, Benson," my dad says. "What is it that you do?"

Ben clears his throat. "You can call me Ben, and I'm in real estate."

My dad nods, even though we all know he will continue to call him Benson. "And do you enjoy it?" I give my dad a look saying *leave him alone*, but he just keeps going. "How long have you been doing that?"

"I do enjoy it," Ben answers, keeping his emotions level. "It's been close to ten years, and I still love what I do."

My dad smiles. "Good," he says.

My mom takes that as her cue to chime in. "How old are you, Ben?"

He smiles. "I turn thirty-one in a few weeks, actually."

"And do you have any siblings?"

Just like that, I can see the light as it leaves his eyes. My parents probably don't notice, but I know him well enough now to notice the subtle shift in his energy. "Not anymore," he says quietly.

I give my mom a glare that says *stop grilling him right now or so help me God*. He told me about his brother a few weeks after we met, maybe on our third or fourth date. I can't keep track anymore. His brother suffered from drug addiction, which led to him take his own life. They were young when it happened. My heart broke listening to him tell me about their relationship as kids. I could feel how lonely he was in that moment, moving through life without his younger brother, his best friend. But it made us stronger... knowing that we each had suffered trauma.

I quickly change the conversation to my dad's latest fishing trip. He can talk about fly fishing forever.

TIME FLIES when you are being questioned, though. We walk back to the car, holding hands as our arms sway back and forth. "I'm sorry." I inhale deeply. "They can be a lot, but it comes from a good place. I just haven't been with anyone in a really, really long time. And they're just excited."

He turns, smiling at me. "Your parents are great. Love them. I can see why you are the way you are." I gasp, punching him lightly in the shoulder. He laughs as he dodges the blow. "Really, though, they were wonderful. Thank you for taking me to meet them." He opens my car door for me before walking around to his side.

"Of course," I say quietly, turning to face him from the passenger's seat. "It means a lot to them. We didn't really talk for a few years. They didn't approve of my ex, and it was complicated. We weren't in touch for a long time, but our relationship is finally back on track." By the time I finish, I realize I'm rambling. I always ramble when I'm nervous.

"I love you."

My chest tightens. "What?"

"I love you," he repeats with just as much conviction, if not more.

"I am happy to meet your parents, and I will spend as much time with them as you want. I want to be a part of your life, as much as you'll allow. Because I love you."

For a split second, I think about running. Then I realize how silly that is. I'm sitting in the passenger's seat of his car, shoes kicked off, sitting cross-legged. It would be ridiculous to fling the door open and take off barefoot. I would probably cut my feet on broken glass or step on some really sharp gravel on the side of the road or something.

Once the impulse to bolt passes, I calm down. I don't have a therapist but if I did, I could imagine her telling me *to acknowledge my feelings and respond appropriately* even though I don't think I've ever done anything appropriately when it comes to my feelings. But I take my imaginary therapist's advice and allow myself to think as the minutes tick by and the words hang heavy between us.

I'm mulling over the past few months in my mind, reflecting on every memory from our time together, and how he makes me feel. Every good morning coffee, every goodnight text. *Is that what this is? Love?*

I thought I was in love once before, but it was nothing like this. The realization knocks the breath from my lungs like a punch in the chest. "I think," I say, trying to get it back. "I think I love you too?"

"Yeah?" he says, fighting a grin. "You think?"

"Yeah," I say more confidently this time. "I'm pretty sure. Maybe."

He shakes his head and chuckles softly. "I'll take it." Putting his car in drive, he pulls out of my parents' driveway. Toward home.

I'm still smiling as I look out my passenger side window and notice a red car parked on the side of the road.

ARIA

I never look forward to wedding season.

Do I love baking? *Yes.*

Am I grateful to have a thriving business? *Absolutely.*

But it's exhausting... baking four to six cakes a week, and spending my entire weekend driving all over the state delivering them. Not to mention, it's just me... a one-woman show.

But now that I have Kate, we are inseparable. Spending every weekend at work is way more fun when I get to be with my best friend.

Today's wedding is going to be magical. I know how hard Kate worked on this one. I witnessed the late nights, the hours spent on the phone finalizing every detail, not to mention her putting up with the mother of the bride at all hours of the day.

As I drive through the winding mountain roads, I steal a glance in the rearview mirror, hoping that my cake is still standing right side up. I'm pleasantly surprised to find it hasn't moved an inch.

Good, because I spent three hours on the fondant alone yesterday.

Colorado is beautiful. I love living here. I've tried a few other places—not because I wanted to, and not because it was my choice—

but I tried them, nonetheless. And nowhere compares to here. This is *home*. The picturesque Rocky Mountain skyline, and the crisp air... I can't think of anywhere else I'd rather be.

Twenty minutes later, I arrive at The Arrabelle in Vail Square, one of the most luxurious venues in Vail, Colorado. Couples fly in from all over the world to get married here. The ceremony deck at the top of the mountain is just one short gondola ride away, offering jaw-dropping views of Vail Valley.

Kate and I have both done weddings at this venue before, but this is our first one together, and I am *so* excited.

I can spot Kate from a mile away, running around with a clipboard in one hand and an iced coffee in the other. She's politely telling people what to do and where to go. I laugh as I walk through the square and toward Kate in the big white tent.

She's having the time of her life. She is completely in her element, and not only does she love being a wedding planner, but she's also really damn good at it. Her designs are next-level, her attention to detail is unparalleled, and she thrives in a creative environment.

Bossing people around a little bit doesn't hurt either. If you know Kate, then you know she likes to be in control. Really, she *needs* to be in control.

Kate spots me from across the square. "Finally! I'm so glad you're here."

I run up and give her a one-armed squeeze, delicately balancing my cake in the other. "Hiiiiiii! Where should I put the cake?"

Kate leads me over to a cocktail table in the corner of the tent. There's an antique pearl-rimmed cake stand, an heirloom from the bride. Alongside it, there are a few trays and platters for me to use for cupcakes and cookies. This couple went all out—splurging for a huge dessert bar along with a decadent champagne pink three-tiered cake with delicate pearls and flowers vining up one side of the layers.

"I'll be back in a minute," Kate says, hurrying off to fix another last-minute detail. I turn, noticing what has Kate in a tizzy. There's a disco ball currently being hung across the dance floor in the wrong spot, and it's way too close to the ground. Anyone over five-foot-ten will easily smack their head on that. I shake my head and laugh.

If I'm lucky enough to only have one cake delivery per day, I always try to stay and hang out for a little bit. I mingle and network with the other vendors. I hang out with Kate and help where I can. Today is one of those days, so I plan to stay through the cocktail hour, at least.

The ceremony is my favorite part of a wedding. I will forever be a hopeless romantic, even after Ryan. Even after everything he put me through. *He didn't know how good he had it.* Maybe I was naive, and maybe I will never find someone who treats me the way I know I deserve, but I still believe in love. I thought I didn't for a while, but now that time has begun to heal my wounds… I'm relieved to at least be *thinking* about the possibility of love again, even if acting upon it is another matter entirely.

"Hey," Kate brings me back to reality, "I'm about to head up the mountain for the ceremony. Do you want to come with me? They hired a local musician to play their ceremony music, and I've heard he's really good and really cute." She smiles. "You should come with me and check him out."

I roll my eyes. "Yes, I'll totally come, but not so that you can try and hook me up with the guitarist."

"Mmmmmm, okay. We'll see about that," she says with a devilish grin. Leaving me for a minute, she trots over to the stage to grab her coffee. The band is deep in sound check for the big show later. The cool beat of drums and jazzy saxophone echoes through the square, setting the tone for what's to come once the sun sets.

The gondola is a sight to see. One-by-one, weddings guests climb into rotating carriages and are swept up the mountain. It's a vibrant summer wedding bursting with color everywhere. The men, dressed in all black, look sharp and polished while the ladies are bringing it to life with their mismatched floral pattern dresses.

I follow Kate into one of the carriages and take a seat.

Weddings make me feel out of place, and it usually comes down to my outfit. Normally I don't stay. Normally I'm in and out. I touch base with the planner, drop the desserts, and leave. But today, I look down and find myself wishing I had something else on other than a dirty pair of sneakers and my most comfortable leggings still smudged with flour from my work this morning.

"You look fine," Kate whispers. "You'll be standing in the back with me. No one will even notice."

I smile apprehensively. Kate always knows what to say to make me feel better. She always has my back, no matter what. I'm not sure of much anymore, but I am sure that fate brought us together. It wasn't coincidence; it was something more. Kate is strength, whereas I am compassion. We need each other.

Kate climbs out of the carriage first, bee-lining to where the wedding party is standing in a cluster, clearly having forgotten everything they were told yesterday at the rehearsal. She starts lining them up, having them stand together more uniformly. Waving her hands around, she's trying to give them tips for what to do with their hands and where to hold the bouquets.

I look around the mountain. The views from up here take my breath away. There's nothing more than a few stone boulders shaped into benches and a winding path leading from the gondola to the edge of the mountain. Couples choose this location for its simplicity and its sheer beauty.

Off to the side, someone catches my eye. A man is carrying a folding chair in one arm and a guitar in another. *That must be the musician.* He's taking his place on the left side of the altar, about three rows back from the front. He's close enough to be heard, but not too close to be the center of attention. In black pants and a white shirt, he looks effortlessly composed.

His sandy blond hair complements his piercing blue eyes. With broad shoulders and a rugged beard, he looks like the kind of man who would live in Colorado. I blink and realize I'm staring. I look away quickly, hoping he hasn't noticed me.

Then, spotting Kate, I hurry over to where she's standing. With perfect timing as always, she asks, "Did you notice the guitarist?"

between sips of her latte, still cold even though it's been sweating in the sun for a few hours now.

I side-eye her, and Kate giggles. "His name is Connor. Let me just introduce you."

"I don't know if I'm ready." I sigh.

It's been years, and I still don't know if I'm ready. Yes, I've had time, and I still believe in love, but now that a situation presents itself, I'm not sure if I'm *actually* ready. The deepest cuts heal so slowly.

Kate loops her arm through mine. "It's been a few years," she says gently. "And no one is telling you to marry the man. Just go say hi. I've only talked to him a few times, but he's really nice, and he seems like your type. You know, as in he's the exact *opposite* of Ryan."

I laugh and look across the field again toward where Connor is seated. He's sitting with his back to the trees, facing the wedding guests. Looking intently down at his guitar, he's focused on the song he's playing as the bride sweeps down the aisle. Kate might be right. He looks like a nice person... like someone who has it all figured out, instead of someone who is a mystery I need to solve.

When the bride reaches the altar, I hear a sniffle and look over at Kate. "Gets me every fucking time," she breathes, wiping her tears away quickly without ruining her mascara.

I look back at Connor. Maybe I will go say hi, or maybe I will let Kate introduce me. *What harm could come from that?* Again, Kate is right. *How does she do that? It's really annoying sometimes.* I don't need to marry the guy. Maybe we can start slow... I wonder if he'd meet me for coffee.

I *have* been single for a few years. It's been fine. Not just fine... but necessary. I needed time. I needed to find my way back to regaining my dignity. But now, maybe it's time.

"Come on," Kate says, still sniffling. "Let's just go say hi. You can have a panic attack when we're back in the gondola."

We walk over to Connor, who's packing up his stuff, getting ready to move locations. He sees us coming and smiles. "Hey," he says, cool and casual, kind of quietly. "I'm heading down the mountain in a few minutes to get set up for cocktail hour."

"Sounds great!" Kate says. "Thank you. That was beautiful by the way, the acoustic version you played for the bride. Really beautiful."

She gestures to me as I'm standing on her right. "Connor, I want to introduce you to Aria. She baked the desserts for the wedding today. And they are out-of-this-world delicious. Make sure you try some before you leave."

I can feel my face heating up. My hands are cold and clammy. *I'm going to kill her.* "Hi. It's nice to meet you." Smiling gently, I extend my clammy hand in his direction.

"Likewise," Connor says, shaking my hand in return. His gaze is piercing. I could drown in his eyes if I'm not careful. "Can't wait to try some of your desserts."

I might die. Right here, in this moment. *Why am I so embarrassed?*

I used to date. Granted it was a long, long time ago... but still. This is ridiculous.

Kate begins slowly walking toward the gondola and I follow as Connor falls into step beside me. "So, how long have you been a baker?" he asks casually.

"Actually, it's a pretty new endeavor for me," I answer quietly. "I've always loved baking, but I only recently decided to make it my career."

I glance over at him to find him watching me with a gentle smile on his lips. He looks like he wants to be the one who lights stars in the places I thought would always stay dark. I smile back cautiously, definitely unsure, but undeniably hopeful. Something in his eyes makes me believe, even just for a minute, that maybe I can trust again.

I DON'T KNOW *if I can do this.*

I'm standing outside of my old ballet studio for the first time in years. I haven't been here since Ryan, since I learned that I was pregnant, since I got into the Paris Ballet, *since I lost everything.*

My instructor used to reach out. Once on my birthday, and once when she was training a new group of girls, just to tell me one of the new girls in her class reminded her of me. I didn't respond, I couldn't. What could I say after all that time? I'm sure she assumed I didn't get into the Paris Opera Ballet, and letting her think that was easier than telling her the truth.

Leaning against the brick wall, I let my back slide down the wall until I'm sitting on the ground. It's just a regular Tuesday morning. The birds are chirping, the sky is overcast with a few scattered clouds scudding across the sky, and commuters are rushing through traffic to make it to work on time. For the rest of the world, nothing looks out of the ordinary. Nothing monumental is happening, and it's a typical weekday filled with typical weekday things. The world is oblivious as I linger here. To me, everything has changed.

What's the worst that could happen? Crying through the whole class would be the worst case scenario, I suppose.

A petite girl with strawberry blonde hair peeks her head around the corner, looking in my direction. "Um, hi. Are you Aria?" She must be new here, I think to myself, even though it's been years since I last stepped foot in these doors. Her voice is soft, gentle.

"Class is about to start. Will you be joining us?"

I swallow, forcing a smile. My face is twisted into a painful expression as I try to keep my emotions neutral. She backs away slowly into the studio without waiting for my response. Peeling myself off of the cold cement, I grab my bag and follow her inside.

The lighting has been upgraded, and the fluorescent bulbs now illuminate every mirror and corner of the sprawling space. But everything else is the same as it was before. Quietly, I make my way over to the wall. Dropping my bag on the floor, it makes a loud thud. Everyone turns to look at me. I raise my hand in an apologetic gesture as I quickly fumble to tie my slippers on.

When I stand up again, my instructor is looking at me with a knowing smile that says *I'm so glad you're here.*

∾

KATE'S PERCHED ON A STOOL, peeling clementines. It's a beautiful sight I thought I'd never get to see. She will be the first one to tell you that she can't cook. Or bake. Or do anything in the kitchen at all. But she loves to come over and help me bake, *or try to help at least,* when she can find the time. She showed up at my door bright and early, eager to hear about my ballet class yesterday.

I'm leaning against the counter with a glass of wine in hand. The afternoon sun is creeping in through the windows giving the room a soft yellow glow. The scent of vanilla and powdered sugar still hangs in the air from a long day of baking. Daisy and Beau are curled up on the sofa, far enough away to not be underfoot, but close enough to keep an eye on the food, should any of it miraculously fall on the floor.

Kate lets out a deep sigh. "You know what the hardest part is for me?"

I look over at her, waiting. I love that we both know who we are speaking about without needing any context. "What?"

"Reminders of everything I missed out on. I had dreams—I wanted to go to cosmetology school, maybe live with some girlfriends in New York for school. I don't know that I would have acted on those dreams, but that's the point of being young, you know? You dream big." She twists the clementine peel between her fingers as she continues.

"But then I met Ryan, and everything changed. I gave up so much before I even realized it. My education. My chance at a career. My independence. I spent months not talking to my parents because I thought they wouldn't understand. He isolated me completely, and I didn't notice I was disappearing until I was already gone." Setting the peeled clementine down abruptly on the counter, she turns to look at me.

"By the time I woke up from that horrible nightmare, it was too late. Time didn't stop just because I was with Ryan."

I walk around the counter, pulling out the bar stool directly across from her. "It's not your fault. I used to think I was so strong for sticking it out. For staying even when it hurt. But now I look back and know that I mistook endurance for love and strength." My voice cracks but I keep going.

"I lost friends too—real friends—because I stopped showing up. I stopped answering calls. I was ashamed. And my family... God, my sister tried to reach out so many times and be there for me. I just couldn't let her see how far I'd fallen."

I look out the window as dusk settles into the trees like a secret. Holding my wine glass between two fingers, I swirl the wine around the glass, lost in thought. "The hardest part for me is thinking I missed out on my one chance to become a mom."

Kate takes a slow and steady breath. "No. Absolutely not. I refuse to accept that." She picks up another clementine, anything to keep her hands busy. "You'll have another chance when the time is right, and when you are so deeply in love that the world feels safe again."

"I know you're right," I say quietly. My lips tremble. "Deep down, I know that. I just can't help but think about the baby... my baby. And about being a mom. It wasn't the right time, ballet and Paris, and it wasn't the right person. I *know* that, but it was still something he took away from me, and it haunts me. What if I never get the chance again?"

I pull my attention back to the island and to the dessert I abandoned. Kate's the only one doing any work at this point. "That's what keeps me up at night."

Silence falls over the kitchen like gentle snow.

I reach over and pick up my phone on the other side of the counter, skimming the messages on the home screen. Time slips away from me when I bake, and the hours pass before I even notice. Moreso when Kate's here, I'll admit. Usually two to three business days go by before I reply to a text message.

Then I see it.

"What?" Kate looks at me when I gasp. "What is it?" She's alarmed now.

"It's Ryan."

Kate pauses, blinking rapidly. Disbelief is written all over on her face. "No, it's not." She hurries around the island, rushing to my side. I angle my phone so Kate can read the message on the screen.

Hey Aria, it's Ryan. I'm in Colorado. Can we meet for dinner? I was hoping we could clear the air. Let me know.

I'm frozen. Kate is squeezing her wine glass so tight I think for a second it might shatter. Even just reading his name causes my heart to start racing, and I suddenly feel dizzy. Thank God I'm already sitting or I might faint.

"What the fuck," Kate whispers under her breath. "You do not owe him anything. You do not need to respond."

"Why now?" The words come out quiet, confused. "It's been years. *Why now?*"

I can feel the weight of the past trying to creep in like an old uninvited friend. My mind is spinning as my eyes scan the words on the screen once more.

How did he get my number? I turn around on instinct, as if he could be watching me through the windows. *How does he know I moved back to Colorado?* I guess he probably assumed as much when I disappeared without a trace. This is *my* home.

Bryce came over one afternoon, shortly after I returned, and forced me to file for divorce from the comfort of my sweatpants. They served him papers at our house in Texas, but he wasn't home. After trying multiple times, they gave up. He was nowhere to be found. I didn't think anything of it, because they granted me a default divorce anyway.

I guess I'd just spent the last few years clinging to the hope that he'd let me go.

"He wants to clear the air," I mutter. "What does that even mean? And after everything, why would I even want to hear him out? He's delusional." Sighing, I let my voice drop an octave. "Maybe we're in a parallel universe right now, and this isn't really happening."

Kate exhales and takes a deep breath. "You don't have to listen to him. Remember, you don't owe him anything. You've worked so hard to get to where you are now. But if you do choose to meet him, we'll go together." She turns to me, forcing a reassuring smile. "Whatever happens, I won't leave your side."

I give her a slight smile in return before my eyes narrow and my grip tightens around my phone. The old familiar feeling of panic begins to overtake me. *Why now?* I repeat to myself. *And why is he even in Colorado?*

Kate interrupts my train of thought. "God, I've been seeing a red Camaro around town for the past few months. Aside from causing a mild panic attack, I didn't think anything of it." I grip the counter until my knuckles turn white.

I can only imagine the rage he felt when he came home to learn I had left. I picture his fist smashing through the walls as he moved through the house, breaking everything I ever loved and everything I had to leave behind. My stomach is twisting into knots.

"I don't care," I say finally, my voice quieter but stronger than I'm used to. "I don't want to meet him. I don't want anything from him. Not after all these years. It's too late for apologies."

Kate loops her arms through mine, grounding me. "I think that's smart. You don't need to meet him, and you don't need to hear him out. You don't need to sit there listening to him justify his actions or beg for your forgiveness. Both of which he probably won't even do." Her voice is firm but gentle, a reminder that we've come so far from the days when Ryan's words controlled every aspect of our lives.

"Just block his number, and pretend like he never existed. We've been doing that so well already." Kate smiles again, bumping her hip against mine.

I nod, but the tension in my shoulders doesn't ease. My body spent years in fight or flight mode. I spent years seeing him every night in my sleep, anticipating every bad dream, sleeping with the light on. *And now that I know he's in Colorado?*

I can't go back there. *I can't.*

I think back to that last week together the day before I left. The day that I decided I'd had enough. I remember him choking me. I remember thinking that this was it, that I was going to die. And I remember being glad, relieved in a sense that he was going to put me out of my misery.

Kate squeezes my arm after a minute, reminding me that she's still here. "Don't forget how far you've come." she says quietly, cautiously. "You've healed more than you think. I'll always be here to remind you who you are now, not who he tried to make you. Who you *are*."

My eyes well up with tears, but there's no shame in them now. No fear. "I don't want to go back," I whisper, almost to myself.

"I know," Kate says softly. "And you won't. Not now. Not ever."

We sit in silence for a minute, the weight of that text hanging between us. But as the minutes pass, I start to feel like my old self. The tension in my shoulders begins to loosen. The smell of buttercream and oranges fills the air once more. The old me, the one who had lived in the shadows of Ryan's anger, is no longer there.

This Aria is stronger and braver. This Aria is a phoenix who rises from the ashes. I rebuilt my life from the ground up. I started over completely. Completely alone and all on my own. I don't need to meet him to prove anything. I don't need his apology, and I'm sure as hell not the same person who had feared being in his presence.

I will not waste another second thinking about him.

I stand abruptly, wiping my tears quickly with an abrupt swipe of my hand and walk back over to my mixer. "Enough of that." I laugh lightly. "What do you say we enjoy a taste test?"

Kate smiles at me. "I love that idea." She moves quickly, joining me at the mixer. Picking up a spoon, she takes a big scoop and puts it in her mouth. "Mmmmmmmm," she says as her eyes roll back into her head. I giggle.

Picking up a spoon, I follow her with my own scoop. "Also," she says while chewing. "How many more clementines do I need to peel because my arms are getting tired."

I laugh loudly, feeling it deep within my core this time.

KATE

As I pull up in front Aria's house and park along the curb, I remember Thursdays used to be my favorite day of the week. Now they're just another day, another thing Ryan took away from me. *Another thing I am determined to get back.*

It's one o'clock. I knock on the door, peering through the glass into Aria's studio. I see her look up quickly, clearly not expecting any visitors, but smiling pleasantly when she sees it's me.

She swings the door open. "Hi! I wasn't expecting you today!" I lean in, careful not to reveal the surprise behind my back, and give her an air kiss. "I need to leave in about an hour to deliver these desserts."

"I know! I won't stay long, I just wanted to bring you a coffee." Swinging my arms out, I reveal the Starbucks I've been holding. Her favorite, a chai tea latte.

She smiles as she takes the cup from my hands, taking a big sip. "Thank you! You saved me."

"Okay so I have an idea, hear me out." I throw my tote off my shoulder, inviting myself in as I sit down on the nearest chair. "I went to bed yesterday thinking about the text, and I think..." I pause. "I think we should have a wake."

Aria nearly chokes on her sip. "I'm sorry, a wake?"

"Yes," I continue. "I think we should write a letter to our younger selves. Actually, I think we need to tell them everything we wish we would have known. I think we should write a letter to ourselves, and then take those letters, along with every other stupid thing we still own that reminds us of him… take it all up to the mountains and set it on fire." I'm smiling now. This might be the best idea I've ever had.

She hesitates for a moment, and I can see her considering my idea. Her wheels are spinning.

"Okay, let's do it," she says decidedly, setting her coffee cup down on the counter, barely missing a pen balancing on a notepad filled with notes from a late night baking session. "Let's go on the next wedding-free weekend we have."

"Perfect." I look around at the boxes of desserts, packaged up tightly, wrapped neatly in bows. There are three dozen cupcakes, two dozen cake pops, and a three-tiered cake. "Can I come to Estes Park with you?"

"Oh you don't have to do that! I can manage."

"I know you can manage," I say as I stand up. "But I want to come. I've got nothing to do this evening, and I'm in the mood for a little girls' trip. Ben can figure out dinner."

"Okay," she says as a smile spreads slowly across her face. "A road trip does sound fun." Picking up a stack of boxes, I follow her out of the studio door and over to her black Mitsubishi. It's not the kind of car you would expect her to have, but I think that's the point. The second she moved back to Colorado after leaving Ryan, she sold the car she had, the car she learned to drive in, the car she had her first kiss in—desperate to start over and remain hidden from him.

As soon as we get on the road, I pull out my phone to text Ben.

"Hey babe. I'm helping Aria with a delivery up in Estes Park, so I won't be home for dinner. See you in a few hours, love you. XX." Pressing send, I watch as my text becomes a permanent fixture on my screen. I chuckle softly, remembering a time when I didn't need to check in with anyone aside from Bandit.

"Now that we've got that taken care of…" I say to myself under my breath. "Let's put on some music."

Grabbing her AUX cord, I plug it into my phone and open Spotify. "I know what we should listen to." Aria looks at me sideways, waiting to see if this is one of those moments where we are in sync or not.

Pushing play, I play the newest album by Gracie Abrams. "Not to be dramatic," she says casually. "But this is literally my favorite album of all time." I laugh because I agree with her, and I love how much we love the same things.

We listen to the whole album, two times, before we reach the Black Canyon Inn. Moments after we pull up to the venue, the wedding planner rushes out to greet us. She's a cute little thing with fiery red hair and a white clipboard in one hand, contrasting the black jumpsuit she's wearing.

"Hi!" she says, out of breath. "So glad you're here. Let me show you where you will be setting up!" Aria and I look at each other and smirk, stifling a laugh. I can't really judge though, because that's me like every other weekend.

I love coming with Aria to her weddings. I love seeing her in motion. She moves so gracefully and with such precision. She sets up her desserts like an artist paints on a canvas. Her desserts are incredible, obviously, but she's known for her meticulous designs.

I help her stack the cake pops, and artfully place the cupcakes on the dessert table. After we make sure our presentation is up to her standards, we walk up the stairs and into another room on the opposite side of the venue where the ceremony is taking place. *Our favorite part.*

We stand in the back and off to the side, making sure to remain out of sight, especially because we're both in sweatpants today. The second the bride reaches the front of the aisle, Aria and I both start choking back tears.

We look at each other and laugh, our hands over our mouths to muffle the noise. We must be a sight to see. We both have tears streaming down our faces, sniffling like we've just caught a cold.

The ceremony is brief. A few "I love you's" followed by a "You may now kiss the bride." Aria glances across the room, making eye contact with the wedding planner. She gives a small wave as we head for the front door.

It's early evening now, and the sun is beginning to set behind the mountains. It only takes a minute for me to spot a TJ Maxx right next to the freeway. I look at her and raise my eyebrows, "Should we?"

"We should," she says without hesitating.

Whipping her steering wheel to the right, the car turns and she pulls into the parking lot. We walk in, heading straight to the kitchen goods area. *Naturally.* We maneuver around a mom with her toddler who's squirming in the shopping cart, fighting the strap buckled across his lap in an attempt to free himself.

Then I spot them. On an end cap, stacked up with a bunch of other coffee mugs in mismatched patterns and colors. Right next to a mug that says *Boss Babe* are two mugs with *World's Okayest Survivors* written in gaudy, bright pink cursive writing. I smile as I pick them up. When I turn, my crossbody whips around, smacking me in the butt. "LOOK," I say, holding them up in front of my face.

"OMG." She chuckles. "Those are an absolute *need*." Pushing the cart in my direction, she adds, "Put them in the cart."

Forty-five minutes and three hundred dollars later, we are back in the car and driving toward home. Aria found some new baking pans and some light blue spatulas that match her latest kitchen aesthetic. I picked up an air fryer because I am determined to learn how to cook now that I have a man to feed.

We drive with the windows down, watching our headlights paint the highway in yellow as we fall into a rhythm talking about love and life, the past and the future.

Just like that, Thursdays feel like mine again.

ARIA

I'm so tired.

But I'm not too tired to see Connor this morning. It's Friday, and our coffee date is finally here. He texted me the day after we met, asking if he could take me out for coffee. I was planning to spin some kind of excuse as to why I would be busy for the next four years, but Kate was over and she said *yes* before I could object.

I rub my eyes, not ready to lift my head from the pillow just yet, when I hear whining coming from the doorway. I sit up, furrowing my brows together, watching Daisy and Beau in the doorway, whimpering with leashes in hand.

I sigh. "Yes, yes, I know. I'm coming."

Groaning, I drag myself out of bed. Last night was so much fun. It was a much later night than I planned to have, but it was still fun. After we got back from Estes Park, Kate came inside for a glass of wine. One glass turned into three and she didn't leave until close to midnight.

I head back inside, only to realize I don't really have anything that would be classified as "cute" for a date.

Connor wants to meet at a new coffee shop in Greenwood Village. It's a little boutique spot on the outskirts of Denver. I'm really excited because this is my ideal first date. It won't be too long like dinner and a movie would be, but it's intimate and we'll be able to have some good conversation.

Leaning against the counter I lift my phone to check the time when I notice four missed texts. *I'm so bad with my phone.*

Three texts are from Kate, and one is from Connor.

I swipe, reading Kate's first.

"Good Morning, Sunshine!"

"I can't wait to hear about your date!"

"Call me immediately on your drive home."

Then I read the one from Connor.

"I'm looking forward to today. See you in an hour 😊"

My eyes widen. *One hour?* I look up at the time stamp on the top of the screen.

What!

I'm always late, for everything, all the time, and I hate it. I am *not* a morning person. But I really, really don't want to be late for this date.

Flinging my dresser open, I grab my favorite pair of jean shorts. Scanning my closet again, I dig through clothes I need to put away and shirts dangling off hangers. It's a total mess in here! I spot my favorite white ruffle top. Throwing it on, I race into the bathroom and run a brush through my tangled hair.

My natural blonde hair is so thin, and it's always in tangles. Sometimes I throw curls in it, but because it's so thin, they don't hold well. Pulling out my curling iron, I decide on the curls anyway, feeling determined to look like I put some effort into my appearance.

After my hair and my eyelashes are curled sufficiently, and I look like I didn't just wake up, I sit down in the living room. Slipping on one sock, then the other, I decide to wear my light yellow flower vans. And as I'm tying the strings on my last shoe, I realize I'm shaking a little bit. I look down at my hands and inhale deeply several times, forcing my breathing to steady.

Is this nerves? It must be.

I haven't been on a date in years. And the last time I did go on a date, that date turned into a marriage that ruined my life. Standing up, I take another deep breath. I will not allow myself to go down that rabbit hole. I already committed to this date. I'm *excited* about this date. I'm going.

Grabbing my purse and my jean jacket, I walk out looking more confident than I feel and lock the door behind me.

I SEE why Connor chose this place. The outside of the building is painted in pastels, with white trim and stained glass windows. It's the kind of place you could stumble into and accidentally stay for hours.

Opening the door, I walk inside. My eyes wander around, taking everything in. It smells like fresh espresso and warm pastries, with a vintage-inspired charm. There are bookshelves every few feet, overflowing with colorful spines and worn pages. The mugs are mismatched, and there is a nook tucked in every corner. Every detail is an intentional work of art.

There's something magical about a good coffee shop, isn't there? I see Connor sitting at a two-person table tucked in the back corner. He's spinning his coffee cup around in small, intentional circles, and he is looking toward the door. When he sees me, his eyes light up and his face breaks into the biggest smile.

I lift my hand in a small wave, returning a shy smile.

I make my way over to the line, inserting myself between a mom with her two kids and a college student with an overflowing backpack. Studying the menu, I can't decide what to have. Everything looks so good... how will I choose? I could get my usual, a chai tea latte, or I could try something new.

"Hey," a voice comes from my left, startling me.

My eyes lock with his—a wave of ocean blue. I stare at him for a moment, forgetting how to speak. I wish I could disappear into the walls and take a minute to gather my thoughts.

Connor notices, adding, "Can I buy your coffee?"

I clear my throat. "Oh. Um, sure. Thank you."

"Hi, what can I get you?" The barista's greeting brings me back to the decision in front of me.

I still have absolutely no idea what I want. The only thing I know is that I will drown in Connor's eyes if I look into them for a second longer.

When I realize that I'm holding up the line, I panic-order my usual. Anything so that I can sit down before I collapse onto the floor, a heap of legs and anxiety. "Can I please get a chai tea latte? Medium, thank you." I smile at the barista, watching as Connor takes his wallet out of his jeans and hands her his card.

"Thank you," I say again.

"Of course. I wanted to." His eyes meet mine again. "I got us a table in the back." He turns around and points. "I'll wait for your coffee and meet you there in a minute."

I follow his line of sight to the small table I noticed he was at when I walked in. It's nestled between a few pretty potted plants and a vintage bookshelf. I sit on the far side, feeling at home among the greenery. I collapse onto the rattan chair, taking a breath. *I can do this.*

Connor sits down a minute later, pushing my chai tea latte across the table. I pick it up and take a sip, desperate to have caffeine coursing through my veins.

Wow. This is the best chai tea latte I've ever had. "Good?" he asks, watching me intently.

"The best I've ever had, actually."

He laughs. "I thought you would like it here! Something about this place reminded me of you." I look around, my heart warming at his declaration. He's right. The coffee shop looks like it was pulled straight from my imagination.

"So, tell me about yourself," he says, bringing his Americano up to his lips. "I know you're a phenomenal baker, but what else do you like to do?"

I pause. "Honestly? That's all I have time for. Baking is my entire world. Once upon a time, I used to dance. I loved ballet. But it's been years since I've been in the studio."

Swallowing, I decide to offer up another kernel of information.

Something about Connor makes me feel comfortable and relaxed. Like I can trust him with my deepest, darkest secrets.

"I was in a pretty toxic relationship a few years ago. I managed to walk away, but my entire world came crashing down. This is my first date in almost five years, actually..." My voice trails off quietly as I feel my cheeks heat up and I look down at my lap.

Connor is watching me. Not with pity, but with understanding. He doesn't say anything, but something in the way that he's listening to me tells me that he knows exactly what I'm feeling.

"Truthfully, I'm not sure how to start over. I poured everything into that relationship. I think I avoided dating for a really long time because I was used to giving everything and coming up empty." I take a sip of my latte.

"But," I smile, "I'm trying to be an optimist."

He smiles back, reaching his hand across the table to grab mine.

"Thank you for sharing that with me." After he squeezes my hand, he lets go. His touch sends a chill up my spine.

"I went through something similar a few years ago. I spent too much time trying to save something that couldn't be fixed." He pauses, considering his next words. "It's hard to walk away. It's hard to rewire your brain, because sometimes it doesn't know the difference between love and pain."

"Yeah, exactly." I look at him, and I feel like I'm really seeing him. Someone who listens. Someone who understands that while some areas of life are gray, most of it is black and white. Right and wrong. *Truth and lies.*

"So." I set my latte down quickly. I decide to change the subject. "When you aren't serenading brides as they walk down the aisle, what else do you like to do?

He laughs. "I don't really know. Music is my whole life. When I'm not playing, I like to be home and spend time with my dog, Jake. I also like to cook."

"I love that." I'm smiling as I say it because I genuinely mean it. "I have two dogs also, Daisy and Beau. When I'm not baking, they consume my time, too."

Then I hear his phone buzz on the table. It's so quick that I don't even realize it, but my body tenses up. I watch as he picks it up, looks at the screen then sets it back down.

He didn't take the time to respond, forgetting he was on a date. He didn't flip his phone face down, like he had something to hide. He didn't do any of that.

I watch him lean back in his chair, crossing one ankle over the other knee. "We should take them to a dog park together sometime."

I study him for a minute. I should trust him; he's given me no reason not to trust him, but it can't be this simple. *Can it?* Something doesn't add up. He's so... normal. My gut is telling me not to trust this. There's no way it can be this easy.

Despite my fear, I respond with, "I would love that."

KATE

I'm in the mood to dance.

Aria comes over every single Monday. It's *our* day. Tonight we're trading the Salvatore brothers for a night out. One of our favorite EDM artists is in town, and on a Monday, nonetheless. We can't pass up the opportunity to see them live; it's kismet.

I bought a sequin crop top just for the occasion. I also bought a top for Aria, knowing she will be stressed about having nothing to wear. She prefers my clothes, anyway.

Speaking of Aria, she's late. *She's always late.*

I glance at the clock, which is hanging a couple of feet above my dresser. Our bedroom is a mix of boho and modern, with a clean finish. The colors are neutral, and it's bright and refreshing. If I had it my way, the apartment would look like Lisa Frank had a baby with Ed Hardy, but Ben is much more reserved than I. And I don't want to scare him off.

It's a quarter past seven and Aria's supposed to be here already. I laugh, pulling my attention back to the mirror in front of me as I swipe on some mascara.

A few minutes later, the doorbell rings. I race down the stairs and bounce up to the door. I swing it open with so much excitement. "Ugh," Aria says. "Sorry I'm late. I couldn't find anything to wear."

"I figured," I say, eyeing her up and down with a smirk. "That's why I picked out an outfit for you." Turning around, I bound up the stairs and leave Aria standing at the front door.

Aria walks in and closes the door. "Oh, thank God."

She passes Ben in the living room, already comfortable on the couch for the evening. He will surely be playing video games the whole time we're out.

When we reach my room, I walk back over to the mirror, putting the finishing touches on my makeup. "Try it on! I'm almost ready." I turn and toss a shirt in Aria's direction.

She holds it up—a fishnet crop top, strung together with a few pieces of black fabric. "Uhhhhh, is this a shirt?"

"Yes." I roll my eyes at her, smiling to myself. "It's basically a rave. You'll fit in. Trust me."

Aria nods as she pulls it over her teal blue sports bra. She walks over to the mirror, and after eyeing her reflection a few times she cracks a smile and admits, "Okay, okay. You were right. I love it!"

"Which sneakers?" I walk out of the closet, holding up a lavender pair and a green and white checkered pair.

"I think purple," Aria says, cocking her head to the side. "It matches your eyeshadow perfectly."

Spinning around, I give myself a once-over in the mirror and wink. "You're so right."

It only takes us a few more minutes to gather the rest of our things. We throw Chapstick and our wallets in matching chromatic fanny packs that Aria bought just for tonight. Mine has a sheen of purple and Aria's has a sheen of blue, bringing our outfits together perfectly.

I yell to Ben as I zoom down the stairs. "Bye, Babe! See you later!"

Just before the door shuts behind us, Ben yells back, "Be safe! I love you!"

Just three minutes later, the Uber pulls up just like I planned. I mapped out every detail, down to the minute, and I love being on time or even early if I can manage it. I prefer to be the first one anywhere. Which is why I scheduled the Uber to be here precisely at seven-thirty, putting us at the venue by eight o'clock. Which means we will be the first ones in line, and the first ones to pick through the merch. All the pieces of my plan for the best girls' night ever are falling into place.

I fling the door open and scoot to the far side of the car. Aria slides in after me, closing the door with a soft slam.

"So…" I look over at Aria, and see her wide-eyed, staring back at me. "How was your date with Connor? Tell me everything."

She turns beet red. "It was amazing." She looks down, fidgeting with her seatbelt. "He's kind and understanding. And hot. " She's smiling now, really, really big. "We're going out again next weekend."

"Yes!" I scream, startling the driver. I watch him jump, swerving the steering wheel for just a moment. Laughing, I throw my hand over my mouth. "Oh. Sorry!" His eyes meet mine in the rear view mirror and he nods slightly.

We double over in laughter as he drives down 6th Avenue, racing through the traffic lights.

THE VENUE LOOKS EMPTY, aside from a few people in line waiting to be let in. We timed this perfectly. I smile to myself as we climb out of the Uber, taking our place in line among the rest of the concertgoers.

When we enter the venue, my eyes immediately lock on a hot pink baby tee hanging high above the merch table. "That one!" I reach out and grab Aria's hand. "I need that one."

Her eyes are frantically scanning the table, bouncing from one item to the next. "What do you think of that one?" She points to a blue tank top with a flower design across the chest.

"I love it! It's so you."

She smiles and pulls out her credit card. "We'll take those two," she says to the merchant as she points to our choices. I open my mouth as I prepare to protest. "You got the tickets, so let me get these!" she says, cutting me off.

I roll my eyes. "Thank you. I love you. I'll buy the first round then."

We wander deeper into the venue, searching for the bar. The electrifying sound of bass pulses through the air. The lights are changing from pink to purple to green, covering every inch of the space. We spot the bar, linking arms as we move through the crowd. Despite the deceptively short line outside, it's busy and filling up quickly in here.

The bartender nods to us, waiting for us to shout an order in his direction.

"Uhhhh." I look at Aria, unprepared to have a decision so quickly. "We'll take two margaritas… on the rocks." I shout before I look over at Aria and shrug. It's too loud to talk in here.

He pushes our margaritas across the sticky bar top, tequila splashing over the side and onto my hand. "Thanks!" I yell in his direction, but he's long gone. I slap a twenty down before we turn and move in the other direction, making room for the group of girls behind us to move in.

Carrying our drinks, we make our way across the dance floor and up to the front. I always like to be right in the action, as much as possible anyway.

We've barely pushed our way to the front when the lights dim and the artist skips onto the stage, hands raised in anticipation. The crowd cheers so loudly, the sound of my own cheering is lost. I look over at Aria and smile, wrapping my free arm around her shoulders, pulling her in close. She wraps an arm around my waist, and together we surrender to the music.

ARIA

"Can I ask you a question?"

Connor looks over at me, my feet resting gently in his lap. I swallow nervously. The last time this question was asked, the answer uprooted everything I thought I knew. I made a decision that changed the trajectory of my life based on the answer to this question. Looking at him, with my stomach in my throat, I force the words out. "Do you want children someday?"

He looks at me for a moment, contemplating his response. I see it in his eyes, the uncertainty. My stomach drops as I feel my future slipping further and further away.

"I am open to it," he says finally. "I've never really considered it. But if the right person comes along, I would definitely be open to it."

Looking away, I let his words sink in. We're on our second date. It's *only* our second date. Maybe I'm testing the waters because I'm sick of being jerked around. *Maybe I'm secretly tying to self-sabotage this.*

I don't know why I needed to ask that. *Well, that's a lie.*

Connor and I took the dogs to the park to play. I packed a picnic and he packed his guitar. Just down the hill, there's a mom, dad, and little boy playing on a swing set. The dad is pushing him really fast and he's laughing and laughing. A deep, belly laugh. The kind of laugh that only someone you love could bring out of you. The kind of laugh that is born from innocence. The mom is sitting on a colorful, quilted blanket, eating snacks, watching her whole world swinging back and forth in the wind.

She looks so close to my age. As I watch her, I wonder if she has everything she ever wanted. The longer I watch them, the more my heart breaks.

The life that I want feels so far away.

At least Connor was honest with me. At least, I *think* he's being honest. I don't know how I'm supposed to tell anymore. He's nothing like Ryan, he's really not, but I've been burned before and it's hard to silence the part of me that feels like everything is a lie.

It's been a lovely day. A really, really nice afternoon. Or was, until I decided to question him about the future. I need to leave it alone. I need to see where this goes. It's only our second date for Christ's sake. It's unfortunate that you can't just erase a bad decision with an oversized rubber eraser.

I look back and him and plaster a smile on my face. "Okay," I say. Lying flat on my back, I watch a group of bees play tag above us. The wine has me feeling a little bit tipsy.

After a few minutes, his voice breaks the silence. "We better get going or we're going to be late," he whispers quietly.

I kick my feet off of his lap, slipping them into my warm sandals, heated from the sun. I gather the snacks and a bottle of sunscreen, shoving it back into my tote bag. We walk toward his car, dogs in tow. I turn back around, looking at the family one last time. I can't quiet the little voice in my head that's telling me that I missed my chance.

When we reach the car, Connor opens the passenger's side door for me. Jake, Daisy, and Beau file in, one after another, before I climb in.

I'm choosing to trust him. I'm choosing to have hope. I'm choosing to believe that there's a possibility that I could be the *right person* for someone. Because if I don't have hope, what else do I have?

KATE

It was an accident, a genuine accident.

I look down at the burn mark stretching down the full length of my forearm. It's still faint, the mark of a fresh burn that hasn't had time to fully form yet. The oven timer still chimes, lost in the chaos of the scene unfolding. I'm staring at my forearm in a daze as I hear Ben in the background, "Shit! Kate, I swear, I didn't mean... are you okay?" He's moving quickly and fumbling through the freezer for an ice pack or some frozen peas.

Thursdays at Rain were slowly replaced with a new recipe every week, moving around each other in our too-small kitchen. Tonight's recipe is a chicken casserole. I don't cook. I never have. My mom doesn't cook much either. And so here I am, approaching thirty, with no real culinary skills. But I try. For Ben, I try. He enjoys it and I've gotten good at pretending I like cooking.

I had tugged open the oven door, heat rolling out in a wave that fogs my glasses. The casserole was heavier than I remembered, and Ben was so eager to help with our masterpiece. He reached past me to grab a potholder and the sudden movement startled me. I shifted my grip just as he leaned in, and his shoulder bumped mine and I lost my balance. The dish tipped and my forearm pressed against the glowing oven rack as I scrambled to steady it.

It was so quick, I barely registered what had happened. I heard the sound first, the sizzle of my skin, and then I felt the white-hot burning pain. I gasped then, dropping the dish on the stovetop. Once the fog clears, I look down and see Ben holding a bag of ice to my arm, which I am clutching to my chest.

"Baby, I'm sorry. I'm so sorry." His voice cracks as he says it over and over, fumbling with the bag of ice. He's scanning up and down my arm as the angry welt continues to rise. The pain is real, but so is the flood of memories and the familiar feeling of being hurt and then blamed for it. I find myself bracing for impact, for the anger in his words, and the accusations.

Instead, Ben's frantic, leading me over to the couch to sit down. "Oh God, Kate. Does it hurt? We should go to urgent care. Please, let me take you." He takes a seat beside me, draping his arms over my shoulder to hold me close.

The panic I see in his eyes isn't anger, it's fear. I fight the urge to shrink and say, "It was an accident." I whisper, almost testing the words.

He's looking at me like I've lost my mind. "Of course it was an accident. I shouldn't have rushed in like that, Babe, I just wanted to help. This is my fault—please let me do something."

I feel my heart crack wide open. I look over at him with tears in my eyes, not just from the pain, but because he's not Ryan. *He's not Ryan.* I don't have to shrink beneath someone's cruelty ever again. The realization is freeing, like running barefoot on the seashore.

"Okay," I say with a little more certainty. "Let's go to urgent care."

He tries to smile, pleased with my answer. I lean down and give Bandit, who has positioned himself between my ankles, a scratch behind the ears. Ben helps me off the couch, holding firmly onto my uninjured arm as I shuffle toward the door. My legs are fine, but the pain is coursing through my whole body now, the welt moving from a dull ache to a sharp sting.

"Let's get takeout on the way home." I look over at him and smile.

He huffs a laugh and rolls his eyes in return. The dish isn't ruined but deep down he knows I hate cooking, and I would choose Panda Express over a home-cooked meal any day.

"Anything you want, Babe." He leans in to kiss my forehead as he leads me to the car.

"I love you," I say before I can stop myself. Saying those three words out loud still gives me a physical reaction. Those words used to come with strings, or judgment, or only were spoken after something terrible happened.

I hate that I still feel this way. I've said it to Ben before; it's not like this is the first time. We've been living together for a while now, and I do love him. I know that, and he knows it too. I finally let myself relax and feel comfortable around another man. I finally let someone else add excitement to my life, and I haven't looked back because he's never given me a reason to. He loves me on a level I've never experienced before; he gives without expecting anything in return. He treasures me, and understands me. *What more could I ask for?*

"I love you," I say again, this time more confidently as I drift toward him, drawn by something I can't describe. *I'm safe.*

He wraps his arms around my waist, holding me close, careful not to touch my injured arm. "I love you more."

Maybe I've finally arrived at the love that I deserve, and damn does it feel good.

ARIA

I glance down at my phone when I reach the stop sign.

"I've got a surprise for you." It's a text from Kate. "Pack a small bag and meet me at the airport at 11:30."

I look up at the clock, and it's a quarter past eight. Curiosity gets the better of me, so I reply with, "What did you do?" even though I know she won't tell me. She loves surprises, and she doesn't care that I don't. I love that about her.

I'm on my way home from a morning delivery. The wedding isn't until tomorrow, but the mother of the bride requested the cake a day early and I'm not complaining. I love having my weekends to myself. *How did Kate know I had this weekend free?* I laugh because that's typical Kate, finding a way to access my Google Calendar.

Pulling into my driveway, I hustle inside. I have forty-five minutes to pack a bag and drop the pups at my mom's. Standing in front of my closet, I survey my options. I don't know where we're going, so I don't know how to pack. I pull my phone out of my back pocket and text Kate. "Can you at least tell me if I should pack for cold weather or warm weather?"

She replies instantly. "Warm weather!"

Hmmmm. I start throwing all of my shorts and tank tops into my suitcase. I add in a light jacket and a pair of jeans, just in case. Scurrying into my bathroom, I grab my curling iron and dump all of my toiletries into a bag. I would rather overpack and be prepared for every scenario.

When I arrive at the airport, I spot Kate leaning against the wall holding something cardboard in her hands. When I get closer, I see that it's two heads, one of Stefan and one of Damon.

"Um, why are you holding cardboard heads?" I ask as I walk up to her. Kate whips her head in my direction when she hears my voice.

"Because," she hands me Stefan's head, "we are going to a *Vampire Diaries* Convention."

"What?" Grabbing the head, I flip it back to front in my hands, trying to figure out where she even got this from.

"In Georgia," she finishes.

"Wait! What?" I ask again, because I don't think I heard her correctly. "Seriously?"

She's grinning now, and it hits me that she's serious. "Oh my God. Where did you even hear about this!"

"Oh, you know..." She kicks off the wall where she was leaning and walks toward the United counter. "An Instagram ad." I shake my head and laugh, following her to drop off our bags. The airport is busy today, full of families with small children who are going on vacation. Kate sets her suitcase on the belt before lifting mine up next. Both register as overweight on the scale. *Shocker*. She turns to look at me with a smirk on her face.

The line at security is even longer than at the check-in counter. Kate goes first, fumbling through her bag for her ID. She's moving so quickly, her sleeve gets caught on the zipper as she maneuvers through each pocket for her wallet, and that's when I see it—a huge burn mark spanning the length of her forearm. As if she can sense me staring, she looks over at me, following my line of sight. She looks down at her arm, then back up at me again. "It was an accident," she says quietly. "A genuine accident." I look up at her, scanning her eyes for any hint of foul play. I'm trying not to read into the situation because I believe her, and she would never lie to me, but my mind just can't help but associate the word *accident* with *abuse.*

"I promise." She flashes me a reassuring smile before moving forward in line, and handing her ID to the TSA agent. I smile back and decide to drop it. I believe her, and more than that, I believe that she would never let someone treat her that way again. She's the strongest person I know. Making our way through security, and then to our gate, we have forty-five minutes to spare.

"Should we get coffee or breakfast? Or both? I'm starving."

"Yes to both." She pulls out her phone, trying to locate the nearest Starbucks, which just so happens to be only a few gates down from ours. "Thank you, Jesus."

I follow her onto the moving walkway, scrolling through my phone and checking my emails. We're sandwiched behind a young couple and a traveling baseball team when Kate suddenly loses her balance, stumbles backward, and steps on my foot.

"Ouch," I say dramatically as I glare at her. She doesn't look at me or apologize. She stands frozen and slowly turns, gripping my forearm tightly. "Again... Ouch! Earth to Kate," I say. "What's wrong?"

Without saying a word, she lifts her arm slowly, pointing across the walkway to the people moving in the opposite direction. First, I spot the faded baseball cap, flipped backward over chocolate brown hair. Next, I spot the tattoo. A faded infinity symbol peeking out from beneath the cuff of his fitted white tee shirt. His arm is draped casually over the shoulder of a girl with blonde hair. Of course she's blonde... *just like us.* Her eyes dart almost frantically around the airport, and she looks like she's trying to make eye contact with someone, anyone.

Ryan.

Kate turns around to look at me fully, finally making eye contact with me, and we stare at each other while having a telepathic conversation. *Why is he still in Colorado? Why is he at the airport? Is he coming or going? Who is that girl? God, he looks exactly the same. Does the devil not age?* So many questions and no answers in sight.

The walkway comes to an end and without saying a word, we take off running. Sprinting through the airport, we pass the Starbucks and we don't stop until we are clear at the other end of the terminal. People are moving out of our way left and right, assuming we are late for a connecting flight. Kate collapses on an empty hard leather sofa, gasping for air. I fold over, resting my hands on my knees, panting like a dog.

After a few moments, when we've had time to catch our breath, she bursts into laughter. "Are you kidding me?" she says between breaths. My heart is racing in my chest, and I'm fighting off a panic attack. I haven't seen him in person since the night he almost killed me. I feel my hands starting to sweat and I think I might be sick. "Are you okay?" Kate reaches her hand out and takes mine, steadying it.

"I-I don't—" I can't find the words. "I don't know." I take a seat next to her, burying my head in my hands. "I just never thought I'd see him again," I whisper.

"I know," she says softly. "But you're safe." I know it. Deep down inside, I know it too. I just need my body to catch up with my mind. *I'm safe*. I'm with Kate, and an airport full of people. I'm not scared of him anymore. Besides—I'm 99% sure he didn't see us.

"I wish we could warn her," I whisper. "Like you tried to do for me."

She's still panting ever so slightly. "What do you mean?"

Digging through my backpack, I pull out my wallet. Sandwiched between my health insurance and Costco cards is the note, the torn piece of paper smudged with crimson. I unfold it and hand it to her.

"Oh my god," she breathes. "You found it. I can't believe you actually found it."

"I did. I wish I would have listened to you, but I didn't. *I couldn't*."

She runs her fingers over the words, lost in memory. "I wrote this the night he pushed me down the stairs." Her lips quiver slightly. "I wasn't sure what would happen to me, but I just knew it was my job to try and save the next girl." She lifts her head, gazing across the terminal in the direction of Ryan and his next conquest.

I follow her gaze, suppressing the anxiety rising in my chest. "She probably wouldn't listen either. He's already got her exactly where he wants her."

~

AFTER TOUCHING DOWN IN ATLANTA, we collect our bags and make our way to the Enterprise counter. The second we step outside, we feel sticky, the southern humidity ruining our perfectly curled hair. We follow the attendant, who leads us through rows of cars. Bypassing the SUVs and the compact cars, he leads us straight to a white Mustang convertible. Kate squeals, popping open the trunk to toss our bags inside.

One thing about Kate—she will *always* get a convertible. Something about her high school boyfriend having one, and she's been obsessed ever since. She loves the top down, hair blowing in the wind, singing at the top of her lungs. Not a care in the world. It's my favorite thing about her, if I'm being honest. Her carefree spirit.

A short drive later, we pull up to the Mystic Falls Inn, located in the quaint town of Covington, Georgia. The whole show was filmed in this town, and to this day it remains a public attraction for fans of the show. Authentic clothing from the television show hangs behind thick glass at the Mystic Grill. Caroline's house is down the block from the clocktower building, running every thirty minutes for a scheduled tour. Memorabilia of *The Vampire Diaries* is on every block, everywhere you look. It's simply magical.

I look over at Kate and see the stars shining in her eyes. "Where do we even begin?" she whispers as she looks around, taking it all in.

"Let's drop off our bags and go have dinner at the Mystic Grill."

She clears her throat. "Okay yes, good plan. I heard they serve red wine out of blood bags and we simply must have one." I laugh as she climbs out of the car, slamming the door behind her. I climb out too, following her to the trunk. I let those words sink in for a moment. *Red wine... out of blood bags.* Because we are in Georgia, in the town our favorite show was filmed, meeting our favorite actors tomorrow.

I was drowning in the ordinary and Kate saved me. She brought me back to life and she makes me feel safe.

She will never know how much I needed her.

KATE

Today is the perfect day for a wake.

It's a warm and slightly overcast September day with wispy clouds stretching across the blue, almost periwinkle sky. The wind in the Colorado Rockies has a kind of honesty to it—sharp, untamed, and unapologetically wild. Despite the warmth of the day, I can feel it stinging my cheeks as we climb. The burn in my thighs is amplified by the weight of my backpack, thumping against my lower back with every step. Beside me, Aria moves with the same quiet purpose. Neither of us speaks, because neither of us can breathe in the thin mountain air.

A zippered pouch in my backpack holds old photos, faded letters, and other bits of memory I haven't thought about in years. I don't know why I kept these mementos, if I'm being honest. It's not nostalgia, but maybe just a way to remind myself of how far I've come since I was with *him*.

Aria has her own collection of things she also hasn't dared to look at in years, stored in a battered shoebox. They're the last remaining pieces of a life she's finally ready to let go of.

We've been anticipating this hike for months now. Calling it "the wake," half-joking, half-serious—it's a funeral for the women we used to be. The name couldn't be more fitting, especially because we nearly die on the way up here—we are not used to hiking and the altitude is no joke.

We reach the ridge just before the golden hour, the aspens glistening yellow in the setting sun. The sky stretches in every direction, painting the horizon in pinks and golds so breathtaking it makes my throat tighten.

"This feels like a good place to die." Aria huffs as she sets down her bag. She doesn't mean it literally, but the irony isn't lost on me.

I laugh. She's right though, this is a good place to *end* something. To bury ghosts from the past.

We build a small fire in the clearing—the air has cooled with the setting sun and we're both feeling chilly now that we've stopped moving. The remnants of previous fires linger, outlining the ground like a roadmap. The sparks ignite and the dry wood hisses, the fire coming to life in the evening air. I sit cross-legged in my Lululemon leggings, setting the pouch of memories in my lap. Inching closer to the fire, the flames keep me warm and I gingerly remove the items from the pouch like they might break.

The first photo I pick up is a snapshot of Ryan and me on our wedding day. My face is blank and I have an empty, vacant smile. This is the one where I look, *and felt*, like I was drowning. I stare at it for a long time. "I remember feeling so trapped the second we said our vows. I remember feeling everything change in the span of a few seconds," I whisper, looking at Aria. She's sitting on my right, knees hugged into her chest, taking in the gravity of the moment.

Then I toss the photo into the fire and watch it curl and blacken into ash.

Aria reaches into her bag and pulls out the shoebox. Lifting the lid, she picks up a sonogram first. Her hands shake as she holds it over the flames.

"No one ever even knew you," she says, her voice breaking. "I bet you had my eyes." The fire consumes the image slowly, like it knows it has to be gentle with this one. Aria doesn't cry. She just exhales a breath that sounds like ten years of silence cracking wide open.

One by one, we burn the fragments of the lives we survived. Photos full of fake smiles, notes scribbled in anger, or desperation, or apology. One necklace. Sticky notes from a proposal. A letter of acceptance into the Paris Opera Ballet.

Each offering feeds the fire, and the fire feeds our freedom.

When the shoebox is empty, and the zippered pouch no longer holds the past, we sit back and let the fire burn. The sun dips low behind the mountains, casting long shadows across our faces. Minutes pass as we soak in the comfortable silence.

She turns to look at me. "Should we read our letters now?"

I nod, staring at the fire. "I think so." Meeting her gaze, I say, "I can go first."

I reach into my backpack and pull out two White Claws, handing one to Aria. This moment requires alcohol if I'm going to make it through. I reach into the backpack a second time, into a small pocket on the front, pulling the zipper down. Inside is a piece of paper, folded in fours to make a perfect square.

The paper doesn't look like anything special from the outside, but inside it holds a powerful truth. Inside it holds the words I wish someone would have said to me. If someone, just one person, would have told me everything would be all right, it might have changed everything.

Kate,

It's hard to be 21. Nothing feels certain, and I know how scary that can be, but you won't always be this lonely. Soon, you will meet someone who ignites your fire, and you think he's the one. He's not, but you won't know that yet. You will have to learn the hard way, I'm sorry.

He is going to hurt you, and he is going to do the unthinkable, and only through that pain are you able to grow. But first, he will take everything from you. Your spirit. Your fire. Your will to live.

It's not fair. None of it will be fair, but it's necessary to shape you into the woman you are meant to become. Only from the ashes can you rise.

You will float adrift for a while, unsure of your place in life. Struggling to find your footing again. You will have to give up on your dreams, if only temporarily. The goals you have for yourself and your life—none of it will seem achievable, as least not for a while. Just know that you will meet someone who loves you for who you are. He will see your faults and your baggage, and love you anyway. He will heal parts of you that you didn't even know were broken, and you just need to be patient.

And then, you will fall in love again. Because love isn't linear. It takes more than one shape; it has more than one voice. You will fall in love again with someone who sees the darkest parts of you and meets you there with an unconditional embrace. She will understand things you've never said out loud, and support you without question. She will become your chosen family.

You will be filled with so much love—more love than you know what to do with. More love than you could have ever imagined as a little girl, growing up alone, unsure of your place in the world. You didn't grow up knowing the freedom of choice, and you won't—not yet anyway.

You just need to hold onto your spark and never let it die. You will have to hide it for a while, bury it deep down, but only for survival. Just remember to hold on.

Tears are streaming down my face uncontrollably now as I fold it up, tossing it into the fire. I look over at Aria, her face hidden in her knees. I hear the quiet sobs.

I lay my head on her shoulder, letting us both live fully in this moment—letting the words burn off the page and turn into ash as she wraps her arm around my shoulder.

Quietly, she opens her shoebox again, lifting the one remaining piece of paper from the bottom. She takes a long sip of her White Claw, then clears her throat and begins.

Aria,

You won't believe me right now, but one day you'll breathe again—really breathe. The air won't feel heavy anymore. You'll laugh without waiting for permission, and you'll wake up without that dull ache in your chest wondering what version of him he'll throw at you today.

Right now, you're walking on eggshells, trying to keep the peace. You think if you love him harder, stay quieter, shrink just a little more, trust him, maybe he'll finally see you. Maybe he will stop cheating on you. Maybe he will stop hurting you—mentally and physically. But here's the truth: you were never the problem. His cruelty was never proof of your inadequacy—it was proof of his emptiness.

You will leave. It will be the hardest thing you will ever do. But piece by piece, you will build a life outside of his shadow. It will take time, but trust me... it will be worth it. You'll rediscover your laughter, your joy, your art, your voice. And you'll meet people—one woman in particular—who understands that kind of darkness because she's walked through it too. Together, you'll turn your pain into your story, your story into your power and your power into everlasting friendship.

And then—when you're no longer searching for someone to save you—you'll meet someone who will love you the way you always deserved to be loved. You'll find the kind of love that doesn't keep score, doesn't silence you, and doesn't make you small. He'll look at you with gentleness instead of with control. He'll make the ordinary days feel safe again. You won't question his intentions or your worth—you'll just know.

So hold on. Even in the quiet moments when it feels like you're disappearing, know this: you're still here. And you are worth saving.

She finishes, and I'm sobbing hysterically. I look at her through the tears pooled in my eyes and smile. She smiles back, knowing the same thing that I do. *We are free.*

We are finally choosing ourselves.

Neither of us feel small anymore. It's as if every loss and every scar has expanded the boundaries of who we are instead of shrinking them down.

When the fire dies down, we bury the ashes beneath a pile of rocks. It stands as a grave marker for a version of us we no longer needed to carry. Our burdens lie beneath those rocks and they will never be ours to carry again.

As we start down the mountain, with the stars shining above us and our shadows trailing behind, we aren't haunted anymore. Because sometimes the bravest thing isn't surviving, it's choosing joy anyway.

Now life is a blank page, and it's ours to rewrite.

ARIA
SIX MONTHS LATER

I'm going to be sick.

As I peer around the heavy velvet curtain, my stomach flips nervously when I see the auditorium is *packed*. There are so many people, *too many people*, seated and waiting for the opening night of the recital. I lock eyes with Kate seated in the front row next to Connor. She smiles at me and mouths the words, "You can do this."

It's my first recital in years, and I feel dread, but also excitement. *I will not throw up.* I move back, taking my place in line. The girl next to me looks over and gives me a nervous smile. I smile back at her, giving her a slight nod. Closing my eyes, I take a deep breath, listening to the hush of the crowd as the curtain lifts.

As I move around the stage, poised and weightless, I remember why I love to dance. It all comes back to me. I twirl around the stage, remembering my years of training. All eyes are on me as I rise onto relevé as the spotlight follows me before my limbs extend in a perfect arabesque. I hear gasps coming from across the theater. The reaction makes me smile.

It feels so good to be back.

FALLING in love isn't for the weak.

It's hard to go from simply enjoying someone's company to craving their presence. It's also hard to discover a new realm of happiness and to accept that I actually wasn't happy before to the point that it ruined my life. I've known that for a while now, but I'm starting to realize how much I've healed and changed since I left him. I am so out of my mind in love with Connor, and I know without a doubt that no other feeling has even come close—certainly not the "love" I thought I felt when I was with Ryan.

Connor is playing at a local bar tonight, and I always get there extra early because I want the best seat in the house. I love watching him play live. I crave the attention he gives me and only me when he is surrounded by a room of women, all pining for him.

Bryce is fidgeting in her seat, and her pleather skirt is sticking and releasing from the seat with each movement. She normally doesn't dress up or wear anything other than a tank top and slacks, but tonight she broke out her short pleather skirt, the one that she bought in high school to impress a boy not worth her time.

I saved her a seat right next to mine in the first row and off to the side. I prefer the seat on the end so I can slip out and go to the bathroom or grab another drink without making a scene. Anything to avoid being the center of attention.

The lights dim as I lift my cocktail to my lips. Moments later, Connor enters through a side door, taking his place on stage. My heart is racing. *I'm a lucky girl.*

He smirks at me as he positions his guitar on his lap, tuning the cords. "Hi everyone, thanks for coming." He addresses the crowd in a confident but soft-spoken way. "It means a lot that you want to spend your Tuesday night with me, so let's have some fun. Shall we?"

He scans the room for a moment, making eye contact with the patrons, taking a minute to give the crowd the attention they deserve, when his eyes lock on mine and he smiles. I melt in my chair.

The sound of his acoustic guitar fills the air, the melody pouring into every corner of the bar. It's magical to watch him, so in his element. The song comes to an end and the audience gives him a well-deserved applause.

"There is someone here tonight who is very special to me," he starts again. "This one's for you, Baby." I feel my cheeks heat up, betraying me even in the dim bar lighting. Thankfully, the crowd is full of strangers and no one knows who I am, except for Bryce.

He strums the chords again, letting himself fall into the song's rhythm. When he starts to sing again, my eyes lock on his. I've never heard this song before. I'm mesmerized as he moves from the bridge to the chorus, lost in his every word.

When he finishes playing, there's not a dry eye in the room. "I wrote that song for my best friend," he says into the mic, while he stares into my soul. He clears his throat as he sets his guitar down on the stand next to him, continuing as he climbs off the bar stool. "I know it hasn't been that long, Aria, but I am so in love with you." He walks off the stage, stopping directly in front of me. I'm frozen like a deer in headlights. I don't think I'm breathing. "I love you more and more every day, and I promise I will always strive to be the man you deserve."

Then he pulls a blue velvet ring box out of his pocket, and drops to one knee.

"Will you marry me?"

KATE

hy am I craving milk?

I hate milk. The smell, the consistency, the taste. Everything about it is repulsive. But right now I want it.

It's been three weeks, and every single day I've woken up craving milk. I drink oat milk in my coffee, strictly because I can't drink coffee black and oat milk is the best option. It's the only thing I can tolerate. But for some reason I just want an overflowing glass of ice cold, whole milk.

Rolling over, I groan dramatically, causing Ben to stir beside me. He reaches over to grab me before I can stand. "Where do you think you're going?" he whispers, pulling me back into his arms. I lean in and give him a kiss on the cheek, letting myself bask in his warmth and attention. After a few minutes, I say, "Going to get a disgusting glass of milk."

He lets go of me, laughing. "You're so weird, Babe."

"I know, I know..."

I stumble into the kitchen with Bandit right on my heels, starting the coffee pot before opening the fridge to grab the milk. There's nothing like double fisting beverages at seven o'clock in the morning.

I like spending my mornings out on the patio, listening to music, and catching up on emails. Alone. Ben knows that I need about thirty minutes to wake up before he is allowed to pepper me with conversation.

Opening the sliding door that leads out of the kitchen to the backyard, I set down my beverages before returning to the kitchen for my AirPods and my laptop. Bandit does his business before chasing a squirrel up a tree, missing him by just a hair.

I pick up my phone to comb through my notifications first, as I start with my glass of milk. I've got a few texts from Aria and one from my mom.

I read the texts from Aria first. "See you tomorrow! Connor and I will pick up Chinese on our way over." I smile. Monday night is my favorite night of the week.

Next, I read a message from my mom. "Will you stop over this week? I've got a puzzle and some cleaning supplies I want to give you." I roll my eyes and chuckle.

The next notification is from my health app. My mom got me a ring for Christmas last year that connects to a health tracking app on my phone. It registers my movements, my cycle and everything in-between. It's almost like a Fitbit, but a ring instead. It's incredible. My ring tells me I'm getting sick before I even experience symptoms. Swiping left on the notification, the words appear on my screen. "Your cycle is three weeks and five days late."

What?

I stare at the words on my screen, my gaze moving from my iPhone in one hand to the remnants of milk at the bottom of the glass in my other hand, and back again.

How have three weeks gone by without me noticing? The pieces start falling into place. *Shit. Shit, shit, shit.* We've been super careful; we are always careful. There is no way.

Setting the empty glass down, I storm inside, phone in hand, and reach for my purse, feet sliding into my sandals. "Babe, I'll be right back!" I yell, already halfway out the door.

I RETURN SHORTLY with a box of pregnancy tests in hand. Kicking my sandals off in the hallway, I head for the bathroom, locking the door behind me.

Glancing up, I look at the girl in the mirror.

This can't be happening. *I can't be pregnant.*

I don't know the first thing about being a mother. I wouldn't be a very good one either, that much I know.

I've barely come around to the idea of being in a relationship again. Well, I guess we've been together for over a year now, but still. Taking care of Ben and Bandit is enough for me.

Where would we even put a baby in this apartment? It's barely big enough for the three of us.

I shake my head to stop my thoughts before they spiral too far out of control. My hands are shaking as I rip open the box, tearing into the first test. Slipping the test beneath me, I pee on the awful little stick—the tiny piece of plastic that holds my future.

When I'm done, I set it on the counter and wash my hands. Then I lean back against the wall and slide down until my butt hits the floor with a thud.

This can't be happening.

And I thought girls craved pickles in the first trimester? Not milk. Gross.

"Babe," I hear Ben calling from the other side of the door. "Are you alright?"

I will myself to speak, keeping my voice as level as humanly possible. "I'm fine. I'll be out in a minute." That seems to be enough for him because he doesn't say anything further. I hear him walk back down the hall, shuffling toward the kitchen.

I don't know how long it's been because I forgot to count the minutes. But after what seems like an eternity, I peel myself off of the floor. Tiptoeing over to the counter, I look down at the test.

Two pink lines. Pregnant.

I promptly lean over and vomit into the toilet. My stomach is in knots, my palms are sweaty and my heart is pounding so loudly it sounds like it's going to crack my ribcage.

Moments later, I hear a rap on the door. "Babe, are you sure you're okay?"

I think back to the last few weeks. We've been so busy lately: we took a weekend trip to the east coast to see Ben's mom and I've already had four weddings this month. I haven't given it any thought, but I just assumed my cycle would come any day now. My app mentioned that something has been "straining my body," but I thought I was just run down from all of the travel, or maybe that I was getting sick.

But pregnant? This is not acceptable. *God has a really ill-timed sense of humor.*

Crawling toward the door, I reach up and unlock it. Ben pushes it open slowly, taking in the sight of me on the floor, and the pregnancy test on the counter. He stares at the test as the moments pass, not moving, not speaking. When he looks toward me again, I force a smile because I don't want him to notice my emotions brewing beneath the surface. His eyes well up with tears, and for a second, I swear that he looks... *happy.*

"Kate, we're going to be parents."

ARIA

I don't know how I've kept this secret from her for nearly a week. Kate is going to lose her mind. She was already upset to miss Connor's show… something about a "wedding walk through she couldn't reschedule," so she's going to be even more pissed when she learns that she missed Connor's proposal to me!

I thought about calling her five seconds after it happened, but I decided to wait and tell her in person. She's so animated that I really just want to see her reaction as it's happening. It would be way less rewarding to tell her over text.

We are on our way to Kate's apartment for Chinese food Mondays. I look down, spinning my ring around in circles on my finger. He did well. Really well. *Of course he did.* He knows exactly what I like because he is my best friend. The ring is white gold, with a turquoise gem in the center flanked by two round diamonds. It's absolutely beautiful.

When we arrive, we let ourselves in. As usual, *Vampire Diaries* is on the TV and Kate is curled up in front of the fireplace with a blanket on her lap. Bandit lifts his head over the back of the sofa, pleased to see that it's just us and not an intruder. Their apartment is more like a condo—two stories with a second living room between the upstairs bedroom and the office. Ben leans over the railing upstairs, waving down to us in the entryway.

"Connor! What's up, man!"

Connor smiles, grabbing a beer from the island before joining Ben upstairs. They take Chinese food Mondays as an opportunity to watch Monday Night Football. I smile as Connor takes the steps two at a time. When I walk deeper into the apartment, I see that Kate has our takeout spread laid across the coffee table and a glass of wine poured just for me. I plop down on the adjoining loveseat and let out a comfortable sigh.

"Hi, Honey," she says casually, zoned out with her attention glued to the TV. It's the episode where Bonnie and Damon get stuck in the prison world, and Elena realizes she's never going to see Damon again. There is no talking to her when she is in this state. I need to wait for this scene to end. A few minutes later, she lets out a breath I didn't even notice she was holding.

She looks over at me this time, her eyes lit up because she's always so happy to see me. "Hi!" she says again, turning her attention to me. "How are you? How was the rest of your week? Tell me everything." Shifting under her wool blanket, she pivots until she's facing me.

I bring my legs up underneath me, fidgeting with my hands in my lap. Then I swallow. "I have something I need to tell you."

Her expression changes and then her face drops. "What happened?"

It's so fun to mess with her, particularly because she spends the entirety of our relationship surprising me even though she knows I hate it. I pause, reveling in it for a minute. I'm staring at her and she's staring right back at me, waiting for me to continue. Finally, I put her out of her misery. Lifting my hand up, I flash my newest accessory at her.

"I'm engaged," I whisper, unable to control the tear that slips down my cheek.

Her eyes go wide as she looks at the ring, then up at me, then back at the ring. This only lasts for a minute before she screams, "Oh.

My. God!" She launches off the sofa and runs over to me, throwing her arms around my neck. We hold each other for I don't know how long as the tears fall. When she finally lets me go, she pulls back and her eyes are glistening. "This is the best news in the world. This is everything you deserve and more." I smile back at her, unable to control the tears any longer. For the first time in a long time, they are happy tears.

Then she screams again. "Connor!" Before she bolts outs of the living room and up the stairs to the second story. I can only imagine the scene unfolding up there. It sounds like she basically tackled Connor in a giant hug because I hear Ben say, "Whoa, Babe. What the hell are you doing?"

"They're engaged!" she screams again before running back down the stairs, joining me and Elena, as we blubber like babies.

"What? Congrats, man! That's amazing!" I hear Ben say faintly, followed by the sound of beer bottles clinking together. The sound makes me smile. It took Ben and Connor no more than a month to bond over music and football. How lucky am I that I get to marry my best friend and that my other best friend's boyfriend is my boyfriend's best friend? Life is perfect.

I pick up my wine glass to take a sip. When I set my glass back down, I notice that Kate is staring at me. This time her expression is different. She seems almost... apprehensive. "What is it?"

"I need to tell you something, too."

My eyes go wide when it hits me that maybe she is engaged, too. She notices me glance at her hand and she quickly adds, "No. No, it's not that."

I furrow my brows together, wondering what else it could be. I'm lost in my own thoughts when she sighs and then says, "I'm pregnant."

"What?" I ask immediately because I'm not sure that I heard her correctly. I look down at the coffee table and suddenly notice that she didn't pour herself a glass of wine. There's only water next to her sesame chicken.

"Yup, I'm pregnant," she says, sounding a little bit defeated.

My lips start trembling as the tears return. "Kate, you are going to be the best mother." I fill the distance between us, grabbing her hand. "I am so unbelievably happy for you."

She tries to force a smile, but she doesn't say anything. "What is it?" I ask.

"I don't know if I can be a mother. I don't know *how* to be a mother. I should be excited. I mean I am somewhat excited… I guess? But I'm scared. I don't know the first thing about babies." She pauses, tilting her head. "I don't even know if I like kids."

I smile at her. "No one knows how to be a mother until they are thrown into the trenches, forced to figure it out as they go." Leaning back against the loveseat, Bandit hops from his spot next to Kate into my lap.

"I, for one, think you will be an incredible mother."

"You have to say that." She rolls her eyes. "You're my best friend."

"Plus," she blurts out, continuing before I can argue. "The timing could not be worse. I have a bachelorette party to plan and a wedding to help you with. How am I supposed to do that if I'm throwing up every five minutes."

"Oh! That reminds me." Standing up, I walk to where my tote bag is draped over her kitchen chair. I dig around until I find the box I'm looking for, wrapped in a hot pink bow. I carry it back to the sofa and hand it to Kate. She waits just three seconds before untying the bow and tearing the box open. The sight makes me laugh.

"Will you be my maid of honor? You'd be sharing the honor with Bryce, of course."

Kate lifts a chocolate chip cookie dough sandwich out of the box, shoving one into her mouth before she can answer. "Of course I will." Between bites she says, "You really know the way to my heart." I laugh again because it's true. I know her better than anyone, and the same goes for me. We are inseparable, fated.

She joins me on the loveseat, slipping her arm through mine.

"Of course I will. It's us against the world."

EPILOGUE

I*'m only here to look*, I tell myself.

Just look. I saw the announcement on the news and I couldn't resist. I needed to be here in person. From across the street, the cafe is glowing from opening day. People gather in clusters with flowers in one hand and a coffee in the other, with a tote bag full of books draped over their shoulder. It's a celebration for a new beginning. The way everyone is coming together, it looks like an inside joke everyone is in on but me.

It shouldn't matter to me. Why does it matter? *Why am I here?*

So many people showed up for the grand opening, despite the weather. As soon as the ribbon hit the ground, the rain started coming down.

I'm huddled under a lamppost, the rain soaking my Patagonia jacket. I watch as the crowd quickly moves inside to get out of the weather.

Then I see them. One of them moves quickly, adjusting a stack of books, her eyes lit up with excitement. Ink cascades down her arm, reaching her wrist before fading out. The other one appears behind her with two croissants in hand. Her smile is small but real. She tucks a strand of hair behind her ear, and as I watch them... they look safe. Like they survived a storm and somehow shipwrecked on the same shore, learning to speak a language only they know.

I can hear the chatter from the crowd from where I stand, half-hidden under this lamppost like a coward. They don't know me. They don't know I exist, not yet.

I press my fingers into the seam of my jacket pocket where the picture hides. My heartbeat is so loud it feels like the thumping might give me away. He doesn't know I took it, and after last night, I can't bring it up.

A gust of wind kicks up, rattling the banner hanging above the door that reads in sprawling type, GRAND OPENING! The fluttering sound makes my insides twist. I stumbled upon their Podcast *Her Voice* late one night while I was listening with headphones in while he slept in the other room.

Inside the cafe, they wrap their arms around each other in a quick, happy squeeze. They look like women who have finally learned how to exhale... women who found their way out.

Fear coils in my stomach. Someone walks past me from behind, bumping my shoulder, and I flinch. My eyes dart back to the cafe door, terrified they've noticed me, but they're busy greeting customers and handing out pastries, joyfully unaware of anything outside the cafe.

A part of me whispers that I should turn around and run before I get caught. Another part whispers this moment might be the only sliver of courage I'll ever have. I didn't come here to meet them. Not yet. I came here to make sure they were real.

With shaking fingers, I pull my phone from my pocket. I look at the cracked screen to make sure the recording of my story with him is already queued. It's the one I made in secret last week after I realized I might not get another chance. My thumb hovers over the send button as my future hangs in the balance.

Inside, the girls turn toward each other at the same time as they burst into laughter.

I look down at my phone. If I do this... if I send my story to *them*, there's no turning back.

But my hesitation is brief. I hit send, then disappear into the crowd before he realizes I'm gone.

BONUS CHAPTER

The Rockies are majestic in the distance with a dusting of spring snow on their peaks, as if nature itself is dressed in white to witness Aria's new beginning. The air is crisp and blooming with the scent of flowers. The venue is tucked in a wildflower-drenched valley just outside Boulder. It's the kind of secluded, sacred place Aria never imagined herself brave enough to step into again.

She stands in the bridal suite as sunlight pours in through the windows. Her dress is soft butter yellow silk, with a halter neck and intricate detail trailing down onto the floor. Bryce and Marissa just slipped away to check in with the outside coordinator, against Kate's wishes but Aria insisted, and Aria's mom is somewhere fussing over flowers.

Kate is behind her, crouching down to adjust the train, her own lavender dress flowing around her like water. She's been by Aria's side since they woke up this morning.

She looks up, her eyes glassy. "You look... like everything you've ever wanted," she whispers.

Aria blinks hard, but the tears come anyway. "I never thought I'd be here again. Not really."

"I know," Kate says. "But I've been betting on you since the beginning."

Aria walks over and sits at the edge of a blue velvet chaise with her bouquet of Calla Lillies cradled in her lap. "I got you something," Kate says, reaching into her Prada clutch. The purse was a gift from Ben when the twins were born three months ago. It's the one she searched for a few times on his phone so the algorithm would suggest exactly what she wanted, of course. Because she had to birth not one baby, but two, and deserved the ultimate push present.

Aria smiles, already teary again. "Of course you did."

Kate pulls out a tiny box with a bracelet inside. It's simple and silver, elegant with a tiny A charm dangling in the front. "Because you healed me. I didn't realize I was still broken until you came along," Kate says softly, leaning down to fasten it around Aria's wrist. "We're soul-bound. It's you and me, always."

Aria holds it up, her eyes shining with tears as she admires the delicate band. She clutches it to her chest, then reaches down into her overnight bag, digging around inside. Slowly, she lifts a small box out of the inside zipper. Kate's eyes go wide. "You aren't supposed to get me something on *your* wedding day!"

Inside is a gold necklace with a shining "K" pendant on a delicate gold chain. "We really are the same person," Aria giggles as she watches Kate's eyes light up.

"You found your way back," she whispers as she stands, clasping the necklace around Kate's neck with shaking fingers. "And you helped me find mine. You made me whole again."

We stand side by side, arms linked together, laughing through the tears that won't stop coming, ruining our makeup. These gifts weren't wrapped in ribbons, but rather in meaning, in the weight of years survived and rebuilt. "No matter what," Aria says, her voice catching, "it's you and me, forever and ever."

"Forever," Kate echoes, reaching for her hand.

Outside, the ceremony space unfolds like a dream. The chairs arranged in a gentle half-moon, all facing the wide-open mountain vista that held the late afternoon sun. The archway stands simple and intentional, draped in flowers, the handiwork of Connor and Aria together.

Connor stands beneath it, guitar in hand, his tie slightly askew, like always. He isn't polished, and he never tries to be. That's part of why Aria loves him, for his quiet confidence, his unshakable calm, and his refusal to pretend. He doesn't chase perfection; he chases truth.

When the first soft chords ring out - familiar, raw, and entirely hers - Aria's breath catches. It's the song Connor wrote just for her. He tucked it away and only played it once before, the night he asked her to marry him.

Now as he strums, his eyes never leaving hers, his voice low and steady as he sings her down the aisle. It feels like time folds in on itself, like every wound and every moment of grace leads to this. She walks toward him slowly, hands trembling, tears slipping freely down her cheeks. And in Connor's gaze, she sees no echoes of her past, only home.

This is a man who has waited, not just for her love, but for her healing. A man who never asked her to shrink, but instead made room for her to expand. He wrote her a love song, yes, but it's more than that, he made space for her to write the rest of her story.

Kate stands beside her during the ceremony, holding the bouquet when it's time, holding her breath during their vows. Aria's voice trembles as she speaks of rebuilding, of starting over, of the kind of love that doesn't seek to own but to understand. When Connor vows to protect not just her heart, but the history it carries, there isn't a dry eye in the place—including the wedding vendors who have come to know Aria and Kate's story over the last year.

The baker. The wedding planner. A new sisterhood formed from our shared courage.

After the ceremony, while guests drink champagne and dance beneath strings of twinkle lights, Aria and Kate slip away to a small ridge overlooking the valley. It has become their ritual over the past year, escaping to quiet places to reflect, to honor what they survived together and because of each other.

With drinks in hand and the soft hum of celebrating in the distance, they talk about the future, not in abstract dreams, but in the concrete details of something they are building together.

Wonderland.

It's a cozy, whimsical blend of a bookstore and bakery. It's their passion project and it will be their sanctuary. It will be full of mismatched chairs, handwritten notes tucked into book spines, pastries named after fantasy heroines, and stories spilling off the shelves. A safe place for women to gather, to heal, to belong. It is a space for beginnings.

The idea was born in quiet conversations and notebooks filled with doodles, but now it feels real. Tangible. Aria will handle the bakery side, her hands already itching to try new recipes. Kate will bring the books and the design, the need to create courses through her veins. They will call it *Wonderland* because that's what they found with each other. A world beyond survival, a place where joy can live again.

As they clink their glasses, they both grin with the kind of giddy excitement that only comes with starting something entirely their own.

Kate and Aria make their way back down the winding path from the ridge, hand-in-hand, cheeks still damp from tears and laughter. The mountains stretch wide behind them, silent witnesses to the promises they made together.

As they step into the reception, the golden-hour light has softened, casting everything in that honeydew glow of early evening. Just in time, they slip through the crowd and back into the heart of the celebration as Connor steps onto the dance floor, reaching his hand out to Aria.

Aria's breath hitches as the first notes of *To the Men Who Love Women After Heartbreak* float through the air. She walks into his arms, and together they move like they've always belonged.

Kate stands at the edge of the dance floor, one hand resting just below her heart. She steals a glance at Ben, standing off to the side with their twin girls nestled in his arms. He smiles at her with a look that holds both love and understanding.

Because survival has given way to softness. Because the future, at last, looks bright. Because for the first time in a long time, Kate doesn't feel the need to run and Aria doesn't feel compelled to look over her shoulder. They have arrived at the life they built with their own hands.

It's not perfect, but they are together and they are free.

ACKNOWLEDGMENTS

Where do I begin? This book was born from a period in my life when I had never felt more alone. I was floating, drifting through life with no purpose. I was young, naive, and full of unrelenting optimism—and because of that, I met someone who I thought could save me.

Plot twist: he didn't.

This story wouldn't exist without my best friend—without the very same person ruining her life, too. It's hard to put into words how it feels to have someone else out there who knows the exact patterns you fell victim to, who understands the shame and the regret without hearing you utter a single word. Our souls are forever intertwined.

Alyce, you are the greatest gift to come out of this chapter in my life—one that I wouldn't change for anything. I would go through the heartache day after day if I knew you would be there waiting at the end. You are the brightest light, and I am infinitely lucky to know you. Writing a book is no small feat, and I am thankful to have you here with me every step of the way. Thank you.

And thank you to my sister Jess and Suzy for believing in us and this story. Thank you for the countless hours you both spent pouring over every detail. This is a story that needs to be told—not just for us, but for others as well. We believe wholeheartedly in spreading awareness around abuse and creating a safe space for women to feel seen and heard.

Everyone told me to write the book for myself—to write the story that I want told. So I did.

This is for me, for Alyce, and for every woman who has ever had a man dim her spark. Set the world on fire.

ABOUT THE AUTHOR

KENNEDY BAKER lives in Colorado with her husband and twin boys. She loves to write women's fiction, romance and thriller novels. When she isn't writing, you can find her at a concert, or impulsively getting a new tattoo. She was born and raised in Michigan, and will always have a soft spot for the Midwest.